Nationhood

To Danielle
and Shanice -
Hope you enjoy
the book. Thanks
for your support.

To order additional copies, please contact
BookSurge, LLC
www.booksurge.com
1-866-308-6235

James
Gordon

Nationhood
A NOVEL

2007

Nationhood

This book is dedicated to the people of Liberia.

Chapter One: And Justice for All

Mecca City. This grand and beautiful metropolis was the capitol of the nation of AUNK, an acronym for the African Union of New Kemet. AUNK was the homeland to all people of African descent. Once called the Western Sahara, AUNK had become the sovereign nation for Black people from all countries.

This new and powerful nation allowed citizenship to be established by any Black person regardless of where they were and has been the single, most populated area for Black residence. Over the years, AUNK has prospered in ways that no other civilization has, even in ancient Egyptian times. Built on what was once a barren desert devoid of life and resources, AUNK soon became the most respected nation in the world. Its four major cities possessed marvelously constructed buildings with ancient Greek, Aztec, art deco, medieval and Asian influences. But the prominence of African architecture, namely the obelisks and pyramid structures, permeated Mecca City, the capital of AUNK.

The history of the great and proud nation was short, but remarkable. Halfway through the twenty-first century, Blacks from all over the world began to see changes in other races' behavior toward their kind. Discrimination was becoming more and more prevalent. Injustice seemed increasingly commonplace in day-to-day interactions. Skirmishes soon erupted in various nations, as the children of Africa became the target of many government operations and hate groups. For two years, the world leaders attempted to quell the rising animosity between Blacks and non-Black, attempting to work toward a peaceful resolution to the problems. But unfortunately, their attempts were futile. Angry words turned to fists of rage, which soon escalated into shootings and other crimes. The culmination of this war came on February 2. On that day, the United States Supreme Court handed down its decision in a discrimination case involving a Black man who'd been promoted over a White man. The case was quickly turned into an attack against Affirmative Action, which caused the urban leaders to rally around the cause. But their actions came too late. The court handed down the verdict that the policy was

James Gordon

unconstitutional, and with that one action came the total dissolution of an act that took centuries of struggle and work by the Black community to create.

African Americans were stunned. Many businesses and corporations quickly hired non-Blacks into executive positions, slyly forcing the minorities currently holding those positions out. It wasn't long before minorities began suing the government and the corporations. But the victories were few and there were even fewer lawyers who would take any of the cases, no matter how strong it was. Finally, Blacks found their way to Africa. How this came to be was still a mystery. Historians would probably say it was some form of mass exodus, people returning to their place of origin after being unfairly treated abroad. But regardless of the reason, Blacks were returning to Africa in droves. Among those individuals was a man named Edward Bolo and his wife, Camille. They brought with them a son named Mbaku, who was only five at the time.

Mbaku didn't understand much of what was happening. All he knew was that he was surrounded by children who had similar skin color to his. In fact, the entire village was filled with people of color. They ranged from those who were very dark to pale individuals who could probably pass for White. Despite the complexion, Mbaku and his family soon found happiness and the tiny village quickly turned into a neighborhood that rivaled the elite areas in suburban American. His father found work and shortly thereafter opened his own business. Many of the people in his neighborhood also found success and Mecca City literally rose from the ground overnight.

Twenty-five years had passed since the day the Bolo family set foot on African soil. Mbaku was now a grown man. As he stared into the distance from the penthouse floor of the Rose Hilton located in the center of the city, Mbaku waited for his benefactor to arrive. His eyes were cold and dark like licorice and when he was angry he had the disposition of a Black Mamba. Yet, he also had the capacity to be a very compassionate individual, especially when it came to the people of this city. That was saying a lot for a man that was considered to be the best in espionage tactics, not to mention one of the deadliest assassins in the world. He wasn't like other spies who used a lot of clever gadgets or state of the art weaponry. Mbaku was skilled with his hands and his techniques were only surpassed by his love for his country, which was what brought him to the Rose Hilton.

Nationhood

Mbaku loved AUNK and he especially loved Mecca City. He witnessed its beginnings and watched as it grew over the years. He loved the people that helped this place become the economic power it was now. They were his neighbors, friends, relatives and associates. His pride and the heritage of this new nation made him take a vow to do whatever he had to in order to protect the people of AUNK and its resources.

He'd gone to college and received his bachelor's degree in business. He later joined the military where he was trained in espionage and combat. He used his aggression and patriotism to quickly rise through the ranks and was often chosen to lead certain expeditions that required special handling. After seven years, he'd had his fill of the military and became a mercenary for hire. He never disappointed his clients and did his part to secure AUNK's prominence in the global market. As he continued to stare at the horizon, Mbaku heard a voice behind him.

"Beautiful, isn't it?" asked the voice.

"Indeed," replied Mbaku, not turning around. "The sun is so beautiful in the late summer months."

"No other place on earth possesses such a scene. Elephants strolling in the distance, giraffes moping in the sunset, herons flying off to wherever they are going. Ah, there is indeed no place like this."

Mbaku smirked. "You're late," he replied.

Just then, an older gentleman with skin colored as dark as coal walked to his side. He had a beard of white that matched the hair on his head. He wore dress slacks, a dress shirt and a wrap sweater that buttoned down the front. In many respects he favored Moses Gunn. He was Mbaku's uncle, Clarence Bolo. Clarence was the dean at the University of Kemet and was one of the more wealthy individuals in the nation.

"Have you eaten dinner yet?" asked Clarence.

"You didn't bring me here to ask me that, did you uncle?" asked Mbaku.

"I suppose not," Clarence replied, tucking his chin. "But what kind of uncle would I be if not concerned for my nephew's well-being."

"I see. And what manner of business do you have for me this time?"

Clarence puckered his lips and rolled his eyes upward to look at his nephew who was still staring out the penthouse window.

"There are many who would love to take this from us. They would destroy it just because we are the ones that possess this paradise,"

James Gordon

said Clarence.

"But you know I wouldn't allow it, right?" asked Mbaku.

"Yes. This I know."

"I made a vow once. Never again will the people of this nation fall under the oppressive hand. This is our home, a home we built when all other homes cast us out. I will die before I allow it or our freedom to be taken again."

"Many share your sentiment. But I'm glad to hear that the flame your soul holds for AUNK still burns brightly. Without you, things might be quite different now."

Mbaku turned his head slightly. "Why have you summoned me?" he asked.

"Do you remember a man by the name of Elijah Pollins?" asked Clarence.

"The Senator from Independence. Yes, I know of him."

"He called me two days ago and informed me of a plot his people uncovered to heist the Romanian crown jewels that were to be on display during the Winter Harvest Festival at the embassy."

"And what does this have to do with me?"

"He and the Romanian ambassador have decided not to display the jewels and secure them in a vault in the basement. After which, the jewels will be transported back to his country. Added security has been hired to ensure that the jewels are not stolen. However, we have reason to believe that the Americans will try and commandeer these national treasures in hopes to use them to barter with Romania and form an alliance, one that might give them a small geographic strategic advantage over our allies in Russia. Needless to say, their concerns are our concerns."

"Interesting. But this sounds like a matter for the United Nations, not me," said Mbaku, turning to walk away.

"Normally, that would be the case. However, I fear that there might be shadow players that are about to show their hands," said Clarence, whose words stopped Mbaku in his tracks. "As you know, are enemies are many since we've developed the new regenerating fertilizer that allows us to transform normal desert sand into lush, fertile ground. Combine that with the oil deposits off the coast... well, I need not bore you with the rest."

"I'm well aware of our resources, Uncle. But tell me more about

Nationhood

these shadow players?" said Mbaku.

"Yes, I figured that would pique your interest." Clarence walked to his nephew's side. "These players have caused great concern throughout the world and are considered to be responsible for many of the terrorist attacks that have been performed, the last one being the bombing in Sri Lanka last week. Although we are not sure who they are, we do know that their intentions will soon turn toward us. We must discover their identity. In order to do that, we must flush them out."

"And I'm assuming this *flushing out* process involves the current predicament the Romanian government has found themselves in?" asked Mbaku.

"You don't miss a trick, do you?" replied Clarence.

"Just what would you have me do, Uncle? Steal the jewels?"

"Exactly."

Mbaku scoffed. "You do realize what could happen?"

"Yes. This could all blow up in our faces. If discovered, we could be viewed as the bad guys and our relations with Romania and our other allies will be jeopardized. But protecting the welfare of AUNK and its territories is your prime directive. This must be done, and I see no better person for the job."

Mbaku pondered the idea for a moment. The embassy would be crawling with security and equipped with the latest in surveillance technology. Even if he were to get past all of that, he still had to get the jewels and escape undetected. It was nearly impossible to perform such a task, but if there was one thing that Mbaku enjoyed it was a challenge.

Just then, he realized something. In his uncle's last statement, he made very specific comments about the job. It was a little trick he liked to pull, placing comments about the mission in his sentences in order to see if Mbaku was paying attention. Clarence was an extremely intelligent man and he chose his words very carefully. In this instance it wasn't so much a matter of what he said, but instead what he didn't say. With a slight smirk, Mbaku turned to look at his uncle with a stare of skepticism.

"You don't want me to go into the embassy. You want me to wait for the person whom the American's send to steal the jewels and then steal it from them," probed Mbaku.

"Perceptive as always. That is why I chose you for the job," Clarence replied.

"What would you like for me to do with the spy?"

James Gordon

"Do as you choose. If at all possible, you might want to glean any information as to who and what we are up against. Just be mindful of the risks involved."

"I always do. I assume the embassy will be providing dinner for this little soirée? That is why you asked if I've eaten, right?"

"Prime rib and lobster."

"Yum. Guess I better break out the old tux."

"That would be appropriate."

Mbaku began walking away. As he reached the entrance to the massive room, he stopped at the threshold, turned and spoke to Clarence.

"We're still on for our weekly game of chess on Sunday, correct?" he asked.

"Indeed. I owe you a thrashing from last week. I still think you cheated, though I haven't figured it out yet," replied Clarence.

Mbaku gave him a nod, turned and exited the room. Clarence stood there staring at the door through which his nephew departed. The expression on his face revealed the troubling thoughts that plagued his mind. If what he feared was validated, and these shadow players indeed have intentions to attack AUNK, it would be the greatest threat to ever confront the nation. In his mind Clarence prayed that his suspicions were wrong.

~~~

"How dare they do this!" shouted Senator Elijah Pollins as he slammed his attaché into the wall of his office. "Who in the hell do these Americans think they are, trying to strong arm the Romanians?"

"Senator, please calm down," said Lucinda Mathews, Senator Pollins' assistant. "Would you like for me to fix you a drink?"

"Hell no!" he exclaimed. "I want to grab those sons of bitches by the neck and squeeze until they're all about to pass out!"

He walked to the window behind his desk and flung open the curtains. He stared at the River of Humanity, the manmade canal that passed through the center of Mecca City. He was seething, almost to the point of shaking.

"I have a good mind to call every newspaper in the world and publicize their actions," he said calmly.

"But if you do that, every country is going to think that this is some sort of smear campaign. The fallout behind such actions would set our progress back generations," Lucinda replied.

Nationhood

She lowered her head, not really knowing what to say next. She had been Senator Pollins' assistant for five years and she'd seen him like this only once. However, she knew that these rare moments were best handled by remaining quiet, looking concerned and allowing him to vent.

Senator Pollins continued to stare out at the famed river. He was starting to calm down now, but he still couldn't believe that something like this would ever happen. Then again, he should have seen this coming. The Americans had been grumbling for years, ever since AUNK became the new agricultural provider for the world. But now, things had been taken to a whole new level.

"Can you imagine, Lucinda? After hundreds of years of Blacks being oppressed and discriminated against, they still have the nerve to grumble about the last few years of progress we've made. For the first time since the fall of the Egyptian Empire, the playing field has become balanced. It seems ludicrous that they would still view us as a threat, even after all the good we've done," said Pollins solemnly.

"Yes, sir," said Lucinda with a sigh.

"You know, I wasn't born when the American Civil Rights Movement in the 60s took place, but it's clear that the fight for equality is far, far from over. I just don't understand why so many people can't see that we are not their enemy and that we are trying to help make this world a better place."

Just then, Teresa Evans, Senator Pollins' secretary came to the door and knocked.

"Excuse me, Senator, but there's a call for you on line two," she said.

"Thank you, Teresa," he replied.

"You know, I'm sure the Romanian Embassy is going to want a response from the members of the legislature about this. I'll go make some calls to some of their aides and set up conferences. Let me know if you want anything," said Lucinda, as she backed out of the office to allow Pollins some privacy for his call.

"Thanks," he said.

As the doors closed, Senator Pollins stood with his hands on his hips, glancing at the blinking light on his phone and debating whether to pick it up. He had an idea who it was. It was probably the Moroccan Embassy calling to say how appalled they were to learn about Romania's decision to not display the jewels. Morocco was once the country that had

James Gordon

some semblance of rule over the land that now composed New Kemet and they'd had this bittersweet relationship with AUNK ever since the new nation came into power.

Even though it has been over twenty-five years since the nation was born, their feelings haven't changed. They've been waiting for AUNK to slip so they could ease back in and take over once more. The Americans have supported their acts of espionage and, as a result, weakened relations between Morocco and AUNK. It would be no surprise that they would already know about the supposed heist. Although he wasn't ready to hear the pretentious apologies from their representatives right now, he had to remain professional at a time like this and play along, for that was what politicians did; they deceived. It's a part of the job. He took a deep breath and forced a smile on his face. He lifted the receiver and pressed line two.

"Senator Pollins," he said with a somewhat chipper salutation.

"Elijah," said a slightly accented voice on the other end.

"Consulate Mendoza," replied Pollins as he rolled his eyes.

"How are things? I trust that you and your family are well?"

"Yes. We are doing nicely. And how are your wives and children?"

"Well. My third wife, Milan, is expecting our third child any day."

"That's great news. So, Consulate, how may I assist you today?"

"It has come to our attention that there might be a bit of trouble at tonight's engagement at the Romanian Embassy."

"Really? You heard that?"

"Well, one does hear things when in politics."

"Yes, nasty how that works, wouldn't you agree?"

"Indeed. But that is not the nature of this call. I wanted to assure you that our country has absolutely nothing to do with any of this. We want nothing more than to continue to strive toward a peaceful relationship with you and your people."

"Is that so?" asked Pollins.

"Oh my. It sounds as if my intentions are not believed?"

Pollins began to allow some of his frustrations to show. "Consulate Mendoza, I deeply appreciate your concern over AUNK's and Romania's delicate situation and it truly relieves me to hear that Morocco intends to seek further civil diplomatic relations with AUNK. But suffer no delusion about what I'm about to say. If we find out that the Americans

Nationhood

are truly behind all of this, our eyes will not only turn toward them, but toward you and your country as well. I'm sure you can understand why, seeing that the two countries are such close personal allies."

"Yes, I understand your concern, and your words will be taken into consideration," said Mendoza. "In an effort to show our good will and civil intent, perhaps we should meet and discuss this further. How about the Safari Lounge, at say, 6:30?"

"Sounds great," replied Pollins.

"See you then."

The phone clicked in his ear and Senator Pollins replaced the headset in the cradle. He sighed in disgust because he was growing weary of this game. For so long, he and other people of his country had fought to make gains and every time these gains were made they would find someone trying to take them away. It was a constant battle and it was beginning to feel as if it was all in vain. He pressed the intercom button on his phone.

"Yes, sir," said Teresa on the speaker.

"Could you get me my navy suit and a fresh shirt? It seems that I have a meeting tonight with Consulate Mendoza," he said.

"Which tie?" she asked.

"You pick it. Something that says *screw you*."

"Right away," she said with a chuckle.

He clicked off the intercom and sat in his plush leather chair behind his massive cherry oak desk. He loosened his tie and braced his head in his hands, massaging his temples and staring at the bookshelf on the opposing wall. For fifteen minutes he did nothing but stare at each of the books, wondering what was going to happen to the nation after tonight. With a deep sigh, he placed his head on his desk and tried to close his eyes for a few moments.

~~~

Washington D.C. The mist of the dawn met the morning joggers as they raced through the park with their leashed pets. Others waited patiently at bus stops, preparing for their morning commute to the city. This was just another day for the folks who worked for a living in America. It wasn't a pleasant start, but it was something most people could live through until quitting time. Then you could put this day to rest and perhaps start another with a little better beginning. But for many, that pleasure would never come again.

James Gordon

When the Affirmative Action policy was ruled unconstitutional, African Americans began leaving the United States and returning to Africa, mainly Mecca City. Once there, they became citizens and were released from any debt owed to the US due to the International Laws of Propriety. These laws stated that no funds earned inside one country could be transferred to better the economy of another nation except through trade. Since African Americans were no longer citizens of the United States, they didn't have to repay the debts they owed. Needless to say, such actions caused a major stock market crash and almost ruined the economy of America.

But then, the United States government made an emergency closed gate policy called the West Wing Act. This policy prevented the departure of any remaining African American that owed any money to any financial institution, regardless of the amount. With Affirmative Action being considered unconstitutional, some Blacks were unable to get work and ultimately found themselves unable to repay their loans. Those who *were* able to find work discovered that their interest rates had become so exaggerated that it made it nearly impossible for them to repay their loans.

In an effort to regain all the money they lost, indebted African Americans were imprisoned and then sold to the government by the financial institutions. These new policies were called the Jack Crow Laws. These laws rescinded the rights of all incarcerated Blacks in the United States and returned them to a new form of slavery called Indentured Servants, or IS, for short. It was around that time when a new organization was formed, Exodus. It was a Black freedom group that was formed right after the Jack Crow Laws went into effect. It fought to free the remaining Blacks who weren't able to flee the United States before the enactment of the West Wing policy. The movement had many supporters, some of whom were from other ethnic groups but the majority of them were Black. But with support comes enemies and there was no other group on the face of the planet that had greater enemies than Exodus.

In a deserted warehouse, fifteen miles outside of the city limits, five shots were heard echoing from inside. Birds that were perched on the windowsill shot into the air and scattered in all directions. Inside, a body lay on the floor as a stream of blood flowed from under it. Standing over the lifeless body were three men. One of them had fired the fatal shots and still stood in his two point shooting stance. He was an older man, perhaps in his mid to late fifties. The scowl on his face wasn't one that illustrated

10

Nationhood

any anger or hatred he possessed for his victim, but instead his expression blatantly displayed the pain he had endured over the years and the endless attempts to suppress the memories of his past deeds. It was etched into every wrinkle and groove. He slowly lowered his pistol as the smoke inside the barrel continued to swirl from the opening.

The others stood by, watching the first man conclude his duty. He was to be feared, even if he wasn't an immediate threat to their lives. The older man turned from the corpse and strolled slowly toward the table in the corner. Dust clouds rose as his feet shuffled across the floor. The building used to be an old steel mill back in the 1930s. Now, it was a home for the destitute and the drug addicts. Its purpose today was to provide a secluded place for a murder and its purpose was fulfilled.

As the older man arrived at the table, he set the murder weapon down and dropped his hands to his sides. He stood for a moment, motionless, as if he were having a moment of silence to remember his victim on the floor. The remaining two men turned to look at the older man. They also stood motionless, as if they were looking to the older man for some sort of signal to execute their next move. Their hands were crossed in front of them; their faces devoid of emotion. They were the epitome of what a secret service agent looked like when they were guarding the president.

As they continued to stare at the older man, he lifted his hand toward the handle of the gun. His effort to grip the weapon seemed to show signs of a mental struggle as his fingers encircled the butt. It almost appeared as if his movement possessed a degree of reluctance to grab the firearm. After a few moments, he finally secured the gun in his hand and slowly lifted it from its resting position on the table. The two stiff guardsmen began to show a little concern. They dropped their hands to their sides and prepared to reach for their sidearm.

The old man dangled the gun in his hand and began to slowly turn to face the other men. He stared into their eyes. They watched him murder someone and did absolutely nothing to stop him. Silence filled the air, as the tension of the moment seemed to overpower the fact that there was a body lying on the floor behind them. The two guardsmen looked at each other and then toward the older man.

"So Doctor Weinkaufen. What is your decision?" questioned the lead guardsman with a hint of a German accent.

"Why do you wish to know? Doesn't it seem obvious what I am

11

doing?" retorted the doctor.

"Come now, Doctor. Don't do anything stupid," said the guard, attempting to reason with him.

"Stupid is what I have been *doing* for the last several years of my life," said Weinkaufen. "The system has taken my pride, my honor and my dignity. I have nothing left to take."

"Don't be an idiot, Doctor. You know this was the right thing to do," said the second guard, who had an even thicker accent.

"Perhaps."

"So I ask again, Herr Doctor. What is your answer?" queried the first guard.

"Here is my answer!" he replied, lifting his gun toward the two guardsmen.

Fear exploded across their faces. Their bodies tightened as the doctor pointed the deadly weapon toward them. The barrel still showed the traces of smoke from its previous firing and the burnt smell of gun power lingered in the air. The second guardsman began pulling his coat back in order to get to his pistol. His actions didn't go unnoticed. The doctor turned the gun toward the second man and slowly began squeezing the trigger. Sweat began to bead on the foreheads of the two guards and panic gnawed at their brains. Their heartbeats raced and sounded like someone pounding on a timpani. Suddenly, the doctor performed a move that was quite unexpected. He quickly turned the gun from the two guards and placed it in his mouth. Without a moments hesitation and before the guards could utter a single word, Weinkaufen pulled the trigger.

The explosion blasted copious amount of blood and flesh across the warehouse floor and on the table where the gun laid moment ago. The doctor's head snapped back and his body convulsed for a moment. Then he flopped to the floor in a bloody heap, twitching from the autonomic reflexes of shock. His eyes were fixed, but possessed a peaceful glaze that gave the impression he had surrendered the ghosts that haunted his life for so long. His body gave one final twitch and the moan of his last breath rushed from his lungs.

The guardsmen dropped their defensive postures and reassumed their straight-faced expressions. They walked over to the doctor's body and knelt beside it. The doctor's mouth still showed streams of smoke from the blast. The lead guard lifted the doctor's head and placed three fingers in the large hole in the back of his neck. He maneuvered his hand

Nationhood

around for a few moments and then removed his brain and blood covered fingers from the hole. He dropped the doctor's head, allowing it to thump against the cold, concrete floor. He stood to his feet, reached into his lapel pocket and removed a handkerchief. He began wiping the chunks of cerebral matter from his hands with a calmness that seemed almost robotic. The second man removed a phone from his inner coat pocket and pressed a single button.

"What!" blurted a voice from the receiver.

"It's done," said the man.

"Good. Return to base," retorted the voice.

The man pressed the button to disconnect the call. Then he crushed the phone in his hand, allowing the crumbled plastic to fall on the chest of the Doctor Weinkaufen. The first guardsman completed cleaning his hands and dropped the blood-soaked handkerchief on the deceased doctor's body. Without saying a word, the two men turned and walked away.

~~~

James Gordon

Chapter Two: Don't Shoot the Messenger

Mbaku stood on top of the roof of the First Kemet National Bank, the tallest building in the city. He stared at the metropolis below, forty-seven floors down to the busy streets. In a few hours he would be attending the Winter Harvest Festival at the Romanian Embassy and stealing the prized Tsar Nicolas Jewels. The act, in and of itself, would most certainly spark riots and accusations in Romania as well as the rest of the world. But it was what his country's government requested of him and what AUNK wanted, he would certainly deliver.

The top of the bank was one of his favorite places. It gave him a perspective of the entire city and the world, for that matter. He could see for miles in every direction and the building was the focal point of all communication network uplinks. At this dizzying height he cleared his head, developed his strategy and prepared himself for his mission. Having been there for over thirty minutes, his preparation was now complete. He knew exactly how he would carry out his duties and now it was time to leave. He walked from the roof's edge and made his way to the elevator inside the catwalk. As he waited for it to arrive, he heard a buzz on his two-way communicator, which was implanted inside his right auditory canal. It was his assistant, Vishepsut Amundo, or as he called her, Vee.

"What is it, Vee?" he asked.

"Have you completed your preparations?" she asked.

"Yes, thank you."

"Your invitation will be in the lobby when you pick up your car. Your equipment has been stored in the trunk and everything is ready to go."

"Good. This should be a night to remember."

"Indeed. I wouldn't be at all surprised to see CNN at the embassy."

"Neither would I. The Americans love to publicize their coup attempts."

"I know I don't have to say this, but do be careful. I'm not sure why but something about all of this has a foul stench surrounding it."

James Gordon

"That's why I like you, Vee. We're always on the same wavelength. I'll call you when I'm done."

Mbaku disconnected by touching the outside of his ear. The elevator finally arrived and he stepped inside. He pressed the button for the basement and the doors closed. As he descended, Mbaku realized that he still wasn't in the frame of mind he needed to be in and with so much at stake he couldn't afford to be distracted. He'd done all the necessary preparations for the mission. Now all that was left was for him to calm his nerves and there was but one way he knew to do that. Her name was Wendy Hughes, owner of one of the local art galleries and a doctor in internal medicine. She was American by birth and one of the few who was able to buy her way out of the country before she could be placed in indentured status. Mbaku pulled out his cell phone and punched in a phone number. A soft voice answered on the other end.

"Hello?"

"It's me," he said.

"Hey, how are you?"

"Okay, I guess. Are you busy?"

"No, not at all. Are you coming over?"

"Yeah, I'll be there in a few minutes."

"I'll be waiting."

His mouth curled at the ends. He closed the flip cover of his phone and placed it in his pocket. The elevator slowed and then stopped. The doors opened and he found himself inside the parking garage, which was beneath the building. He exited the cabin and made his way to the attendant's desk, where he gave his normal ten-dollar tip to Leroy, the parking attendant.

"Thank you, sir. How are you doing today?" asked Leroy.

"Very good, Leroy. Would you be so kind as to get my car, please?" asked Mbaku.

"Yes, sir. Right away, sir."

Leroy dashed off toward the reserve parking area to retrieve Mbaku's car. Still feeling stressed, Mbaku took a deep breath and attempted to collect himself. He shifted his mind on Wendy and the things he wanted to do with her when he got there. She was very sensual and had an insatiable appetite for sex. Aside from the fact that she was one of the most erotic and extraordinary women he'd ever been with, she was also one of the smartest. She could nonchalantly say something that often

16

Nationhood

caused him to experience great insight on many issues. However, it wasn't her intellect he sought at this moment. He simply wanted to relieve some stress and she enjoyed taking the edge off before he left for these missions. She would say it was her patriotic duty.

After a few moments of waiting, the squeal of car tires was heard and a Black Mercedes sedan pulled to a stop by the attendant's desk. Leroy hopped out and held the car door open for Mbaku.

"Here you go, sir, all clean and ready to go," said Leroy.

Mbaku walked to the driver's side and got in. "Thank you, Leroy. Tell your family I said hello," he replied.

"Thank you, sir. Have a good day, sir," said Leroy as he closed the door.

Mbaku pulled off and exited the parking garage. As he turned on East Capitol Street, he began wondering about tonight. If things didn't go as he'd planned it could jeopardize the welfare of the nation, not to mention the freedom of his people. Just then, his concentration was broken by the ringing of his communication device in his ear. He traced his hand over his ear lobe and activated the uplink.

"Yes?" he answered.

"It's Vee again."

"What's up?"

"I just watched a broadcast on A.E.T. about something you might find interesting."

"And what would that be?"

"They were talking about the release of an IS. Supposedly, he'd repaid his debt to the government and was being released today. His plans are to come to Mecca City and meet with a few members of the Imperial Senate to discuss aid in helping others do the same thing."

"And why would you think that would interest me?"

"Have you ever heard of any Black person being released from indentured status since the Americans instituted the Jack Crow Laws?"

Mbaku thought for a moment. "Come to think of it, no," he replied.

"My point exactly," Vee continued. "I find it hardly a coincidence that he would be released and want to speak with the single most powerful legislative body in our land."

"Yes, that does sound odd. Tell you what, do some checking and call me if anything important comes up."

James Gordon

"No problem."

Mbaku disconnected and continued driving toward Ngunde, a ritzy area north of Mecca City. Traffic was congested, more so today than normal, it seemed. As he drove, he found himself wrestling with his thoughts. He never truly believed that things had changed in America, nor had they accepted AUNK into the global community. He also didn't believe, despite America's patriotic propaganda, that life for Blacks in that nation was better and that a true understanding had been developed amongst them and their oppressors. But now he was beginning to wonder what the Americans were really up to. This recent release of an indentured servant had to be some sort of ploy. In fact, he feared that this situation was about to lead to a far worse state of affairs. As the possibilities raced through his head, Mbaku hadn't realized that ten minutes had passed and he was nearing his destination.

He soon arrived at the Ngunde subdivision, where he turned into the driveway of a brick Ranch style home with a sloping green lawn surrounded by medium sized oak trees. The entire area was the result of the regenerating fertilizer created by AUNK scientists. The lawns were lusciously green and no one would have ever thought that this area was once a barren desert. He parked his car in the driveway, turned off the motor. He sat there for a few moments, debating whether to go in, especially after the troubled thoughts he'd been pondering. He could feel that there was much unrest in the country, like the spirit of Africa was talking to its children. This made him even more anxious about tonight's mission. Everything had to be executed like clockwork and nothing could be left to chance. After rationalizing that he needed to calm himself, along with the fact that he didn't want to waste a trip to Wendy's house, he got out of his car, checking around him to ensure no one was watching. The tall trees and heavily bushed landscaping provided excellent camouflage. He closed the car door, walked up to the house and pressed the doorbell once. A few moments later, a slender, yet busty, cream-skinned woman with shoulder length blonde highlighted hair opened the door. Dressed only in a sheer, full-length, angel white caftan with matching four-inch stilettos, she stood with her hip cocked slightly to the right and her hand braced on it.

"Welcome," she said.

"Hello, Wendy," replied Mbaku.

She opened the door wider, allowing him to walk in. She slowly

Nationhood

closed the door behind him, then propped herself against it as if she were waiting to be taken. He looked at her, still sporting a somewhat serious expression. Wendy picked up on his solemn mood and walked over to him.

"What's wrong?" she asked with a pretentiously pouting face.

Mbaku could not answer. He simply wanted to put the mission out of his mind for a while. He pulled Wendy close and began kissing her passionately. She cupped the sides of his face and tried to keep up with his ravenous fondling. He pressed her against the door hard, then lowered her to the floor where they writhed against each other like two animals in heat. Mbaku was more aggressive than normal and his actions made Wendy feel more desirable. He was like a man possessed and she loved it. She imagined his passionate hunger for her had grown completely out of control and he was lost in the thralls of desire.

For several moments, they engaged in a frenzy of fondling, suckling and kissing. Suddenly, Mbaku stopped and turned Wendy around, positioning her on all fours. He lifted her caftan and unzipped his pants. His entrance made Wendy yelp, then grimace, arching her back due to the pain she felt from his forceful entry. Her nails scratched across the wooden floor as Mbaku aggressively began thrusting himself inside of her. His emotions came to a boil and with each stroke his tension was being released. His mind was no longer focused on Wendy. Instead, the raw passion that he'd tried to suppress came out and she was the hapless instrument he used for his release. Wendy moaned and screamed as Mbaku continued his unbridled moment of passion. Then, with a muffled groan, he concluded his aggressiveness with a release. Wendy dug her fingernails so deeply into the wood grain of her floor that she scarred a portion of its polished finish. As he concluded his orgasm and relaxed his body, her moans of pain died into whimpers. Mbaku slowly slid himself from inside of her and lowered his head. Wendy began crawling away from him slowly, her vagina throbbing from the vicious battering she just took. She backed herself into the far wall, pulling her knees to her chest and staring at him through a veil of tears. Traces of moisture glistened on her cheeks as her emotion-filled eyes glared at Mbaku, who sat on the backs of his legs in the middle of the hallway. A stunned look blanketed his face and his eyes had a far away gaze. A few moments of uncomfortable silence passed. Then, Wendy decided to speak.

"You've never done that before. It was almost as if you were trying to hurt me," she said.

Mbaku lifted his head and looked at her.

"I was," he replied, somberly.

"Why? What did I do wrong?"

A look of uncertainty bloomed across his face.

"I don't know," he replied.

Wendy's eyes lowered and she stared at the floor. A few more tears fell from her eyes. Despite the fact that her relationship with Mbaku had always been a purely sexual one, Wendy was somewhat fond of Mbaku and she'd never considered the fact that he would ever harm her. But she could also tell he wasn't himself. He seemed despondent and she had a good idea why. Knowing that he would not make the first move, she inched her way across the floor and sat next to him. She gently placed her hand on the other side of his head and guided him to lay on her lap. She began stroking his head, gently using the tips of her fingernails to calm him.

"I'm sorry I hurt you," he said softly.

"Are you sure?" she replied. "I mean, that is what you said you were trying to do."

"Yes, I'm sure."

A few more quiet moments passed, and once more Wendy broke the silence.

"I've never seen you like this before. Wanna talk?" she asked.

Mbaku wanted to, but he couldn't, at least not yet. He wasn't sure that Wendy would understand. Although she'd been with him for many years, she could never fully grasp the impact these missions had on him. Each time there was something different, another plot from another country to destroy his country. All of the accomplishments and progress they made was constantly being placed in jeopardy and he was starting to get tired of it. Perhaps it was time to tell Wendy what was going on. It would, at the very least, give him someone to confide in. He lifted his head off of her lap and looked into her hazel eyes. He then stood to his feet, zipped his pants and helped her up. As he looked at her, he was almost too emotional to speak.

"What do they want you to do this time?" she asked.

Mbaku gulped, second-guessing whether to say anything to her.

"Something that could change the complexion of this country forever," Mbaku replied.

Nationhood

"Does it have anything to do with tonight's gala at the embassy?"

"Yes," he replied after a mild pause.

Wendy placed her right hand over her mouth and the other around her waist. She thought for a moment, then walked to the entrance of her living room, grabbed the remote from a nearby table and turned on the television. The news was on and the anchorperson was talking about the very thing she'd just asked Mbaku about.

"I'm sorry, baby. I don't know what to say," said Wendy, lifting her hand over her mouth once more.

"There's nothing you can say," Mbaku replied.

"But why do they have to keep calling on you? Why can't they train someone else?"

Mbaku walked toward her and placed his hands on her shoulders. "Because no one else loves this country more than I."

"Bullshit!" exclaimed Wendy, turning to look at him. "There are hundreds of soldiers out there just waiting to defend the righteous AUNK! Why does it always have to be you? Haven't you done enough? Haven't they taken enough from you?"

Suddenly, Wendy felt faint and began collapsing to the floor. Mbaku caught her before she fell. He helped her down to the floor and laid her against the wall. Wendy was hyperventilating, a problem that she often had when she felt emotionally overwhelmed. Mbaku began talking to her and calming her down. She took deep breaths and fanned herself. Soon, she felt her anxiety lessening and her skin became flushed and formed small beads of sweat.

"How are you feeling?" asked Mbaku.

"I think I'm okay," replied Wendy.

"You want me to get you a glass of water?"

"No, I'll be fine in a minute. Just let me sit here and catch my breath."

Mbaku sat next to her and held her hand. Within moments, Wendy had calmed herself completely. She took one more deep breath, then pushed herself from the floor and attempted to stand.

"Are you ready to do that?" asked Mbaku.

"Yes, I'm okay," she said.

Wendy began walking into the living room. Mbaku stood from the floor and followed. They sat down on a plush virgin white sectional as Wendy, still holding the remote control, began channel surfing on the flat

21

James Gordon

screen television on the far wall. The news of tonight's big event was still being broadcasted. On MSNBC, however, broadcaster Bob Durham was in America covering the story about the IS that was about to board an airplane and depart the United States. The crawler across the bottom of the screen read, "First IS freed from indentured status." Behind Durham was a mob of angry White people screaming insults and voicing their protest over the release. Durham had to actually scream over the chants of the crowd in order to deliver his report.

"Not since the ruling of Kessler vs. Southwest Natural has there been this much turmoil. Victor Johnson, a Black man from New Orleans, has been given clearance to leave the US. In just over five years, he was able to repay his debt and now he walks on this commercial airliner a free man. Many Whites are voicing their opinions, claiming that he doesn't deserve freedom. In the Black community, however, they are calling this a victory for equality," said Durham.

Wendy turned down the volume as people from both sides began speaking to the media. She laid back and rested herself on Mbaku's chest.

"Well, there you have it," she said.

"Yep, the continuance of a very bitter and bloody struggle," said Mbaku. "Black people in that country are right back where they started. They're probably in worse condition than before the Civil Rights Movement."

Wendy just shook her head.

"You know this was the plan from the start," Mbaku continued. "They only enacted Affirmative Action because they knew they were going to take it away. They just played along so Blacks could get comfortable and settle into the belief that change had taken place. But all along, things remained the same. Just when we believe we are catching up to the game, we find out that we are still way, way behind."

"I wouldn't worry about it. We've come too far to slide back now. Just have a little faith," said Wendy.

"Faith?" asked Mbaku as he pushed up and stood to his feet. "Faith is something I don't have much of right now! Those White folks have taken everything our people had in America! They tricked them and sold them right back into slavery! Now they have the audacity to say we don't deserve our freedom, after everything they've done!"

"Baby, all I'm saying is injustice never prospers. They'll get there's. You just have to wait on God to handle things."

22

Nationhood

"God? What manner of God are you speaking of? The God that rules over our people isn't the one they speak of in the bible. The God in that book talks about being subservient and bowing down to a more powerful entity. That God is more of an egomaniac than a merciful giver. He could have stopped all of this injustice if he truly existed. But he doesn't. It's just a gimmick to keep people of color passive and accepting of things that are unjust. It has been the single, most destructive tool against our people."

"And just what would you have everyone believe in?"

"The gods that brought us to glory—Amen-Ra and Isis, Osiris and Anubis. When we believed in our gods, we were a powerful people. We created a kingdom that has been unmatched ever since. The Orthodox Church of Kemet is the only religion of our people because those gods did not teach their children to be footstools to those who would destroy them."

"You sound like a Black Muslim."

Mbaku's expression became deadly serious. "I should have expected that kind of talk from you, especially since you could pass for White!" he said.

Wendy took offense to his comment. "Why are you attacking me? I'm not your enemy here! I care about you and you know this! Yes, you are Black and I am so light skinned that I could pass for White. But don't think for one, single, solitary second that I'm any less Black than you are just because my skin isn't as dark as yours. In fact, I believe I have more anger and hatred in my heart than you do. I was there when the gates closed. I was there when they broke into people's homes and dragged them out in the middle of the night, separating families who did nothing more than try to exist. But just because I saw, first hand, what depths these people would stoop to doesn't mean that I have to lower myself to their standards. It doesn't mean that everything that has happened has to affects us. I don't want to think that way, and I thought you didn't either."

She stood and walked toward the living room entrance. She was noticeably upset and Mbaku knew that he'd crossed the line. He didn't mean to say what he said. It was just a matter of him letting his feelings get away from him.

"Wendy," he called to her.

Wendy stopped at the entrance, keeping her back turned toward him.

"I'm –I'm sorry," Mbaku continued. "You're right; I'm taking my

23

James Gordon

frustrations out on the wrong person. I didn't mean what I said."

Wendy turned around and looked at him. She was very sensitive and any little word Mbaku said harshly would cause her to cry. They'd been seeing each other for over five years and she thought of them as more than just sexual partners. Even thought they had developed a relationship, his comments made her feel that he'd lumped her in with the rest of the despicable people of the world.

"You know, you hurt me," said Wendy as tears streamed down her face. "Even though I was born an American doesn't mean I subscribe to the rules that now govern them. I didn't deserve that. You know what I went through to get out of there. You know what they put me through. I paid a king's ransom for my freedom and it still wasn't enough. I lost my pride, my dignity and my home, Mbaku. They took everything from me and I didn't deserve the things you said to me."

With a look of shame, Mbaku shook his head. "No, you didn't," he replied. "I know what you went through, as well as what my parents went through when they left. No one left America without some form of loss. I should not have demeaned you."

He walked toward her and hugged her tightly. She wrapped her arms around his back and hugged him as well and allowed herself to cry. Mbaku held her for as long as she needed him to. For several minutes Wendy cried, then she began to gather her composure. She pulled back from Mbaku and wiped her eyes with her hands. Mbaku removed a handkerchief from his back pocket and handed it to her. She was about to wipe her face when she stopped, looked at the handkerchief and then looked at Mbaku.

"This hasn't been used, has it?" she asked.

Mbaku chuckled. "No, it hasn't."

The two enjoyed a mild chuckle. But their mirth was quickly interrupted by the chimes of Wendy's grandfather clock in the hallway. They both looked at it and then at each other, their expression turning serious.

"I have to leave," said Mbaku.

"I know," Wendy replied.

"There may be unrest on the streets tonight. You should stay inside for the rest of the evening."

"I intend to. I'll be here for you when you're done."

Mbaku and Wendy kissed one last time. He fixed his clothes as

24

Nationhood

she helped straighten his shirt and wipe the lipstick from his lips. They walked to the front door and paused. Mbaku stared at Wendy like a sailor who was about to leave for his six-month duty. He wanted to remember her just the way she was right now. Oddly, before now he never realized just how important she really was to him. In fact, he almost felt sad about leaving her.

"Thank you for keeping my head straight, as always," said Mbaku, giving Wendy a wink.

"You're welcome, baby. Stay strong and remember I believe in you," said Wendy.

She opened the front door and saw that the sun was now completely set. Mbaku walked out and quickly made his way to his car. He got in and fastened his seat belt. He cranked the motor and backed out of the driveway. Wendy waved as he began pulling away from her house. As he got to the end of her street, he turned right and started his trip back toward the city. Wendy released a heavy sigh and closed her door.

~~~

Washington, D.C. USA. The morning sun continued to rise over the city, spreading its warmth and glow over the nation's capitol. The hustle and bustle of the country's movers and shakers had already begun and the buzzing of humanity made the city take on a life of its own. Just outside the city limits, a huge mansion sat majestically off the road. Once rumored to be the home of one of former president Andrew Jackson's mistresses, it now was the domicile of another woman. Inside, massive curtains were drawn apart via remote control. The sunlight beamed through the opened drapes and brightened the room immensely. The plush surroundings became more visible as the curtains widened. Roman style décor was the theme. Huge marble pillars stretched toward the eighteen-foot high barrel-vaulted ceiling that was covered with Michelangelo style paintings. The walls were trimmed with white marble that had been chiseled by hand. A massive chandelier of crystal hung from the ceiling center, refracting the sunlight into tiny-orbed rainbows that danced against the wall.

Atop a three-tiered platform in the middle of the bedroom sat a huge canopy bed that had been carved from pure cherry oak. Its size alone commanded the attention from everything else in the room. The covers were rumpled, as if someone had been sleeping in it. Dual Sheratons graced the casual area at the foot of the bed and a full gourmet breakfast

James Gordon

sat on a table on the terrace. A single rose stood in a green crystal vase in the middle of the table and a gentle breeze danced with the panels that draped the massive doors to the patio.

Amidst this scene of luxury was something even more enchanting in the next room. Adjacent to this palatial paradise was the bathing room. Inside, a huge one hundred thirty-gallon, floor level, Jacuzzi-style tub made of marble was filled with a warm bubble bath. Rose pedals littered the floor of onyx and the steam from the heated water clouded the room in a blanket of mist. Gold trimmings accented the room and the theme was of Egyptian design. Suddenly, the shapely legs of a woman erupted from beneath the soapy water. Gently, her feet rested against the rim of the tub as droplets fell from her skin and tapped against the water's surface. These legs and feet belonged to the lady of the manor; a woman of extreme power. She was a living, breathing goddess whose mere glance could mean someone's death.

The dainty feet slid down the side of the tub and submerged beneath the suds with a splash. The soothing hum of the whirlpool, along with the sauna-like heat, was enough to make the tensest person relax. But as all peaceful moment go, it was soon interrupted by a knock on the bathroom door. She lifted her head just enough for her lips to break the water's surface.

"Come!" she shouted.

The doors of the bathroom opened as her mouth sunk beneath the water's surface once again. In stepped a man who appeared to be in his mid fifties, part Asian and part Black, dressed in a formal butler's suit. He had a slightly muscular build and his hair was peppered with faint strands of gray. In his hands he reverently carried a platinum serving tray that had an extremely high polish. His name was Jaquimo and he was the butler of the woman in the tub. He walked to the massive floor-level bathing basin and stopped at the edge. He glanced down to see the woman lying beneath the sudsy water. He rolled his eyes in exasperation, then announced the reason for his intrusion.

"There is a transmission for you. Would you like to take it in here?" he asked, kneeling down.

The woman erupted from beneath the water and sat up. She maneuvered herself to the tub's edge, reached toward the platinum tray held by Jaquimo and removed a slender silver rod measuring the length of a common fountain pen.

Nationhood

"Thank you, Jaquimo," she said as she brushed the water and soap from her face.

"Would Madam like anything else? Perhaps a snorkel?" he asked jestingly.

"No." she said. "But thanks for asking."

"I'll leave you to your business then."

"I'll ring you when I'm done."

Her name was Katura Ishtar and she was the world's most wanted woman, a tagline that wasn't directed solely toward her stunning beauty. Her list of titles read like an international criminal report. She was a mercenary, a spy, an assassin and a thief, among other things. She was wanted in more than fifteen countries and was at the top of Interpol's terrorist list. She was also an indentured servant. She fancied herself as a gun for hire, renting her services to whomever could afford her. For the most part she was contracted by financial institutions and insurance companies to go after international clients who seemingly forgot to pay their normal premiums. Sadly for them that meant a severe penalty, the kind they didn't walk away from unscathed. She was good at what she did, performing her duties with unnerving accuracy. She was the most preferred agent in America's espionage arsenal and although she was still the property of the United States government, she was treated like royalty. Anything she wanted was given to her. Homes, cars, jets and tons of money to spend. But even with all the riches and toys she was still a slave, a fact she found to be most ironic.

Jaquimo turned and walked to the door of the bathroom. He grabbed the doorknobs and closed the French doors behind him. Katura pressed a small flashing button on the side of the rod and then placed it on the edge of the tub. She pushed herself to the opposing wall, reclined against the side and rested her head on the edge, waiting for the transmission to begin. Just then, the rod projected a three dimensional image in front of her face. It was the image of a gray haired man in a smart looking suit tailored to fit him perfectly. His skin was slightly tanned and he had Arabic features. He was known as Prime, a high-ranking member of the United States government.

"Good morning, Ms. Ishtar. Glad to see you up and about!" said the image of Prime.

"Good morning, Prime!" Katura replied.

He began surveying Katura in her nude state.

James Gordon

"I say, Ms. Ishtar, of all the suits you have, this has to be my favorite!" he jested.

"Keep dreaming, old man. Now, what do you want? You're disturbing my bath," she replied, writhing beneath the water's surface.

"Quite right. You'll be happy to know that the Tsar Nicholas Jewels have been returned to their guarded location, deep within the embassy's underground vault. Your normal half-fee of 6.7 million dollars has been deposited into your standard accounts. The President sends his gratitude," said Prime.

Katura smiled, scooped a handful of sudsy water and poured it over her breasts.

"You have a funny way of relaying my orders. Just because you deposited that hefty dollar amount into my bank account already doesn't mean that I'll take your mission. I don't know if I want to go to the embassy's basement and steal the jewels for you. And tell the President he owes me more than his gratitude," she replied.

"You don't have a choice. Now, make sure the job is done well and do your best to avert a major international incident. Recover the priceless collection of jewels, that are older than any jewelry known I might add, and quite possibly you'll have earned something more valuable than the money we deposited—your freedom. I'd say that alone should make you take the job," stated Prime.

Katura smirked at Prime's comments. She braced her hands on the edge of the tub and stood up. The water cascaded down the curves of her shapely and well toned body. Her skin glistened as she reached for a towel and began drying off. Prime watched Katura with a look of euphoria. She performed a quick wipe across her face, then wrapped the towel around her body. After she made herself decent, she turned to face Prime and continue the conversation.

"You actually expect me to believe that all I need to do is this one little mission and all of a sudden you're gonna set me free? Do I look like an idiot to you, Prime?" she asked with clenched teeth. "Spare me the insults to my intelligence. I know you didn't come here to make fun of me. What's going on?"

Prime sighed deeply and quickly developed a more serious expression.

"Have you been keeping up with current national events?" he asked.

28

Nationhood

"Depends. What events are you referring to?" she asked.

Prime's expression worsened.

"Dr. Weinkaufen was killed earlier this morning. The details are sketchy, but from what we've been able to gather, he was shot through the head. Reports say it was a suicide, but I'm sure you know better," Prime explained.

Katura sighed and bowed her head. She closed her eyes tightly trying not to cry. Durst Weinkaufen was like her father. He practically raised her since she was six years old and Marina, his third wife, treated her like her own daughter. Marina never had any children, and she and Katura were very close. But she was especially close to Durst. The news of his death felt as if a knife had been plunged into his chest.

"Do you think he committed suicide?" she asked.

"We don't know. His fingerprints were on the gun," Prime retorted.

"Any witnesses?"

"Not at this time. A couple of homeless people found him this morning."

"Has Marina been told?" she asked, turning away.

"Yes, she knows."

"She must be a nervous wreck right now."

"She is being taken care of. However, it is you that I'm concerned with. Now that I've told you this bit of information, I'm wondering whether you are in the right frame of mind to carry out this mission."

"I'm fine. Please make my arrangements," said Katura with a tearful tone.

"Are you sure you're up to this? Operations suggested that I not tell you about Doctor Weinkaufen. They believed that if I told you about him you'd become unstable. They say you are too close to the matter. They said that if I told you they would send Viper."

"Viper? He's way over his head on this. Besides, I sense there's some connection between this mission you're sending me on and the death of my..." her voice trailed off. "Durst Weinkaufen wasn't some pastry chef on third and main, he was a doctor in biomedical research. You know as well as I do that his death had something to do with his work," said Katura.

"Perhaps. But I'll ask you again. Are you up to this?"

"Don't toy with me, Prime. Either you send me or I'm going in

29

James Gordon

anyway. Now, which would you prefer?"

After a few seconds of deliberating, Prime realized what he needed to do. It was better to have an agent he could keep in contact with than some rogue agent running around un-patrolled. That was exactly the course of action Katura would have taken if he didn't send her.

"Very well," he said with a sigh. "However, I only want you to get the jewels. Don't attempt to investigate. I don't want anything drawing more attention to this issue."

"*Don't Investigate*? What do you mean by *don't investigate*? The man that raised me for most of my life is dead and you want me to steal the crown jewels of the people who sponsored his research, and you tell me not to investigate?" asked Katura with a tearful, angry tone.

"Yes. That's the deal, either take it or leave it. Remember, your freedom is at stake, unless you *want* to spend the rest of your life as a slave to the United States Government," said Prime, with a sarcastic tone.

Katura pondered for a moment. "Guess it's like you said. I have no choice."

"Very well. By the way, you should know that M-5, Interpol and others are monitoring the embassy. Supposedly, there will be added security, but that shouldn't be a problem for you," said Prime.

Katura wiped her eyes and turned her back to Prime's image.

"What weapon was used?" she queried.

"Sorry?" asked Prime with puzzlement.

"What weapon was used to kill Durst?"

"Police reports indicate that Weinkaufen was killed with a lazar V77. The President has ordered the feds to keep a lid on this one," Prime continued.

Katura eyes widened and she stared into space with an astonished expression.

"A V77?" she asked with fear in her voice.

"Yes, Ms. Ishtar," Prime replied. "That means our friends, Exodus, are involved."

Katura turned and frowned from the revelation. Being an IS herself, Katura was forced to fight with Exodus for over eight years, ever since her enslavement to the system. Even though they fought to free the enslaved people, she was made to counter their attacks. Her last encounter ended with the total destruction of the Exodus headquarters in Los Angeles, a mission that almost ended her life. It was reported that she'd

30

Nationhood

wiped most of them out. It was now clear that the rumors, like the interest rates, were grossly exaggerated.

As a stipulation of her acceptance by the institution that sold her, Katura had been placed under torturous conditions and fed manipulated information that brainwashed her over the years. This conditioning made her, for the most part, a truly loyal soldier who would do anything for her government. Despite the fact that she knew Exodus was fighting for the freedom of people like her, the programming in her head kicked in. They were terrorists, criminals who'd taken things a little too far, especially now that they'd killed her father.

As she stood there pondering the implications this new information Prime had given her suggested, she began wondering whether her loyalties had been misplaced. For reasons unknown, a weapon that was manufactured and used by Exodus, the V77, was used to murder him. Everything pointed toward Exodus and by all rights they needed to be stopped. But Katura was no fool. She knew full well the possibility that there was more to the story than what she was told. For now, she needed to play along until she found a break and uncovered what really happened to Doctor Weinkaufen. She quickly collected herself and addressed Prime once more.

"Do we have any more information?" asked Katura.

"There was another body found with Weinkaufen. It was Senator Lindsay."

Katura sighed softly with despair and walked into the other room. She made her way to the table where the food was set and picked up a saucer holding a cup filled with tea. She took a sip, then replaced the cup on the saucer and held it as she pondered a little more. The image of Prime followed her into the other room and stood near the bathroom entrance.

"His birthday was only six days away?" said Katura, referring to Weinkaufen.

Prime sighed deeply.

"I know," he replied.

Katura placed the cup and saucer on the table, turned and walked toward the balcony. She stopped at the door and placed her hands on her waist.

"What's the connection with Lindsay?" she asked.

"We don't know. Weinkaufen was working with something very hush-hush. We knew he had some very generous funding from Romania,

31

but we haven't been able to find out what he was working on. We believe Lindsay was connected in someway and if they were involved with Exodus, you can bet it will have something to do with Romania's recent friendliness with AUNK," said Prime.

"Then I guess I'm off to the embassy. I'll be ready in one hour," said Katura.

"The necessary arrangements are being made as we speak. Ms. Ishtar, don't disappoint us," said Prime.

Suddenly, the transmission ended and the pen-like devise melted and oozed into the water. Katura walked outside on the balcony and pondered her newest mission. Her worst nightmare had come true. A loved one had been killed and all signs indicated that Exodus was responsible. She couldn't believe this was happening. In her heart she always rooted for them, even though she was forced to fight against them. Now, she once more had to face them and attempt to stop their plans. The only problem was that the circumstances surrounding her mission had become very personal.

Supposing they did do the murder, why would they kill Durst Weinkaufen? What did they have to gain from his death? Another good question was why their brand of weapons was left at the scene? The more Katura thought, the more she realized that things were a little too convenient. First she was given a mission and then she was told that the greatest network of freedom fighters were involved. It was as if somebody was trying to push her into doing something or accomplishing some task other than retrieving the jewels. Maybe they thought that by killing Weinkaufen she would become blinded by rage and run off half-cocked. Perhaps this was a trap. Something certainly didn't seem right about all of this. There had to be something more going on than just a simple plot to have her killed. If that was the case, they'd have done it by now.

This was too sloppy, a characteristic that was not expected by any member of Exodus or the United States government. She looked at the clock on the wall. It was time for her to prepare. The flight to AUNK was going to be a short one, especially using the mode of transportation she was riding in, a speed-of-sound stealth jet called the White Bolt. With it, she would be in AUNK in a little over an hour.

She marched from the balcony and into the room. She walked toward a huge painting on the wall, which instantly disappeared like a hologram. She made her way down a massive hallway measuring twenty

Nationhood

feet in diameter. Movement sensors triggered the lights behind the wall panels to come on as she journeyed down the corridor. This was the entrance to her private situation room, the place especially designed to prepare her for her missions. Jaquimo followed her in, then waved his hand across an illuminated panel on the wall, reactivating the holographic image.

As they entered the main chamber, the mega computer system, known as Auntie, activated and quickly identified Katura using retinal scans, body configuration probes and DNA matching, all of which was done as she sauntered into the huge chamber. The scans were completed in seconds and the surveillance systems activated automatically. Three-dimensional holographs mapping the Romanian Embassy appeared. A huge laser globe spun in the middle of the room, showing weather conditions, satellite locations and thermal activity inside the earth and beneath the oceans. Jaquimo walked to the edge of the platform and stood behind her.

"I assume that we are going to download Strategy Level Seven-Delta?" he asked.

"Yes, that would seem appropriate considering the security level of this operation," said Katura. "It may even be a good idea to prepare Tactical Profile Beta One."

She walked over to the spinning apparition of the Earth. A panel board surrounded the orb. She began pressing various symbols that matched correlating locations on the globe. Jaquimo walked over to the control board on the mega computer behind her. He, too, pressed a series of buttons, then both of them stopped simultaneously.

"Strategy Level Seven-Delta and Tactical Profile Beta One ready for download," said Jaquimo.

Katura nodded, then walked to a disc-shaped platform in the middle of the floor. She loosened her towel and allowed it to bundle around her feet. She tilted her head upward and closed her eyes. Suddenly, beams of light shot from a cone-shaped apparatus on the ceiling. The lights shined on various parts of her head, fluctuating in color and design. This was part of her normal preparation for a mission. Katura Ishtar wasn't just a spy, nor was she an ordinary woman. As a condition of her indentured status, she became a living, breathing hybrid of technology and humanity. She was a human with cybernetic enhancements. Her brain was laced with nano circuitry, technology that improved her mental and physical abilities. They stored information and maximized her mental capacity. They also allowed her to do physical things normal individuals could not. The fluctuating lights were tactical and strategic data compressed into digital format and downloaded using laser transmission. The process allowed her to interface with the master computer, Auntie. It was briefing her, installing various encrypted data into her head. She was gaining all of the information she needed for this mission and in a few minutes she would be ready to depart.

Jaquimo watched as Katura continued the briefing. After a few minutes, he turned and pressed a button. The flickering lights ceased and a long hallway began opening behind her. She lowered her head and stood motionless for a moment. Then she stepped off the disc and walked into the antechamber. Minutes later, she emerged fully dressed in a skirt suit ensemble.

"Will madam be needing a pre-flight cocktail?" asked Jaquimo.

"Indeed," she replied, making some final adjustments on her outfit. "Make sure that it's strong."

"Certainly, madam. Might I also suggest, in order to ensure our safe return, that a more commercial form of travel on the way back might be in order?"

Katura looked at him and smirked.

"What's the matter, you don't trust Uncle Sam to bring us back in one piece?" she asked.

"Let's just say that under the current situation, a backup form of transportation might be appropriate. Flying the *White Bolt* might be a little, shall we say, ostentatious, especially for someone who could potentially be starting World War III."

Katura snickered and shook her head.

"Very well, Jaquimo. Have a private jet ready, just in case."

"Yes, madam."

~~~

Chapter Three: Fear of a Direct Hit

One hour had passed since Mbaku left Wendy's house. He'd changed his clothes and donned a midnight-colored tuxedo, white shirt and matching black bowtie. He crouched atop a nearby roof, scanning the area to examine the various routes and entry points the thief might take. It was a rather simple trek to figure out. They would most likely come from the north, scale the fence, take out a few guards and then enter through one of the ventilation shafts on the roof. If he had to steal the jewels, that would be the path he would take. In a few moments he would leave this perch and monitor the situation from inside the embassy. Then, he would wait for the intruder to make their escape. They would probably cause some commotion in order to vanish amongst the crowd of people. If they did, he had to be ready. As he was about to leave, he received a beep on his communicator. He touched his ear and activated it.

"Yes, Vee?" he answered.

"There is an emergency call from Senator Pollins. He asked to be connected to you. Are you available to take the call?" she asked.

"Yes. Feed him through. Make sure the encryption is on the line."

"I always do. Here he is."

Mbaku waited for a moment. Then he heard background noise, which meant the senator was on the line.

"Senator Pollins. What can I do for you?" asked Mbaku.

"Mbaku. I'm on my way to a dinner with Consulate Mendoza from Morocco. I just wanted to wish you well on your mission tonight. I don't have to remind you just how important all of this is," said Pollins.

"No, Senator, you don't have to remind me. I'll get your jewels. But after that, it will be you that deals with the aftermath."

"Yes, well, I just wanted to..."

"I know what you wanted to do. But your strong-arm tactics don't work on me. I know more about what is at stake than you do. You forget, I was here when Mecca City was nothing more than one dirt road and a few shacks. I know how each person gave their blood, sweat and tears to make this city and this nation what it is. It would serve you well to remember that."

"I appreciate the history lesson. But I must remind you to whom you are speaking."

"And I'll remind *you* once more that you'd better be thinking about what you're doing rather than worrying about me and what I'm doing. Now, if you'll excuse me..."

"Wait. Maybe we got off on the wrong foot. I didn't mean to insult you. I'm just a little uneasy about all of this."

"Then I suggest you get your issues in order. I'll have the jewels to you by tomorrow morning. Enjoy your dinner, Senator."

"Thank you."

"Out."

Mbaku pressed his ear once more and disconnected the call. He stewed in his anger for a moment, wondering what the hell that was all about. He despised politicians because he felt that none of them could be trusted. It was advice his father had given him long ago and he never forgot it. The politicians in America made their pockets fat, even the Black ones, all the while knowing that the Affirmative Action policy was under attack. Yet they did nothing except try to convince their constituents that they had everything under control. When things started going badly for African Americans and the policy was defeated, the Black leaders were the first to leave the country, shouting rebellious jargon from across the water in some foreign country like Spain or France. He felt that Pollins was no different, ready to bail on a moment's notice. But now, Mbaku realized he was off his game plan and his mind was consumed with anger. He needed something to bring him down. He touched his ear and connected to Vee.

"I take it the conversation went well?" she asked jokingly.

"Yeah. I just love speaking to fascist," said Mbaku.

"Want some company to help get your mind back in the game?"

"That would be nice."

Vee downloaded a symphony that made Mbaku instantly calm down. It was Urondu Gunde's, *Angola Sunrise in D minor*. He took a deep breath and closed his eyes for a moment. He thought about the years when Mecca City was just as he'd explained to Pollins—the dusty roads and the shacks that barely stood on their foundations. He remembered the morning calls when the minister would awaken everyone by singing hymns in the middle of the village. Everyone would come out of their huts and join him

Nationhood

in morning praise. It brought so much unity to the people and it gave them hope that that day was going to be better than the previous one.

He opened his eyes and stared at the panorama of downtown Mecca City. Much had happened in the last twenty-five years and to look at it no one would ever suspect it was once nothing more than desert. The regeneration formula caused the ground to become rich with nutrients and allowed unparalleled growth of a plethora of vegetation. Grass, flowers, trees and an assortment of produce were literally created over night. The fertilizer turned this once barren land into a tropical paradise.

After a few moments more, Mbaku found that he'd calmed his anger and took a slow, deep breath to regroup. Vee heard his exhale and knew it was safe to engage a conversation.

"You shouldn't let them get to you. I know they do not have the legacy you possess to this city and nation, but they are trying, nonetheless. Perhaps you should give them a chance," she said.

"A chance to do what, destroy everything my family and friends fought so hard and long to create? They know nothing of this place. Everyday some new Negro comes here looking for a way to turn this nation into a third world ghetto."

"Kind of strong, don't you think?"

"Guilty until proven innocent, I say. They're all a bunch of lip service agents, talking bad until there's something that needs to be done. The original settlers made this country into a major superpower. We have nuclear capability as well as the status of being the world's largest food supplier. We have control of all the crude oil resources off the coast and we have harnessed nuclear energy into a new source of power. We are the world's most powerful nation and yet we are still proving our worth to some of our fellow nations."

"But that doesn't mean that others don't see what we've done. I caution you to not be so judgmental."

Mbaku rolled his tongue across his teeth.

"Since the birth of this nation there have been moments so monumental that it literally changed the course of history," he said. "Such a moment is upon us once more. It is a moment that can either define us as a great civilization or destroy us all. The decision whether we live or die rests in the hands of a few, and even though I do not have all of the answers or possess the power to change the world, I can say that sacrifices will be made, sacrifices that, once made, can never be undone. I took a vow to defend the rights and liberties of the people of AUNK. I will die carrying out that oath. Tonight, I go to the Romanian Embassy to perform a duty for my nation, a nation I am willing to die defending. I just hope the leaders of my nation don't do anything that would jeopardize the good name our people fought so hard to establish or the liberties we struggle to maintain."

Vee seemed a little lost for words. She took a deep breath just as the last note of the symphony ended. All was quiet for a moment. Only the gentle breeze from the east could be heard rustling the leaves in the trees. Mbaku leered once more at the embassy. His mind was now settled and he was focused on his mission.

"Thanks for the talk, Vee. I gotta go," he said.

"Herago, Mbaku," said Vee, which meant goodbye in Nubi.

"Dua Netjer en etj," replied Mbaku, which meant thank you in Egyptian.

He disconnected communications and settled into battle mode. The time to act would soon be at hand.

~~~

Night had fallen over the city of Kashmir, India. A majestic mansion resembling the beautiful Taj Mahal sat on a massive stretch of green grassland east of the city center. A half moon hung high in the sky and its faint glow shone through one of the Victorian style windows of the inner manor. The sheer panels danced with the west-blowing breeze looking like a wraith that was haunting the chamber. A plush high back leather chair sat in the middle of the room facing the window. The faint image of someone could be seen sitting in it. They were motionless, seemingly caught in deep meditation.

Suddenly, the silence was broken by the ring of a telephone on the coffee table next to the individual. Their hand reached for the headset and lifted the receiver from its cradle. On the other end, a masculine voice with a thick South African accent could be heard.

"Phase one is complete. The package is being delivered," he said.

"Excellent. Let me know when it lands," said the strong Arabic-accented voice of the person in the room.

After replacing the receiver in its cradle, the double French doors behind the person opened and a sinister-looking man donned in a white kurta stood in the doorway. His dark beard was full and groomed and his eyes shined like polished pieces of onyx. His slender form gave a hint of

Nationhood

muscularity as he clasped his hands in front of him and waited patiently near the door.

"Have the doctor notified right away that the first phase has been completed," said the seated man.

The man by the door bowed and backed out of the room, securing the doors behind him. The seated man resumed his stare out of the window at the beautiful glow of the city. He reached to the coffee table and retrieved a cup filled with tea. He took a sip and released a deep sigh as the curtains wafted in the dry evening breeze.

~~~

Thirty minutes had passed and now Katura Ishtar was sitting in the plush Sky Room of a private airport located on Ronald Reagan National. She slowly sipped on a glass of red wine, staring out at the runway while the attendants prepared the private jet, *The White Bolt,* for departure. She sat the glass down and playfully traced her fingertips around the rim. Although her main thoughts were occupied with getting to Mecca City and retrieving the jewels, part of her mind was on her foster mother, Marina, and making sure she was okay. Her instincts told her that she needed to get to her soon. But first there was work to do. Suddenly, she detected the scent of a strong cologne and felt the eyes of someone watching her.

"Miss Ishtar," said a masculine voice.

Katura turned and found her eyes resting on a tall and rather attractive man with broad shoulders and a very well groomed, yet wavy, hairstyle. His navy-blue, tailored suit fit him nicely, bringing out the bronze flesh tones of his face. His mannerism was stately and suave, a characteristic that many of the wealthy playboy types possessed when they were engaging someone they wanted to take to bed. If she weren't so confident in herself, she might have been intimidated by him.

With the collection of the data she gathered from scanning this impressive man, Katura instantly knew who he was. His name was Thomas Thurgood, a former Congressman who stayed behind in America after the enactment of the Jack Crow Laws in order to lobby for the reinstatement of the Civil Rights Act. They'd met once before at a benefit in Los Angeles, where he gawked at her all night while massaging the hips of the woman he'd brought to the event.

"Mister Thurgood. How nice to see you again," said Katura.

"Wow! I'm surprised you remembered me," said Thurgood with

James Gordon

widened eyes.

"Now, how could I forget such a handsome man," she said flirtatiously.

They shook hands and exchanged a few more formal pleasantries. Katura invited him to sit, which prompted Thurgood to quickly pull his chair closer, sit down, cross his legs and recline.

"I'm headed to a rally in California. We're trying to raise money to begin Project Renaissance," said Thurgood boastfully. "It's a project to re-establish the voting rights for African Americans."

"That's wonderful," said Katura. "I hope it's successful."

"Thank you. Where are you headed?"

"Mecca City."

"Whoa. Are you going for good?"

"No, just business."

As the stench of his cologne filled her nostrils, Katura began to regret asking him to sit. She grabbed her glass of wine, took another sip and stared out at the tarmac, wondering how much longer before her plane was ready. Thurgood loosened his tie and rested his arm on the back of her chair. His eyes scanned down at Katura's crossed legs that were visible through the slit of her skirt. They were perfectly toned and looked as smooth as silk. He couldn't help feeling somewhat turned on by what he saw.

Katura, on the other hand, glanced at him from the corner of her eye. She saw him admiring her legs and fought to keep from laughing at his antics. She knew all about Thurgood. He was attractive, from a very wealthy African American family and was quickly becoming one of the major forces in the movement to reclaim African American Civil Rights. He was the opposite of Exodus, attempting to make gains through lobbying and not with terrorism. However, he also had a reputation for being a lady's man.

Normally she could have a great deal of fun with him, toying with his ego and watching him make a fool of himself in order to sleep with her. She knew she could raise his spirits in one instant and tear them down in the next. However, neither her mind nor her heart was in the mood for such games at the moment. In fact, Thurgood's cologne was starting to get to Katura. She slightly scrunched her nose and hoped that the attendant would arrive soon to take her to her plane.

Thurgood saw Katura's expression, but was oblivious to the fact

40

Nationhood

that his cologne smelled to high heaven. In his mind he thought that she was a little disturbed about something and perhaps wanted to talk about it. He decided to use that as a starting point for a conversation.

"I couldn't help but notice that you seem a little distracted. Is there anything wrong?" he asked.

Katura glanced at him. She didn't want to tell him that she thought his cologne was a little much nor would she divulge the nature of her trip to Mecca City. Instead, she decided to tell him about the tragedy concerning Weinkaufen. That should be sufficient to keep him at bay.

"Yes, I am a little distracted. I've just experienced a loss. Perhaps you heard about Doctor Durst Weinkaufen's death?" she said.

Thurgood's eyes widened.

"Oh yes, Doctor Weinkaufen. I did hear he had died. Was he a friend of yours?" he asked.

"He was much more than a friend. He was like a father to me."

"My deepest condolences," said Thurgood sympathetically.

Suddenly, it occurred to Katura that perhaps Thurgood knew something about his death, being connected to the government. With Senator Lindsay's body being found with Weinkaufen's, perhaps Thurgood might know something that could link their two murders and perhaps give her a clue as to who did this to Weinkaufen. She decided to play a cerebral game of cat and mouse, just to see what she could find.

"They say he committed suicide, you know," said Katura.

"Yes, that is what the reports say," replied Thurgood.

Katura squinted slightly.

"You don't sound convinced."

"Let's just say, I don't place much stock in governmental inquiries or reports."

Katura's interests were starting to pique. She knew now that the former Congressman knew more than what he was letting on. If the government had done an inquiry, there was more to the story than a simple suicide or homicide. She needed to find out what that inquiry said and Thurgood was the one who seemed to have some answers.

"I also heard that there was a Senator who died with him," she said.

Thurgood shot her a frowning glance.

"How did you know that? That information was classified. Even I barely got that info," said Thurgood.

James Gordon

"I'm a lady of influence, Mister Thurgood. It should pay you well to remember that there is very little I can't find out," said Katura.

"I see. Well, since you already know, then yes, Senator Lindsay's body was found at the scene."

"A Bio-nuclear physicist and a Senator, both shot to death in the same place. Sounds like someone's trying to cover something up, don't you think?"

Thurgood seemed a little uneasy with her questions. Katura was about to open her mouth to pose another one when the flight attendant walked over to her table.

"Excuse me, Miss Ishtar, but your flight is ready," she said.

Katura gracefully refrained from pursuing the issue. There would come another time for her to pick the brain of Thurgood, she would see to it. She reached into her hand-sized purse and pulled out a business card. It had neither a name nor any business information on it, only a phone number. She slid it on the table and closed her purse. Then, she stood, as did Thurgood. She stared into his eyes and lifted her hand. Thurgood quickly cupped it in his and kissed the back of it.

"It was a pleasure seeing you again, Mister Thurgood. Good luck at your rally. I should be back in a few days. Perhaps we can meet again and discuss things in a more intimate and appropriate setting," said Katura.

Thurgood didn't really know how to respond. Although he was flustered by her questions, he was also totally captivated with Katura's eyes, stunning beauty and sultry curvaceous figure. He attempted to be as cool and suave as he could be, but knew he couldn't resist accepting an invitation such as this.

"Ah, yes, yes, that would be great. I'll call you in a few days. Maybe we can have dinner?" asked Thurgood.

"Dinner would be fine. I love lobster," said Katura.

"Lobster it is."

"Until then."

Katura turned and followed the attendant to the door of the Sky Room. She felt Thurgood's eyes scanning her the entire time. But that was what she wanted him to do. She had his attention and he also had hers, but not in the same way. She knew that Thurgood knew or heard something about Weinkaufen's death. She also knew that if he did know something, he might somehow be connected to Exodus, even though on the surface they appeared to have separate agendas.

42

Nationhood

As she exited the room, another thought entered her head. What if Thurgood had something to do with Weinkaufen's death? What if he was there when he was killed? If he were somehow connected, Thomas Thurgood would be the first casualty on her list of revenge. Regardless, he definitely knew something and she was determined to find out what he knew.

She followed the attendant to the boarding gate and onto the air pad where the *White Bolt* was waiting. She boarded as the roar of the engines intensified. Within moments she would be airborne and landing in Mecca City inside of an hour.

~~~

Mbaku entered the embassy and began scanning the interior, looking for vantage points and flaws in the security. In a matter of seconds he found several deficiencies, the kind of deficiencies that should not exist. There were a scant number of guards inside and only a few more scouting the perimeter. The surveillance cameras weren't in sync and left large gaps in their scanning patterns. There was far too much traffic coming in and going out of the embassy, and the security guarding the entrance was uncomfortably lax. With the level of alert being as high as it was, especially when there was news that the jewels were targeted, it almost seemed to Mbaku that they were inviting disaster.

He continued further inside, making mental notes of the guests. He saw an assortment of dignitaries, ranging from Saudi princes to German baronesses. Various ministers and secretaries were also on hand and the spread of food they had was unparalleled.

But despite the pomp and circumstance, he remembered what was at stake and he knew that something didn't seem right. He touched his ear and up-linked to Vee.

"Aren't you supposed to be inside the embassy by now?" she asked.

"I am inside," Mbaku replied.

"Why are you calling me? Is something wrong?"

"Very. The security is way too sloppy for my tastes."

"What do you see?"

"Cameras are not synchronized, the entry is not secure for the most part and the guards are definitely not professionals. This is not what I would expect from the Romanians."

"You think they're setting a trap?"

James Gordon

"Any spy or thief would know right off the bat that something was wrong. They would see all these flaws and know right away that things weren't right. So to answer your question, no, I don't think this is a trap."

"What, then?" asked Vee.

"If I didn't know better, I'd swear they wanted someone to waltz right in and take the jewels," said Mbaku.

"That's crazy? Why would the Romanians want someone to steal their crown jewels?"

"That's a good question, Vee. But right now I don't have the answers. Stay on alert status. You never know when I might need you."

"Roger."

Just then, an elegant yet older woman strolled to Mbaku and wrapped her arm inside of his. He turned abruptly and stared at her. His eyes widened with surprise as he looked at the face of his mother, Helena.

"Mother?" he asked.

"Yes, I was just as surprised to see you here, as well," Helena replied. "What are you doing here, looking for someone to bust?"

Mbaku pruned his lips, fighting the urge to reply with a flippant comment.

"I thought it would be a good idea for the boy to have a night out," said Clarence Bolo as he approached them both from behind.

"I didn't know you would be here also, Uncle," Mbaku replied.

"Well, you know me. I hate to miss a good party," Clarence replied.

"Have you eaten anything?" asked Helena.

"As a matter of fact, no," Mbaku replied.

"Then come with me. You simply must try the stuffed lobster," said Helena, pulling Mbaku by the arm.

"Helena," said Clarence, stopping her in her tracks. "Do you mind if I had a word with Mbaku for a moment? I promise I'll send him straight over in a minute."

"Yes, I do mind," she replied.

"Mother, I'll only be a moment, I promise," said Mbaku.

She looked at the both of them with a disappointed, but skeptical, expression. Then, she leered at Clarence. "Do not get my son into any trouble," she said assertively.

"Now, Helena. Would I do something like that?" asked Clarence

Nationhood

patronizingly.

Helena continued to look at her brother-in-law harshly, then turned and walked toward the tables. Mbaku and Clarence watched her leave, smiling at her as she glanced back at them. Once she disappeared into the crowd, they looked at each other, assuming a more serious expression.

"You should have warned me she would be here," said Mbaku.

"I didn't know until the last minute, which is why I'm here," said Clarence. "I'll make sure she is safe. No doubt she knows that something is up, now that she has seen you. But that's my problem. However, it seems that you may have some problems of your own. Notice anything peculiar?"

"If you're talking about the level of security, then, yes, I do see something peculiar."

"Seems awfully light for such a serious threat, don't you think?"

"Indeed, Uncle. Is there something you forgot to mention?"

"No, but I will suggest that you be on your guard. Something tells me that we are about to stumble on to something very scary. Now, I suggest you join your mother and get something to eat. No sense letting all this good food go to waste."

Mbaku nodded, then walked in the direction his mother went. As he made his way through the crowd, he took note of all the people he passed. Many of them were the social groupies who always showed up for these parties. They were the women hoping to marry into wealth or the men trying to rub elbows with the real power players. Each of them was oblivious to the actual dealings taking place during these functions. The real party happened elsewhere in the building. That's what he needed to check out. But first, he would have some lobster with his mother. Then, he would go in search of the real reason behind this farce.

~~~

He sat on his couch with his elbow propped atop the arm. Since his return from his less-than-cordial dinner with Consulate Mendoza, Senator Elijah Pollins had been watching the television screen like a mad scientist who was studying a specimen under a microscope. He didn't move an inch as his assistant, Lucinda, stood next to his desk and poured him a glass of water. She walked to him and placed the glass on the coffee table in front of him, all the while his eyes remained glued to the set.

She turned to look at the screen. The news report crawler said

45

that the IS from America had landed at the New Kemet International Airport. Every major network was covering the event. Lucinda turned to look at Pollins once again. He still hadn't moved. She placed the carafe of water on the table and stared at him with eyes filled with uneasiness. Pollins finally shifted his eyes to look at her.

"What?" he asked.

"You seem tense," said Lucinda. "Is something wrong?"

"No, nothing's wrong," he said with a troubled expression.

"I take it the dinner with Consulate Mendoza didn't go so well."

"He's an idiot, not worthy of me giving a second thought to."

"Then what's with the intense stare? If you look any harder at the screen it might catch fire."

A brief, but annoyed, look was given to Lucinda, one that caused her to raise her brows. "My, that was quite the look," she said.

"Lucinda, please don't make this into some sort of ordeal."

"I'm not doing anything. But I see you are in need of some time alone. Is there anything else you need?"

Pollins shook his head. Lucinda was about to leave when the senator realized that he was being rude. He took a deep breath to regain his senses and attempt to be more civil.

"I'm sorry, Lucinda. It's just this damn situation surrounding this IS, Victor Johnson," said Pollins, pointing at the screen.

"What about him?" Lucinda asked, sitting on the couch.

"There's something strange about all of this. The whole situation about him being here is strange. I can't put my finger on it but something about this deal stinks to high heaven. I know that the Nation of AUNK will regret him coming here. I fear that there are some bad things coming over the horizon."

Pollins stood to his feet and began pacing the floor. On the television, the police officers continued their struggle to restrain the crowd of reporters as they attempted to get a word with the newly freed Black man.

As Johnson got to the elevator doors leading to the lower floors of the airport, Lucinda stood up and walked toward Pollins. He released another sigh, still showing his displeasure with Victor Johnson's arrival. He hoped it was just his suspicions getting the better of him.

He glanced at Lucinda as she stood quietly and patiently behind him. She was a fairly pleasant looking woman, he thought, conservatively

Nationhood

dressed yet possessing an air of inconspicuous promiscuity. Her hair was neatly done, pulled back from her face in a ponytail and kept in place with gel. Her salmon-colored skirt suit and matching pumps complimented her cinnamon complexion.

Normally, Lucinda was quite a conversationalist. However, right now, she was quiet and noticeably uncomfortable, staring at Pollins like a woman scared to speak. Pollins knew that he was causing her to feel this way and decided to try to break the ice.

"Sorry I troubled you," he said.

"It's okay," she replied.

"No, it isn't. I should learn to control my emotions."

"If you did I wouldn't want to work for you any longer. You'd be no fun."

They both exchanged smiles, then Lucinda became serious. "Do you really think there is something suspicious about this guy? Do you think his presence here is going to be that big of a deal?" she asked.

Pollins turned and looked at her, his brow furrowing.

"I don't know. But what I can say is there is much unrest in our country. The Romanians are uneasy and now we have a new refugee on our doorstep being treated like a returning hero. The whole thing is just a little fishy," Pollins replied.

"I know I'm in the minority, but I think it's good that we allowed him here. I just feel that so much pain has come from their ordeal and now that his is over we can move ahead and try to get more of them freed."

"You do, huh?"

"Why, yes," Lucinda said, walking closer. "As you know, my major in college was history. Early in the century, Blacks thought things were equal and they were given various positions that appeared to be a show of good faith. But when the Affirmative Action policy was ruled unconstitutional, they were set up to fail, just so someone could say that Blacks weren't equipped to be in those positions to begin with. They were subsequently fired and many of them were sold into slavery by the banks. At least now we have a home to come to, a place where we can prove our worth and not be given token positions that present the appearance of equality."

"Well that's a very optimistic and altruistic statement, Lucinda. But what about our enemies who continue to beat at our door because they covet our resources? Isn't that just as bad?"

James Gordon

"I know I will sound naïve in saying this, but I believe the people of the world see the necessity of creating a diverse global community, especially in this day and age of global business. To not have that sort of cooperative environment would be disastrous. But I'm confident that we as a country will continue to do the right thing, and allowing Mister Johnson citizenship is, indeed, doing the right thing."

"I hope you're right about all of this, Lucinda."

"I think I am. We've come a long way, Senator."

"But there is still a long way to go."

Just then, the reporter announced that Victor Johnson had just entered the elevator and was descending to the second level where he would meet with AUNK officials.

"Well, it's getting late and you have a banquet to attend," said Lucinda, walking to the door and gathering her things off the chair next to it. "You have a good night, Senator Pollins."

"You, too, Lucinda. Be careful on your way home."

Lucinda walked out of the office and closed the door behind her. As he stood in the middle of the floor, Pollins thought about what Lucinda said and pondered whether she was right. Was this arrival of Victor Johnson a good thing or was it a ticking time bomb? If worked properly, this could potentially be one of the best things to happen for Blacks in a long time. When the American Civil Rights Act was put into place, some believed it would bring an end to racism and that equality would reign forever. But scant years later, Blacks had experienced more struggles than ever before, and it has gotten worse ever since.

Even with the birth of New Kemet, Blacks were still not given the respect they deserved. Although Pollins wanted to share Lucinda's optimism, he simply couldn't bring himself to shake his feeling of dread, especially after everything he'd seen. The question now was how he would deal with things if his suspicions were correct.

He turned to look at the television again. This time he saw a report about a recent rally being held in California. It was a fundraiser to help lobbyists continue their struggles to regain the civil rights of Blacks through negotiations. However, protesters staged a counter rally and the networks were there to pick up every moment of it. With the departure of Victor Johnson to the Nation of AUNK, civil unrest had already begun throughout America. Blacks and other oppressed minorities were taking to the streets, voicing their opinions and shouting chants that demanded

Nationhood

their complete and total freedom. Speakers from both sides voiced their respective courses of action. Some spoke of violent retaliation while others stressed more civil and strategic measures.

The report switched to Atlanta, where the attention was being focused on a small community center. A few hundred people had gathered to discuss their plans to regain their freedoms. But the real focus was on the speaker. His name was Reverend Mohammed Aziz, leader of the National Coalition of Social Reform. But to many, he was the voice of Exodus, the common name for the militant faction of the group.

Reverend Aziz was one of the most outspoken activists for civil rights. He'd been preaching for years, pleading with Blacks around the world to organize their efforts and help the indentured servants get to Africa. They could aid in furthering the efforts of AUNK, helping it to become the sole economic superpower in the world. It was his belief that by cooperating, the Black race would achieve economic and social supremacy throughout the world and abolish the Jack Crow Laws forever. He stood in front of the crowd of emotionally charged Black Americans and delivered his emotional speech.

"Today is a day that will live in our minds forever!" he bellowed. "It is a day when the nation that we bled for, sweated for, died for and cried for; set one of our people free!"

An arousing and explosive applause followed his statement. But as Pollins continued to stare at the television, he could tell that emotions were high and a very agitated atmosphere had filled the room. People were on their feet, their faces showing the pain that consumed their hearts. Aziz continued to fan the flames of their anger, telling everyone exactly what they wanted to hear.

"The bell has tolled and the fat lady has left the building! We did not heed the warning or read the writing on the wall when we had the chance! But now, we have no choice but to accept the fact that equality isn't something that is given simply by writing some words on a piece of paper and passing it as law! Equality is a fundamental right, just as the right to life, liberty and the pursuit of happiness! It is a right that must be fought for! It is a right that we must have!"

The crowd was growing even more volatile and Pollins was feeling more uneasy. Clapping hands, angry screams and stomping feet followed Aziz's words. It seemed that the people were coming closer by the moment to mutiny. Camerapersons scanned the room as the

49

emotionally charged group began to show near riotous behavior. Some of the news people stayed close to the door, preparing to make a hasty exit should things get out of control. The room was filled with tension, thick and destructive. Like the earthquakes that stirred the magma before a volcanic eruption, conditions were perfect for an explosive insurrection, the kind that could erupt at any moment.

But instead of trying to calm the crowd, Aziz continued to preach. With every word, the crowd grew more and more hostile. Closed fists were lifted into the air. Even children too young to truly understand what was going on shouted words of anger. This was his goal, to wake the masses. He felt that the time had come for Blacks to stop living in denial, and from the response he was getting, they finally had.

Pollins was deeply disturbed by their actions. He knew that if they rioted, many of them would be killed. As the drama continued to unfold, he walked over to his desk and picked up his phone. He dialed a few numbers and waited for someone to pick up. Moments later, he heard the voice of an operator on the other end.

"Yes, this is Senator Pollins. Get me in contact with Reverend Aziz," he said.

~~~

Chapter Four: Green Eyes in the Night

The *White Bolt* had just entered AUNK airspace, crossing the Atlantic in just under an hour. This was a record time, faster than any aircraft had ever traveled. However, that was of no consequence to Katura Ishtar, who sat comfortably in her chair while Jaquimo looked at his global satellite-positioning device.

"I believe we are almost there. That should be the Cairo River below," said Jaquimo.

Katura looked out of the window as Jaquimo turned his attention from the GSP and looked over her left shoulder.

"I believe you're right," she replied.

"At our current rate of speed, we should be landing at New Kemet International Airport within the next two minutes," he said, standing erect.

"One minute, fifty one seconds to be exact, depending on weather conditions," Katura replied, shooting him a sly look.

Jaquimo rolled his eyes.

"I do wish you'd stop doing that. No wonder you don't have many male friends, let alone female ones."

Katura stood and walked over to the wet bar. She poured herself a glass of water and drank it without stopping to take a breath. When she finished, she placed her glass on the bar and then looked at Jaquimo.

"Are you suggesting I should play dumb?" she asked with a wry smile. "You think that will buy me some friendship?"

Jaquimo placed his GSP on the table and looked at her.

"I'm only suggesting that madam would enjoy more company if she weren't so...um, how do the youth say this...ah yes, anal?"

"I am not anal. I just have a penchant for exactness, a touch of OCD. Call it one of my idiosyncrasies."

"Sounds more like a problem to me."

"You should be thankful I like you," said Katura flatly. "Otherwise, I would have killed you for a comment like that."

"I'll thank Allah later," Jaquimo replied, even more flatly. "Now, if you'll excuse me, I'm going to go prepare you a small meal before your

James Gordon

night on the town."

As he left the room, Katura chuckled beneath her breath at the tongue and cheek banter that took place between them. It was something she and Jaquimo had often, and it kept her in good spirits. He was the only one she could trust and the only one she would ever let get close enough to her. But then she began to wonder whether he had a point. In his teasing, did he make an observation that wasn't necessarily false?

Katura began thinking about her life. After she lost her freedom due to the Jack Crow Laws, she also lost contact with friends and family. Although it wasn't by choice, everyone she'd ever known was suddenly gone from her life. She became a slave and was cut off from everything she ever knew and loved. She was conditioned to follow orders and was sent on missions that were supposed to help ensure her eventual freedom. But each mission became more and more dangerous, and when she returned alive she was treated more like a commodity instead of a person. It wasn't long before she realized that she had become the property of the United States government and their guarantee of freedom was nothing more than an empty promise.

In that instant, Katura's mind shifted and she began to realize that there were many instances she had an opportunity to escape. The plethora of chances flooded her mind and it bothered her that during her missions she was unable to recognize the openings she had to escape her enslavement and, perhaps, find the loved ones from her past.

Each times she was sent out on missions she could have used some of that time to locate the people she'd loved, like Durst and Marina. But for reasons unknown to her, those thoughts never crossed her mind. Instead, she was consumed with her missions and missed out on those opportunities as well as all the joyful moments she could have had with the people she missed. It was as if her ability to think of such things were blocked, forcing her to focus on the orders Prime and his superiors wanted her to focus upon.

Although she puzzled over her past inability to think, Katura found that she was now devoid of the restrictions that prevented her mind from wandering in the past. Such moments were few and far between and often resulted in some release of pent up emotions.

She began thinking about Durst Weinkaufen and the last time she saw him alive. He'd just been awarded the Global Star, a prestigious award given to scientists who achieve a monumental discovery or cure.

Nationhood

His contribution to science was a formula that was able to destroy carcinogenic cells. It was a combination of genetics and nuclear fusion. He'd created a cell that could be injected into the human body that could identify cancerous cells, dissolve them and then totally disintegrate into a concentrated protein that would help to heal the infected tissue.

In the years that followed, his discovery saved the lives of hundreds of thousands of cancer patients. Most of them made full recoveries. When he received the award, it was the proudest day of his life and remembering it brought tears to Katura's eyes. She bowed her head, trying not to let anyone see her loss of composure. She quickly traced her fingers around the rims of her eyelids and quietly sniffed.

As she lifted her head to look out of the window, she found that Jaquimo had returned with her food. He placed the tray on the table in front of her and handed her a tissue. His compassionate eyes said everything he didn't need to say. Katura took the tissue from his hands and dried her eyes. Then, she gave him an embarrassed glance. Jaquimo didn't want to broach the subject, but knew that she was reminiscing again. It was one of the few things that made her emotional. Instead of asking her what was wrong, he decided to take a different approach.

"Perhaps you'd like a little wine...to relax you, of course," Jaquimo suggested.

"No, but thanks," she replied hoarsely.

"Forgive me if I said anything out of line."

"You didn't. In fact, you spoke the truth. I have been very preoccupied with my missions and it cost me time, time I should have spent with people I love. I don't know why it's taken me this long to see that. However, it took Durst's death and your words to show me that. The only problem is he'll never know how much he meant to me and that hurts me, deeply."

Jaquimo saw how hard she was taking things and wanted to make her feel better.

"Perhaps you should get some rest. Three minutes of cyber-sleep should do the trick. We're making our descent now and it should take about that long to taxi and begin de-boarding. Why not use that time to relax," he said.

Katura nodded, then released a deep sigh. She rested her head on the back of her chair as Jaquimo took the tray to refrigerate her meal until she awakened. But Katura knew that she might not fall asleep. Her mind was racing with guilt and worry. She regretted being away from Durst and Marina for as long as she had and worried about Marina's mental condition during this most difficult time. She had to be totally distraught and right now Katura simply wanted to get to her.

Although they weren't blood relatives, Marina was the only family Katura had left and her yearning to be with family had totally consumed her mind. She turned her head and looked out of the window. The lines of streetlights stretched into the horizon like endless strings of pearls. They looked so beautiful and she wished she could open the hatch and do some skydiving just so she could soak in the entire panorama.

Just then, a beep was heard coming from her watch. The time on it read nine o'clock. It had adjusted to local time, but that wasn't the reason for the beep. The watch was also her communication link to the master computer, Auntie. Unbeknownst to Thomas Thurgood, Katura's card with her number on it was actually a tracking and surveillance device. Inside the fabric of the card was a nano recording device that stored the conversations that Thurgood had since the time he left the airport. It transmitted the information to Auntie via laser digital uplink with Sky Cam, the government's spy computer. Auntie then downloaded the entire file to her communicator and the beep signified that the entire file had been received.

"Well, well. I wonder what the good Senator had to say," she said curiously.

~~~

Thurgood sprawled back in his chair, his hands clasped behind his head and his feet resting on the seat in front of him. His sleeves were rolled up and his tie hung limply and loosely around his neck. He stared at the ceiling of his hotel room, beaming a smile that made him resemble the Cheshire Cat. His thoughts were of Katura. For some reason he just couldn't get her off his mind. He still saw her face and imagined his hands caressing her smooth, toned body. She stirred something in him, something he hadn't felt about other women. She was different, sophisticated and elegant, yet there was this toughness about her that transcended her beauty and allure. It was as if she was a tom girl packaged in the shell of a goddess.

As he continued to indulge his fantasies, Thurgood's aide, Lela, watched with amazement. She'd never seen him this comfortable and happy before. Her expression changed from one of wonder into one of

Nationhood

curiosity as she tried to figure out what had gotten into him.

The rally didn't go so well and he hadn't raised all the money he need. Yet, he seemed to be in extremely good spirits. Most of the time sex or money were the things that made him this way and since he hadn't raised a lot of money she wondered whom his new conquest was. She hesitated to ask, thinking that she might be overstepping her place. But she and Thurgood were beyond a simple friendship. They'd grown up together and although nothing sexual ever transpired between them, they were intimately close. She knew everything about him, even the women he'd been with. She decided to be nosy and see what was causing his glee.

"What's got your nose open?" she asked.

Thurgood snapped out of his delightful daydream state with a start. He craned his neck and looked at Lela, whose wide-eyed leer indicated that she was waiting for an answer. With arms folded, she gave him her best sister-girl pose, tapping her finger against her forearms and resting against the back of an executive-style swivel chair. Thurgood leaned forward, then turned to rest his arms on the table that sat next to him. He locked his fingers and leered at Lela curiously.

"What?" he asked sneeringly.

"You heard me," she said, snaking her neck.

"No, I didn't. What did you say?"

"I said, who is the woman that has your nose all open. Whoever she is, she did one hell of a job on you. You're over there smiling; your eyes are all glassy. If I didn't know better, I'd swear you were in love."

"Me? In love?" Psst, right?" he said, blowing it off.

"You can deny it all you want. But you look sad. Not in depressed, but sad as in you got it bad for this woman," said Lela.

"You're crazy. I don't know what it is you're seeing, but I don't have anything. You know me, I'm not the marrying kind," said Thurgood.

"I hear what your mouth is saying, but your eyes tell a different story."

Thurgood was starting to feel a little uncomfortable with Lela's inquisition. It was worse than being in front of a Senate committee. She could look at him in such a way that made him crumble. He could never figure out how she did that.

"There *is* no one, okay? Now, what do you have for me?" he asked, trying to change the subject.

Lela pruned her lips and unfolded her arms. Her eyes continued to stare at Thurgood disbelievingly. She slowly leaned forward and began opening her files, loosening her full lips into a smirk. He might have gotten off the hook this time, but the subject *would* come up again, she would see to it.

"You have a meeting with the National Security Council concerning the unrest in the New York and Los Angeles areas," said Lela, looking at her files.

"Anything new with that?" asked Thurgood.

"Not really. There still seems to be rallying taking place. Rumor has it that Al Qaida members are providing arms to the rebel IS forces. The reports to the President from Central Intel indicates that things can escalate real fast."

"Do they plan any attacks?"

"Possibly. Deployment has already begun and security is beefing up in some of the occupied territories around South Central, Long Beach, Queens and the Bronx. It's been said that refugees who escaped some of the IS camps are held up there. The government is demanding their return by midnight tonight or they are going in and using force to secure them. I don't think they are going to back down from their threats."

"What should we do?"

"Although some of this information is unconfirmed, it has been reported that Exodus members have gone in and helped to fortify the areas. I think you should stay in Los Angeles and try to defuse the situation, otherwise there could be a major blood bath and a lot of casualties, mainly innocent ones."

"Great. That's all we need, more gunfights with terrorists running around blowing up things," said Thurgood with exasperation. He locked his fingers behind his head and looked up at the roof of the cabin. "What else you got?"

"Well, we've been getting reports that the explosion that took place in Wisconsin at that night club was the act of a sleeper cell. No confirmation of the affiliation yet. However, intelligence seems to think it was some of the hiding Taliban members taking advantage of the free press and not any of the escaped IS people or anyone from Exodus. Agents have been dispatched to do some snooping, but nothing has come back yet."

"Is it just me or is the world going to hell in a hand basket?"

"It's just you," replied Lela nonchalantly.

Nationhood

Thurgood leaned forward and resumed his clasped hand pose. "We have Exodus, who is nothing more than a domestic terrorist group, joining up with known international terrorist groups who want to destroy the country. Don't they realize they aren't helping?"

"You don't see the reason behind their actions? I mean, what do you expect for them to do, sit back and wait for the government to come hunting them down while they lay in their sleep?"

"But there has to be another way."

"There is, and getting you back to Los Angeles is part of it. The President has formally addressed the issue with Exodus, stating that he will use force to quell the attacks and bring the culprits to justice. I'm sure the group didn't take that too well. He's stated that any attacks made on his men would be met with attacks on each and every one of them."

"That's crazy. This is going to turn out to be a mass slaughter."

"It would seem. That's why you need to go there and help defuse things. But, before you go leaping to the rescue, there's something else you should know."

"What is it?"

"Remember that comment you made about international terrorist groups? Well, there's more going on than you think. Here's where things are beginning to get interesting."

Lela pulled a photograph from her folder and slid it to Thurgood. He picked up the photo and stared at it for a few minutes.

"Hey, isn't this Omar Fahad?" he asked.

"Yes it is. Check out the guy standing next to him," said Lela.

"He looks familiar."

"That's William O'Reilly, the leader of the IRA who defected to South Africa three years ago. However, British intelligence took that picture two months ago in Belfast."

Thurgood laid the picture on the table and pondered.

"Why would a Saudi general and an IRA leader living in South Africa be meeting in Belfast?"

"I'm sure you'll come up with the answer. That's why they pay you the big bucks," said Lela.

Just then, the intercom system buzzed.

"Mister Thurgood. Your dinner is ready," blared the voice from the speaker.

"Thank you. Bring it up," Thurgood replied.

James Gordon

He turned to look at Lela with a puzzled expression. The information she just gave to him was disturbing, more than he cared to say. Something big was going on and many pieces of the puzzle were missing. His eyes showed the processing of the information she gave him. His face displayed his worry in every frown wrinkle. Answers were all his mind craved, yet he did not know the first place to start searching for them. He decided to take Lela's advice and stay in LA tonight. Things had become too volatile and he hoped that somewhere in the afore-mentioned area he would find some of the answers he craved.

~~~

Katura pressed a button on her watch, ending the transmission of information that Auntie downloaded to her. She smiled, relishing the way she was able to eavesdrop on the conversation Thurgood had with Lela. Although there were no items of particular importance discussed, she did, however, hear how Lela poked fun at Thurgood and imagined how giddy he must have looked. She could only wonder if he was thinking about her. Just then, Jaquimo entered the cabin and walked to her.

"All the bags have been unloaded," he announced. "It's time for you to get suited up."

Katura released a deep sigh. "You know, I've been thinking. I think you're right about me," she said. "I think I have been a little too *anal*. Perhaps, after this mission I'll find me a friend, someone that will pique my mental and physical interests."

Jaquimo smiled with relief. "There's hope for you after all."

~~~

After waiting ten minutes for Reverend Aziz to come to the phone, Senator Pollins received an answer he didn't like.

"What do you mean, he's busy?" he yelled at the person on the other end. "I told you this was an emergency!"

"Yes, sir. I'm sorry for the inconvenience, but if you'd like to leave a name or a message, I can give it to him," said the male voice on the other end.

"Well, make sure that you do! This is Senator Elijah Pollins of the African Union of New Kemet! Tell Reverend Aziz to call me as soon as possible! This is a matter of national security!"

"Yes, sir. I'll give him the..."

Pollins hung up before the man could finish his sentence. He looked back at the television, expecting to see more of Aziz's speech. But

Nationhood

ten minutes had passed and now they were showing scenes from outside the airport where the reporter was explaining the situation surrounding Victor Johnson's visit with the members of the legislature. Pollins picked up the remote and turned up the sound in order to hear the reporter.

"...as expected, the Senate will discuss the possibility of assisting more IS refugees in attaining deals for their release. Although Johnson is the first person since the passing of the Jack Crow Laws in the US to receive his freedom and be released from the country, it is expected that the US will try to push more assertively for exclusive deals with the New Kemet Energy Council to secure rights for the use of Q-76, the nuclear energy experimentation project controlled by the N.K.E.C. The negotiations are scheduled to begin next week between the US energy council and the very members who are meeting with Victor Johnson tonight. If the US does push for an energy deal with N.K.E.C., immigration officials say there will be a huge influx of refugees. The only question remaining is where will the country place them."

Pollins raised the remote and lowered the volume a little bit. He was bothered by the reporters comment. Although tasteless, he did have a point. AUNK had already made deals for other refugees from other parts of the world. In Germany, members of a German energy group who wanted more secure drilling rights for oil had held the very doctor that helped to create Q-76 captive. The negotiation of his release was crucial to AUNK's rise in the global market and made the deal with the Germans insignificant.

Throughout the following years, more and more individuals were released under similar circumstances. But now, the cities were becoming crowded. There were four major metropolitans in New Kemet; Independence, Kenté, Langston and Mecca City. Each of them was the capitol city in their respective providences, with Mecca City being the nation's capitol. Spaced within one hundred miles of each other, AUNK had a network unsurpassed by any other country. Each city had it's own industry, independent yet connected to the whole. But with so many new people moving to AUNK everyday, it was becoming quite difficult to keep up with the rising costs of growth.

Pollins rubbed his hand over his mouth and tried to continue his attempt to calm himself. Although the question of housing would be a potential issue, he still had one problem that he needed to contend with now. He hoped that Reverend Aziz would return his call soon. He really

James Gordon

wanted to talk to him about the state of affairs he'd witnessed on the television. Whether he knew this or not, Aziz had to keep the people calm. If they revolted, there was sure to be deaths and the majority of them would be on the side of the Blacks. Just then, Pollins' ears picked up something, a change in the reporter's tone.

"...I'm getting word from Internal Security that there has been an emergency inside the conference area where Senate members were meeting with Victor Johnson," said the reporter, pressing his hand on his earpiece. "We're not sure at this time what has happened, but we do understand that the members are being evacuated as we speak. We're trying to get close to the action, so I'll turn things over to Carla Snipes who's near the scene."

Just then, the network split the screen in half and the image of a quaffed caramel complexioned woman appeared.

"Carla, can you tell us what's happening?" the reporter continued.

"Yes, Paul," Carla began. "Only moments ago, a fleet of emergency personnel raced into the conference area where Victor Johnson met with members of the New Kemet Senate. We're not sure just what has taken place inside, but there were at least ten paramedics, all donning chemical gear. Security has pushed us back to the outer halls of the conference area, stating that it was in our best interests not to come any closer. At this point we're waiting for word of what has transpired and we will stay here and inform you as soon as we know something."

Pollins leered at the television, his eyes sparkling from the light of the screen. His mind was reeling from the news he just heard, but he wasn't too surprised. He expected something was going to happen and now he knew his suspicions were true. With a deep sigh filled with exasperation, he mumbled, "They didn't waste any time, did they?"

~~~

Mbaku was like an impatient child that couldn't wait to finish eating so he could go play. The entire time he sat next to his mother his mind was on his mission. He needed to scout the place and check things out. As they both ate their stuffed lobster, he remained silent while his eyes scanned the main ballroom.

Every once in a while he would sigh heavily and then slide another piece of lobster into his mouth. Helena chuckled beneath her breath at her son's antics. She knew the only reason he was sitting with her

60

Nationhood

was because he was being hospitable. However, she enjoyed the fact that he was spending some time with her, regardless of how fidgety he was.

Mbaku ate another mouthful of lobster, then lifted his glass of water and took a sip in order to help him swallow. Helena glanced at him as she sliced off another sliver of meat. The sides of her mouth turned up as she reminisced about him as a young boy. He was just as squirmy then, especially when she was preventing him from doing what he really wanted. But tonight she was being selfish and his uneasiness was something she was willing to ignore. She decided to ease the tension and strike up a conversation, one she knew he would most certainly engage in.

"You look more and more like your father every day," she said.

Mbaku stopped eating, turned and gave her a perplexed look.

"Where did that come from?" he asked.

"Just an observational comment. You're beginning to look so much like him. He was such a handsome man, stately and imposing. I remember when we first met. I thought he was some sort of gangster or convict, coming in to the store I worked like he owned the damn place. But then we spoke, and from that moment on I knew he was the man for me."

Mbaku smiled. "I miss him, too."

Helena placed her knife and folk down, then stared straight ahead. "Watching you sit there eating reminded me of some of the times your father and I went out. I remember the time he took me to dinner for our tenth wedding anniversary. We didn't have much money at the time, but he managed to secure a secluded corner and put up dividers so we could have some privacy. He had candles all over the area and a violinist that played for us the entire time."

Helena paused the story for a moment due to the overwhelming flood of emotions caused by her walk down memory lane. Mbaku placed his hand atop of hers, grasping it slightly and shaking it for comfort.

"Mbaku, I know I can be a little smothering at times, but it's because I lost your father due to some of the things you're involved with. I know your uncle, Clarence, and he has but one thing on his mind, to make sure that this country doesn't fall into the hands of those who would place our people back into bondage. He has noble ideals, but I just don't want to lose you like I lost your father," said Helena.

Mbaku looked his mother squarely in the eyes, seeing the struggle she possessed in trying not to cry. But she may as well have. The emotion in her voice relayed the desperateness of her plea, as if her words weren't enough. She loved him dearly and he knew that if something were to happen to him she would be more devastated than when his father was killed.

But Mbaku also knew that he was one of the few that stood between his mother and those individuals who would enslave her and their people. He had to continue fighting, even if it placed his life in jeopardy. It was a lesson he learned from his father. He knew the risks involved. Still he continued to hold the line, a decision that eventually cost him his life. Now he was the one carrying the gauntlet and he was determined not to drop it.

"Mother," said Mbaku. "I understand your fears. Everyday I wonder when our enemies will make their move and cross the line that should not be crossed. If that day should come, we as a nation have to be ready. I cannot stand by in good conscience knowing that there are people out there that would do you harm. I cannot stand by and not do something to prevent that."

"I'm a big girl, son. I know how to take care of myself," Helena replied.

"Perhaps. But I don't want you to ever have to. I want you to sleep easy at night and not have to worry about an air raid or someone knocking down your door in the middle of the night and taking you away forever. That's why Dad continued to do what he did. He didn't want either of us to find ourselves in that predicament, and that is why I continue to fight the fight."

"But you've done so much already. Don't you think it's time to let someone else do the fighting?"

"There will come a time when I've fought my last fight. When that time comes, I will gladly turn the reigns of the movement over to someone else. When that happens, I want to be able to rest easy knowing I've made this country safe from all predators."

"And what if that day never comes? What if the forces against us continue to mount? Will you not stop fighting until they kill you?" asked Helena with a trembling voice.

"If that day never comes, Mother, then, yes, I will continue to fight. I will not let anyone take away your or anyone else's freedom. I will not!"

Helena stared at her son, his anger and pride beaming in the

Nationhood

reflection of light in his eyes. The determination in his voice left very little doubt of his devotion to the nation. He would make whatever sacrifice he needed to in order to ensure the safety of her and his countrymen. His level of patriotism was honorable and reminded her of the same level of commitment her late husband possessed. In fact, in that moment she could almost see him instead of her son. He was still strong and determined, the kind of man who could not be easily deterred from anything once he set his mind to it. That was the man her son turned out to be also. Mbaku possessed the very same characteristics of the man she fell in love with all those years ago. And even though she did not want to lose him, she knew that he was definitely his father's son, almost a clone in some respects. It was a thought that was disturbing as well as inspiring and prideful.

"So, I guess you have some work to do, huh?" she said in a tongue and cheek manner.

Mbaku snickered. "Yes. But I'm glad we had this time together. I'd forgotten how nice it was to sit with you and enjoy a meal."

"You should come by more often, and perhaps bring a date. I'm sure there is some young woman out there that has captured your eye."

Mbaku released another deep sigh. "Still trying to marry me off, are you?" he asked.

"Well, there needs to be someone to carry on the fight," Helena replied. "Besides, where's the harm in wanting grandchildren."

"There's no harm at all."

Helena stood from her seat and grabbed her purse. "Well, that's enough lobster for me tonight. I better get home before it's too late," she said.

Mbaku stood also. "You sure you want to leave now? I didn't mean to ruin your plans of staying. In fact, you won't even know I'm doing anything."

"All the same, I'll know you're doing something. But don't worry, you're not ruining anything. I'm going to call up a friend I haven't seen in a while and pay them a visit. But I will say this. Be careful. I don't know why but something about this night doesn't feel right. I guess that's why I wanted you to sit with me a while before you went off to do your duty."

"You're pretty astute, Mother."

"You act surprised. I managed to learn a few things from your father. Like I said, son, I know how to take care of myself."

63

James Gordon

"Would you like for me to call you a cab?"

"No, mother is fine," she said, speaking of herself in third person. "Anyway, call me tomorrow. You have a good night, son."

Helena placed a kiss on her son's cheek. Mbaku returned a kiss of his own, then watched as his mother walked toward the door. In his mind she reaffirmed what he needed to do. Now that she was gone he could go about his business without having to worry about whether he was placing her in any danger. Just then, his uncle, Clarence, walked to his side.

"I thought she'd never leave," he said smugly.

"Any updates?" asked Mbaku.

"You already know everything there is to know. Now, I suggest you get to you duties."

"You sound worried, old man."

"Too much time has already been wasted. Let me know when you get the jewels."

"As you wish."

~~~

Outside the regal embassy, tuxedos and fancy gowns donned the invitees who stood in the courtyard. Limousines paraded down the main driveway carrying the elite of the elite. Senators, ambassadors and the wealthy converged on this most auspicious happening. The festive atmosphere sent a wave of celebration throughout the city that rivaled that of the Mardi Gras.

As the party continued, a long stretch Lexus limo drove to the entrance of the embassy. The windows were tinted to the darkest shade. The lavish chariot was champagne in color and trimmed with glittering gold accents. It stopped in front of the velvet-carpeted walkway as the valet rushed to the rear door and opened it. As he stood waiting for the occupants to exit, a pair of long, shapely legs could be seen through the hip high slit of a royal purple gown.

The woman gracefully placed her matching shoes on the carpeted runway as socializing gentlemen acknowledged the strong, toned legs. A golden blonde haired woman emerged from the vehicle as the valet assisted her by gently holding her hand with his fingertips. She stood still, allowing her gown to drop to its full flowing magnificence. She walked a couple of steps and waited for the rest of the entourage to emerge from the vehicle. She daintily held her purse with both hands in front of her, arching

Nationhood

her back and showcasing her full and round breasts. Her bright full smile created a stir amidst the adoring men who stood outside.

Just then, another pair of legs emerged from the vehicle. These belong to a platinum-gowned brunette who followed the same social etiquettes as the preceding blonde. She completed her exit and stood opposite the first woman. They passed whispered comments while they patiently waited for their escort to emerge.

As the other women were reprimanding their gawking gentlemen companions, another person stepped from the vehicle. A stunning pair of shiny black tie-ups clumped onto the velvet walkway. Then, a stout gentleman slid out of the limo and stood with a huff, adjusting his jacket and straightening his bowtie. His name was Ambassador Nikolai Ishevsky and he was overjoyed at the turnout of tonight's extravaganza.

The flash of the paparazzo's cameras illuminated the entrance like a million tiny flashing spotlights. The charismatic ambassador strolled through the near riotous mob of photographers with his escorts waving at the attendees and socialites. This was a very important night for the Romanian Embassy. It was the culmination of months of negotiations with the nation of AUNK, all climaxing on this night. The security guards raced along side of the ambassador as he marched up the steps leading to the entrance of the building. All eyes were focused on the leader of the Romanian embassy. The elite, the rich and the powerful were all present for this night. In a matter of moments, the ambassador and members of the AUNK government would unveil a new peace settlement, one that would bring huge opportunities for both countries. As a token of goodwill, the Supreme Chancellor entrusted the royal jewels of Tsar Nicholas II to the embassy and AUNK. The importance of this event was far reaching and had the eyes of the world focused on this one night.

Despite the festivities and the light show that illuminated the skies of Mecca City, not all who watched this momentous occasion were joyous. A pair of green eyes stared through a set of high-powered binoculars from the top of a building a couple of miles away. A dark hooded figure peered at the embassy and the activities that surrounded the building. As the Ambassador disappeared inside, the figure reached down and grabbed a backpack, then secured it on its back. Without any hesitation, the figure leaped off the roof of the seven-story building. A pair of glider wings whipped open beneath their arms, allowing them to gently and silently glide to the ground below.

James Gordon

After landing, the figure began running toward the embassy, disappearing into the shadows of the surrounding trees. Its stealth-like movements mimicked a panther and its gracefulness and speed matched that of a gazelle. Within moments, the figure reached its destination. It crouched along the outside perimeter of the gates of the consulate, peeking just above the lower cement border. As the guests continued to parade into the building, the figure performed a quick scan of the area, then darted behind one of the pillars, camouflaging itself in the shadows. It performed another quick scan of the surroundings for cameras or anyone that could hamper its mission.

Two guards were walking nearby, performing their customary lackadaisical patrol of the area. The figure went unnoticed. It was well concealed, peering at the guards with an icy cold gaze. After the guards had passed, the figure turned to survey the wall. It felt the surface for cracks or loose masonry or even a loosened bar or tie. Unable to locate a weakness in the gate's structure, it extended its arm upward and fired a silent projectile from its wrist. The object lodged into the upper carving of one of the pillars. A thin, but strong, wire was attached to the dart-like hook and a small hoisting device began to silently raise the dark figure to the top of the brick pillar.

With skillful acrobatics, the figure dislodged the projectile and flipped over the pillar, gliding to the ground after executing a three hundred sixty-degree summersault. It landed mere feet from a guard that had just completed its scan of the area. The figure spied the patrolling officer and ducked into the bushes as the guard turned and looked behind him.

"Hello?" he asked.

The guard then shined his flashlight around the entire area. However, he saw nothing. Still a little unsure about his findings, he ventured closer to make sure the area was secure. He shined his light into the shrubs. As the beam pierced the foliage, he saw what he thought was a pair of green eyes staring back at him. He slowly placed his hand on the thirty-eight strapped to his hip.

The figure was motionless in the bushes as the guard approached. Suddenly, just as the officer was about to remove his gun from its holster, a pair of headlights flashed behind him. The guard turned quickly to see what caused the lights. He saw a black stretch vehicle pulling to a stop in front of the walkway. The guard turned and resumed his inspection of the shrubs. As he peered into the dense leaves, he found that the eyes he thought he saw were gone. He began shining the light in different angles hoping that what he saw was a reflection of the leaves or another article in the brush. Then, a voice blurted from the two-way radio on his belt.

"Unit thirteen, please report to base. Over!" said the monotone voice.

A puzzled look appeared on the officer's face as he reached for his radio and removed it to respond.

"Unit thirteen, copy," he answered as the scratch of the radio signaled the end of his transmission.

The guard shined the light once more into the bushes, still puzzled by what he thought he saw. If there was something in there, it was gone now. But he couldn't believe that in that split second of time, something vanished from that location. He reserved himself to believing that it was a reflection off the condensation on the leaves, one that he didn't have time to duplicate through experiment with his flashlight. The guard turned and began walking toward the embassy to check in with the guard station. However, as he walked away, the dark figure stood glaring at the officer from atop the embassy. In that short amount of time it had crossed the grounds, scaled the wall and was now on the roof. It silently gazed at the departing officer, who was now whistling as he walked toward the guard station. The dark figure turned and disappeared into the shadows of the rooftop.

~~~

James Gordon

Chapter Five: Pyrrhic Victory

The jubilant atmosphere inside the embassy was beyond comprehension. The acoustics of the main chamber was magnificent and echoed the music throughout the entire area like the hall of an opera house. Guests began dancing in the center of the floor as the festivities continued. Loud eruptive laughter was heard from various tables and the smell of lamb and lobster faintly drifted in the air.

In an upstairs room, two lovers escaped the party for a moment of lustful play. They were excited by the prospect of being able to have sex in one of the embassy's upper rooms. As they embraced, the shadows from the trees danced on the wall as the two ravenously explored each other's bodies and mouths. Her moaning and his grunting filled the room with a chorus that resonated their erotic desires. She locked her legs around his lower back and he pushed her against the wall and kissed her breasts passionately. Despite their attempts to find a secluded spot, their actions did not go undetected. As they began their love making, a security camera in the north corner of the room spied their every action. Downstairs in the basement, two guards sat with their eyes glued to the monitor, enjoying the free peep show and making fun of the couple's antics.

"She's cute," said the first guard.

"What do women like that see in a guy like him?" asked the second guard.

"It sure as hell ain't the sex. He's small and he doesn't have any rhythm."

"Yeah! But he's getting some ass and we're stuck in this control room."

"Think we should bust them?"

"Nah! Let 'em have their fun. This probably won't be the only two that will try this tonight. I only wish we had a recorder."

As they adjust the camera and move in for a close-up, the dark figure that had made its way to the roof had entered their secured viewing station and was standing behind them, watching.

James Gordon

"She's got some nice ones, eh?" asked the first guard.

"Man, I'd like to have those babies in my mouth for fifteen minutes!" the second guard replied.

The figure lifted a small tube-like device and fired a projectile toward the control panel in front of the guards. A brief trail of mist was emitted as the projectile disintegrated before striking the panel. It was a light, but concentrated, form of chloroform. The guards saw the trail, but fell to the ground unconscious before they could do anything.

As the security guards lay on the floor, the dark figure rushed to the control panel and began manipulating some of the controls. They quickly found the camera it was looking for, one that observed a small room in the basement. With lightning speed, the figure zeroed in on an object. It was a well-guarded attaché attached to another guard's wrist.

Suddenly, the figure detected a noise and ducked away from the panel and into a corner. Another security guard came through the door with a carrier filled with cups of coffee.

"Hey, Joe, they didn't have any sugar so I brought you some sweet and ..."

The entering guard stopped in his tracks, shocked by what he saw. Two of his comrades were lying on the floor unconscious. He dropped the coffee, which exploded on the floor and drenched his pants. He reached to the right side of his utility belt and popped open the restraining strap to his gun.

Just then, a black boot kicked him in his chest and knocked him into the door of the security office, slamming it shut. Stunned by the blow, the guard attempted to shake off the effects and zero in on his attacker. As his vision cleared, he saw another roundhouse kick just before it connected to the right side of his face. He slammed into the wall, then slumped to the ground unconscious.

As the guard lay on the floor, the figure returned to the control panel. They scanned the basement of the embassy and discovered that the guard with the handcuffed attaché to his wrist was alone and his gun was drawn. The intruder ducked out of the room and began to make their way down the stairs. Along the way, they saw other members of the Romanian consulate walking up the huge spiraling staircase.

The dark figure smoothly moved into the shadowed entryway of one of the stairwells. As they stood motionless in the shadows, they began picking the lock, just in case they needed to duck in. The intruder watched

Nationhood

as the members walked by, continuing their conversation as they pass the figures shadowed location.

Suddenly, the rear member stopped, detecting something in the doorway. He turned to stare into the corner where the figure was hiding. He began to move slowly toward the shadowed entrance of the stairwell. As he got closer, he found that there was no one there. He examined the area, even though he could see nothing. He was certain that someone was there.

As the rest of the consulate members turned to notice their colleague's actions, they questioned him in their native tongue to ensure that everything was all right. After a moment of deep thought, the inquisitive man turned to the group and reassured them that all was well. He walked away from the exit and rejoined the group.

Meanwhile, the figure had made their way to the main hallway. Another group of guards ran down the corridor, causing the intruder to duck into one of the rooms. Inside, the couple that was being spied on during their lovemaking had just finished with their moment of passion. A few moments of pillow talk passed, then they decided to get dressed. As they began putting their clothes back on, the woman noticed that it was much colder in the room and saw that the window was open.

"Baby, please close that window. I'm getting a chill," she said with a slight accent.

The man took a deep breath as he fastened his belt. He looked at his lover as she adjusted her stockings, enticing him with her beautiful legs to partake in one more session. She traced her hands around her calves and up her thighs, ensuring that there were no runs in her hose. She looked up and saw that the man was still standing there, admiring how she looked.

"If you don't close that window, I might be too cold to take off my clothes again," the woman cooed.

The man rushed to the window and pulled it shut. He turned to walk back toward her, but paused in thought. He suddenly realized that the windows weren't open when they arrived. He turned and looked at them with a puzzled expression.

"I don't remember those windows being open when we got here," he said.

"There were a few things that weren't open when you first got here," said the woman as she opened her legs.

Seeing the opportunity for one more lay, he quickly shrugged off

James Gordon

his suspicions, gave the woman a pleasing smile and raced back over to the bed, burying his head between her legs as she giggled from his antics.

As the two lovers attempt to steal another moment of passion, the dark figure had already darted through the room, escaped out of the window and stood on the ledge outside. The open window was because of their hasty retreat. They managed to attach a wire line to the wall and were lowering themselves to the ground. The drop was quick and quiet. In five seconds, thirty feet had been covered and the figure's feet were on the ground. They quickly unfastened themselves and ducked into the shrubs as the lights of a patrol car shine on their location.

The figure remained motionless as the car passed. Then, they ran toward the rear of the building, tracing their hands against the wall. Peeking around the corner, they spied a lone plain-clothed guard patrolling the area. The figure reached back and threw a dart-like object that lodged into the neck of the guard, who fell immediately to the ground unconscious.

The intruder jumped across the body and proceeded to the rear of the embassy. They stopped at the corner of the building and peered at the rear door. Next to it, a small window was seen at the base of the building. The figure swiftly moved over to the side of the steps and blended into the shadows. They studied the small window, then quickly removed a handled suction cup from the pouch on their side, fastening it to the window. Then the figure removed a small vile and squirted a few drops on the hinges and lock area. They fastened the top to the solution and returned it to the pouch.

Pulling on the handle of the suction cups, the window was removed without a squeak. The figure then slipped their legs into the small opening and repositioned the suction cups on the opposite side of the window. Then, they slid into the opening, pulling the small window behind them and resealing it in its original place.

Now inside the lower chamber of the embassy, the intruder quickly surveyed the area, releasing the suction cups from the window and placing the device back into the pouch. They began to maneuver through the clutter of the storage area. They could hear the pacing of the shackled guard—he was just around the corner.

The figure scurried to his location and positioned themselves for an attack. The guard was now mere feet away. Through the darkness of the shadows, green eyes peered through the eye openings of the mask, sizing

Nationhood

up the guard like a tiger watching an antelope. The intruder crouched down and glided around the clutter. After a few moments of maneuvering, they were in perfect position and ready to pounce.

Just then, another guard appeared. His gun was drawn and a look of urgency was on his face.

"The guards in the station were attacked. Someone's in here!" he said.

They both began scanning the room, looking for any signs of movement or intrusion. Suddenly from the shadows, a dark blur streaked through the room and delivered a kick to the chest of the informing guard. The air burst from his lungs as he fell backwards into the far corner, crashing into some wooden shelves and reducing them to pieces of kindling. The initial guard with the handcuffed attaché stood in awe of the swift attack. As he turned to lift his gun, he was met with a kick that knocked the barrel of the gun backwards, pointing at his chest. The figure grabbed the guard's hand and with a quick twist downward, forced the guard to fire one shot that severed the handcuff's chain. The briefcase dropped to the ground with a thud.

The guards down the hall heard the shot and rushed to the room while radioing an alert to the others.

The burn from the exploding chain caused the guard to relinquish his concentration for a moment and turn his attention to his hand. With the guard's attention diverted, the intruder delivered a sharp upward elbow to his chin followed by an equally devastating forward thrust to the chest. The guard stumbled backward and fell on the sacks of cement on the floor. As he struggled to catch his breath and his senses, the figure closed in for the finish.

"Get away from me!" the man screamed.

At that moment, another set of guards burst through the door with weapons drawn. They spied the disabled guard and the dark figure looming over him. They began firing at the intruder, who dashed into the shadows as the rain of bullets ripped into the darkness. Unfortunately, their aim was off and they inadvertently shredded the incapacitated guard. His body jerked as the Teflon coated projectiles pummeled his flesh. After a few brief seconds, the arriving guards ceased their shooting as the lifeless body of their colleague slumped to the ground in a crimson heap.

The shooters rushed to their fallen comrade's location and performed a sweeping survey. One guard knelt down to check on the

James Gordon

condition of their associate.

"He's dead," he said.

The other two guards continued their survey. They looked at his wrist and noticed that the briefcase was gone. They began to cautiously creep into the shadows where the figure had dashed. Their guns were ready. Their senses were fully alert as they crept into the darkness. They wondered whether they'd shot the individual. But, their training taught them to never underestimate anyone, especially when they don't see a body.

They continued to quietly venture into the far corner of the room. As their eyes adjusted to the darkness, the light shining through a small window from the outside lent some assistance in their search. It beamed through the basement window and illuminated the darkened corner. The assistance allowed the guards to see something on the floor in the far corner. It looked like the intruder squatting on the floor.

They quickly fired several rounds at the image and after a few moments of gunman bravado, they ceased their firing and began closing in on the subject. One of the other guards found a flashlight and shined it on the image on the floor.

As they approached, they noticed that the figure they saw lacked human characteristics. It seemed to be more of a pile of clothing than a body. They drew closer to examine what it was. As they did, they discovered that it was, indeed, a pile of clothing. As a matter of fact, it was the same outfit that the figure donned. They abruptly turned and scanned the area to ensure their safety.

"Quick, go to night vision!" said one of the guards.

They each pressed a button on the side of their goggles and their night vision was activated. But despite their attempts, they could not locate their illusive target. However, the glasses did detect a reading from the clothing. One of the guards switched his scope to infrared. It appeared to be a signal and it was blinking. Curious, the guard slowly and cautiously knelt down to investigate. Using his gun barrel, he slowly peeled back the top layer of clothing in the pile, and then another. Finally, he saw what it was.

It was small, round, clear and plastic, with its circuitry visible on the inside. A light on one of the panels blinked as if it were a timer. It was then the guard realized it was a bomb. The terror of his discovery sent a chill up his spine and he slowly lowered the layers of clothing and

Nationhood

attempted to make a run for it. As the guard stood up to escape, the blinking stopped.

Instead of an explosion, a small spray of smoke shot from various positions on the basement floor. They appeared to be coming from small star-shaped devices that were scattered around the guards. The spray of smoke filtrated throughout the room in seconds, blanketing the entire area with a foul stench. The guards scrambled to escape the basement as the smoke made them cough and their eyes tear.

As they ran up the stairs and into the hallway, they noticed that this path was also littered with the accursed star-like devices, which were also bellowing the same smoke. They soon realized that they weren't going to make it. Using their radio ear set affixed in the temples of their glasses, they broadcasted their situation to the rest of the guards.

"Unit t-three to c-command! We a-are under attack!" coughed the guard. Then, he passed out in the hallway.

Meanwhile, the smoke had filtered into the upper chamber. Its rapid movement and thick concentration set off the smoke alarm instantly. The signal echoed though the embassy with an annoying buzz and everyone was instantly placed into a state of distress. The festivities had reached its height when the alarming signal blared throughout the facility, drowning out the performance of the orchestra. The patrons' look of bewilderment spread quickly as an automated announcement was made.

"Ladies and gentlemen, may I have your attention please! Due to safety precautions, we ask that you exit the building at this time! This is not a test!" said the recording, repetitiously.

The bewildered guests began to calmly, but anxiously, head toward the nearest exit. The smoke was still in the lower chamber and hadn't reached the main ballroom yet.

In the midst of the ruckus, a young woman wearing a golden sequin gown calmly walked from the hallway and toward the exit. Her skin was caramel and her eyes were green. Her lips were the perfect shade of glitter gold, matching her dress. Her strapless V-cut neckline accented her breasts, which had a sheen of perspiration. The gown's waist high slit displayed Katura Ishtar's shapely legs and hips as she gracefully proceeded to the door.

As she walked toward the exit, men suddenly turned and began staring at her. Each step she made was perfect and well placed. The attempts by the hoards of men to speak to her were met with uninterested

James Gordon

hand gestures and glance, which caused the men much embarrassment and disappointment. She sidestepped every effort when they tried to corner her. With flirting green eyes, she toyed with the single-minded males, almost encouraging them to try to win her favor as she pranced to the embassy entryway. Ironically, she was the one thing that kept calmness in these men during a moment of certain chaos.

Despite the efforts of her wanna-be suitors to deter her from leaving, Katura arrived at the exit. The pack of men filed behind her as the other women of the party stared at her, envious of the effortless bewitching. She stepped to the door guards as they perform a one hundred percent search of those who participated in tonight's events. The guard stared at her as she approached and began to develop knots of panic in his stomach, instantly entranced by her beauty and grace. She walked with a slink toward the young sentinel with widened eyes and a gleam of flirtation on her lips. A smile began to unconsciously erupt across his lips, overjoyed that he'd captured her attention. The guard cleared his throat and struggled to remain professional as she stood within inches of him.

"May I see your identification, Miss?" asked the guard.

Katura gracefully opened her purse. Her beautifully manicured nails traced the edge of her passport and then pulled it from its sleeve. As she teasingly handed the guard her identification, she dropped the content of her purse on the floor. The guard looked down at the spilled items, but was quickly distracted by another sight.

The breeze blew across her gown, causing the waist-high slit to become even more revealing. The full beauty of her toned, shapely legs caught the young man's attention, mesmerizing him instantly. He struggled to maintain his composure, pretending to assist her with the retrieval of her items.

"Here, let me help you with that," he said as he bent down and began collecting her things.

Just then, another individual walked up and stood behind the bewitching green-eyed beauty. It was Mbaku. He'd just completed his inspection with the other guards and was preparing to leave. But instead of walking around Katura and the kneeling guard, he stood waiting as the sentry continued to scoop the items off the floor. At that moment, he leaned forward and whispered in her ear.

"I doubt if you'll make it to the front door with those diamonds," he said.

Nationhood

From the corner of her eye, Katura looked at Mbaku and the corners of her mouth turned up.

"I have no idea what you're talking about," she whispered back. Mbaku returned a sly glance and a smirk.

"Have it your way," he retorted.

He took a step back and waited patiently while the guard picked up the remaining items.

Katura realized that she'd been found out and the moment she walked toward that door the man standing behind her would make his move. It was clear that this mystery man knew that she was the dark-clothed intruder, which meant he also knew about her heist of the crown jewels. She quickly glanced down at the mesmerized guard who'd finished retrieving her belongings but was sneaking peeks at her legs.

Katura felt the panic beginning to build. She couldn't risk being caught, especially with the diamonds. She wasn't worried about the guards. Getting passed them was the easy part. It was the feeling she had about the man standing behind her, a feeling that she wanted to explore. If he were security, he would have arrested her by now. But instead, he simply whispered enough information in her ear to let her know that he could help her.

Suddenly, she thought of an idea. She performed an intentional ploy, stumbling backwards and bumping into Mbaku. He steadied himself and Katura by holding her in his arms. Her eyes stared into his and her beauty instantly entranced him.

"Are you okay?" he asked with concern.

"Yes, thank you," she replied. "I guess I lost my footing."

"Well, these things do happen."

Moments passed while the two of them continued to hold and stare at each other. Mbaku looked as if he were hypnotized. Katura was one of the most beautiful and elegant women he'd ever seen. Likewise, Katura was quite impressed with his ability to catch what she'd done. She stared back at Mbaku with warm, begging eyes. Her mouth hinted a flirting smile as the scent of her perfume drifted into his nose. Finally, after what seemed to be an eternity, Katura looked away and Mbaku released her.

He began adjusting himself as the guard finally returned to his feet. He stared menacingly at Mbaku who excused himself and exited the building. As he departed, he glanced back at the angelic woman he held in his arms. Katura returned a look of curiosity, watching the handsome gentleman as he descended the steps. The guard handed her the recomposed purse as she feigned a look of embarrassment.

"Here you go, Miss," he said.

"Thank you so much," she replied.

"Now I need to examine your person. Would you please raise your arms out to the side," asked the guard.

"What are you going to do, frisk me?" she questioned in a teasing tone.

The guard blushed. She consented to his requested and lifted her arms. The guard lifted a wand that performed an X-ray examination of her entire body. He passed it across her front and then behind her. The scan instantaneously displayed on the screen next to him. He lowered the wand and began looking at the screen.

"See anything?" she asked, peeking at the display.

"No," he said after a quick examination. "You're free to go, Miss."

Katura gave the guard one more flirting glance, then turned and sauntered down the steps of the embassy. As she passed, the guards momentarily ceased their exit searches to admire the graceful sultriness of her walk, floating downward and completing her descent off the steps. More admiring men paused their conversations and other activities as she passed. Women stared at their men angrily when their attention was diverted from them momentarily.

A limousine pulled to the entryway of the embassy and came to a stop directly in front of her. She stood poised at the edge of the curb staring at the obstructing vehicle. The window in the rear lowered and its occupant rested in the shadows. Katura stood waiting for the person inside to reveal themselves. Then, a face appeared from the shadows. It was Mbaku once again.

"Would you like a ride?" he asked.

She smiled, but did not reply. The limo driver opened his door and proceeded around the car to the rear where she stood. Mbaku slid over as the driver opened the door and waited for Katura to enter. She raised her gown slightly and then stepped into the limousine. She settled in and crossed her legs to reveal her beautifully shaped thighs.

Mbaku's eyes sparkled.

The chauffeur closed the door, scurried to the driver's side and

Nationhood

re-entered.

As the limo drove into the night, the two passengers non-verbally flirted with each other. Mbaku patted his hair with his palms while Katura seductively wet her lips with her tongue. She had hungry eyes and an insatiable curiosity, wanting to know how he knew she had the diamonds. She knew she wasn't sloppy, so it could only mean that this guy was a professional thief just like her. That thought alone made her very interested.

The two of them continued to stare at each other, silently sizing up the other. Mbaku reached into his inner coat pocket and removed a beautiful necklace. It was one of the crown jewels Katura stole from the embassy.

"Nice maneuver back there, using me as your accomplice," said Mbaku.

"It was the least you could do, insulting me by watching my every move," Katura replied.

"Hard not to do, considering how beautiful you are."

Katura smiled. "Was that supposed to flatter me?" she asked.

"Just stating a fact. But suffer no delusions. I do have a job to do."

"And would that job include me, a martini and some pillow talk? If so, you've certainly been reading too many European spy books."

With a pleasant smile, Mbaku replied, "You do know I was sent to take these from you?"

"Really? And here I thought you were only trying to get me in the bed," Katura replied sarcastically.

"I must admit, the Americans have some very beautiful loyalists," said Mbaku.

"Trust me, loyalty had nothing to do with it."

"Then what? Did they offer you freedom? Please tell me you aren't that naïve?"

Katura gave him a look that indicated he'd come too close to the truth and was about to overstep his liberties.

"When I kill someone of breeding, I usually like to know their names. It makes things a lot more personal," she replied.

"Mbaku. Mbaku Bolo."

"Katura Ishtar."

"Pleasure."

James Gordon

"Likewise."

"So why do you want to kill me, Mrs. Ishtar?"

"It's Miss, and you may call me Katura."

"Very well. Why do you want to kill me... Katura?"

"Because you're a smart ass. You already know why I'm here and why I'm doing what I'm doing. In order for my mission to be successful, I can't leave any loose ends, therefore, I have to kill you."

"But what if I'm trying to help you?"

"Help me? Now you're insulting my intelligence."

"No, really. I can help you get out of here."

"And why would you want to do something like that?"

"That's for me to know. But I give you my word that I will help you to get out of the country. No tricks, no small print."

"And I'm supposed to believe that you'd allow me to waltz into your country, take the Tsar Nicholas Jewels and leave, knowing what this could do to your relations with Romania? Gosh, I must have my look-at-me-I'm-stupid makeup on."

"I don't know about makeup, but I can tell you this. There are individuals who are so deeply entrenched in power that to remove them would cause the world to spiral into chaos. Those are the people who must be brought down and those are the people you work for."

"My, don't we sound self-righteous."

"Indeed. I have read the Bible, the Torah and the Koran, studying their teachings from cover to cover. Those people who believe in them and followed their words have either been the victims of injustice or the victimizers. It boggles my mind why anyone would put their faith in such things. Bow down, turn the other cheek and accept the crumbs that have been given to you, those are the teachings of servants, not for a people that live in the most powerful civilization this planet has ever seen."

"And what civilization would that be?" asked Katura, leaning forward.

"Our civilization," replied Mbaku, also leaning forward.

"You can't be serious. The United States is a just and righteous nation. Our people are God-fearing people who only want what's best for the world. On principal alone we aren't going to let this upstart nation gain anymore power. To believe such a thing would be total lunacy."

"Ah. I see you are still under the influence of their deceit. But the Nation of AUNK has already begun our rise. When our people were taken

Nationhood

to the shores of the supposed *New World*, we were forced to abandon our gods—Amen-Ra, Isis, Anubis. With our abandonment came the wrath for our disobedience. We were subsequently fed to the lions of a people who coveted our country. Before AUNK, Black people owned none of Africa. We were taught to be subservient and those lessons were further engrained into our minds by this so-called religion of yours. To this day, scientists still marvel at the accomplishments we, as a people, made all those centuries ago. But instead of glorifying us, they wish to erase us from history. For so long we allowed them to put White faces on our Black kings and queens, the original rulers of this world. *Our* people ruled this planet once and we are destined to rule again. All we need is a leader to make that happen."

"And just who do you think that person will be?"

"I'm not sure. We are a people of faith. But we are also warriors. We will fight for a just cause. If that cause embraces our faith, a faith that teaches us that New Kemet is not a nation of ne'er-do-wells or servants, but a powerful nation whose existence still impacts other cultures today, we will give our lives. It's long been said that people of color aren't patriotic. What hasn't been said is that we are very patriotic, just not to the same countries that would lie to us and make us feel inferior. You've been a fool for too long, Katura Ishtar. It's time you opened your eyes."

"Such pretty words," said Katura. "But I'm still not impressed. No matter how powerful you may think you are, the Americans will find a way to bring you down. So, if you don't mind I'd like to leave now. The only question is whether you are going to give me the jewels voluntarily or will I have to carry through with my threat and kill you?"

Mbaku saw that she was no longer listening. He extended his hand and lackadaisically handed her the necklace. Then, he reached to his side, picked up a silk bag and handed her the rest of the jewels. Katura took them from him, giving him a skeptical look.

"I must say I'm a little disappointed. After all that talk I thought you'd give me a tussle. And here I was so looking forward to getting sweaty," she said teasingly.

"My job is simple. I only needed to give you back the jewels. But I must warn you, my Arabic beauty. Your masters will not let such a prize as you go," said Mbaku.

"That's my problem."

Just then, the driver stopped. Katura opened the door and got out

James Gordon

of the car, slamming the door closed behind her. A loud screech could be heard outside. Mbaku lunged to the door, but found that he was unable to get it open. He quickly lowered the window and looked out. To his surprise he found another vehicle pulled extremely close to the limo, blocking the door from being opened. He then looked into the sky and spied a small helicopter rising into the heavens. Inside, Katura blew him a kiss as the chopper disappeared into the star-lit night sky.

With a slight chuckle, Mbaku sat back onto his seat. He reached into his inner coat pocket and removed a moderate-sized diamond. It was one of the jewels he managed to chisel from the necklace. He was certain she would eventually notice it was missing, which ensured he would see this entrancing beauty again.

Although he just met her, Mbaku knew that Katura was one of the best. This was just his way of making sure she came looking for him when the time was right. But he also knew that there was more to the story and she was a principle part of it.

He found it interesting that the Americans would send someone to commit such a terrorist act knowing that it could damage their relations with other countries. If he'd stopped Katura from stealing the diamonds, the blame for their theft could have easily been placed on the Nation of AUNK, especially when the government officials attempted to return the diamonds. From a tactical standpoint, it made sense to allow her to escape. But to stoop to such measures meant there was something about those diamonds that went beyond simple diplomatic sabotage. He recalled the lax security and how everything about the gala seemed more like a half-assed façade to protect the jewels. It was as if they wanted the jewels to be taken, which was why he allowed Katura to take them.

But he knew that something didn't seem right, something beyond the smoke and mirrors, and the more he thought about it the more Mbaku saw that Katura, whether she realized it or not, was being set up. If she was being made to be the patsy, he needed to stay close to the action because it wouldn't be long before she would be needing his help. But first, he had to see what mysteries surrounded the sparkling gem he now held in his hand. There had to be a reason why the US would go to such lengths to get them.

"There's more to these diamonds than meets the eye," said Mbaku. "And I intend on finding out what that is."

Meanwhile, in the helicopter that Katura escaped in, the ringing

82

Nationhood

of a phone could be heard. She lifted the headset off its cradle, pulled her hair back and placed the earpiece to her ear.

"How did it go, Miss Ishtar?" asked the voice on the receiver.

"Why do you ask me such stupid questions, Prime?" she replied.

"Why? It's my job. I trust that all went well?"

"Yes, everything went perfectly," she said, reaching into a bag and removing the jewels.

She smiled as she remembered how she smuggled them from the embassy. But most of all, she smiled as she reminisced about the mystery man named Mbaku Bolo. He was handsome and well mannered, a quality she'd found missing in most men. But above all his tangible qualities, it was his ability to potentially match her skills as a thief that really impressed her. He knew what she did and even agreed to help her. Under different circumstances, she might even want to see him again, if for nothing more than to see if he could catch her in the act of another heist.

She slid the jewels back into the bag and faced forward in her seat, wiping the glistened perspiration off her forehead.

"We are en route to deliver the jewels to the drop zone. However, there are a few loose ends I need to take care of," she said.

"Very well," replied Prime. "I'll see you soon."

She removed the earpiece, then reached above her head and pressed the intercom button. It rang the helicopter pilot, Jaquimo, who turned to look at her with a smirk.

"Told you you'd need an alternate vehicle of escape," he said.

"Yes, Jaquimo, you did," she replied.

"So where to now? I heard you mention something about loose ends?"

"Yes. Let's swing by Barron's first. I've got a taste for some shrimp ettoufee."

"Would madam like to change into something more comfortable first? I brought some extra outfits that might be a little less conspicuous. They're all laid out at the hotel. You could change and then we could get you that ettoufee."

Katura glanced at the beautiful gown she was wearing and pondered for a second.

"Yes, I think that would be best, Jaquimo," she replied.

~~~

James Gordon

Chapter Six: Destined to revolt

Carla Snipes stood in front of the camera, her right hand gripping her crumpled script so tightly that her knuckles were almost pale. She possessed a look of horror, as if the information she was about to deliver was extremely terrible and that she almost didn't want to deliver it. The cameraman, Abraham, looked away from the monitor and did a double take at the nearly motionless Carla. He saw the blank expression and the presence of fear that was frozen in her gaze. He glanced at his watch. Only two minutes before they went live again. He needed to get her head back into the game because any moment they would up-link to the satellite and shortly thereafter be giving their report to the rest of the world.

"Psst! Hey, Carla," said Abraham in a whisper.

She almost didn't hear him calling to her. She turned to stare at him with a far away gaze, the kind that indicated her thoughts were nowhere near the place she needed to be in order to give this report.

"Hey, you okay?" Abraham asked.

Still, Carla did not answer. Only a faint nod of her head was the response she gave. Abraham sighed deeply. He walked from behind the tripod-perched camera and stood next to her.

"Listen, if you need for me to do the report, I can," he offered. "I can show you what you need to do to operate the camera…"

"I'm fine, Abraham," Carla said snippily.

"No offense, but you don't look like your mind is here. I know what we just found out was awful, but we still have a job to do."

"I know that, Abe. Still, it doesn't make this any easier."

"Yes, you're right. Are you sure you're ready? We go live in thirty seconds."

"I'm okay. Now go do your thing. Let's do our job."

Abraham looked at her skeptically, then nodded. He walked back behind the camera and began making his final adjustments. The announcement through his headset gave him the signal the network was ready. He looked through the monitor and gave Carla the standard countdown with his fingers…three, two, one.

James Gordon

At that moment, the voice of Paul LeBlanc, the anchorman, blared threw the mini speakers introducing Carla to the viewing public once more. "And now we go live to the conference area of New Kemet International Airport where Carla Snipes is ready with an update. Carla."

"Yes, Paul," Carla replied. "Just moments ago, airport officials and emergency medical personnel raced out of the conference area with three Senate members on gurneys. They rushed them into waiting ambulances and took them to a local hospital where, officials say, they will be treated. There's been no official release on exactly what happened, but one of the aides was heard to say that Senator Kwane Kefata was quote, *spitting up blood*. We tried to find out what happened to the other senators but..." Carla suddenly pushed her hand against her earpiece. "Wait, we're getting information that Constable Al-Shahir of the Mecca City Police Department is on his way here to make an announcement. I believe I see him approaching."

Carla watched as Constable Al-Shahir pushed his way through the crowd of reporters and stop just behind her. He had a disturbed expression on his face, one that foretold the news he was about to deliver. The flash of camera bulbs and the jockeying for position of news teams almost looked like a circus of performers struggling to take center stage position. Constable Al-Shahir adjusted his coat and cleared his throat.

"I'm saddened to report that there has been an incident with the recently released IS member named Victor Johnson and the members of the New Kemet Senate," said Al-Shahir. "It appears that a form of biological weapon had been released, causing the Senators to become violently ill. At this time containment teams are checking the area to find out what happened and what may have caused the sudden illnesses. The senators have been taken to Mecca City Memorial Hospital where they will be treated."

Just then, Carla chimed in with the questions.

"What were the symptoms the senators exhibited?" she asked.

"They each showed violent vomiting spells, sweating and shortness of breath," Al-Shahir replied.

"About when did these symptoms occur?" asked Carla.

"About ten minutes into the discussions we saw the senators acting peculiar. Then they suddenly began to show the symptoms."

"How are they now?"

"We do not know the condition of the senators at this time."

Nationhood

"And what of Victor Johnson? Did he also suffer from the same symptoms?"

"I regret to report that Mister Johnson died just moments ago from severe internal hemorrhaging. He, too, suffered from the same symptoms, but the paramedics were unable to control the bleeding."

A hush fell over the crowd as the news of Victor Johnson's death sank in. Then, Carla proceeded with the questions once more.

"You said they couldn't control his bleeding and that he was hemorrhaging. What sort of trauma did he have?" she asked.

"There were no signs of trauma. He simply began vomiting violently and there was blood in it," replied Al-Shahir.

Just then, a man who looked as if he was one of the emergency crewmembers came to Constable Al-Shahir and whispered in his ear. The Constable's eyes bulged, like he'd just been told he had ten minutes to live. Carla saw his changed expression, even though he avoided looking into the crowd in an attempt to maintain his composure. After about thirty seconds of whispering, the crewmember turned and walked back up the hall. Al-Shahir looked out at the sea of media, sucking in a deep breath and pruning his lips. By his expression alone, Carla knew that something was wrong. She turned to look at Abraham, who continued to look through his camera monitor. All the other news teams seemed equally oblivious to the change in the Constable's demeanor, standing patiently as he collected himself. Carla looked back at him, the fear gripping her chest like a vice and causing her to feel a shortness of breath and a sense of panic.

"Constable," shouted one of the other reporters. "Are the senators expected to survive?"

Al-Shahir had regrouped and returned to his stoic persona. "At this time we have no report on the senators' condition. However, the hospital officials will have a full report later today," he replied.

As the shouting of questions began, Al-Shahir held up his hands and attempted to calm the crowd.

"Members of the media, this concludes this press conference," he said.

Seconds later, all the power to the cameras was cut. The satellite transmissions were blocked and to the viewers watching it appeared to have been a break in the feed from the airport. Only a black screen was seen and the anchor people attempted to fill in while the technicians tried to find out what was going on.

James Gordon

Meanwhile, inside the airport, the ruckus continued. The media began clamoring for answers and wondering why their uplinks were cut. Al-Shahir held up his hands as his officers began what appeared to be an attempt to corral the mob of angry reporters.

"I'd like for each of you to give me your undivided attention. This is a matter of extreme importance," he said.

The disgruntled masses slowly began to calm themselves, eager eyes staring at Al-Shahir waiting to get a good explanation for what just happened. Carla's fear was becoming more intense. Perspiration began to bead on her forehead and her heart raced even faster as she waited to hear what the Constable had to say. But whatever it was, she knew that after having the power cut and their feed to the network interrupted, it wasn't going to be good.

"We'd like each of you to go into the very next room and set up your equipment there. We apologize for the inconvenience, but we had to go to an instant media shutdown for national security purposes. We understand that the President of New Kemet is on his way here and should be here in about fifteen minutes. If you'll follow the deputies into the other room, we'll get you situated as quickly as possible," said Al-Shahir.

Clamor erupted as the reporters quickly began to gather their things and move into the other room. They wanted to get a good spot so they could have perfect camera positioning for when the President spoke. Abraham was about to disassemble his camera and tripod when Carla touched him on the arm and stopped him. Abraham looked at her, his brow furrowing. Carla watched as the other members of the media began hustling into the other room. However, she noticed that the Constable was looking right at her. She leaned closer to Abraham and whispered in his ear.

"We're not going into that room," she said.

Abraham noticed the glare from the Constable.

"I think you're right," he replied.

By now, the other news teams were in the other room, continuing their clamoring for the best spots. Now it was just the Constable, Carla and Abraham. Carla walked closer to Al-Shahir and stared him squarely in the eyes. She'd become a lot calmer now, realizing that she was going to get the real story as to what was going on.

"The President isn't coming here, is he?" she asked.

"You're a bright woman, Miss Snipes. I knew you'd pick up on

Nationhood

the ploy," said Al-Shahir.

"So, is it safe to say that the senators are dead, also?"

"Not yet. But I'm afraid that they don't have long to live."

Carla stared into Al-Shahir's eyes, seeing the powerful restraint he was using to keep his composure.

"What aren't you telling me, Constable?" she asked.

"Miss Snipes, how badly to you wish to know the truth?" he asked.

"It's my job to uncover the truth. Why do you ask?"

"Any reporter can uncover the truth. But you have a special talent for seeing those things that are missed by others. You have a natural talent for uncovering those secrets that others wish to remain unfound. Seeing as that is the case here, I decided to cut to the chase and offer you exclusivity to what has to be deemed the biggest story of the century. Are you interested?"

"You know that I am."

"Good. I just needed confirmation. But before we get to the matter at hand, I need for you to come with me."

Carla and Abraham gathered his camera and other gear. They followed Al-Shahir to a room located near the rear of the conference area. A foul stench hung in the air and an eerie presence filled the hallway. It was like walking between two lines of ghosts that were staring at them as they passed.

Carla was seriously spooked. Her heart pounded in her chest and her breath carried the scent of fear in each exhale.

They finally made it to a well-lit room at the end. The smell had lessened and the bright light was nearly blinding. As they walked through the door, a group of men grabbed Carla and Abraham. They took the camera and other gear away from them, then held them in place while another person walked up to them and gave them both an injection using an inoculation gun. It all happened so fast that they barely had time flinch. After a few seconds, the men released them both and backed away. Both Carla and Abraham looked at them with startled expressions and a simmering anger building in their chest.

"What the hell was that all about, Al-Shahir!" screamed Abraham.

The men began returning their things as the Constable walked closer to Carla and Abraham.

James Gordon

"I apologize for the roughness. But it was necessary in order to inject the serum into you before the virus took affect," said Al-Shahir, stopping in front of them.

"What the hell are you talking about? What virus?" Abraham retorted.

A look of revelation appeared over Carla's face.

"The one that killed Johnson," she said just above a whisper.

Abraham turned and looked at her with a puzzled expression. Carla returned a look, sporting a slight smirk.

"I think I understand now," she said, facing Al-Shahir once again. "The President isn't coming here. That was all a ruse to get the other reporters into a quarantined area. The virus that killed Johnson is airborne."

"Correct. But the serum I gave you isn't a cure. It's a vaccine that will help to slow down the process of the virus. Understand, Miss Snipes, that what we are dealing with here isn't a simple outbreak of a contagious disease. What happened here tonight was an act of terrorism."

"Terrorism? Are you saying that someone released a biological virus into the air?"

"Not just someone. Victor Johnson."

"The IS? Why would he do that?" asked Abraham.

"He didn't know. He was only the carrier of the virus," said Al-Shahir.

"I'm sorry. You lost me," said Carla. "If he didn't know, how could he release it?"

"It was in his blood," said Al-Shahir. "Allow me to explain. About a year ago, our intelligence department came across plans that a rebel South African group was going to release a biological weapon on the Nation of AUNK. The virus, called Crimson Night, is a rabid carcinogen that eats its host from the inside out in a matter of hours. Naturally, we found the conspirators and disposed of them. We even found strains of the virus they were going to release. Our scientists have been working on an antidote to counter the effects of the virus. So far, we've been unsuccessful due to the virus' mutating capability. The closest we could come was to create a vaccine that would slow down the cancerous effects."

"My God," said Carla, with a look of horror.

"And this vaccine, is that what you injected us with?" asked Abraham, with a disturbed expression.

Nationhood

"Precisely," said Al-Shahir.

"But what about the other reporters?" asked Carla. "Weren't they exposed and shouldn't they be vaccinated also?"

"There's nothing we can do for them. We only have a small supply of the vaccine and we needed to use it wisely. They'll all be dead within the hour."

Abraham and Carla stared at the constable with stunned expressions. They each searched for a way to handle what they heard, but the news was just too horrific to grasp.

"I can't believe this. I really can't believe this," said Carla, bracing herself against the wall. "It's like a nightmare."

"So what you're saying is we're all going to die," said Abraham. Reluctantly, Al-Shahir nodded.

It took a few minutes for the situation to settle. Thirty minutes passed before anyone said a word. Then Carla asked a question. "How long do we have?"

"A day, maybe two," said the constable.

Carla stood to her feet. "I guess we need to get to the hospital," she said.

"That's not going to be possible, Miss Snipes," said Al-Shahir.

"Why not?" asked Abraham.

"Currently, the virus has been contained to this lower conference area. We've sealed off all exits and made the lower floors a quarantine area. But, if that virus was to ever escape this conference area or another carrier were to release that virus on the populace of the city, it could decimate the entire nation. The reason why I chose you, Miss Snipes, is because you have the ability to tell this story in a way that the people of the world need to hear it. Even if we do not make it out of here alive, the world needs to know what happened here."

"You mean to tell me we're prisoners?" asked Carla.

"I'm afraid so," replied Al-Shahir.

"Screw this! I'm getting the hell out of here!" said Abraham.

As he began gathering his things to leave, Carla remained still, allowing the troubling and overwhelming information to settle. So much had been thrown at them that it was hard to get everything to fit. She was still having a hard time handling all that she now knew, but she realized what needed to be done. In that brief span of time, she understood the implications of the virus spreading and the need for them to stay inside.

James Gordon

She braced her hand against Abraham's chest, stopping him from collecting the rest of his stuff. He looked at her with widened eyes filled with panic and anxiety.

"Listen, Abe. I know this isn't easy, but we must think of the bigger picture," she said.

"Screw the bigger picture!" he replied.

"No, you have to listen. If that virus were to leave this place it could kill a lot of innocent people. Think of the devastation it would cause. All the work we've done and the success we've achieved as a nation over the last twenty-five years will be for nothing. We can't let the people responsible for this attack against our country get away with this. The Constable is right. We have to make a sacrifice for the sake of the nation."

Abraham looked at her with a stare of disbelief. "You should listen to yourself, Carla. You sound like a frigging politician."

"No, Abe. I'm just a woman who is scared out of her mind. I don't like this anymore than you do. But I also have friends and family out there in Mecca City, Independence and the rest of the country. You have a daughter and a wife. Neither of us want any of them to end up like Johnson or the senators, and if we must remain here to ensure that happens, then that is what we need to do."

"But I don't want this," said Abraham as tears welled in his eyes. "This isn't the way things were supposed to be. I was supposed to go to work, do my job and then go home. I wasn't supposed to become some goddamn martyr, Carla!"

"I know. I hadn't planned on this either. But we have to stay here. No one should ever have to go through this again. We need to expose this attack and help bring these people to justice. We have to make sure that the events that happened here are never forgotten and that our family and friends never again have to go through this."

Abraham and Carla looked at each other for a few seconds more. Then, he placed his camera and his bag on the floor. Carla wrapped her arms around his neck and hugged him. She then released him and they both turned to look at the constable.

"You couldn't have left anyway," said Al-Shahir. "If you tried you would have been shot."

"Well, that's nice to know," said Abraham sarcastically.

A few more moments passed. There was cursing and crying, anger was released and prayers were offered, all a futile attempt to wish

Nationhood

this away and make it become some horrible dream that they'd soon awaken from. It was a lot to absorb and even more to accept. To ask someone to acknowledge their own impending death was too much, even for Al-Shahir.

Suggestions were given and bargains were presented. More talking took place to find some way of making all of this vanish. Finally, Carla and Abraham came to the belief that someone was going to find a way to stop the virus. All they needed to do was be patient and wait this ordeal out. They decided the best way to do that was by doing their jobs. Carla approached Al-Shahir, putting her best fearless face on.

"Constable, you still haven't answered how Johnson released the virus," Carla asked, trying to focus on the issue.

"We believe it exited Mister Johnson's wounds or perhaps when he vomited," Al-Shahir replied.

"Then, there is the possibility that the virus has already been spread before he met with the senators."

"There is that possibility."

"Oh, that's just blooming great!" said Abraham. "Then why keep us here?"

"On the other hand, it might have been incubating. Our scientists believe that he was only contagious when he began showing the symptoms. After all, the virus was carried in his blood and only when he began bleeding was the virus exposed to the air," said Al-Shahir.

"But you don't know for certain, right?" asked Abraham argumentatively.

"No, we aren't certain," replied Al-Shahir with a slight degree of annoyance in his tone.

Carla turned sharply toward Abraham.

"Listen, Abe, why don't you go set up the camera over there in the corner. I want to talk to the Constable for a moment," she said, trying to defuse the air of tension.

"Sure thing," Abraham replied smugly.

As he walked away to set up the equipment, Carla turned to look at Al-Shahir.

"Okay, Constable. Since we've cleared up the fact that we're stuck here, the first question should seem obvious. How long do we really have?" she asked.

"Your fellow reporters have less than an hour. We should have a day, like I said, maybe two," he replied.

"Then let's make those two days count. Let's start off with the number one question of the day. Who do you think is responsible for all of this?"

Al-Shahir smiled, like the cat that swallowed the canary.

"Yes, that is the question," he replied. "Tell me, Miss Snipes. Have you ever heard of an organization called...The Illuminati?"

~~~

Night had fallen when Thurgood and Lela exited the Wilshire Grand Hotel. They immediately made their way to a waiting town car parked out front. When they entered, Lela gave the driver instructions, then thanked him for his assistance. Thurgood stretched and looked out the window as they pulled from the front of the hotel.

"Nice, but definitely not worth the money we paid," he said, commenting about the hotel.

"It's the location and the view," Lela replied. "Besides, there aren't that many places that would allow us to stay. We were lucky to get this one."

Thurgood shook his head. "There was a time when a Black person could go anywhere in this town and not have to deal with such things."

"Yes. But those days are long gone. Which is why you needed to stay here and check things out."

Thurgood turned to look at her. "But what am I really here to check out, Lela? The same problems people have here are the same ones they're having all over this nation. Jack Crow has a firm grip on this country's pulse and it ain't letting up."

"You're letting things get to you, Thomas. Maybe we needed to stay in the hotel a bit longer."

"No, you were right to suggest we got out for a minute. I was starting to get a little claustrophobic in there."

Lela turned to look out of the window. "You know," she said. "I've always liked Los Angeles. It's always sunny and the city seems so alive."

"I've not been here that much, only stopping through for a night or two when I was meeting with some of the members of congress. Even then, most of my time was spent talking to them. I have to admit, I don't feel that I was missing too much. The city looks abandoned. Those damn

Nationhood

Jack Crow Laws, putting a curfew on the Blacks within the city limits," Thurgood replied.

"Oh, it's not that bad. Sure, things are not as they once were, people out and about, handling their different affairs. But L.A is a nice place. You just have to give it a chance…"

Suddenly, the car came to a screeching stop, jarring both Lela and Thurgood forward. As they regrouped, they both looked ahead to see what had happened. The lights from the town car revealed that their way had been blocked by a brown van that had to be, at least, ten years old. The side door slid open and armed men with bandanas wrapped across their mouths raced toward the car. Thurgood and Lela were immediately stunned and horrified by what they saw.

"Tell me these are guys who are aggressively wanting to clean our windows," said Thurgood, turning to look at Lela.

The armed men stormed the car, crashing through the driver's glass and reaching in to unlock the door. Once opened, the driver was immediately pulled out and another person entered. A second man opened the passenger side front door and also entered, pointing a semi-automatic gun in Thurgood's face. They quickly closed the doors and pulled off. Thurgood raised his hands, staring at the gunman with wild looking eyes. Lela began crying, too scared to say anything. Thurgood was about to grab her hand in order to calm her when the gunman intervened.

"Leave her alone!" he barked.

Thurgood stopped and lifted his hand back into the air. "I——I was only tr-trying to calm her down," he replied nervously.

"She'll be fine. In fact, you both will be fine as long as you follow orders," said the gunman.

"Wh——Where are you taking us?"

"Someone wants to see you, someone very important."

"Do you mind if I put my hands down. It's quite uncomfortable like this."

"Go ahead, but don't get any stupid ideas."

Thurgood slowly placed his hands on his lap. He tried to take a deep breath and calm himself, but it was no use. He was scared and Lela's whimpering indicated she was petrified. He wanted to put his arm around her, but doing so might get them shot. He began feeling guilty because he knew that he was the target. Anytime a person went up against the government they always became a target. But he really didn't want to get

95

James Gordon

Lela involved. Perhaps, he thought, he could persuade them to let her go and just take him. It was worth a shot.

"Excuse me," he said to the gunman. "But I was hoping that you could stop the car and let my assistant go. She is of no benefit to you and I promise I'll go peacefully."

The gunman snickered at Thurgood's bargaining.

"Sorry, Homes, but she's coming, too. As I said, everything is going to be okay, just as long as you don't do something stupid. Besides, she'd be better off with us than out here on the streets. If the cops didn't get her for breaking curfew some psycho with a taste for chocolate would do something far worse to her," he said.

Thurgood looked at Lela, and for the first time he realized just how serious things had gotten here. The reports that she'd given him hinted of trouble brewing in the city. But now, he saw just how bad things were. To make matters worse, both he and Lela were in the thick of it and the only thing he could do was go with the flow, at least for now. He turned to stare at the gunman again. He realized that they had no intention of killing them. If that was their intent, they would have been goners by now. He took a deep breath and decided to see if he could get more information from them.

"Don't expect you're going to tell me whom we're going to see?" he asked.

"You suspect well, Homes," the gunman replied. "You'll know when you get there. Now shut up before you make me do something you might regret."

"Just one other thing. Is there any way you could point that gun someplace else instead of in my face. I wouldn't want any unforeseen bumps in the road to cause you to slip and blow my brains out."

The gunman lowered the barrel and pointed it at Thurgood's groin region. "Is that better?" he asked.

"Not really," said Thurgood. "But thanks all the same."

The rest of the ride was relatively quiet. Lela managed to calm herself a bit. Thurgood, however, kept his eyes on the road, trying to see where these men were taking them. They soon drove into the area known as South Central. They pulled down a narrow alley, creeping along like someone about to perform a drive by. They came to an opening and turned into it. A couple of men were standing next to what appeared to be an old car garage. They opened the doors and allowed the town car to enter. It

Nationhood

was dark, very dark. Lela scooted closer to Thurgood, who finally wrapped his arms around her. As the garage doors were shut, the gunman opened the door as his accomplice turned off the engine.

"Okay, folks. We're here. Get out," he said.

Thurgood and Lela looked at each other. They were reluctant to leave, but knew they didn't have much of a choice. The back door was opened. Lela pondered for a moment, then slid across the seat and got out with Thurgood following closely behind.

They were taken to a modest-size room and the door was closed behind them. The gunmen coaxed them toward a table toward the back where the dimming sunlight was masked by the dingy windowpanes the table sat in front of. Sitting behind the table was a man. He was stocky and had tattoos of sphinxes, pharaoh's heads, pyramids and other Egyptian articles and gods over his arms. He looked like a walking hieroglyph and his presence was very intimidating.

Thurgood and Lela walked to the table and stopped before it. The man was working on a carburetor, using a toothbrush to sweep the inside of the breather valve. He did not look up, but was aware of their presence.

"You know, the Quadrajet is one of the best carburetors there is," said the man. "Only one problem. They all hesitate on acceleration. Not good when one is trying to make a get away."

"Excuse me," said Thurgood with a furrowed brow. "Not to be rude, but your men brought us here because they said that someone wanted to speak to us. I'm assuming that someone is you and if I may say I'm sure you didn't bring us here to chat about carburetors or getaways."

"You assume?" the man said with a chuckle. "To assume is to chance a man's dignity. I would hope you would not be so foolish as to sacrifice such a precious commodity."

"Dignity is irrelevant, especially in the face of the unknown," Thurgood replied.

The man put down his toothbrush, lifted his head and stared at Thurgood. He grabbed a towel, then walked to the sink located a few feet away. He began washing his hands as both Lela and Thurgood looked at him with frowning faces.

"Can we leave now?" asked Lela with somewhat of an attitude.

"You act as if you're prisoners," said the man, keeping his back turned while continuing to wash his hands.

"And we're not?" asked Thurgood.

"That is not for me to say. I tend to look at you as my guests."

"Guests?" asked Lela. "What kind of host holds his *guests* at gunpoint?"

"The guns were not for your capture or containment. They were to make sure no one tried to hurt you," the man replied.

"Hurt us? The only person that seems to be a danger to Lela and I is you," said Thurgood.

"Now, why would you say that? You don't even know me," said the man.

"You know, you're right. Normally, I'd like to know whom I'm speaking with," said Thurgood. "For the last minute we've been playing some sort of Shakespearian badminton. You seem to know who we are, but who the hell are you?"

The man turned off the water, picked up a towel and dried his hands. He turned and began walking toward Thurgood and Lela, placing the towel on the table next to the carburetor. For the first time they could see his entire face. He stopped in front of Thurgood and stared him in the eyes.

"Pardon my rudeness," said the man. "I did not intend to offend. I simply wanted to wash my hands before I shook the hand of the man I most admire."

"You have a funny way of showing your admiration," said Thurgood.

"Looks can be deceiving, especially in this day and age. Had to make sure you were, indeed, Thomas Thurgood. Couldn't have our new location compromised."

"And just what is this location?"

"Mister Thurgood, welcome to Exodus. My name is Ramses."

Thurgood stared at the man before him with an expression of complete disbelief. Ramses extended his hand, but Thurgood was too shocked to notice.

"I hope that my hands are clean enough for you to shake," said Ramses.

Thurgood snapped out of his shocked state and shook hands. Ramses waved for his men to bring some chairs for Thurgood and Lela to sit. The seats were quickly brought to the table. Ramses walked to the other side, slid the carburetor out of the way and braced his arms on the table. Lela and Thurgood took their seats, still in a state of disbelief that

Nationhood

they were sitting with a man who was considered to be the most ruthless terrorist since Bin Laden.

"I have to say, it is an honor to have you among us," said Ramses.

"I wish I could say the same. Your reputation of being a man of moral fiber isn't what's being distributed," Thurgood replied.

"Propaganda. Lies and falsities to discredit me and my people's attempts to bring equality to all people of African descent."

"Ramses. I'd always thought your name was somewhat of a misnomer, given the name of the organization."

"On the contrary. What better name to have. The supposed defeated Pharaoh who lost to Moses when he parted the Red Sea in order to free the Hebrews. Even the holy book has its share of one sided stories."

"And you? Are you telling me that the *propaganda* you alluded to is skewed?"

"Yes, that is what I am telling you."

"But what about the New Orleans Massacre or the bombing of Freedom Square? Weren't your people responsible for that?"

"Yes and no."

"What does that mean?" asked Lela, interjecting. "Either you killed those people or you didn't. There is no ambiguity. Your thugs have been known to be a bit violent."

"I'll admit we have some who are more prone to do such vicious acts than others, but the random taking of innocent lives is not in our agenda," said Ramses. "We were at New Orleans and at Freedom Square. But what we did was secure information to perform cyber terrorism."

"But what about the people, the deaths?"

"We had nothing to do with that. It was the government. *They* performed all those acts, bombing the protesting civilians in order to cover up what really happened there."

"And what was that?" asked Thurgood.

"In New Orleans we deleted files that listed every known member of Exodus. That way we could move more freely without constantly looking over our shoulders," Ramses explained.

"But that doesn't make sense."

"Of course it does. They created a state of terror in order to make us into public enemy number one. They hoped that their actions would turn people against us. They almost succeeded until we managed to seize some secure footing."

James Gordon

"And what would that be?"

"Freedom Square was our greatest move. It was there we managed to take their technology and use it against them. Come, let me show you what I'm talking about."

They stood and walked to another room adjacent to the garage. Inside was an entire area filled with computerized satellite monitors, thermo readings and ultraviolet imaging. The place looked like a mini NASA control room, equipped with every single tracking device imaginable. Lela and Thurgood were dumbfounded as they gazed at the set up. Nothing they'd ever seen could compare to this.

"Not bad, huh? We tapped into the U.S. defense satellite systems in order to know what they are doing at all times. We are able to track their every move. That's how we found you. They'd been tailing you ever since you left Washington D.C. The driver was one of them. The Agency, I suspect," said Ramses.

"I don't believe this," said Thurgood. "This is incredible."

Just then, Lela turned and looked at Ramses. "If they'd been following us using this sky camera, don't you think they would have continued to follow us to this place? Your little hideout could already be compromised."

"That's pretty smart," said Ramses, turning to Thurgood. "I can see why you have her as your aide. But not to worry. We jammed the transmission and replaced it with one of our own. For about five minutes they were watching the car just before it pulled up to the Wilshire Hotel. By the time they realized what was happening, we were safely inside our hideout and the system returned to normal."

Lela seemed impressed with the setup and nodded her head in approval. Thurgood turned and looked at Ramses, his expression a little more skeptical.

"So, you're tapped into the government's satellite systems and you're armed to the teeth. This is all well and good, but the question I have is why are you doing this? We should be seeking peaceful means to fixing our problems," said Thurgood.

"You really must get out more often, Mister Thurgood," said Ramses. He turned to a young woman at one of the terminals. "Desi, show him the images from last night."

She punched a few keys and brought up a scene where police were severely beating a man. He was screaming at the top of his lungs for

Nationhood

them to stop. But they didn't. They kept hammering him with billy clubs and nightsticks. He lay on the ground in a fetal position trying to shield himself as best he could. His blue shirt was covered with blood and soon he could no longer hold his hands up to defend himself. But that didn't stop the officers. They continued to strike the nearly unconscious man, yelling slanderous words at him. The sights were so violent that Lela turned away, sickened and angered by the scene. Thurgood, however, stared at them with horror and disgust.

"This man made the mistake of working a little overtime last night. He was on his way home, several minutes before curfew began. But the LAPD decided that he was too close to the curfew time and this is the result. He tried pleading with them, saying that his daughter was sick and he was only trying to make some extra money so he could take her to the doctor. They denied him insurance at his job because the Jack Crow Laws don't view people of African descent as true citizens anymore. Now do you see why we do this? If we do not stand up for ourselves, who will?" asked Ramses.

Thurgood turned to look at him. "Me."

Ramses chuckled. "No offense, Mister Thurgood, but I've seen your rallies. They are inspiring, but all I see is a bunch of lip service. Don't get me wrong, you are trying to do the right thing, the Martin Luther King approach of turning the cheek and non-violence. But that is not my style. You slap my cheek, I cut out your heart. You beat up one of my people, I'll blow up an entire neighborhood of yours. The folks who run this country only know violence, Mister Thurgood. That is how you gain respect from them."

"All that you are going to do is start a war where millions of lives are going to be lost."

"I said this to you once before, you need to get out more often. We are already at war. All I'm doing is making sure they don't wipe us out completely. I invited you here so you could see that we are not defenseless. With that knowledge, I also urge you to stay out of my way. I have no qualms with you, but should you decide to side with our enemy, you will become our enemy. The government and the powerful ones of this country have no intention of giving us our freedom or our rights back. If we are to be free, we must take what is ours, not beg for it like orphan children."

"Even if that means sacrificing our own people to what you just showed me?"

Ramses stepped closer to Thurgood. "What if that was you, Mister Thurgood? Or better yet, what if that was your assistant lying on the ground begging for mercy while those cops had their way with her? If that were to happen, would you be as open to the option of a nonviolent resolution...I wonder? There are people who preach about being law-abiding citizens, defending the just and the weak. Yet these are the same people who will break the very laws they created when it suits their purposes. Someone has to be there to provide the check and balance. If not, tyrannical governments will be formed and everyone will lose their basic right to live. That is why we exist, Mister Thurgood, to ensure that our people continue to have that basic right as well as all the other rights we are entitled to."

Thurgood didn't respond. Everything Ramses said made perfect sense. But still, the violent extremes he and his followers were willing to take made him very uneasy. Ramses waved for the men to come and take Lela and Thurgood back to their car. The soldiers escorted them away, guns drawn and prepared to fire at a moment's notice. Thurgood and Lela made it back to the town car and as they entered Ramses came to the opened back door and peered inside.

"It was a real pleasure meeting you," he said.

"Just one question before we go," said Thurgood. "Why haven't you and your group left to go to AUNK. I mean, if you have such strong feelings about the people in this country, why stay?"

Ramses thought about it for a moment. "I suspect it is for the same reasons you stay here. I was born here and this is just as much my country as it is theirs. My ancestors helped build this nation and I'm not about to let a bunch of people who are the true terrorists take that away from me. If it is my destiny to leave, then I shall follow my fate. Until then, I shall fight to reclaim my rights. After all, that's how this country began, fighting oppression and tyranny. Who am I, being a natural born citizen of America, to not exercise that basic privilege."

Thurgood nodded. "And how do you know I won't betray you?"

Ramses smiled. "You won't. Remember, we're always watching."

"I look forward to the day we meet again."

Ramses bowed, then backed away from the door. The gunmen who originally brought Thurgood and Lela to the garage climbed back into the front seat. The doors were secured and the engine started. The car

Nationhood

slowly backed out of the garage and within moments was on its way toward the hotel. Thurgood looked out his window with a pensive expression. Lela was quiet for a few moments, then turned toward Thurgood.

"Well, that was interesting," she said, trying to be light-hearted.

Thurgood released a chuckle, still staring out of his window.

"Yes, Lela, it *was* interesting. More than either of us realizes," he said.

"I don't know about you, but I could certainly use a drink."

"Yeah, that sounds real good right about now."

~~~

James Gordon

Chapter Seven: Paradoxes and Paradigms

After a very exhausting ride to the Bantu Building, the upper congressional house of the AUNK Senate, Pollins walked in to a room filled with lively chatter. As he stopped and stood in the doorway for a moment, he could hear and see the heated debates taking place as well as solemn expressions from those who were still in shock from what had happened to their colleagues. In that instant, Pollins realized that this was going to be a very long night.

Just moments ago, the President called an emergency meeting of all senate members as well as his top aides and military leaders. Pollins plotted out the series of events that would take place during this high level assembly. First, there would be a sounding off period. Then, there'd be the recommendations period in which the suggestions would probably get batted back and forth for a few hours. Finally, there would be a summit period to discuss the viable solutions and actions. It was pretty much the congressional shuffle, and Pollins felt uncomfortable with that.

Like most of the senators in attendance, he wanted justice. In a few moments, the President would arrive and Pollins was sure he would be spitting fire and breathing smoke. The condition of the other senators hadn't been confirmed yet, but from what he'd been told it wasn't going to be long before they died. If they did, he feared what would come after that. Senate members would want blood and their attentions would turn directly toward the United States. After all, they were the ones that released Victor Johnson and potentially had the ability to inject him with the virus. It was just the kind of thing they would do in order to get the upper hand. But Pollins knew they didn't have proof the Americans did this, and without that proof pointing fingers at them would do nothing more than strain their already delicate relationship. Somehow, he had to be the voice of reason. However, he had no idea how he was going to do that. He tightened his grip on his attaché and walked over to his reserved spot on the panel. He sat down next to Shirley Adele, who was busily scribbling notes on her notepad.

"Good morning, Congresswoman," said Pollins.

"Yes, it is morning, Senator," Shirley replied. "Normally, I'm still sleeping at this hour.

"Me, too. I see the circus has already started."

"Very much so. They've been at it for over thirty minutes."

Pollins shook his head. Just then, Lucinda Matthews tapped him on the shoulder.

"Good morning, Senator. I took the liberty of getting you a white chocolate mocha," she said, pushing a cup of coffee to him.

"Thank you," he replied, taking the cup from her and placing it on the table.

"I also prepared some notes for you. I inserted some key points your analysts thought you might want to look over."

"Lucinda, you're the best."

Lucinda tapped the side of the Senator's chair and then scurried off the platform, taking her seat along the side. Pollins opened his organizer and looked over the documents Lucinda prepared. After a few moments, he lifted his head and look out at the room filled with his colleagues. They were slowly beginning to find their way to their seats. Just then, Senator Thomas Donaldson stepped to the podium and tapped his gavel.

"Ladies and Gentlemen, the President of the African Union of New Kemet," he announced.

Everyone instantly stood to his or her feet as President Landau DeVeaux entered the assembly hall and made his way to the Presidential seating area flocked by a number of security agents. The air was thick with tension as everyone watched him march passed. His expression was laden with anger and his walk was accented with determination. He reached his area and turned to stare at the assembly. Donaldson walked back to the podium and addressed his colleges.

"You may be seated," he said.

The legislators took their seats and stared attentively at their president. DeVeaux puckered his lips and cleared his throat. He placed his hands on the edges of his podium and stared sternly into the gathering.

"I will be brief," he said. "Just over an hour ago our country was attacked using a form of biological warfare. Three of our senators have been taken to the hospital and are in serious condition. Currently the virus is contained, but we don't know if the populace has been infected. We have a lot to do over the next few hours and there is but one question that

Nationhood

needs to be asked. What are we going to do? I don't want you to answer me right now. However, tomorrow morning I'd like the cabinet members to meet with the majority and minority leaders of both the upper and lower houses. I want that meeting to have some answers and a course of action. Have I made myself clear?"

The members nodded. DeVeaux began descending the platform area. Donaldson and the other members stood as he left. After he'd departed the room, the doors were closed and Donaldson took his place behind the House Speaker podium.

"If we could all take our seats we can begin this meeting," he said. The members sat back down and got comfortable. Donaldson picked up the gavel and slammed it down once. "I'd like to call this meeting to order. We have a lot to do and a very short period of time to do it. To get things moving, I'd like to call Congresswoman Shirley Adele to begin proceedings."

The Congresswoman stood from her seat and walked toward the podium.

"Thank you, Senator Donaldson," she said. "I'd like to say that we were meeting under joyous circumstances, but unfortunately and sadly, this is not the case. One hour ago, out country was dealt a tremendous blow. Three of our beloved senators were victims of a serous attack by individuals who wish to do our nation harm. We are uncertain at this time who is responsible, but the message was clear and it was shocking. They will stop at nothing to make sure that we fall as a people. The challenge that lies before us will be to show that we will rise above this and gather evidence that will uncover the people behind this dastardly attack. We must show that we as citizens of the African Union of New Kemet deserve justice and that we will not stop until we get precisely that."

As the congresswoman continued her speech, Pollins sat quietly, elbows braced on the table with his hands clasped before him. As he listened to Adele's speech, he could only think about his family and how he wished he could be with them right now. This was the first moment he had to simply sit and allow his mind to wander. His son, Charles, his daughter, Mia, and his wife, Mary—he wondered how they were doing as well as how they were taking the news about the virus. Mary had to be worried sick about him, seeing as though he hadn't called her since the incident at the airport happened. Security protocols were immediately put into place after the outbreak and he was unable to make any calls except to other legislative or military members. However, as soon as an available moment came, he would call them and let them know he was all right.

Congresswoman Adele concluded her speech and relinquished the floor to Senator Donaldson. The Senator continued where the congresswoman left off, stressing the importance of the council to show discretion and control. He began outlining a strategy on how to petition the other countries to assist in investigating the matter. Affidavits would need to be taken as well as testimonials and statistics to support the need for the international inquiry. Donaldson was relentless with his presentation, using the hospitalized members of the council in his examples to support the move to, as he coined it, *limit the terrorists*. Pollins kept a straight face, but inside he was a tumultuous sea of emotions. The more he listened to Donaldson's speech, the more he questioned his thinking of whether this was the correct course of action.

When all of this first happened, he relied on his political instincts, remembering not to jump to any conclusions or make any assumptions. However, some time had passed and the senators who'd been victimized by the virus were friends of his. He began to wonder whether an immediate retaliation would, indeed, be the right thing to do. Perhaps they'd been looking at this all wrong. Maybe they already knew who the terrorists were, but were being too diplomatic to admit it. Maybe war was the answer, an all-out, no-holds-barred confrontation. Perhaps if they did that, the nation of AUNK could, once and for all, eliminate the ones that have been conspiring against them since their inception. Maybe it was time to show the world their might.

Donaldson concluded his pitch and sat down in his seat. Then, it was the other members of the panel's turn to voice their concerns. The first to stand was Congressman James Beckett, representative of the Kenté Providence.

"Speaking on behalf of the Kenté contingent, I applaud Senator Donaldson's zeal in addressing this issue. This has been a very harrowing few hours and many of my constituents are very interested in how we handle this issue. Over the last several years, many events similar to this, both in New Kemet and internationally, have drawn a tremendous amount of attention, and justifiably so. However, it is my humble opinion that the policies of civility and restraint have outlived their usefulness. We knew that when this country was created that it would only be a matter of time before someone found a way to harm its citizens. We've tried to have

Nationhood

summits and attempted to handle things in a diplomatic manner. But to think that we can continue down this path is foolish. We must devise a program that will allow our children and their children to maintain their future freedoms and opportunities without having to get permission from these tyrannical terrorists who claim to be the voice of the free world. We must decisively show our entitlement to the rights we so vehemently cried out for and earned, and we must do so without compromise."

Just then, Congresswoman Adele spoke.

"And what would you suggest, Congressman?" she asked. "Your speech echoes the simmering mantra of war."

"Well now, that is the question, isn't it? That's why we are all here, to voice our opinions and come to some sort of consensus to present to our nation," replied Beckett.

Adele seemed visibly disturbed.

"It isn't our nation I'm concerned with Senator, it's our people. There are several million Africans in this country, not to mention our brethren in America and abroad, who will suffer if we continue down this path you're suggesting," said Adele.

Pollins smirked. He was always impressed with the way Congresswoman Adele conducted herself. On this platform she was a dynamo, an unstoppable force who had more than one way of proving her point. But Beckett was no neophyte. He was one of the most articulate and clever orators in the upper house. The impending discussion was going to be most intriguing.

"Begging the congresswoman's pardon, but we all have something to lose. I do sympathize with your views. We are people of color and the decision we make will affect us globally. My statement is one of preemption. We must stop this now before it gets any worse. Mind you, I'm not suggesting that this be addressed as a racial issue, but instead one of national and international concern. We must show that it is in the best interest of all nations to have this assertive stance and defend the basic rights of the global community. We cannot afford to alienate ourselves and turn this into a race war," said Beckett.

Pollins continued to smirk and looked once more at Shirley to see how she would respond.

"If this were simply a matter of race, then a confrontation should have taken place years ago. This isn't about race, it's about equality. You know as well as I do, Congressman, that had it not been for the establishment of this nation we would not have the opportunities we now possess. This country, our country, provides diverse representation in education, business, government and to life on this planet. No longer are we the orphan children asking to be recognized or requesting special privileges from a group of oppressors. We aren't welfare cases and we don't need to have a coalition of nations to support the decisions we make about our people. I resent the implication that we address this as some international problem and involve countries who have no interest in this matter other than seeing it as an opportunity to swindle a deal in exchange for their participation," said Adele.

Just then, Donaldson intervened.

"It seems that this discussion is getting a little heated. I will remind the members to keep their comments professional as well as their behavior," he said.

Adele adjusted her papers and scribbled a few more notes. Beckett nodded and returned to his seat. Donaldson turned and looked down the row of panel members. He saw Pollins sitting forward with his chin resting in his hand.

"Senator Pollins, we've not heard from you yet. Might we hear what you have to say?" asked Donaldson.

Pollins chuckled slightly. He leaned forward and adjusted his microphone, then clasped his hands before him.

"My fellow legislators," he said in a stately manner. "I've heard the comments from my colleagues as well as those of aides and friends. On my way over here, I listened to the news reports and the analysts discussing this issue. I've seen and heard the angry crowds outside the Bantu Building who demand justice and scream for vengeance. But nothing disturbed me more or brought greater revelation than what I've seen right here in this room. For far too long, we as Africans speak about world unity, yet there is none. We speak of equality and justice, yet there is none. We march and protest, boycott and riot. Yet nothing ever changes. We gain ground and then we lose it with the stroke of a pen. We bicker and argue, but the result is always the same. We look to others to blame, but the real problem isn't with them, it's with us. We have done this to ourselves. We didn't prepare for this sort of threat and we allowed ourselves to become lazy. We didn't press forward to ensure that we had a backup plan in case something like this happened. That was our mistake. Now instead of trying to find a way to fix the problem, we'd rather bicker

Nationhood

over the insignificant options of retaliation or protection. Congressman Beckett and Congresswoman Adele were both right. We must look out for the nation as well as the people. We should have seen this coming, yet we failed to be visionaries and prepare for this possibility. However, the solution to this problem isn't to petition other nations for assistance or to ostracize ourselves from the world, but one that will forever solidify our rights and freedoms, not just nationally, but internationally."

"Sounds to me like you have an idea," said Donaldson.

Pollins smiled and nodded his head.

"Perhaps I do. But I am not going to divulge it at this time. I'd like to work out the details first, then I'll make my presentation. So now, if you'll excuse me, I have some issues to attend to," said Pollins.

A slight rumble echoed in the room as Pollins scooted his chair back and stood. He gathered his things and began leaving the platform. The remaining members watched in shock as Pollins and his aide, Lucinda, left the chamber. A roar of commotion exploded as the huge oak doors closed behind him. Pollins stopped for a moment and listened to the chaos he'd caused, and a smile came to his lips. Lucinda walked over to him.

"You sure caused quite a stir," she said.

"That was the intent, Lucinda," said Pollins as he began walking down the hall. "The solution to this issue does not lie in that room. In there are a bunch of politicians who are more concerned with keeping their offices than fixing the problem. But just like someone once said, if you want something done right, you have to do it yourself. We can't sit back here and debate this issue. We have to take action now."

"You know your phone lines are going to be flooded for the next few days."

"Indeed. I intend on being away for the next few days."

"Like I wouldn't have guessed. So what's your plan?"

"Like I said, I want to work a few things out before I say. Cancel all my meetings for the rest of the week."

"You got it."

Pollins and Lucinda walked out of the Bantu Building and onto the main mall. As they walked, they came across a young Black woman passing out leaflets. For reasons unknown, Pollins stopped and looked at the woman.

"What's wrong?' asked Lucinda.

111

"What is she handing out?" asked Pollins.

"I don't know. Probably some paraphernalia about some rally. That's what most of the kids I see are passing out."

Pollins walked over to her. Lucinda followed.

"May I have one of those flyers?" he asked.

"Here you are," said the woman. "Hey, wait a minute. Aren't you Senator Elijah Pollins?"

"Yes I am."

"Oh, sir, it's a pleasure to meet you. I'm a big supporter of yours."

"Well thank you Miss..."

"Debra Reynolds," said the woman holding out her hand.

"Well, Miss Reynolds, thank you for your support and the flyer," said Pollins shaking her hand. "This is my aide, Lucinda Mathews."

"Very nice to meet you," said Debra as she shook Lucinda's hand. "Are you coming out to the rally tomorrow night?"

"I might."

"Oh, you'll love it. Have you ever heard Reverend Aziz speak?"

Pollins' brow raised. "Reverend Mohammed Aziz?" he asked.

"Why, yes," Debra replied.

"Once."

Pollins looked down at the flyer and saw that Reverend Mohammed Aziz was going to be speaking at the convention center tomorrow night. He'd been trying to get in contact with him concerning the speech the reverend gave in Atlanta a few hours ago. He must have hopped onto a flight shortly thereafter to come here. Like an epiphany, Pollins knew that this was a sign that his plan was the right way to go. Now all he needed was to get in touch with the individuals that were crucial to his strategy's overall success.

"Yes," he said, looking at the woman once more. "I think I will attend."

"Excellent!" she said, enthusiastically. "He is so dynamic and it would be great to have someone of your stature at the speech."

"Well, then, I'll see you at the rally, Miss Reynolds. I must be going now. Thanks again for the flyer."

"You're welcome, Senator."

Lucinda and Pollins began walking away. Lucinda fought to keep from laughing at the spectacle that just took place. She turned and looked

Nationhood

at Pollins with a slightly crooked smile.

"Well, you sure made her day. I almost thought she was going to attack you and smother you with kisses," she said.

"You're funny," said Pollins as he looked once more at the flyer.

"So, are you really thinking about going to that?"

"That depends. Would you do me a few favors, please?"

"What's that?"

"First, get the president on the phone. I want to tell him what I'm going to do. Then, I need for you to find out where Aziz is staying. I want to have a little chat with him before he goes to this gathering tomorrow night."

"Anything else?"

"Yes, get my wife on the phone. I have the feeling this might be one of the few chances I'll get to speak to her for a while."

~~~

Sudan Pier sat along the western side of Mecca City. Here, amidst the dark and barren loading docks, Katura was to make the drop of the jewels. The beautiful gown that she wore to the Romanian gala no longer donned her shapely form. Instead, she figured a black jumpsuit was fitting attire for dropping off the diamonds. In her hand she clutched the handle of a metal attaché case. She was alone, giving orders to Jaquimo to stay out of sight, at least until the deal was done. She walked down a barely lit driveway between two massive warehouse sheds. At the end she could see three men; one leaning against the hood of the car and two at the trunk. They were each wearing dark suits and looked like the typical CIA agent types. She walked to the man leaning against the hood and stopped a few feet away, making sure she could see the other two. She lifted the attaché in front of her, then placed it on the ground. The man looked at it and then at her.

"Nicely done," he said.

"Do you have my emancipation papers?" Katura asked.

The man turned to one of the other men near the trunk and motioned for him to come forward. He walked toward Katura and removed an envelope from his inner coat pocket. He placed it on the ground next to the attaché and took a few steps back. Katura looked at the envelope and then at the briefcase. She lifted her eyes to stare at the two men in front of her. Next, she scanned the car as well as the positioning of all three men. The sides of her mouth curled upward and she faintly shook

113

her head.

"You know, I could have sold these diamonds on the black market and gotten quite a hefty sum for them," she said. "The going price was thirty million easily. What do you say we find us a buyer and split the earnings?"

"That wouldn't be a wise thing to do," said the man.

Katura looked at the man addressing her and realized he looked quite familiar.

"If I'm not mistaken, you're Henderson, correct?" she asked.

"Very nice. You do know your agents," Henderson replied.

"Yes, well, I pride myself on being thorough. So, are you sure I can't interest you in going in with me on this deal?"

"I'm afraid not."

"That's a shame. I really hate being turned down."

"I'm afraid this is more than a simple turndown."

"I see. So this is how the American government repays me for all that I've done...by sending five flunkies to try and kill me?" Katura asked.

Henderson stood erect from leaning against the car.

"Now, Miss Ishtar. Who said anything about killing you?" Henderson asked. "And what do you mean by five of us? There's only three agents here."

"Let's not play games, Henderson. I know why you're here. But allow me to answer the question of the five men. I can see those other two agents lying inside the car with their guns. Did your people fail to mention my enhancements during your briefing?"

Henderson looked a little uncomfortable, which meant he had no idea what she was capable of. Katura knew that these men were grossly misinformed, a mistake quite unusual for her former employer to make. A playful smile bloomed across Katura's lips as she realized that there was something odd about this scene. She needed to play along for the moment and see where this was going. Once she found out the real score, she would make her move.

"I guess they also forgot to mention some of my other attributes as well as my preference in men," she said teasingly.

"Miss Ishtar, I'm not here to listen to your drivel. I'm here to inform you that you are now free from all services to the United States government. Your talents are no longer required," said Henderson.

"Cut the crap, Henderson. I know why you're really here. It

Nationhood

didn't take five men to pick up some diamonds and to give me my emancipation papers. In fact, I'm guessing that you are the B-team, the diversion sent in to distract me from the real killers. So at the risk of being rude, let's get this shootout started. I'd like to be in bed within the hour."

Henderson was noticeably anxious and angered by Katura's comments. The look on his face showed the mental debate on whether he should make the first move. He had been given some information on Katura's abilities and he knew she was a dangerous woman. She was right in the respect that it didn't take all five of them to perform this task. In fact, all he needed to do was shoot her once in the head and it would be over. In a moment of selfish bravado, Henderson decided to end this. He reached into his coat and removed his gun from the holster. Almost simultaneously, the other men did the same. The ones lying inside the car rose from the floor, hoisted their guns and pointed them at Katura, who stared back at them with icy, green eyes. In her mind she'd already devised a strategy and before they could squeeze off the first round, she will have already won this battle.

Two darts that were concealed inside compartments within her sleeves slid down into her hands. With the swiftness of a cobra she threw one at the man who presented her the emancipation papers and the other at one of the men inside the car. Both darts stuck into the men's necks, paralyzing them instantly. Henderson squeezed off a round, but Katura performed a split, allowing the bullets to whiz over her head.

A quick reach behind her revealed her Tassen, a folding Japanese fan with an iron frame. She uppercut Henderson's gun to point into the darkened sky, allowing her an easy shot to his groin area. With a kick, she launched him into the air and crashing on top of the hood, jarring the entire car. The other gunman inside misfired into the roof, blowing a hole approximately two feet in diameter.

Katura ran toward the fallen Henderson and leaped onto his chest. The air burst from his body with an agonizing groan. With a swiping kick she knocked his head into the windshield causing the glass to shatter in a spider web design. The other gunman who was at the back of the car ran to intercept Katura with his gun ready to fire. Katura performed a perfect three-and-a-half turn dismount, bringing the razor-like edge of her Tassen across the wrist of the approaching agent, slicing his hand off in the process. The gun-grasping hand smacked against the concrete like a slab of meat while the shocked agent stared at his severed appendage with

James Gordon

disbelief. Katura performed a roundhouse kick and nailed the agent on the side of his face, smashing his head into the passenger side window.

Just then, she could see the gunman inside of the car turning to fire his double-barrel shot. She raced toward the back of the car, making him turn in ways that would throw him off balance. She leaped into the air and over the trunk. Using a version of a baseball slide, she crashed through the back window and nailed the gunman in the chest. The force of the blow was so powerful that it drove him into the floor, crimping his neck and snapping his spinal cord. The gunman lay on the floor twitching, drool slowly seeping from the corner of his mouth. With a gurgle, the man exhaled one last time and collapsed. His eyes were still open.

Katura stared at her last victim, watching his life drift away with his last breath. She didn't want to do this and it bothered her that she had to. She only wanted to complete her mission and earn her freedom. After that, her plan was to find Marina and help her get through this time of mourning after the death of her husband, Durst Weinkaufen. She felt she deserved to be free, especially after everything she'd done for the United States government. To think they would send mercenaries after her was insulting and heartbreaking. It meant she was not free and, oddly enough, a threat to national security. Confusion filled her head and she couldn't think straight. What she did know was that she needed to get out of there and figure things out. She grabbed the doorknob and opened the back door. She exited and walked to the front of the car where one of the men she used her darts on was still awake, but unable to move. She knelt beside him and grabbed his collar. She pulled him close and whispered in his ear.

"Your friends are all dead, except for the one in the front seat. The poison in the dart I stuck in his neck will wear off soon, as will yours. I spared your lives because I wanted you two to deliver a message to Prime for me. Tell him I didn't appreciate this little soirée and one day he's going to have to pay for his deceit. If you know what's good for you, you'll find another job as soon as you get back. If you don't, I'll kill you the next time I see you."

Katura didn't get a reply due to the man's paralysis, but she knew he understood. She released him and stood to her feet. She walked to the attaché case, picked it up and threw it into the car. She then grabbed her envelope and opened it. As she pulled out the form letter, her eyes widened. Inside, she didn't find a letter of emancipation like she'd hoped. Instead, she found something very disheartening—a note from Prime.

116

Nationhood

Dear Miss Ishtar,

If you are reading this it means that you have killed a good many of the men I sent after you. That being the case, you will understand that I can't allow you to live. You've been a great asset to the U.S. government but your usefulness has come to an end. Therefore, I've arranged for another surprise.

At that moment, a Blackhawk helicopter rose from behind one of the warehouses and flew directly toward Katura's location. She dropped the envelope and stared in disbelief. A rain of bullets rattled through the air and ripped up the ground. Katura raced behind the car, hoping to use it for a shield. However, as she crouched on the ground another helicopter came from the other side, trapping her between them. She crawled beneath the car as the shower of bullets began to make Swiss cheese out of the vehicle. Katura knew she couldn't stay there much longer. She scanned from beneath the car and saw that she was next to the docks. It was only a few feet away and if she ran as fast as she could she just might be able to make it. If she could get to the water she would be safe and possibly make it out of there alive.

The bullets continued to pelt the car and some were now punching through the floorboard. Katura knew that it was now or never. She rolled from under the car and stood to her feet. Like a sprinting decathlete, she raced to the docks with all the speed she could muster. The helicopters turned and pursued her, the whirling of their blades echoing off the surrounding buildings. Katura kept running, staying focused on the water and not daring to look back. She could hear the helicopters getting closer, but she could not focus on that. She had to make it to the water in order to survive. Just a few more feet and she was there.

The gunman on the choppers fired another round, ripping up the ground as she stayed a few inches ahead of the bullets. Katura kept running, looking more like a long jumper getting ready to make their leap. She panted heavily and could feel a slight stitch developing in her side. But she couldn't let that slow her down. She was now within inches of the water, She took a few more steps and then leaped into the air. As her feet left the ground, one of the gunmen fired one more round. Just before she splashed into the water, one of the bullets found Katura's right shoulder. The impact pushed her forward and she dove headfirst into the murky waters of the docks. Now beneath the surface, she swam as fast as she could toward the bottom, trying to place as much distance between her and

James Gordon

the bullets that continued to whiz passed her in the water.

As she swam further, the bullets became motionless pieces of debris floating in the dark depths. She removed a portable breather from a pouch in her waist and placed it over her mouth. This would allow her to breath underwater for about thirty minutes. That should be long enough for the choppers to be gone. They were already in violation of the International Firearms Treaty, which prevented nations from using weapons in a foreign country. Soon, the authorities would be arriving and the US could ill afford such a violation of international policy.

As she reached the bottom, she could feel the pain in her arm beginning to worsen. The wound from the bullet that tore through her shoulder was probably being exacerbated by the contaminated water in the river. However, she had to remain submerged for just a little while longer. Once she felt that her would-be assassins were gone, she would emerge from this murky depth and find Jaquimo. Hopefully, he heard all the commotion and took the proper actions to avoid detection. He was her only hope for survival and she prayed he was okay. She came to one of the support beams to the docks overhead, settled near its base and rested against it. Now, she would wait for the time to pass and hoped that somehow she would make it out of this alive.

~~~

Chapter Eight: What Wonders Never Cease

Mbaku pressed a button on his car console that opened the door to an underground garage located beneath what appeared to be an abandoned building. He pulled his late model Mercedes inside and proceeded down the spiraling driveway. The doors closed and darkness surrounded him momentarily. Lights quickly popped on illuminating the sides of the driveway. He continued to follow the downward, corkscrew path, finally ending at a parking bay. Mbaku pulled into a vacant space and turned off the engine. He got out and proceeded toward a platform near the far wall. In his hand he carried a black pouch that contained the diamond he plucked from the crown jewels. He stood upon the platform, which automatically began lowering. A trap door quickly concealed the open shaft and moments later all the tracking lights went out.

Mbaku was tired. He'd been up for a while and this was the last leg of his mission. Within a few moments the platform reached its destination. Mbaku stepped off and walked toward an open laboratory area that resembled a scene out of a mad scientist movie. Behind a desk, feverishly typing on a computer, was a dark complexioned woman who looked to be in her thirties. Her thick glasses and uncombed hair gave the impression that this person was one who buried herself so deeply into whatever she was doing that basic hygiene and grooming was of little concern. Her name was Vishepsut Amundo, Vee for short. Mbaku stopped in front of her desk, slamming the pouch upon it. The woman stopped typing and looked toward the small bag.

"Gold is up fifteen points on the NASDAQ. You might want to sell in the next day or two," she said.

"And what need have I of gold when I have the world as my prize?" Mbaku replied.

"Even Santa Clause likes presents."

"And even a Messiah requires saving."

This was the code they used to ensure that the person who was before them was, indeed, whom they should be speaking with. It was the checking system Vee created due to the fact that she was blind. Although unable to see, her other senses were acute and unless Mbaku said his lines just right, she would activate a self-destruct program that would level this entire complex before the person could turn and attempt to run. Mbaku looked at his comrade, a smug smile appearing on his lips.

"I don't know why you wear those glasses, Vee. Blind people have no need for such things," he said.

"It's the look. I like to keep everyone confused. Is that what I think it is?" she asked, alluding to the pouch he slammed on the table in front of her.

"If you're guessing an engagement ring, then you'd be wrong."

"You're a bastard, Mbaku. Set it on the table over there," she said, motioning with her hand.

Mbaku did what he was asked. He then saw some vials containing odd colored liquids in them. He walked to one of them and took a whiff. He scrunched his nose and began backing away immediately.

"You might want to be more careful, Vee. The fumes from this one can kill you," said Mbaku.

"If you knock that over, the fumes will be the last thing you'll need to worry about," Vee replied.

Mbaku gave her a wary look, placing more distance between he and the vials. He walked back to the desk where Vee was continuing to type her notes into the computer. She paused for a moment and turned her face toward Mbaku.

"I sense you are disturbed. Did something go wrong during the mission?" she asked.

"I don't know," said Mbaku, placing his hands in his pockets. "I confronted the American who was sent to make the heist. It was her, the woman that Intel called Katura Ishtar."

"Ugly? Cute?"

"Very nice."

"I see. Did you let her escape?"

"Only as a tactical move. Although she had things well planned, I was able to figure out her strategy and intercept her. I allowed her to take the diamonds to the individuals who are truly responsible for all of this. No sense catching the little fish when there are much bigger fish that can be fried."

"Yes. And what bait did you use to help you find these big fish?"

Nationhood

"The nano probes you invented. When I took the diamonds from her, I released some into the pouch they were contained in. I'm sure she switched bags or perhaps placed them in a briefcase, but there were more than enough of them to filter into the jewelry. By now I'm certain the individuals she was supposed to deliver them to have them. I want to get moving on this as soon as possible before they leave the country."

Mbaku started walking toward the exit when Vee said something that stopped him in his tracks.

"I don't think you have to worry about that," she said.

Looking back at her, Mbaku posed the obvious question. "Why not?"

"Because all manner of departure out of Mecca City have been closed. The media just released information that there was a terrorist attack at the airport earlier. Seems as though someone released a virus during the conference between the American IS, Victor Johnson, and the three senators."

"A virus?"

"Yes. The area has been quarantined and the international CCD is there investigating. No one is being allowed anywhere near the place and no one is being permitted to leave the country."

"Were there any casualties?"

"The American. He died at the scene. Seems as though he bled to death."

"And the senators?"

"Critical condition at Memorial Hospital. But if I had to wager, I'd say that their chances of survival are almost non-existent...professionally speaking, of course."

Mbaku pondered for a moment. "Odd that all of this would be happening simultaneously," he said.

"My thoughts exactly," Vee replied.

"Something tells me that those diamonds are connected somehow to the virus that was released."

"Interesting hypothesis. But what's your basis?"

"No basis," said Mbaku. "Just a hunch. However, Vee, I want you to check out that diamond I brought. See if there is anything that could help us unravel the clues to this little mystery."

"Yeah, I'll *see* what I can do," she replied sarcastically. "What are you going to do?"

James Gordon

"I'm going to pay Senator Pollins a little visit. With everything going on I'm sure the President will have something to say about all of this. I wouldn't be surprised if they are making war plans."

"War?"

"Yes, and that's something I have to try and stop. This was too conveniently planned and it has the stench of espionage all over it. But before you begin dissecting the stone, I have something else I want you to do."

"What's that?"

"Get a fix on all of the nano probes I planted on the diamonds. It's my guess you'll find three readings. One strong reading will be where the bag they were originally in is located. The second strongest reading will be where the diamonds are now. But it's the third and weakest reading I'm concerned with."

"Why is that?"

"Because that reading will lead me to Katura Ishtar. She had to handle the diamonds and some of the nano probes are probably still affixed to her. She, no doubt, knows something and I intend to find out what that is."

"But why not go after the people who have the diamonds. Surely they will know something also."

"Too risky. The diamonds are probably well guarded and since I don't know what I'm up against it is best that I start with the one thing I do know something about."

"Be careful, Mbaku. I'm told she's a dangerous woman and if she is connected in all of this she might not hesitate to kill you," Vee warned.

"I'll keep that in mind," he replied. "For now, I'm going to head toward the Senator's office. Let me know when you pick something up."

"Will do."

~~~

Carla Snipes stared at Constable Al-Shahir with eyes filled with fear. She'd asked who he thought was responsible for the terrorist attack on the senators, to which he replied in a way she never dreamed.

"The Illuminati?" she asked. "There's no such thing."

"That's what they said about God and the devil," said Al-Shahir. "But just because we are unable to show evidence that suggests they do exist doesn't mean they don't. The same could be said about the Illuminati. Many would say they are just a myth, an urban legend created to fortify the ranting of conspiracy theorists. But make no mistake, they are real and they are a serious threat to this nation."

"But why? Why would they attack us?"

"Because we are a nation not under their control. Throughout time, the Illuminati have conducted coupes and insurgences to bring down independent nations and weaken their infrastructure. They released viruses that would wipe out large portions of the country's population, like they did during World War II and the Korean War. Once the country was considered a hot zone they would conveniently produce a cure for the disease and use it to barter for power. That very scenario is what's happening now. What took place today is a part of a much bigger plan by this organization to bring the Nation of AUNK under its control."

"Unbelievable."

"Yes. But as unbelievable as it sounds we are now caught in the reality of war. We are the casualties that will be offered up as sacrifices for the greater good. Sadly, this was not the way I planned to spend my day, nor was it the way I expected my life to end."

"You give up way too easily, Constable," said Carla. "Our lives aren't over yet. We still have a job to do. Just like I said earlier, if this must be our last few hours, then let's make them count. If the Illuminati are behind this attack, the world must be made aware. We must present irrefutable evidence that no government can deny. They must be exposed and the people must see the true terrorists."

"I knew you'd have the right perspective about this," said Al-Shahir. "So, where do we begin?"

"First, we must make sure that the virus is contained. We must assure the people that everything is okay in order to reduce the chances of a nationwide panic."

"Very good. And once that is done?"

"Then, we go after the real story."

The Constable was please with her answer, and even prouder of the fact that he chose her to cover the story. He had been an admirer of Carla's for a long time. He even had a mild crush on her. He would watch her news reports and marvel at how graceful she was in relaying the information, no matter how terrible or heartbreaking it was. She was gifted in her craft and displayed a comfortable and trusting air about her. She made people believe in what she reported and captivated audiences with her smooth sultry voice and dreamy brown eyes. Perhaps, Al-Shahir thought, that he should have made a move toward her sooner. Maybe they could have shared something other than this pitiful excuse for a last stand. If he had it to do all over again, he would certainly have included her in his life much sooner. For now, he would help her deliver the news and reveal the Illuminati. If nothing else, they would have that to share.

~~~

Lucinda had been on the phone for the better half of an hour trying to locate where Reverend Mohammed Aziz was staying while he was in New Kemet. His speech was slated for tomorrow night in Mecca City's Shrine Auditorium, a palatial hall that was so large it had its own zip code. But every lead she tried turned up bad. It was as if he didn't want to be found. But that made Lucinda all the more determined. She loved a challenge and if she had to comb the entire nation to find him she was going to do just that.

She placed a few more calls, which were routed back to a central number that simply rang. After running down a few more leads, she realized that her determination was about to reach its limits. Frustrated, she decided to take a break and call her mother, Mabel, to see how she was doing. With all the news about the attack, Lucinda was certain she was a little uneasy. She dialed her number and waited for her to pick up. After three rings, a raspy voice answered on the other end.

"Yes?"

"Mother, is that you?" asked Lucinda.

"Hey, sweetheart. How are you?" Mabel replied after clearing her throat.

"I'm fine. But you don't sound well."

"Oh, I'm just fighting a cold, is all."

"I see."

"I should be asking you how you are doing."

"So you heard about the airport deal, huh?"

"Are you kidding? They interrupted my favorite TV show with all these news bulletins. Shoot, it's on every channel. I decided to turn off the television and go to bed. May as well get some rest."

Lucinda chuckled. "And here I was thinking you'd be upset or worried," she said.

"Child, I'm an old woman. If it's my time to go, then it's my time. God knows what he's doing. You need to remember that. Anyway, shouldn't you be doing something for that boss of yours instead of calling

Nationhood

me?"

"I am. I'm just taking a break." Lucinda paused and sighed heavily. "I never knew how much trouble it was to find one person."

"Who you trying to find?"

"Can't tell you, Mom. National security and all."

"Well, I hope you find them. As for me, I'm going back to bed. But just remember this. Finding a person is easy if you know where to look. You just have to think like them."

With those words, an idea came to Lucinda. Her mother touched on something she hadn't thought of. She'd been thinking that Aziz would be behaving like a diplomat, staying at a luxurious hotel or perhaps with one of the politicians. But the good reverend was nothing like that. He was a down home person that shunned such extravagance. He would much rather stay with a friend instead of in a hotel. With that thought she had a hunch where to look for him.

"Mom, I have to go. Thanks for everything and you get some rest, all right?" said Lucinda, with a slightly hurried tone.

"I will," said Mabel. "You be careful out there. Things are getting kind of rough."

"I will. I'll call you later."

They both said their good-byes and hung up. Lucinda pressed another line and called information. She asked for Doctor Earl Bennett, who was the head of the New Kemet Orthodox Temple located in downtown Mecca City. The operator transferred her to the number, which rang a couple of times and then someone picked up.

"Hello?"

"Hi, my name is Lucinda Mathews, Senator Pollins' assistant."

"Senator Pollins? You mean *the Senator Pollins*?"

"Yes, I was..."

"Good evening, Miss Mathews. This is a real honor to be talking to you. How can I help you?"

"Well, I was looking for a Reverend Doctor Earl Bennett. Information said this was his number."

"Yes, I'm Doctor Bennett."

"Thank goodness. I was hoping you could help me. You see, Senator Pollins was trying to get in touch with Reverend Mohammed Aziz. He's speaking at the Shrine tomorrow night and the Senator was hoping to have a word with him before then."

James Gordon

"Well, you came to the right place. The reverend is staying with me."

"Really?"

"Yes, ma'am. Would you like to speak with him?"

"That would be great."

Lucinda released a deep sigh of relief, the kind that seemed to sap all the energy out of her. She heard Bennett walk away from the phone and the mumbled conversation taking place in the background. Moments passed. She waited anxiously, listening intently to the muffled dialog. Finally, the shuffling of shoes could be heard approaching the phone and then a husky voice answered on the other end.

"Hello?"

"Reverend Mohammed Aziz?" Lucinda asked.

"Yes?"

"My name is Lucinda Mathews. How are you?"

"Very well, thank you."

"You have no idea how happy I am to finally get in contact with you. Anyway, I'm calling on behalf of Senator Elijah Pollins, who would like a few moments of your time to discuss some pressing issues."

"I see. Well then, I would be delighted to meet with the senator. What would be a good time?"

"Do you mind me setting a meeting with the two of you for tomorrow morning, say around eight o'clock."

"That would be excellent."

"I'll arrange to have a car pick you up in front of Doctor Bennett's house at 7:30. Will that be all right?"

"Yes. That would be perfect."

"Very well. We'll see you tomorrow."

Lucinda hung up and drummed her palms on her table, delighted that she actually found him. She stood from her chair and walked toward the senator's door. He'd been inside for the last few moments talking to his wife, Mary. She placed her ear to the door to hear if it was okay for her to enter. When she heard silence, she knocked. The muffled sound of Pollins telling her to come in could barely be heard. She opened the door slowly, peeking her head in to see if everything was okay.

The room was dark, not a light on anywhere. Near the picture window of his office, Lucinda could see the image of Pollins standing in front of it. His office was several stories above the city and from his

Nationhood

window he could see every part of Mecca City. Lucinda crept into the room and raised the lights partially. She stood by the door, watching as Pollins stared out upon the city.

"I found Reverend Aziz. He has agreed to meet with you tomorrow morning for breakfast around eight," she said.

"That's good," Pollins replied.

Lucinda frowned, slightly puzzled that he wasn't a little more enthusiastic about her success.

"He seemed very happy to meet with you. This should be a very enriching get-together," she added.

"Yes, it should be," Pollins replied unenthusiastically.

Lucinda became slightly annoyed by his cavalier attitude. She folded her arms across her chest and stood with her hip slightly cocked to the side.

"Is that all you have to say?" she asked.

Pollins turned and looked at her, his brown eyes seemingly filled with lament. Lucinda could see that something was really bothering him and she immediately dropped her defensive attitude.

"What's wrong?" she asked.

Pollins slowly walked to his chair and sat down. He rubbed his head, almost as if he were trying to massage away a melancholy hangover. Lucinda lowered her arms and walked a little closer.

"Senator, are you okay?" she asked.

Pollins took a deep breath and exhaled forcefully. "I just got off the phone with Mary," he said.

"Is she okay?"

"Yes, she's fine."

"The kids?"

"Fine, also."

"Then why the long face?"

He looked up and stared at her. Even though the room lights were barely lit, she could see the welling of tears in his eyes.

"They're dead. All three of them," he said.

"Who's dead?" Lucinda asked.

"The three senators, the ones from the airport. They're all dead. They died just a few moments ago."

Lucinda was stunned. She eased into one of the chairs in front of Pollins' desk, attempting to process the news she was just told. Three

# James Gordon

senators, three of the nation's leaders, were dead. It was almost too fantastic and horrible to accept. She lifted her hands to her mouth trying to keep the yelp of emotions from leaping from her lips. Tears rolled across her cinnamon cheeks and her breath shuddered ever so slightly. A slight tremble shook her body as she fought to maintain some level of composure.

Conversely, Pollins had the look of a man possessed. In one fell swoop a portion of the nation's legislature had been eliminated. This was an unprecedented catastrophe, one that was sure to have horrific repercussions. The thought that a virus had killed three AUNK senators was an uneasy fact to deal with. However, Pollins knew that he had to stay strong. Although he mourned for his friends, he couldn't allow himself the time to grieve. He had to keep his wits because the threat to the country was far from over. He looked at Lucinda, who was now into a full fledged cry.

"I'm so sorry, Senator," she said tearfully.

He stood and walked to the other side of the desk. He guided Lucinda to stand and hugged her tightly. Her arms limply rested on his waist, burying her face into his lapel. She continued to allow her pain to show, too distraught to summon the energy to do much else. The more she cried the more Pollins' anger swelled. He blinked his tears away and sucked in deep breaths in order to collect himself. He pulled back slightly, resting his hands on Lucinda's shoulders. She tried to avoid looking directly at him, using her hands to cover her face.

"Thank you for your condolences. But we don't have time for tears. The bastards that did this are still out there. They killed my friends, Lucinda...my friends. That could have been Mary or my children instead of them. They drew first blood and now they will have to suffer the consequences."

Lucinda managed to catch her breath. But instead of an expression of sorrow, a fearful look came over her face. She gazed into his eyes, like a woman who wasn't sure about his state of mind. "Senator, you sound very emotional," she said.

"I am emotional," he replied. "Those bastards killed my friends. They came into my country and took the lives of three good men, men who had families that loved them and needed them. Well, if they think they are going to get away with this, they're wrong. If it's a war they want, then it is a war they will get. I will not stand by and allow them to get away with

0128

Nationhood

this."

"Senator, what are you going to do?" asked Lucinda with a fearful tone.

"What am I going to do? I'm going to meet with Aziz tomorrow for breakfast. Then I'm going to meet with the president and give him my plan."

"Senator, you're scaring me. I know that you're hurt, but I'm thinking this is all too soon. Don't you think you should wait a day or so before you give the president your input?"

"No, I don't. I see everything just as I should see it. I attempted to deal with things from a logical perspective, trying to do the right thing and be diplomatic. All along, while I was trying to be the good politician we were having our diplomacy grinded into our faces like cheap cigars. However, a new day is dawning, one that will change the complexion of this planet forever. By sundown tomorrow a new era will be born and the Americans are going to rue the day they crossed the line. Tomorrow, the Nation of AUNK will confront our enemies and deal with these terrorists. Tomorrow, World War Three begins!"

~~~

Jaquimo did well to stay out of sight until the agents in the helicopters left. They searched the waters and the surrounding areas of the docks looking for any remains of Katura Ishtar. Some of the troopers even performed ground sweeps of the area, scanning warehouses and as many containers as they could. When the sirens from approaching police cars were heard, they got back into their choppers and disappeared into the darkness. Now the police officers were checking the area, helping paramedics place the dead bodies caused by Katura's rampage onto gurneys.

Believing she was still alive, Jaquimo stayed hidden, lurking in the shadows like a thief and waiting for his moment to do his own searching. He knew that Katura had her breathing apparatus, but she was well passed the thirty minute mark and it wasn't much good after that. He glanced at his watch. Nearly fifty minutes had passed. Worry was starting to settle in the mind of the faithful attendant. He began wondering whether she was okay. Perhaps she was wounded, or worse, they did get her. If that were so, they would certainly find her body soon. He prayed that wasn't the case.

Suddenly, his Global Satellite Positioning tracking device began to beep for only a few seconds and then stopped. Jaquimo reached into his pocket and removed the GSP detector. He stared at it anxiously, hoping that it would beep once more. Several anxious moments passed. No beeps. He shook it, hoping that the nickel cadmium batteries weren't going dead. Still no beeps. He then heard the sound of police officers talking, they were too close for comfort. They sounded like they were only a few feet away, discussing the shooting and who might have been responsible for all the dead bodies. Slowly, Jaquimo backed further into the shadows and began distancing himself as far from the conversing officers as he could.

Just as he turned the corner of one of the warehouses, the GSP beeped again. He lifted it and looked at the display. It had a reading that was just a few yards from where he was standing. He quickly got a fix on the location and began trotting toward it.

Once he arrived, he slid the GSP back into his pocket and began looking around. He was in the loading area of the docks, surrounded by open stock crates and empty pallets. This was the location of the signal and according to Jaquimo's calculations whatever was sending the signal should have been right where he was standing. However, there was nothing there. He hoped that it was Katura, figured she had to be hiding. He decided to call out to her and hope no one else was around.

"Miss Ishtar," he said in a whisper.

"Here, Jaquimo," said a voice from inside one of the containers.

Just then, an injured Katura stepped from the darkness, clutching her right shoulder as her arm dangled by her side. Jaquimo ran to her and caught her just before her knees buckled.

"Steady, there," he said. "How bad is it?"

"I think it's infected. The water had sewage in it," Katura replied.

"Then we need to get you to a doctor."

"No doctor. I'm certain they've alerted the police and fingered me as the person who swiped the diamonds. They probably told them I might be injured, either from diving into the water or from injuries caused by this skirmish. In a matter of minutes there will be a nationwide manhunt for me and I'm positive they'll have every hospital on the lookout for me. I can't let them catch me."

Katura grunted, trying to fight the pain that riddled her entire body.

"Come, let's get you out of here," said Jaquimo.

He wrapped her good arm around his neck and helped her toward

Nationhood

the car that was parked a few hundred feet away from the scene. Once there, he assisted her inside. She flopped across the back seat, a groan escaping from her mouth. Jaquimo took out a pocketknife and began cutting away the material surrounding her shoulder. Finally, he was able to see the wound. The bullet was still lodged inside and the redness further validated her statement that it was, indeed, infected.

"This is pretty bad. You're going to need surgery and a powerful antibiotic. I need to get you to the hospital," he said.

"No," she said panting. "That's just what they'll be expecting me to do. Those bastards tr-tried to kill me. I will not give them a s-second shot at me."

"But, My Lady, I'm afraid that all I can do is remove the bullet and perform a meager patch job. There's the chance you could bleed to death and you still need something to kill the infection."

"I know."

A sharp pain ripped through Katura's body as the infection began it's spread. Jaquimo knew that the only way he could save her was to get her some medical attention. With the U.S. government looking to finish the job, potentially scouring every medical facility waiting for Katura to show up, he knew that if he took her to any hospital was sending her to her grave. There had to be someone who could help her. But who in this country would give aid to someone who stole the royal jewels of Romania and potentially placed this country on the brink of war?

Just then, Jaquimo remembered the gentleman who helped Katura sneak the jewels out of the embassy. If memory served him correctly he'd offered to help her, according to Katura. If ever she needed help it was now. The real question was how would he get in contact with him. There had to be someway to find him, something he left that would give Jaquimo a clue to his whereabouts. Perhaps he left something with Katura, he thought. Hopefully she had a business card or an address, something that would help him make contact. There was only one person who had the answer to that question.

"My Lady, I think I know who can help us," said Jaquimo. "But I must ask you a question. The man who was in the limousine the night you heisted the jewels, he said he could help you, correct?"

"Man?" she asked with a pant and a grunt. "What man?"

"The one who helped you get the jewels out of the embassy."

She thought for a moment. "Yes, Mbaku, I believe his name

James Gordon

was."

"Did he leave you a way to contact him?"
Another few moments of thought passed. "No."
Jaquimo lowered his head with despair.
"However," Katura added. "If he is a spy worth a grain of salt, he slipped something into the bag of jewels."
"A tracer, perhaps?"
"Maybe."
"Then we can use it to send him a message. Let's get you to someplace safe. The bag that the jewels were in is in the trunk. We'll use his tracer to find him and get you some help."
"Please hurry, Jaquimo. The pain is getting worse."
"Hang on, My Lady. I'll find him and I'll get him to help us."
Jaquimo stepped out of the back of the car and closed the door. Quickly seating himself behind the steering wheel, he started the vehicle and drove a little over a mile away. He stopped at a rest area, got out and raced to the trunk. He opened it, grabbed the bag the jewels were in. Removing a device from his pocket that looked more like a pen, Jaquimo shined a series of infrared, X-ray and ultraviolet beams inside the bag. Millions of tiny transistors were found, each of them sending long-wave location transmissions. Jaquimo quickly pulled out his GSP detector and opened the back. He did some quick rewiring, grabbed his pen-like device and began shining it on the small monitor screen. Using a bit of ingenuity, he managed to create a device that blocked the steady flow of the nano trackers intermission and turned it into a series of blimps that resembled Morse code. It was his hope that the man who offered to help Katura was tracking the transmission and would get the message.

He placed the device in the bag, allowed it to continue sending the message. He closed the trunk and walked to the back door. He opened it, got in and gazing down at Katura whose condition was worsening by the minute. He prayed that Mbaku would get the signal soon. He simply didn't want to consider the alternative.

He noticed a blanket laying on the floor. He picked it up and spread it over Katura. She was strong and if there was anyone who could beat this it was her. With a brush of his hand across her head, Jaquimo attempted to reassure her.

"Hang on, My Lady. Help is on the way," he said.

~~~

Chapter Nine: Secrets of an Unmarked Grave

Mbaku was circling the inner highway, the one that looped downtown Mecca City. He was about to exit the freeway and head toward the Senator's office when his communicator buzzed in his ear. It was Vee. He tapped the outside of his ear, up-linked with the satellite and answered.

"What's up, Vee?"

"You'll be interested to know I found something very peculiar as it relates to the trackers you placed on the diamonds," she said.

"What was that?"

"I managed to get a fix on them, getting two signals, not three. One is strong, but it's coming from inside the Romanian embassy."

"The embassy? But why would it be coming from there?"

"Beats me. You're the criminologist-slash-spy-slash-assassin-slash…"

"All right, already."

"Anyway, it appears the diamonds, or should I say *fake diamonds*, are back in the bowels of the building."

"Fakes?"

"Yes. The one you gave me isn't a diamond, it's a form of crystal, very rare. I'm placing it in the analyzer to see if I can find out anything on its structure, composition, origin. All I know is there's more to this crystal than meets the eye."

"Interesting. And you say the other crystals are back at the embassy?"

"According to the readings I'm getting from the nano trackers."

"Perhaps it's time to take another tour of the place, see what there is to see."

"Perhaps."

"What about the other signal?"

"Now that's the odd thing. The second signal is a lot weaker than the first, but it's emitting a pattern, a series of short and long blips, like it was sending a message."

"Any idea what it could mean?"

"Yes, as a matter of fact. It's Morse code. The signal is an S.O.S."

"S.O.S.? Where is this signal coming from?"

"Near the docks. I attempted to correlate the location but the metal in the area is interfering with the reception."

Mbaku pulled to a stop outside the Senator's office. He'd planned to get there and be waiting for him when he arrived in a few hours. Little did he know the Senator was still inside. Thinking that his meeting with Pollins could wait, he decided to take advantage of the opportunity and find out more about this patterned signal being sent from the docks.

"Check the scanner to see if there's any unusual activity there," said Mbaku.

"Already did. Seems as though there was some shooting going on earlier. Cops arrived shortly thereafter and found three dead bodies, one of them had a severed hand. There was also a bullet-riddled car, armor piercing stuff. They've combed the area but haven't found anything. Think this was your girl, Ishtar, in action?"

"Could be. However, our records indicate she doesn't do this sort of sloppy work. I *will* say that it sounds like an attempt by someone to cut loose ends. I'm thinking the dead men was her doing, but the bullets in the car was someone else. Sounds as though she might have learned the hard way what I was trying to tell her."

"And what was that?"

"Don't outlive your usefulness, especially to the Americans."

"So what are you going to do now?"

"Check things out, of course. Someone is sending that signal and I'm willing to bet it's Ishtar. She could need my help and that's just the bargaining chip I need to find out all there is to know about these fake diamonds and who is responsible for releasing the virus."

"You don't think the Americans are behind this?"

"Don't know. But there's only one way to know for certain and that is to find Ishtar."

"Keep in contact. I'll alert your uncle of the situation."

"Roger."

Mbaku tapped his ear and disconnected. He drove toward the inner highway once more to make his way toward the docks. Anxiousness cruised through his veins, an uneasiness that things were about to take a

Nationhood

change for the worse. Viruses being released and fake diamonds that were now back at the very place they'd been stolen—this had all the makings of espionage, terrorists playing with the welfare of his country. There were a lot of questions, the kind that made him wonder who and what he was fighting. The road to answers started with Katura Ishtar. She was the one who was the link in all of this. First he had to find her, then persuade her to help him unravel this puzzle. Once that was done, the real battle would begin.

~~~

Thurgood was on his way back to Washington, flight three-twenty-two, the redeye. He stared out of his window, gazing at silhouettes of fluffy white clouds stretching for miles. Looked like someone threw cotton balls everywhere. A full moon peeked through the cloud breaks, adding a shimmer of magic to the bland blanket of cumuli.

Lela sat next to Thurgood, hadn't said an entire paragraph since their run-in with Ramses and Exodus. She was still suffering from shock.

A Black flight attendant came to his seat, leaned slightly toward him and holding a folded piece of paper in her hands. She pushed it toward Thurgood, who sluggishly relinquished his stare from the band of clouds to look into her brown eyes.

"Mister Thurgood, this is from the gentleman in the first-class section. He said if you wouldn't mind giving him a few moments of your time he has something he wishes to discuss with you," she said.

Thurgood took the note from her, giving Lela a puzzled glance in the process. He opened it and silently read. *'We have much to discuss.'*

A tension-filled sigh floated from his mouth, panic beaming in his pupils. The hairs on the back of his neck stood on end and the muscles in his stomach tightened. Five words never sounded more menacing in his life. They screamed the message that he'd screwed up and now there will be hell to pay. Thurgood surmised that it had to have something to do with the incident with the agent that was driving the car when Ramses and his mob attacked. After that, he never saw the guy again.

When the members of Exodus dropped them off at the hotel, Lela immediately called the airlines, rescheduled their departure and they were out of the room within thirty minutes. The had the driver get them to the airport as quickly as he could, taking back streets and driving up medians to bypass traffic. He thought they'd gotten away as quickly as they could.

James Gordon

Clearly, the note proved how wrong he was.

He lifted his eyes, stared at the flight attendant who couldn't be more than twenty-five.

"Lead the way," he said.

He stood from his seat, squirmed passed Lela who'd pulled her legs tight against the seat to allow him to pass. The attendant began walking toward the front of the plane, Thurgood following with a nervous expression on his face, looking like the kid who was being taken to the principal's office. When they got to the curtains that separated first class from coach, the attendant motioned toward the entrance with her hand, looking like Vana what's-her-name off that Wheel show.

Thurgood stopped and stared at the curtain, asking himself whether he should go in or not. He looked at the attendant who tried to be comforting, pressing her lips together and trying to muster a smile. She looked more like she had constipation. He gulped, feeling the lump in his throat restricting his ability to breathe. He was here now. Bad form to turn and walk back to his seat. He summoned a chunk of courage, parted the curtains and walked in.

Rows of White faces wheeled around, returning scowling expressions, their eyes asking what the hell he was doing in their part of the plane. For a moment his feet got stuck to the floor and Thurgood was certain he would hear a gunshot if he moved. His eyes gravitated toward the floor, trying not to look at any of them. However, he kept his head up, thinking all the while to himself that he made a mistake accepting this invitation.

He was about to turn and make his way back to his seat when he saw a White female attendant waving at him near the front of the aisle. A quick scan around the cabin to see if she were waving at someone else revealed that he was the one she was beckoning.

His legs felt like they were filled with lead, taking steps he was certain would have him tossed out of the plane without a parachute. Mumbled conversations and whispered insults met his ears as he passed the other passengers. Finally, he arrived at the very front of the plane, face to face with the White flight attendant.

"You may sit here," she said, motioning to the seat.

His eyes looked at the seat and then at the man sitting next to it. He was White, late fifties or early sixties. His fingers were combing through a copy of *Time*, inquisitive eyes scanning the pages. He was well

136

Nationhood

groomed, *Brooks Brothers* bifocals balanced on the bridge of his nose. Liver spot freckles dotted the area around his eyes and his skin was in desperate need of some sun. His tan khakis, cream pullover and slip-on loafers had *Macy's* written all over them.

Thurgood glanced at the attendant who shifted her eyes away and quickly made her exit. The knot in his stomach was strangling his liver and he felt on the verge of asphyxiation due to the lump in his throat.

"Please, sit," said the man, still flipping through the pages.

Thurgood walked into the aisle and eased down into the seat, trying his best to maintain some semblance of dignity and strength. He felt like the kid who was waiting for his father to finish looking over his report card before receiving *the talk* and then the ass-whipping. Thurgood decided to make the first move, ask a question before he was lectured to and patronized.

"You wanted to see me?" he asked, thinking to himself after the words left his mouth what a chicken-shit question that was.

The man closed the magazine, slid it between him and the seat. Thurgood turned his head and looked at him, waiting with baited breath as his host finally made eye contact with him.

"Nice to see you, Mister Thurgood," said the man who had a massive Southern drawl.

"Who are you?" asked Thurgood.

"My name is Senator Richard Greene."

Thurgood's eyes widened. "The senator from Georgia?"

"Yes. I hope you don't mind me asking you up here. Might have been quite a stir if I'd ventured toward the back of the plane. Figured we'd have a little more privacy here."

"Yes, that would have been quite a stir, seeing that the back is where all the Black folks are."

Greene smiled. "I've been an admirer of your work, lobbying to regain the rights of your people. Reminds me of the Civil Rights movement back in the sixties. Grandpa told me about it. Of course, he wasn't one that subscribed to the belief that Blacks should be treated equal. Seems that most of America feels the same way."

"You mean in the White parts of the country."

"Of course," Greene said, lifting a hand in the air as a form of apologizing. "Still, there are some factions that are making things difficult for Congress to pass a law that reinstates the rights of Black folks. Your friends, for example."

"What friends?"

"Come now, Thurgood. The ones that ambushed your car and took you away."

"They aren't my friends."

"Yes, yes, you're right. Which is why I'm coming to you for a favor."

"And what might that be?"

"Not much, just that should they make contact with you again that you allow us to track you and find out their whereabouts."

"You mean, you don't know where they are."

"Cockroaches are hard to track."

"So you think they're cockroaches?"

Greene dropped his cavalier attitude and assumed a more assertive one.

"Anyone that threatens the livelihood of this country and its people is a cockroach. Exodus is a known terrorist group that has killed innocent people and undermined the security of this country. They even threaten negotiations with your people with their outlandish demands and their radical behavior."

"Some could say the same for the government, Senator. Stripping African Americans and other minorities of their rights, placing them in another form of slavery and treating them like second-class citizens is just as bad, if not worse, than what these folks are doing."

"Is that what you believe?"

"Did you bring me here to ask my opinion about Exodus or did you have something else on your mind?"

At that moment the attendant walked up carrying two glasses filled with scotch. She handed the first one to Greene and the other to Thurgood. She then walked away as the senator swirled his drink and took a whiff.

"Ah," he said with a satisfying sigh. "There's nothing like the smell of scotch."

Thurgood held his drink in his hands, unsure whether to take a sip. He didn't have a taste for scotch, was more of a brandy man. Greene placed his glass to his lips, swigged half, pruned his lips while his eyes watered slightly.

"Country isn't what it used to be, Thurgood. We need to calm the

Nationhood

masses. Too much hatred filling the streets," said Greene.

The switch in messages he was getting from Greene bothered Thurgood. One moment he asked for permission to follow him should Exodus contact him and the next he was saying how the country wasn't the same. Made him wonder if the man shouldn't be on medications. Before he could catch himself, he blurted out his thoughts. "Are you bipolar?"

"No," Greene replied. "What I'm trying to say is we as a country need to put a stop to all of this. African Americans' rights should be restored. Your people have just as much right to citizenship as everyone else."

"Then why the interest in Exodus?"

"What you're doing in lobbying is the right way to do things. We need to sit and discuss things like rationale people, not fight and quibble like savages."

"Should have thought of that when they ruled Affirmative Action unconstitutional and took away our right to vote."

"Before my time, I'm afraid. Those were the actions of a corrupt party and a president who was more a corporate puppet than a leader. He sold your people out, Thurgood, as well as the rest of the American public. He did it because the real people of power made him do it."

"You making excuses for him?"

"Nope, just stating facts."

"And how do you know this?"

"I'm a Senator, Thurgood. You should know better than anyone we have our ways of getting information. Besides, the logistics of the matter isn't the issue. What *is* important is the real threat that faces the American public, the real people calling the shots."

"And whom might these people be?"

"Ever been to Elbert County, Georgia?"

"Nope."

"Go there and climb to the top of one of the highest hills. You'll find something that looks like Stonehenge, a geometric assemblage of stone pillars. On them are inscriptions, guidelines more or less."

"I'm familiar with the tale. Commandments engraved in eight different languages on four giant stones. Supposed to be the commandments of the New World Order."

"You know the legend well."

"To a degree. I always thought it was a marker where a bunch of

James Gordon

dead bodies were buried."

"There's more buried at that place than you realize."

"This is all very fascinating, but I find it very hard to believe what you're saying, that the Illuminati are the ones responsible for the president and his people overturning the civil rights of over two million Americans?"

"Read the commandments and then you decide. All I'm saying is our country has suffered and it is time to end the suffering. If you're willing to help, we can bring an end to the conflict that is tearing our nation apart from the inside. I will call you in twenty-four hours. You can let me know what you decide. However, research the stones, find out for yourself who the true power is. Then, let your conscience be your guide. Now, I must take a nap and you should be getting back to your seat."

Greene placed his glass in the holder and rested his head on the back of his seat. Thurgood leered at him for what seemed to be minutes. He wasn't sure what to make of all of this. One thing was for certain, he had a lot to research within the next twenty-four hours. He placed his drink in the seat holder, stood and walked toward the rear of the first class section. The faces of the White people who still had displeased expressions didn't matter to him anymore. They were inconsequential, idiots who'd fallen victim to the propaganda machine of society.

He exited the first-class cabin, raking through the curtains and marching toward his seat like a man on a mission. Lela snapped awake when she saw him, standing up to allow him to sit. Thurgood shuffled his way to his seat, sat down and puffed breaths like a bull ready to charge the matador. His eyes bulging, skin glistening with a thin layer of perspiration, nostrils flaring. Lela settled back in her seat, her eyes wide and expectant, staring at him with the hope that she wouldn't have to ask what his meeting was all about. After a few minutes of watching him seethe, she knew he wouldn't be forthcoming with the answers.

"Well?" she asked.

Thurgood looked at her. "Well, what?"

"What was that all about?"

"I'll tell you later."

Lela seemed bothered that he was putting her off, shifting in her seat and assuming her sista-girl, neck-snaking pose. "Thomas Thurgood, you better tell me what's going on."

"I will, Lela, as soon as we land. Just be patient."

Nationhood

His answer didn't sit well with her. She sucked in her cheeks and puckered her lips, the way a Black woman does when she is so mad that she could scratch a man's eyes out with her nails but is trying to be cool and not overreact, yet. She folded her arms and crossed her legs, letting the top leg dangle in the aisles as she bounced it on her knee in order to maintain some composure.

Thurgood turned and looked out of his window, his mind completely overwhelmed. He couldn't believe what he'd been told, searching for a way amidst the darkened sky to find a handle on the situation. The clouds were less puffy now, more like stringy and thin. That meant they were about an hour away from Washington D.C., beginning their descent from their cruising altitude. It would be dawn when they landed, but that didn't matter. He had twenty-four hours to unlock a mystery and piece together as much information as he could. He only hoped that Lela wouldn't strangle him before he could tell her what was going on.

~~~

Carla was noticeably distracted. She played with her cuticles, face devoid of expression, eyes staring into space. To say she looked detached from where she was had to be the understatement of the year. Her mind was reeling, a number of emotional conflicts taking place simultaneously. Her past now played like a slow motion movie in her head, every memory being savored, her heart wishing she had more time to relive them all.

It had been a few hours since she and Constable Al-Shahir had their discussion about the Illuminati and the current state of affairs in New Kemet. The country was under attack by a virus so deadly that it had already captured the lives on three senators and the IS that carried the disease. But now she was infected with the same illness that took their lives. Although she was trying to be strong, the anguish in her heart over the idea that she was going to die soon began to erode her composure. She felt the strings of sanity snapping and the unbridled fear bulging at the seems, aching to be released in one giant explosion.

Abraham came to her and saw the far away look in her eyes, instantly knowing what was causing it. He sat next to her, nudging her shoulder with his in a playful manner. She looked at him, her eyes dead, her face drained of all emotions.

"You okay?" he asked.

"No," she replied like a scared little girl. "I'm terrified right now."

"I know. I called Samantha, told her what was going on. She didn't take the news well."

"Can you blame her? You should have spared her the heartache, waited for the station to contact her and give her the bad news."

"No. She deserved better than that. Didn't want my last action on earth to be that of a coward."

"You have more guts than I do. I don't think I could have done what you just did."

"We all have our moments of strength. Yours was earlier, when you helped me to get a grip when Al-Shahir told us the bad news. I wanted to rip his head off for doing this to us."

"Wasn't his fault. He didn't release the disease."

"Did he say who's behind all of this?"

"Yes. But before I go on about this, I want to ask you a question. Are there any regrets you have about your life, any at all?"

Abraham thought the question odd. He looked at Carla with a frown, not sure where she was going with this.

"Just humor me, Abe," she continued.

"Well, there are some things I wished I'd gotten around to. Mostly it was spending more time with Sam, and Shanice, my daughter. Always thought that I'd take them on a fabulous vacation to someplace tropical, perhaps visit the US when relations got better. I always wanted to visit New York."

"Yeah, I went there once. It was nice, crowded, but nice."

"Are the buildings as huge as they say?"

Carla nodded. "There were some massive skyscrapers, looked like they almost touched the heavens. I went to the top of the Empire State Building."

"Like on the movie *King Kong*?"

"Uh-huh. It was the most breath-taking sight I'd ever seen. You could see for miles in every direction." Carla's breath shuddered. She lowered her head for an instant, fighting to hold back her tears. "I dreamed of taking my children there one day, when I had some. Doesn't look like I'll have that opportunity now."

Abraham placed his arm around her, hugged her close. Carla allowed a few tears to fall, used her handkerchief to wipe her eyes and pat her nose.

"At least you had the chance to have a family," said Carla. "I was too concerned with my career, trying to show I can do anything a man could. Too obsessed with proving myself. If I could do it all again I would…"

"That still wouldn't make this any easier," Abraham interjected. "In fact, it would make it harder, knowing you're leaving loved ones to mourn, to know that your daughter will grow up without you, to never take them on that vacation, to never kiss your wife in the morning or tuck your child in at night. No, it's much harder having that burden than not having it."

Carla released a heavy sigh, pondering the perspective Abraham just revealed. She looked at him with emotional eyes, realizing just how hard this was for him.

"You are taking this rather well," she said.

"I'm banking on the long shot, that somehow we just might make it out of here alive," he replied.

"But what if we don't."

"Then I'll cross that bridge when I come to it."

Carla smiled. "Ever the optimist," she said.

"Better than the alternative."

Carla stood to her feet, straightened her pantsuit and worked the kinks out of her neck. She sucked in a deep breath and regained the emotional strength that waned before her talk with Abraham. She looked at her colleague, her eyes showing a little more life than before.

"Thanks for the talk, Abe. You really are something," she said.

Abraham stood to his feet, a pleased look blanketing his face. "No problem. But I should be thanking you. After all, you were the one that helped me be strong. I was only giving some of that strength back. Now, what about this report. What do you have?"

With a devious smile, Carla replied. "We are going to do something that will rock the entire world. We are going after the Illuminati."

Just then, a blood-curdling scream was heard in one of the outer hallways. Abraham and Carla raced from the room and approached the entrance to the area they were being contained. In the outer hallway, they saw a man lying on the floor. It was one of the members from a rival news station's crew. A female teammate knelt next to him, screaming for someone to help him. He was convulsing, spitting up blood, his eyes rolling to the back of his head.

The agents knelt next to him, attempting to take his vitals and restrain him as best they could. But Abe and Carla knew the deal. He was in the advanced stages of the disease and it would only be a matter of time before he was dead. Carla turned, looked at Constable Al-Shahir whose eyes stared blankly at the convulsing man on the floor.

"Make him as comfortable as you can, guys," he said.

He looked at Carla, neither of them knowing what to say. He turned, began walking toward the inner room. Carla could only watch him walk away, realizing that this was the fate that awaited them all. She was a little disappointed in his actions, but also knew that there was nothing he could do, nothing any of them could do. She looked at Abraham. His eyes were wide with fear, staring at his future lying on the floor. Carla nudged him, awakening him from his dazed state.

"C'mon, Abe. There's nothing we can do here. Let's get started on our report," she said.

~~~

Mbaku arrived at the location where the blips were emitting. He parked his car a quarter mile away and placed the vehicle on voice control in case of an emergency. Donned in his Alpha-One combat suit, which was specially made for him, he jogged the rest of the way, taking care to remain undetected. He used the suit's thermo optics to blend with the surroundings, blocking any heat emissions so he wouldn't be spotted using ultraviolet or infrared detectors. He also activated a sonar inhibitor that would prevent him from being identified using sound blips.

As he arrived at the area where the signal was being transmitted, he saw a car parked in a shaded area. He walked over to it, checking around himself to make sure it wasn't a trap. His optic goggles picked up a single life source inside, lying on the back seat and emitting readings that indicated they'd been hurt.

He slowly proceeded toward the car, then stopped. He looked to his left, picked up a blip on his visual and audio sensors that quickly faded. A smile came to his lips, realizing that the person inside wasn't alone. He reached to his belt, turned on his sonic scrambler. The device emitted a ultra high frequency that would do two things, annoy all dogs within a two-mile radius and send a nearly deafening screech to ultra sensitive listening equipment. If someone was listening or using any

Nationhood

surveillance devices, they were in for one serious headache.

Feeling that he'd taken care of everything, Mbaku prepared to move in. Suddenly, he heard a click when he'd taken his first step. When he looked down, he saw that his foot was stepping on a small explosive trigger, the kind connected to a PMA-2 landmine. If he moved, it would detonate. It was then a man came through the brush, looking at him with disappointed eyes. It was Jaquimo.

"That was way too easy," he said. "Figured you to be a little smarter than that."

Mbaku smiled broadly, then took his foot off the detonation trigger. Jaquimo flinched, covering his face with his arms thinking that would shield him from the expected blast. Seconds passed. It was then Jaquimo realized that the mine didn't explode. He looked at Mbaku, wondering how he did that.

"I activated a powerful magnet in my shoe, polarized the detonating mechanism. Then using my microwave emitter, I burned the fuses and wiring," he explained.

"Well done," said Jaquimo. "I can see why she remembered you."

"I assume you're talking about Miss Ishtar?"

"Indeed."

"Interesting how you used my nano transmitters to send me a message."

"We figured a person of your skill would *get* the message"

"I would further guess that she's in some sort of trouble."

"I will explain. Please, follow me."

The two men trotted toward the car, Jaquimo explaining along the way about the ambush Katura encountered. When they arrived, Mbaku saw the beautiful young woman in the back seat, grasping her arm but managing to sit upright and look right at him. Jaquimo got in, sat behind the steering wheel, ready to leave at a moment's notice.

"We meet again," said Mbaku.

"Funny how we keep bumping into each other," Katura replied.

"May I," he asked, alluding to her injury.

He pulled back the bandage, saw the bullet wound in her shoulder. Jaquimo had already performed field surgery, removed the bullet and attempted to control the bleeding by packing the wound with gauze. But it was still bleeding badly and was terribly infected. She was in desperate need of an antibiotic.

James Gordon

"I have a safe house not too far from here. Follow me," said Mbaku.

Just then a police helicopter few overhead, shining a light on the car. Officers with their guns drawn exploded through the bushes and surrounded them.

"This is the MCPD! Please step out of the vehicle and put your hands in the air!" rang a voice over a bullhorn.

"My, my," said Jaquimo, nonchalantly. "I do believe we have company."

"And me without my party dress," said Katura with a grunt.

"I'm hoping you've retrofitted this vehicle with stealth cloaking?" asked Mbaku.

"Wouldn't leave home without it," said Katura.

"Then I suggest we depart. Least wise our friends will insist that we accompany them to the station. Figured you'd want to avoid that whole sordid affair," said Mbaku.

Jaquimo activated the MIRROR, a device that bended light rays around the car, made it appear virtually invisible. Instantly the officers began shooting. Jaquimo floored the accelerator, speeding off into the night like a bat out of hell. The officers continued shooting at the train of dust but soon ceased when they were no longer able to find the target with certainty.

Meanwhile, inside the car, Mbaku and Katura were crouched in the seat. When the shooting appeared to be over, they eased up, checking around to see if the coast was clear. Mbaku lifted his arm, pressed a button on the side of his watch, spoke toward the dial like it was a walkie-talkie.

"Alpha evac protocol, sub program 2," he said.

He released the button, then turned to look at Katura who'd leaned against the door, her eyes closed like she was focusing on controlling the pain. He removed a vial from his utility belt, shook out a couple of pills.

"A doctor will be at the safe house when we arrive. Try to hold on. Meanwhile, take these," he said, pushing the pills toward her.

Katura took them, opened her mouth and swallowed. "An Opioid, Oxycodone, if I'm not mistaken," she said.

"Yes. You can tell that by taste."

Katura smiled, then grimaced. The pain in her shoulder was getting worse, but she knew that with the painkillers Mbaku just gave her, she should be fine shortly. She sucked in a deep breath, attempted to mentally block out the throbbing in her shoulder. "So, that code you rambled off. Was that to call your buddies to come get me?" she asked.

"If I wanted to do that I could have turned you over to Mecca City's Finest back there. No, that code was to alert my vehicle, have it accompany us back to the safe house," Mbaku replied.

"And just where is this safe house?" Jaquimo asked.

Suddenly, Mbaku's car roared down a cross street and swerved in front of them. Jaquimo was caught a little off guard, but managed to maintain control of the vehicle. He looked into the rearview mirror at a smirking Mbaku.

"You could've, at least, warned me," he said.

"Follow my vehicle. It will take you right to the safe house," said Mbaku.

Jaquimo shook his head. "Maniac," he mumbled.

~~~

James Gordon

Chapter Ten: Strange Bedfellows

It had been a couple of hours since the member of a rival news team fell just outside the door vomiting blood and convulsing. Whether it was considered a blessing or not, he died shortly thereafter. The virus had ravaged his body so completely that by the time he died he'd lost all skin tone. He was hemorrhaging severely and had broken several bones due to his uncontrollable shaking.

Since then, five more people had died, all of them suffering from the same symptoms. The conference area where we were being kept was in a state of panic and the agents were now trying to contain the remaining crew members inside the quarantine zone.

Abe and Carla sat next to each other, drenched with perspiration and looking like they were ready to fall asleep any moment. Their eyes were bloodshot and their eyelids would close and then snap back open every so often. The fear of not waking back up kept them going, kept them from dozing off and not making the most of the time they had.

While they'd been cooped up in the confined area, they managed to complete the interview with Constable Al-Shahir. He told them about the Illuminati, the history of the secret organization and how they managed to infiltrate every single powerful nation over the last millennia. He even mentioned some of the suspected members who were in the New Kemet legislature.

He'd gone into great detail, divulging assassination attempts, plots to overthrow various governments and even the London copycat version of the terrorist attacks that took place in the United States on September 11, 2001.

Everything had been recorded. All that was needed was to uplink to the satellite and feed the report to the station. But fatigue was setting in, perhaps the onset of the initial stages of the virus. Carla sat with her back braced against the wall, looking like she'd been drained of most of her energy. Her arms hung limply to her side and her sweat-drenched clothing enhanced her dowdiness. Abraham sat next to her, looking equally tired and listless. Just then, Constable Al-Shahir walked into the room, saw them lounging against the wall and made a beeline to them.

James Gordon

Kneeling beside Carla, he asked, "Would you like a cot to lie down on for a while?"

Carla drew in a deep breath through her nose. She sat forward, stared at Al-Shahir with glazed eyes and an expression that said she would love to take a nap.

"I'm afraid that if I close my eyes I might not wake back up," she said.

"The vaccine is still working. You can take a nap if you like."

"The way I see it, I'll be sleeping enough. I'd rather stay awake for as long as I can. Could be the last time I'll get the chance."

Carla forced a smile on her lips, a tired pretentious smile. Then, her eyes turned down to the floor, like a sad thought had just swept across her mind. Al-Shahir reached forward, placed his hand on top of her. "Come with me for a moment."

He helped her up. She looked down at Abraham. "I'll be back," she said.

The Constable ushered her toward one of the rooms near the rear of the conference areas. It was filled with oval shaped tables made from real oak. High back chairs that resembled mini thrones encircled each of the tables. The walls were covered with Rembrandt style tapestry and white crown molding along the top and the baseboard.

Once inside, Al-Shahir offered Carla a seat. He pulled out one for himself and sat opposite of her.

"What is this about, Constable?" she asked.

"It's about regret, Miss Snipes."

"Regrets?"

He coughed. "Yes. When a person approaches the end of their life, they tend to think about the things they regret doing and the things they regret not doing."

"Yes. I found myself doing that very thing."

"As have I. But I wish to correct something."

"Really?"

"Yes. I wanted to say something to you, something I should have said a long time ago." He coughed again. Carla frowned. "You see, I've been an admirer of yours for quite some time. In fact, I've never missed a single one of your reports."

"Really?" she asked.

Al-Shahir nodded "I've always wanted to tell you this, but I was

Nationhood

never able to gather the nerve to do it. Funny that I'm finding the nerve now."

Carla blushed. "Well, thank you. I'm very flattered."

They shared a smile. "Tell me, Miss Snipes. What are your regrets?" asked Al-Shahir.

Carla snickered. "Funny you should ask that. Abe and I were discussing that very subject just before we did the interview with you, just before the other news crew member, well, you know..." Her voice trailed off.

"Yeah, I know," Al-Shahir replied.

"Anyway, I was telling him how I wished I'd started a family. I was always so preoccupied with my career that I never stopped to consider that one day my opportunity to have children might just fly by. Like you said, when a person nears death, they think of these things."

A pained smile came to the Constable's lips. "I don't have any children, either."

Carla tilted her head to the side, looked at Al-Shahir with a curious frown. "You should have. You would have made a great father."

The Constable looked up and stared into Carla's almond colored eyes. They were so clear, unpolluted by anger and innocent. It was like staring into the eyes of an angel, seeing the endless possibilities and the heaven that he could have had. He felt a tug at his heart; the rumble of butterflies in his stomach almost made him nauseous.

Carla returned his gaze, her breath trembling. In that instant, her mind played with exotic and erotic thoughts. For reasons she could not explain, she felt a burning desire to kiss Al-Shahir. She tried to shrug it off, but the more she tried the more the sensation grew. Her mind raced with wonder and lust as she attempted to figure out why she was feeling this way. This was not the time to be having sex. People were dying and her life was hanging by a thread. Perhaps it was the fact that she was nearing the end of her life and she wanted one last fling before she bought the farm.

Suddenly, she turned away, tried to hide the sparkle that momentarily shined in her eyes. She told herself she shouldn't be thinking like this. She was the victim of an accursed virus and potentially moments away from dying. The entire situation seemed so wrong, so unfair. She wasn't ready to go, didn't want to leave this world alone and empty.

She looked once more at Al-Shahir, saw the gleam in his eyes, felt the warmth of desire brewing in her chest once more. She felt excited and ashamed at the same time, thinking to herself that such thoughts should not be entertained at a time like this yet wanting to have him hold her and make love to her just once.

"I wish I could have saved you from all of this," he said. "This wasn't your time to go."

"Well," Carla replied with a sigh. "No use crying about..."

Her face scrunched, eyes watered, a slow deep whine came from way deep inside. She leaned forward, buried her face in her hands. Al-Shahir knelt before her, placed his arms around her, pulled her close and hugged her tightly. She wrapped her arms around his waist, hugged him like he was her protector. She released her pain, allowed it to flow like the tears on her face. Her cries were muffled by her face being buried in his chest.

Al-Shahir felt her pain. He wanted to release his own but knew he had to be strong, had to be there for her. He stroked her wavy auburn-colored hair and made gentle shushing sounds as he tried to brush her fears away with his hands. For five minutes Carla poured out the agony contained in her soul, her anguish taking the form of pain-filled tears.

After she'd released most of her sorrow, she lifted her face from the Constable's chest and breathed in heavily to regain her composure. Al-Shahir handed her a handkerchief. She wiped her face and patted her eyes dry. An embarrassed expression bloomed, followed by a slight chuckle.

She said, "I'm sorry."

The Constable smiled, kissed her on her forehead. Carla lifted her face, her moistened eyes looking into his. His warm lips gave her the courage to do something chancy, something unexpected, something she needed to do.

"Do that again," she said assertively.

Al-Shahir gave her a frown, at first. Then his expression loosened. He moved to kiss her forehead again, but this time Carla suddenly turned her face upward, intercepted his lips with her. Pressed lips soon evolved into a luscious kiss, their mouths tasting the other's with ravenous passion.

Carla's hands explored the contours of the constable's body, his hands gliding across the curves of hers. Shirts began to come off, shoes flipped from their feet and bounced across the floor. Carla shimmied out of her skirt while Al-Shahir loosened his pants and allowed them to slide

Nationhood

down his legs to the floor. Bras, panties, boxers, T-shirts, socks, panty hose; all were removed without their lips parting for an instant.

They lay on the floor like battling lovers, each trying to release the pent up frustration and desire that came from the life-threatening events. Carla wrapped her legs around the Constable's waist as he slowly slid himself inside her. She gasped lightly, feeling the tingling sensation of being filled completely. They began to love each other like savages, the room echoing with grunts, pants, heavy breathing, moans and groans. Their lovemaking was intense, almost as if they were trying to hurt one another, perhaps making themselves feel pain in order to validate they were still alive.

Sweat began to bead from their entwined bodies, dripping to the carpet that now burned their knees, arms and back. Their mouths hungrily kissed, tasting once more the sweet nectar that they believed would be their last. Their bodies danced, resembling the movements of a sideways piston, grinding against each other with intensity, like two obsessed nymphomaniacs.

Carla was the first to come, her mouth ripping away from Al-Shahir's, opening in the shape of an O, loudly crying coos that echoed throughout the room. Her arms were wrapped tightly around his neck, holding him close as she entwined her legs around his and strained out the rest of her orgasm.

Seconds later, Al-Shahir released a long groan, sounding like a wild beast. He pushed hard and tight into Carla, his body ridged, his hands clutching her hips to the point of pain. His release was eruptive, his very soul being poured into her. He felt the warmth of their mixed juices, the desperate clutching of her hands, the angelic sound of her sighs and pants. A salty taste filled his mouth, it was the flavor of her skin, the brackish tang of lust taken to the nth degree.

Sighs faded, moans trailing off, Carla's arms loosened from around the Constable's neck, his hands releasing their steel-like grip on her hips. He pushed himself up, hovered just above her face. He gently brushed the perspiration from her brow, felt the softness of her skin, looked into her eyes and wished he'd made a move toward her sooner.

"This is how I would have liked to leave this world, in your arms," he said.

Carla smiled, a tear streamed across her temple and into her hair. They kissed once more, then Al-Shahir stood up. He made his way to his

James Gordon

pants, rummaged through his pockets. Carla sat up, braced herself on her elbows and stared at the Constable with a perplexed expression.

"What are you looking for?" she asked.

He suddenly dropped his pants, turned and looked at her. He came back to her side and lay on the floor next to her. His eyes stared into hers, her lips turning into a faint smile. She felt a prick in her thigh, jerked away quickly and distanced herself from Al-Shahir.

"What was that?" she asked, rubbing her leg.

He lifted his hand in the air and revealed a syringe and needle.

"It was my gift to you. It was my way of trying to preserve any hope for the future. If there's anyone who needs to survive this ordeal, it's you."

"What did you just give me?"

"Another inoculation. It was the last of the serum. It should hold you for another three hours. I'm hoping our government and scientists will have something figured out by then."

Carla didn't know what to say. Her mouth opened slightly, but nothing came out.

"Why?" she finally asked.

"Because...I love you."

She stared back at him with a look of disbelief, wondering if this was really happening or if this was a dream induced by the trauma or the drugs circulating inside her body. Suddenly, a violent cough erupted from the Constable, causing him to get on all fours. Carla quickly crawled toward him, started rubbing his back trying to help calm him down. She lowered her head trying to look at his face and make sure he was all right. Her eyes eased toward the floor, did a double take, then widened exponentially. She saw blood.

~~~

His search was exhaustive. Over one hundred books and a plethora of online pages were read, all of this in a span of a few hours. Thompson began researching the information Senator Greene mentioned to him on the plane. He hadn't slept since he arrived in Washington, his mind abuzz with curiosity.

Elbert County, Georgia was the subject. He searched the history books, scanned the Internet looking for anything related to what was rumored to be there. His search was not in vain.

On one of the highest hilltops in Elbert County, Georgia, there

Nationhood

stood a huge granite monument, engraved in eight different languages on four giant stones supporting the common capstone. Ten guides, or commandments, were written. The name given to that monument was The Georgia Guidestones, also known as the American Stonehenge.

Although its existence is relatively unknown to most Americans, let alone the rest of the world, it was considered by many to be a link to an occult hierarchy that dominated the world.

The creation and the people responsible for its erection are shrouded in mystery, has been for decades. All that is known about the guidestones is that they provided very specific direction on the course of action those followers would take. The commandments are as follows: Maintain humanity under 500,000,000 in perpetual balance with nature; guide reproduction wisely - improving fitness and diversity; unite humanity with a living new language; rule passion - faith - tradition - and all things with tempered reason; protect people and nations with fair laws and just courts; let all nations rule internally resolving external disputes in a world court; avoid petty laws and useless officials; balance personal rights with social duties; prize truth - beauty - love - seeking harmony with the infinite; be not a cancer on the earth - Leave room for nature - Leave room for nature.

Most of the information Thurgood already knew. Nothing new was found in any of the information he read. So what did Greene mean when he spoke of the guidestones and the real people who control this country?

He read certain passages again, particularly the ones referenced by members of the religious community stating that the monument had occult ties. Could that be what the senator was referring to? Was the true source of power connected to beings in the occult?

The whole issue seemed too far-fetched. Sounded like something out of a science fiction story. There was no way the world could be controlled by a single organization hell bent on dramatically reducing the population of the world, establishing a world government, promoting environmentalism and a new spirituality.

Then again, why would someone erect a one hundred and nineteen ton monolith in a small county in Georgia?

Thompson checked his watch, saw that he had exhausted most of his twenty-four hour allotment from Greene. He stood from his desk, pinched the bridge of his nose, stretched and yawned, felt the sleep he'd avoided catching up to him.

He heard a beep from his computer, saw a message that he'd received an email. He looked at the title, it said, 'Just for your eyes'.

Thinking that it was simply a piece of junk mail, he pressed the delete button. An instant later it was gone. He was about to walk away and lie down when he heard another beep. At first he was going to ignore it, but curiosity got the better of him. Besides, if he stayed connected, his inbox would be filled with junk mail by the time he got up. He walked back to his laptop, got ready to press the delete button and shut the system down when his eyes saw something peculiar in the subject line.

Just for your eyes, Thurgood.

This could be a virus, he thought, probably something that would shut his system down and destroy his hard drive. He was about to delete it when an instant message came up. 'It's not a virus.'

Spooked by the ordeal, Thurgood did a scan around his apartment. He checked under his bed, in his closet and even inside the shower of his bathroom. No one was there. He walked back to the computer, stared at it like it was possessed. Could this have something to do with what he had been researching?

He really didn't want to open the email, fear gripping his chest at the can of worms he could potentially open if he did. But something was happening, something that obviously affected him. Thurgood knew that even those who didn't want to get involved in things like this normally found themselves in the midst of greater turmoil when they tried to avoid getting involved. If he went in willingly, he just might be able to avoid any problems from finding him.

He lifted his hand, his index finger hovering over the enter key. A long, silent moment of deliberation took place. If he pressed this key, his life would be irreparably changed forever. However, if he didn't, there was a great possibility that he would find himself in deep trouble, real quick.

He allowed his finger to drop, pressing down the enter key. The email popped up, a timer ticking down on the screen. In huge letters was the message.

'This is how much time you have left before trouble finds you. Get out of the apartment now and go to Lou's bar down the street. I will have one of my people meet you there. R'

Thurgood's eyes widened. He looked at the timer. Thirty seconds

Nationhood

was left. He quickly ran to the door, slid he feet into his shoes, grabbed his coat and barreled out of the door. He raced down the steps, stopping at the bottom.

Just then, he saw a black Jaguar coupe pulling to the gate entry in front of his building. Thurgood quickly hid in the bushes near the entrance. His breath trembled as he peered through the branches of the trees, trying to be as silent as he could.

Two European men stepped out of the car, conservatively dressed, nicely groomed. They walked to his apartment entrance and disappeared up the stairwell. Thurgood remained hidden, listening intently as the clop of their shoes resonated inside the stairwell. He scanned the area, looking to see if anyone else was around. When he saw that the coast was clear, he dashed from the bushes and to the edge of the apartment building. He looked up and saw the shadows of the men inside his apartment. It looked as if they were going through his things, tossing papers and other articles in the air.

Thurgood was instantly filled with horror. Who were those men and why had they come to his apartment. If it hadn't been for that email, they would have walked in on him and done God knows what to him, perhaps even killed him.

Realizing that he'd stuck around longer than he should, he dashed to the back gate and raced toward Lou's. When he got there, the place was closed. The doors were locked and the bar abandoned. It was cold, the nippy night air chilling him to the bone. He'd forgotten his cell phone and had no way to call anyone, not even Lela.

Just then, an old Chrysler New Yorker zoomed to the front of the building. It came to a screeching halt and the door flew open.

"Get in," screamed a voice from inside.

By now, Thurgood was terrified. He wasn't sure whether to take the invitation. He began backing away, not sure what to do.

"Mister Thurgood, we don't have time. They've already ransacked your apartment and are searching the neighborhood for you now. They may be here any minute, now get it!"

Thurgood was still uncertain, but crept closer. Just then, the echo of a ricocheting bullet caused him to duck down to the ground. The black Jaguar was flying up the street, the sound of bullets being fired from a silenced automatic weapon pelted the front of Lou's bar.

"LET'S GO, MISTER THURGOOD!" the person in the car

exclaimed.

Realizing that he either got in and risked being killed or stood there and be gunned down on the sidewalk, Thurgood ran to the car and hopped in just as a bullet cracked the rear window of the New Yorker. However, the pane of glass stayed in tact, suffering only a spider web like fissure.

"Stay down!" said the driver.

He peeled off, tires squealing, a cloud of smoke rising from the burning rubber of the tires. The driver raced around the corner, speeding like he was one of those guys trying to get away on one of those televised police chase shows.

Another rain of bullets rattled against the back of the car and battered the rear window. The driver kept going, zigzagging across the street like a drunkard. During the whole ordeal he was calm, like this was no big thing or as if he'd done this sort of thing before.

"What the hell is going on?" Thurgood exclaimed.

"You've been targeted! Those guys behind us were sent to kill you!" said the driver.

"Kill me? Why do they want to..."

"You stumbled across something, something they didn't want you to see!"

"So, who the hell are you?"

"I'm the guy that's trying to save your ass!"

He banked a mean curve to the right, slamming Thurgood head first into the rear left door. "Shit, if you're trying to save me, this is a hell of a way to do it!" he exclaimed.

"Sorry, but this ride is almost over!"

"What the hell is that supposed to mean?"

Just then, a massive explosion boomed from behind them, nearly knocked the car into a spin. Thurgood saw the reddish hue brightening the streets behind them. The driver brought the car to an abrupt stop, slamming Thurgood against the front seat and then onto the floor.

Annoyed by the stop, but more intrigued by what just happened behind them, he pushed himself from the floor and slowly peeked up at the driver. He was staring at Thurgood, a young man with handsome features, thick eyebrows and caramel complexion, a smile beaming across his face.

The driver looked toward the rear window. The red hue reflecting off his face. Thurgood eased up a little more, cautiously inched his head

Nationhood

up to where he saw through the rear glass. The black Jaguar was ablaze, bellowing dark smoke and red flames into the air. The sight was too fantastic to believe and even more frightening.

Slowly, Thurgood turned and looked at the young man, his eyes showing utter bewilderment. "What the hell happened?" he asked.

"You're safe now," said the driver.

"Safe? I don't know the meaning of the word! Who the hell are you and why were those guys after me?"

"My name is Huey, I'm a member of Exodus. Ramses sent me to get you. Are you all right?"

"Hell no, I'm not all right! I've been shot at and chased through the streets of Washington D.C.! What could be *all right* about that?"

"Nothing. But at least you're not in that car," Huey said, motioning to the burning Jaguar behind them.

"I guess that's supposed to make me feel better."

Huey smiled. "Where would you like for me to take you?" he asked, turning to face forward once again.

"Can I go back to my apartment?"

"I don't think so. Soon the police will arrive and no doubt they'll find some of your papers in that car once the fire is put out. They will surely send others after you. It would probably be best to hide at a safe place."

"And just where would that be?"

Huey turned his head slightly and smiled again. Thurgood just shook his head. Then, his expression exploded into a look of fright. "Lela!" he exclaimed.

"Already taken care of," said Huey. "We picked her up the same time we went to get you. She's at the safe house now, figured that when they didn't find you they would be going after her."

"And Ramses figured all of this out?"

"He's a clever man, Mister Thurgood, just like you are. The only difference is he knows what we're up against. You're just starting to figure it out."

"Which brings me back to one of my original questions. Who were those people?"

"An excellent question. However, I feel that it would be appropriate if you heard it from the man himself."

"Ramses is here?"

James Gordon

"In a manner. Let's get you off the streets. We can discuss more when we arrive at the safe house," said Huey.

He pulled off, just as the distant sound of sirens could be heard approaching the area. A group of people had already started running toward the flaming vehicle. Within moments, the New Yorker had turned the corner and disappeared from sight.

~~~

Once his coughing stopped, it allowed Carla to get her clothes back on and helped to redress Constable Al-Shahir. She allowed his head to rest on her lap, her hand brushing across his slightly grimacing face while tears welled in her eyes as she rocked back and forth attempting to keep him calm. The virus had already begun ravaging his body, reducing his organs to little more than mush. It was only a matter of time before he became the latest victim of the terrorist attack, something Carla was having a hard time accepting.

The Constable's eyes were fixed on Carla's, his breathing labored, smeared blood staining his cheeks and lips. The pain was immense, his body shaking slightly. He fought to keep himself still, not wanting Carla to see him turn into a convulsing mess like the others who'd died before him. But it was growing more difficult and he wasn't sure how much longer he would last.

Carla did everything she could for him, patted his face with damp cold cloths and supported his head to allow any drainage in his mouth to flow. However, she knew that she could only make him comfortable as best she could. She's seen a few of the people who'd already died, saw how they trembled and spewed blood everywhere. She was amazed that the Constable hadn't allowed himself to fall that far, a testament to his sheer will and strength. A tear rolled down her cheek, but didn't drop from her face.

Al-Shahir lifted his hand, brushed away the tear, looked at her and managed to push a smile across his lips.

"Don't cry. I'm no longer leaving this world with regrets," he said softly.

"But you *are* leaving," Carla replied. "You're leaving me. I just found you and now I'm going to lose you."

"It was meant to be, this was how it was supposed to be."

"But why? This isn't fair, none of this is!"

Carla began to cry harder, bowing her head and allowing her

Nationhood

tears to fall across her chest. Al-Shahir brushed back her hair, his hand resting against the side of her face. His touch was comforting, relayed a contradicting message that he did have one regret, leaving her.

"You are so beautiful," he said.

Carla stopped crying for a moment, smiled when she heard his compliment, attempted to collect herself and be strong.

"You have a job to do" Al-Shahir continued. "You have to tell the world about the real threat to our country. You must not give up, never stop fighting."

Carla gave him a long stare.

"Promise me, you won't give up," said Al-Shahir.

She nodded. "I won't stop fighting. I promise," she replied.

He smiled. "You have given me something that I'd only hoped to have."

"What's that?" she asked.

"Your love."

A serene smile came to his face. Carla closed her eyes, soaked in the meaning of his statement. Al-Shahir began humming a song, *With you I'm born again*, by Billy Preston and Syreeta. His tone was clear and even, not once did he waver or crack. As he finished the first stanza, Carla took the second one, humming it so beautifully that it would have soothed *Godzilla* if he heard it.

She paused, releasing a snicker that was blanketed by her smile. "I loved that song, loved it from the moment I heard it," she said. "It's hard to believe that it was recorded so long ago. I always wished I'd find someone to make me feel that way, loved and safe, lying in the arms of the man I adored."

She waited for him to reply. Instead, the room was silent, too silent. Fear gripped her chest as she pressed her lips together, felt her breath choking in her throat. She inhaled deeply, then allowed it to slowly ease from her lungs. She opened her eyes, looked down at Al-Shahir. His eyes were closed, but he was still sporting that same serene smile. His chest wasn't moving and his body was limp.

Carla's tears flowed. She leaned closer to his face and kissed him on the lips, using her thumb to caress his cheeks.

"I'll never forget you," she said tearfully.

Just then, Abraham appeared at the door carrying some medical supplies and bottles of water. He saw Carla sitting on the floor crying, saw the lifeless body of Constable Al-Shahir lying with his head in her lap. He instantly knew what had happened. He approached, slowly and reverently. He stopped and stood just off to the side.

Carla lifted her head. As she looked at him, her moistened face told the horrific truth of why Constable Al-Shahir was lying on her lap looking like he was asleep.

Abraham bowed his head, pressed his palms together and said a prayer. Then, he walked closer, knelt down and looked at Carla.

"He looks peaceful," he said.

Carla's breath shuddered. "He was singing...and then...he..."

"It's okay." Abraham placed his hand on hers. "At least you were here with him."

"Yeah."

"I'm going to go get someone to take care of him."

"Thank you."

Abraham stood, then somberly walked out of the room. Carla looked back down at Al-Shahir's face, caressed his cheeks some more.

"I'm going to do what you said," she whispered. "The people responsible for this will pay. I won't stop fighting until this is done, I promise."

She leaned forward and kissed Al-Shahir one last time on the lips.

~~~

Chapter Eleven: The Next Great Tragedy

Morning had come, and Pollins was eager for this day to begin. He walked into the main dining area of the embassy. Lines of guards stood against the wall, their guns shouldered but ready to bring into firing position should the need arise.

Inside the dining room, aides and serving personnel were busily bringing trays and whatnots to the table. Pollins proceeded toward a rather stout man wearing glasses. He was conversing with another gentleman who was feverishly scribbling notes into a palm pilot.

"Reverend Aziz," said Pollins, as he came to a stop and extended his hand.

Aziz turned, extended his hand and shook. "Senator Pollins."

"Thank you for meeting me so early. I trust you haven't been waiting long."

"Not at all. I was just admiring your dining area. This is a most magnificent place."

"Thank you. Our government has been good to us. Shall we sit and begin eating."

The two men took their seats. The individual taking notes bowed and then left the room, as did other members of the Senator's aide staff. Their meals were served, a cornucopia of fruits, pastries, and assorted breakfast items. Aziz sampled each, which was expected for a man with his pear-like shape. Pollins ate mostly fruit and a few eggs. After they'd gotten their fill and a battery of pleasant compliments had been exchanged, Pollins turned to the good reverend and began to relay the real reason for the breakfast.

"Reverend, I'm sure you are familiar with the recent terrorist attack on our nation, correct?" asked Pollins.

"Yes, I am, Senator," Aziz replied.

"This is distressing for my country and our president wishes to have this issue resolved permanently."

"I see."

James Gordon

"We have reason to believe that the Americans are behind this. However, their tracks are well hidden. They created a virus and used the IS, Victor Johnson, to bring their disease to my country. Now three of my fellow senators, dear friends of mine I might add, are dead along with the Trojan Horse they used to infect my people."

Aziz adjusted the glasses that rested on his nose. "My condolences," he said, remorsefully.

"Pardon my abruptness, but it is not your condolences I am seeking," Pollins fired back.

"What, then?"

Pollins sat back in his seat, clasped his hands before him. "Tell me, Reverend, have you heard the story of Gilgamesh?"

"The old Sumerian tale?"

"Babylonian, actually. But yes, that one."

"Religion is tied to history, Senator. What historian or preacher isn't fascinated with this story."

"Then you should recall that Gilgamesh was considered to be the greatest king on earth, two-thirds god and one-third human. This mix gave him supernatural strength. But his people complained that he was too harsh, too directive for their tastes."

"Yes, and then the sky-god, Anu, created the wild-man called Enkidu to be his rival, sort of a balance to his power."

"Exactly."

"I fail to see the connection here."

"You will. Just mentally walk with me for a moment. Do you recall the rest of the story, especially the part about what happened to Enkidu?"

"He was supposedly tamed by a seductive priestess named Shamhat."

"That's right. So the wild man became tamed. Eventually Enkidu challenged Gilgamesh and a mighty battle ensured. Seeing that the gods were against him and that he could not continue to fight this battle on his own, Gilgamesh broke off the fight and proposed that he and Enkidu go into the Cedar Forest to kill the demon, Humbaba."

"If memory serves me correctly, Enkidu becomes ill shortly there after and dies."

"Very good."

"Although I am grateful for the walk down History Row, I still

164

Nationhood

don't get the meaning of all this."

"There comes a time when the ties to those you align yourself with have to be evaluated. The children of the sun that still live in America exist on the whims of a government that would try to subjugate the only bastion of their independence. This country, like many others, works to gain global and economic independence. We've worked within the laws governing the global community to achieve harmony, even when a fellow nation holds our people hostage by using diplomacy and trade as bargaining chips."

"What's your point, Senator?"

"I know why you're here. You're here to seek assistance for the organization you are affiliated with."

"And what organization is that?"

"Don't be coy, Reverend. I know you are a member of Exodus."

Aziz smiled pretentiously, neither confirming nor denying the accusation.

"Although it has been the policy of our nation not to associate in the affairs of foreign nations, this latest attack was proof that we can no longer abide by the rules of the international community when our fellow nations see fit to abuse and disregard those same rules," said Pollins.

"You make a very valid point. How can I be of assistance?" asked Aziz.

Pollins leaned forward, rested his elbows on the table, stared at Aziz with unflinching eyes. "It is time to teach those who shroud their greedy actions under a flag of patriotism that we will not be bullied, nor will we continue to play by the rules when the lives of my countrymen are at stake," he said.

Aziz bowed his head and adjusted his glasses again. "Exodus is a powerful organization, but we are but a few compared to the reach of the American Empire. They seem to have connections in various countries, perhaps even your own."

"True. But it is time to slice that hand and shorten its reach."

"How would you go about doing that?"

"By creating our own consortium of nations. Just as Gilgamesh aligned himself with Enkidu to slay the demon of the wood, there are many disillusioned countries that have grown tired of the manipulative actions of the Americans and wish to align themselves with a league of countries that will not sit back and allow the actions of a tyrannical nation

James Gordon

to go unchecked. By this time tomorrow, I will be proposing a bill that will give the president the ability to declare war on the United States. A declaration of allegiance will be sent to all nations in Africa, as well as friendly nations in the middle east and far east. Already I've heard from China, Japan, Russia, India, Iraq, Iran, Pakistan, Afghanistan and most of the northern territories in Africa. They each plan to sign the agreement and are prepared to take action when we give the signal."

Aziz stared at Pollins, his eyes filled with a fear that erupted the moment his last few words fell from his lips. "My God," he said. "You're preparing to start World War III."

"Wrong," Pollins retorted. "It was not our country that drew first blood, it was the Americans. They're the ones who did this and now they will have to pay for their actions."

"Have you tried talking with someone, perhaps an American Senator or the president himself?"

"The time for talking has ended. We need to take action. However, the course of diplomacy isn't the reason why I called you here today. I wanted to make a request."

"What is that?"

"I wanted you to get me in touch with the leader of Exodus. I want you to set up a meeting between me and Ramses."

Aziz bowed his head, allowed a deep breath to hiss from his nose as he exhaled.

"I'll see what I can do," he said.

"That's all I ask," Pollins replied.

"One thing bothers me, though. You seem to refer to AUNK as Gilgamesh and the rest of the nations as a scattered version of Enkidu."

"A loose analogy, but yes."

"Enkidu died. Is that the same future you see for us?"

"No, Reverend," said Pollins reassuringly. "Enkidu's demise was partly brought on by his weakened condition due to him being seduced by the priestess. Had he remained strong and wild, he might not have suffered such a fate."

"So, by joining with AUNK, the associated nations will remain strong, is that what you're suggesting?"

"America has seduced many nations into believing that their diplomatic society is the doorway to prosperity. But all they've done is turned the lesser nations into another version of an indentured servant.

166

Nationhood

Oppression weakens the spirit of the people over time. Even the mighty Exodus will suffer this fate should they continue on the course they are on. New leadership is needed and the time to act is now."

Aziz continued to ponder the proposal. Then, he looked at Pollins.

"When would you like this meeting to take place?" he asked.

"Seeing that I will be giving the president the bill tomorrow morning, as soon as possible," Pollins replied.

~~~

Her eyes fluttered open, like butterfly wings that were testing the wind currents in preparation of flight. Katura turned her head to the right. She was inside a bedroom. She blinked her eyes again, attempting to make them adjust. Straining, she sat up, bracing herself on her left arm. She felt groggy, and there was a slight twinge of pain in her right shoulder.

Slowly, her memories returned. She recalled being brought here by Mbaku right after her run in with agents she thought were on her side. She lay once more on her back, lifted her hand and checked her wounded shoulder. A bandage now covered the spot where the bullet entered. However, the soreness had subsided a great deal and the burning from the infection had lessened substantially. She was about to pull it off when the bedroom door opened.

She immediately took to the defensive, rolling off the bed and snapping to her feet, placing the bed between herself and the intruder, assuming a martial arts pose like that of a ninja. As she waited, Clarence walked into the room carrying a tray of food.

"Ah," he said warmly. "You're awake."

He sat the tray on a table next to the bed, then turned to look at Katura.

"I trust you rested well. You were in pretty bad shape when you arrived."

Katura remained silent, still holding her tiger-paw stance.

"Let's take a look at your arm, shall we," said Clarence as he walked toward her.

He lifted his hands toward her bandaged wound. Katura swatted them away.

"Here, now," he replied.

"Who are you?" she asked.

"My name is Clarence. I'm a friend."

167

James Gordon

"A friend to whom?"

"He's my uncle, actually," said Mbaku walking into the room.

Following right behind him was Jaquimo, Wendy Hughes and Vee, who used her walking stick to guide her.

"My Lady," said Jaquimo. "How are you feeling?"

He walked toward Katura, who gave him a wary look. She pulled away from him as he reached toward her, but Jaquimo gave her a reassuring look that told her everything was okay.

"We're just going to have a look at your wound," he said.

With a degree of reluctance, she allowed Jaquimo to pull back the bandage. The tug of the tape tearing away from her skin caused her to wince a bit. But soon the discharge-tainted gauze was off, revealing a rather remarkably healed but scabbed suture job beneath.

Wendy walked toward Katura to see the condition of her handy work. But the savvy spy became defensive, stared at Wendy with a frown that made the good doctor stop in her tracks. Mbaku saw the tension between the two and immediately piped in to diffuse the situation.

"Miss Ishtar, this is Doctor Wendy Hughes," he said. "She's the one who has been attending to your injuries since you arrived."

Wendy stepped a little closer. "I only want to examine your wounds," she said.

Katura looked at Mbaku, then scanned the room surveying everyone else. Her eyes finally rested upon Wendy, scrutinizing her particularly hard. The lady assassin was still a little off kilter but surmised that if they wanted to do something to her, they could have already. Adding the fact that Jaquimo was seemingly comfortable around them eased her trepidations a bit. She nodded faintly, but her guard would still be up, just in case. Wendy drew a little closer. She stared at the wound, her *Vogue* glasses resting on the bridge of her nose.

"Hmm, looks like you're healing astonishingly well," said Wendy. "It's only been hours, but you've managed to regenerate well beyond all normal expectations."

"Miss Ishtar is an enhanced super agent. The United States government did some experiments on her, fortifying her regenerative abilities and strengths," Jaquimo added.

Katura frowned, then leaned closer to Jaquimo. "Aren't you being a little too casual with your conversation," she said in a whisper.

"My Lady," Jaquimo replied in a like manner. "These people

Nationhood

helped us when our own government tried to have you killed. They nursed you, took care of you. I doubt they would do all of that just to try and kill you."

They stared at each other briefly. Katura understood his point, however, she still remembered her training and the one lesson that was pounded into her head day in and day out; never trust anyone. Her eyes eased toward Wendy and then to Mbaku. Although this was the second time she'd come in contact with him, on both occasions he seemed sincere in his assistance. But she still had to be on her guard. The people she was supposed to trust had betrayed her, tried to kill her, damn near did, then left her for dead. With an experience like that, she knew that it wasn't out of the question or too unreasonable to be a little cautious.

"Your wound looks good. At this rate you should be completely healed in a day. I'll check back with you later just to make sure everything is all right," said Wendy.

She turned and walked toward the door. She and Mbaku exchanged flirting smiles just before she left. Katura caught that, smirked at this added bit of information she now stored as a mental note for future use. Just then, Clarence stepped a little closer to Katura. She flinched like she was going to strike any moment. He held up his hands, but continued to inch forward.

"I can understand your circumspection to trust during a time like this, Miss Ishtar, but you must understand that we mean you no harm," he said.

"Sorry, but my trust level is a little low right now," she replied, tightening her stance like a cobra.

Clarence stopped. "That I can appreciate. However, this is a time of grave concern for my country. We were hoping that you might have some answers."

"Once again, my apologies. I'm not in the business of lending answers."

Clarence nodded, then turned and began walking in the other direction.

"I'm sure you are aware that Ishtar was the ancient Sumero-Babylonian goddess of love and fertility. She was the daughter of Anu, the god of the air. In most of the stories concerning her, she was described as a beautiful but evil and heartless women who destroyed her lovers once she was done with them."

James Gordon

Katura loosened her stance a bit. "I am what I am," she said with a chuckle.

"Yes, but my qualms are not with you, but those that sent you."
Clarence nodded for Mbaku to finish filling her in.

"There has been much turmoil in my country over the last twenty-four hours. For example, you were involved with the taking of the Crown Jewels of Romania, an act that could have placed my country at odds with one of our closest allies," he said.

After a slight snicker Katura replied, "I fail to see where this is my problem."

"Shortly after that, a virus was released at the New Kemet International Airport. Three senators died and the area has been quarantined. There are a lot of people still there, held captive because of the National Disease Control Agency's efforts to contain the virus and keep it from spreading."

"Still don't see..."

"My Lady, please," Jaquimo urged.

Katura gave him a glance, then resumed her stare at Mbaku as he continued.

"Preliminary reports show the virus to be manmade. It was also concealed in the body of the recently released indentured servant named Victor Johnson, who met with the very senators who died. Johnson is also dead, a victim of the virus he helped to smuggle into my country."

"So why not talk to the US government about this?"

"We intend to. But first, we need to stop the virus before it is somehow released into the populace. If it does get out, it could not only wipe out all of New Kemet, but the rest of the world."

"What about an antidote?" asked Jaquimo. "Can't your scientists make one up?"

"Vee," said Clarence. "Why don't you tell them what you know."

Vee moved forward, tapping the floor with her walking stick, stopping just by the bed that Katura lain upon.

"The virus is complex, more so than any other virus I've encountered," she said. "It's symptoms mirror those of cancer, but at a greatly accelerated rate and with much more severe effects. The person is literally eaten from the inside out."

"Good lord," said Jaquimo.

"Sounds like a blood agent the government used during the

170

Nationhood

Vietnam War and during the Gulf War conflict," said Katura.

"Indeed," Vee continued. "Only this virus' composition changes with each person it comes in contact with, like it maps its host's DNA and modifies itself into a new strain. The most we've been able to do is come up with a cloaking vaccine that shields the cells from potential attack. But the virus adjusts and eventually eats through the vaccine."

Mbaku stepped forward. "The night that you heisted the diamonds, I managed to remove one of the smaller jewels from the crown," he said.

"Suspected you would," said Katura.

"What we found was the jewels weren't diamonds at all, but an elaborate and highly sophisticated crystal."

"A crystal?"

"It gets better. The crystal was a miniature storage device, holding secret information that appeared to be of a scientific nature. There seems to be parts of a chemical formula stored inside of the one I took. We believe it could be the antidote for the virus. We need to get the rest of those crystals back so we can create the antidote and stop this disease before it kills every single person on this planet."

Katura stared blankly at Mbaku as the information he just relayed settled in her head. All of this was quite familiar. Her adopted father, Durst Weinkaufen, performed work involving nuclear biology. This was right up his alley and she couldn't help but wonder if this had anything to do with his death.

For an instant, her mind drifted away. She thought about Marina, about Durst, about a life that seemed so far away now. Childhood memories of family outings, riding horses and playing on their ranch filled her head.

Katura then realized that she still hadn't called Marina, knew that her mother was worried about her, probably was wondering why Katura hadn't called to let her know she was on the way. Certainly she needed some help in dealing with Durst's death and attending to funeral arrangements. She hoped to have been back by now, walking with Marina on the ranch and recalling memories that honored the legacy of the man she called her father.

But she wasn't back in the states. Instead, she was still in New Kemet talking to a group of people about a problem she had no interest in whatsoever. Her mind returned from its stroll down memory lane to the

171

here and now. She lost the far away gaze and looked at Mbaku with eyes filled with uncertainty. Her lips pressed together as she pushed her sentimental thoughts to the back of her mind.

"I want to thank you for your assistance in nursing me back to health. I wish you luck on your quest," said Katura. "I have other issues I need to attend to."

She was about to leave when Clarence made a statement. "We know about your father."

The statement made Katura stop in her tracks. She turned, faced the older member of Mbaku's family, stared at him with a gaze of ice.

"You watch what you say about him," she warned.

"I have nothing bad to say about Doctor Weinkaufen. In fact, we knew each other."

"You're lying. My father never mentioned you before."

"He couldn't. If he did he would have been considered a threat to national security, consorting with a nation that wasn't on the United States' list of favorite ass-kissing nations. However, is it a coincidence that you would be chosen to come to this country and perform a covert act the very time a virus that is linked to your father's research was released into the populace?"

It was as if he read her thoughts. Clarence nailed the very suspicion her mind breezed across when the information about the virus was relayed. Durst Weinkaufen had been working with the US government to create a vaccine that could destroy carcinogenic cells spreading throughout the body. He'd been working on it for years and it was rumored that he actually created a cure for cancer.

But now, Katura was starting to wonder whether his discovery had been bastardized, altered to fit the purposes of corrupt people who intended to use this contribution of science to further their political and financial goals. It wasn't a ridiculous theory and the possibility that this was actually happening bothered her. To think that her father's creation would actually be used for such a diabolical purpose made her physically ill. But she knew it would be something people in power would do and she knew if that was the case she needed to get involved, if not for her sake or the security of the world, for Durst and his legacy.

She fell silent for a moment, pondered the statement Clarence made. Could it actually be possible that her being here wasn't sheer coincidence? If it weren't it wouldn't be the first time she had been wrong.

Nationhood

In fact, there were at least two things Katura had been mislead about within the last few hours. One was the fact that she thought the government would be there for her when she was through with her assignment. The second was the fact that Durst's research was potentially being used for other than honorable purposes. Katura could only wonder what other lies she'd been told.

Her mind wanted to believe her father had nothing to do with all of this, however, she also knew the price for naivety, it could cost lives. Durst was a good man and Katura wanted to believe that he would never have created the curing virus had he known the intent it would be used for later. He was a kind man, always showing compassion and being the kind of father a child would be proud to have. Someone was taking his research and life-long works and was turning it into a weapon to be used for their own glorifying purposes, something Katura felt besmirched the legacy of her father. That was something she could not allow.

Her eyes gravitated to Jaquimo, who had been standing by her side patiently and silently waiting. She felt confused, wondered if she was being told the truth and was looking to him to see if he could confirm or deny the information she'd just been given. His expression was unreadable, a result of his training with the government. Never let them see you sweat, that was the motto. She looked at Mbaku and Clarence once more.

"Do you mind if we have a few moments?" she asked.

"Certainly," Clarence replied.

He, Vee and Mbaku left the room, closing the door behind them. Katura faced Jaquimo, who now looked a little dopey. An expectant glare was in her eyes and she had a commanding posture in her stance.

"What are your thoughts," she asked.

"You sure you want to discuss this now? I thought you had a problem with security and all," Jaquimo replied in a tongue and cheek manner.

"Get serious. I'm concerned about what they said about my father. Do you think he had anything to do with all of this?"

"I have to admit that the effects of this virus are strangely similar to the research your father had been conducting, only in reverse. I wouldn't be at all surprised if the government changed it around to create a weapon, of sorts. The real question is whether *you* believe he had anything to do with all of this."

James Gordon

"I don't know. I want to believe he didn't, but life has always been a smoke and mirror marathon for me."

"Regardless of whether the two issues are related or not, you have a duty to find the truth. Durst was a good man, a good father, and we cannot let his work be trashed, even if it is the US government doing this. The only way we'll know for certain is to check out the story and we can only do that by sticking around and exploring the issue a little further."

"So, you think we should work with these folks and use them to find out what we can."

"Wouldn't hurt. Besides, it might be fun. We no longer have our country's support. They proved that with the little ambush they sprung on you. At least these folks are giving us info. Perhaps if we try cooperating, we might find the truth. Who knows, it might also give you a chance to get back at the people who shot at you on the pier."

"That it would," Katura replied pensively.

Before they could conclude their conversation, the bedroom door opened and Mbaku walked in. Katura was a little alarmed by the intrusion, as was Jaquimo. Mbaku quickly held up his hands to show he meant no disrespect.

"Sorry to interrupt," he said apologetically. "However, I think there's something you need to see. If you will follow me..."

He turned and walked back out. Katura and Jaquimo shot befuddled glances at each other, then followed Mbaku out of the room. They soon arrived in a palatial study room that was just as extravagant as Katura's place in Washington D.C.

As they marveled at the décor, Jaquimo saw that Clarence was standing in front of a big screen television staring at it intently. Vee was sitting on the couch, her walking stick resting against her shoulder and her head turned slightly with her ear directed toward the television.

Without turning his head, Clarence began speaking. "It seems that things have spiraled out of control much more quickly than I had anticipated," he said.

"What are you talking about?" asked Jaquimo as he and Katura came to stop next to him.

Mbaku picked up the remote and increased the volume.

"...and the president indicated that he will not tolerate terrorism. He has already signed a Decree of Conflict, accusing the United States of conducting hostile and covert actions against the people of New Kemet.

Nationhood

Unless the United States meets the demands of the New Kemet legislature, the president stated that there will be swift and deadly retaliation. The US has until 7:00 PM tonight to agree to the government's demands or, as one spokesperson called it, *face severe consequences*."

The reporter continued, but the words that were already said painted a very clear picture of what was about to happen. The legislative and executive branches had agreed to declare war on the US, blaming them for the events that have taken place in New Kemet over the last twenty-four to forty-eight hours. Mbaku lowered the volume, placed the remote on the coffee table.

"As you can see, the stakes have just gotten higher," he said.

"This is terrible," said Katura. "I can't believe this is happening. Your country is about to go to war with my country."

"Yes. All over a bunch of crystals, because that's what it all boils down to."

"What do you think your country's demands are?" asked Jaquimo.

"The antidote, of course," Mbaku replied. "That's why we need to get to those crystals."

Katura's eyes shifted as she mulled over the thoughts racing through her head.

"That settles it," she said.

"Settles what, My Lady?" asked Jaquimo, looking at her uneasily.

"We have to help them get back the crystals and stop this war before it starts."

"Why?" asked Mbaku. "This is no more than what your country deserves. For far too long they've been running around the globe, extorting smaller, weaker nations like a mob boss. Now, they are about to bear witness to the resistance. They're reaping what they've sowed. If it wasn't for the fact that I want to save the lives of my fellow countrymen, I'd let nature take its course."

"You don't get it, do you?" Katura snapped back. "While you're sitting here all comfy in your mansion, our people will stand to lose everything. If this war takes place, the Americans will send the indentured servants to the front line first. That's hundreds of thousands of people. We would be killing the ones we should be trying to save. You have no idea the atrocities we've been through over the last twenty-five years. I, myself, have been the victim of experiments, something I wouldn't wish on an enemy. But I was lucky, I got to live. That will not be the case if we don't stop this war. Besides that, the people of your country will suffer the inhumanities of war, leaving you defenseless and vulnerable. Are you willing to let your countrymen face that?"

"We cannot allow this issue to go unanswered," Mbaku fired back. "Besides, we have a strong coalition to support us."

"A coalition who *say* they want to bring down the American Empire, but when the move is made, you will find out just who is your ally. I fear that the revelation will be most costly."

"She does have a point," said Clarence.

"Then what should we do?" asked Mbaku. "The government has already signed the decree."

"First, we need to find those crystals," Vee chimed in surprisingly. "Then, we need to somehow fortify our forces, at least until certain provisions are put into place."

"Good idea, Vee" Mbaku replied. He turned to look at Katura. "You game to go crystal hunting with me?"

"Thought you'd never ask," Katura replied.

"There's still one thing that bothers me," said Clarence. "It would seem that we are flying blind on this. I think I'll go have a talk with my friend, Elijah Pollins, try to convince him to hold off on the attacks, buy us some time. I just wish there was some way we could get some information about what the Americans are doing."

Katura thought for a second, then her eyes ballooned wide with revelation.

"Perhaps there is a way to get that information…and I think I know just the person who could get it."

"Who's that?" Mbaku asked.

"Someone who's aching to take me to bed—Thomas Thurgood."

~~~

176

Chapter Twelve: A Meeting of the Minds

Huey and Thurgood walked down the steps of a long hall with a steep decline that seemed to stretch for miles. A dank, musty odor filled the air. It smelled like crap and vomit. Thurgood felt himself getting lightheaded. He stopped for a second and bent over to allow the blood to flow to his head. Huey knelt beside him, placed his hand on his back.

"You okay?" he asked.

"I feel sick. What the hell is that smell?" asked Thurgood.

"Ah, that. That's the sweet smell of drainage courtesy of the Washington D.C. Waste Management Department."

"Sewage?" asked Thurgood alarmingly.

"I guess you could call it that," said Huey nonchalantly.

"No wonder I'm feeling lightheaded."

"Don't worry, Mister Thurgood. A few more feet and you'll have nothing but clean air to breath."

Huey grabbed Thurgood by the arm and assisted him down the stepped hallway. Just as he promised, a few feet later they'd come to a door. Huey gave a knock consisting of several short ones with pauses haphazardly placed. Suddenly, the door opened, sliding into the wall and releasing a burst of clean smelling air from inside. Thurgood trotted in looking like he was about to collapse any moment. He knelt to the floor, breathed deeply and exhaled forcefully, like he was trying to breath out all the bad air.

As his senses returned, he noticed that the floor was carpeted. He thought, *what sort of place would be carpeted in a sewer?* Slowly, he lifted his head and looked around him. To his amazement he saw a host of people standing around him, staring at him as if he were some lower form of alien life. Most of them were Black and all of them were donned in white clinical jackets or camouflage combat uniforms. The ones in the fatigues had their guns drawn and pointed directly at Thurgood, who gulped down the lump of fear that had developed in his throat.

"At ease," said Huey, as he reached down and hooked Thurgood beneath his arm.

He lifted him up, the combat ready guards shouldered their weapons.

"Welcome to Shangri-La," said Huey.

Thurgood was still trying to deal with the methane he'd inhaled and the near death experience he felt with the guns being pointed at him. He eventually allowed himself to calm down, scanning the room and noticing that it looked like a laboratory. Slowly, he began walking down the aisle, his brow furrowed, perplexity grounded deeply into his expression. Glass walls were everywhere, experiments taking place in each one of them.

Thurgood pointed at one of the rooms where men dressed in shiny silver suits that covered them from head to toe were cautiously loading missile-looking devices into storage containers. The area was littered with nuclear hazard signs plastered all around. He turned and looked at Huey.

"Is that what I think it is?" he asked.

"If you are thinking those are nuclear warheads, you'd be right," said Huey.

Thurgood's eyes widened. "You guys have nuclear capability?"

Huey simply smiled, neither confirming nor denying the question. He extended his hand toward a hallway that veered to the right. "Let's get you into something a little more comfortable," he said.

Realizing that he'd left his apartment with little more than the shirt on his back, Thurgood nodded to the offer. However, he felt very uneasy about what he just saw. He knew that he was in no position to ask a lot of questions or that Huey wasn't the one whom he should be directing his questions to, but he had questions nonetheless and hopefully they would be answered when he spoke to Ramses.

He proceeded down the hallway, followed by Huey and a few of the armed guards. They passed a lot of doors along the way, some had strange noises coming from behind them, like someone was being tortured. Screams and shouts along with lashing sounds rang down the empty corridor. Thurgood felt a chill run up his spine. Was this something he had to look forward to?

When they reached the midway point, Huey stopped in front of a door. He placed his hand on the keypad and the sliding door opened. He walked in but Thurgood stood there until the guards motioned with their guns for him to enter, which he did reluctantly.

Nationhood

The room looked like something right out of a sci-fi movie. Exotic plants were in crystal vases shaped like planets, beautiful and colorful murals hung on the walls, futuristic furniture made of highly polished titanium were tastefully arranged, various colored lights illuminated the perimeter of the room and a huge aquarium filled with every color of tropical fish imaginable was embedded in the wall above the headboard of the bed. It was the most breathtaking thing Thurgood had ever seen and the look on his face was reminiscent of a child who was entering an amusement park for the first time.

"Ho...ly shit," he said with awe in his voice.

Huey looked at him, a pompous smile fixed on his lips. "These will be your quarters. I trust they are to your liking?" he asked.

"Very much so," Thurgood replied.

"Good. I'm having your dinner prepared. You and Miss Lela Washington will be eating in the dining room. That's when Ramses will speak to you." Huey pointed to a wall on the far side of the room. "There is a panel just ahead. Behind it are several closets filled with clothes of various styles and color. I trust you will find something to your liking. Feel free to try on as many as you like."

The guards began to file out of the room followed by Huey who stopped at the doorway. "You are our guest, Mister Thurgood. Please act accordingly," he said.

Thurgood took offense to the comment. "I'll try not to wipe my ass on the furniture," he replied.

Huey smiled once more, then left the room. The sliding door closed and Thurgood found himself alone in a room that was so extravagant that he didn't want to touch anything. Although there was plenty of room, the lack of windows coupled with the fact that he was probably miles beneath the earth's surface made him feel a little claustrophobic.

He walked to the aquarium and placed his hand on the glass. The fish didn't seem bothered by him at all and continued to swim without a care or a worry. He looked up at the lights. The beams were smaller than the point of a pen, yet they emitted a huge amount of light.

With his curiosity growing, he checked out the murals and the flowers. He sat in the chairs, touched the desks and jumping onto the bed. Everything seemed so foreign, but lavish, far from the lifestyle he was used to living. All his things were traditional or contemporary, made of

James Gordon

wood or some sort of compressed wood-like substance. But this, this was far more than what he ever dreamed of enjoying and it was even harder to believe that Exodus had the funds to furnish such a room.

It was then he remembered that he was to meet Ramses soon and join Lela in the dining room. He figured it was time to get dressed. He stood from the bed and walked to the far wall of the room, the one Huey had pointed to. There were no doors and the wall seemed completely solid. He pressed against the wall, thinking it was one of those pressure release panels where you pushed on it and then it popped open. He started off with a light push, which gradually turned into a full body press against the wall. Nothing happened.

Growing slightly frustrated. He began scanning the wall, finally seeing a light sensor just off to the left. He placed his hand over it and immediately the wall collapsed into sections, then disappeared into a compartment in the floor, which was then covered by a sliding door that matched the rest of the floor.

Shocked and amazed, he took a moment to let what just happened settle in his head. This place had more gadgets than Japan. When his astonishment faded, his eyes beheld a sight that was too fantastic to describe.

Behind the collapsed door was, for lack of a better term, a warehouse sized closet of garments all hung according to color, style, fabric texture and size. There were three aisles and four rows of clothes. The room was the size of a small department store and the aisles were wide enough for him to walk through without touching any of the articles.

Stunned beyond all logical thought, he gazed at the assortment of articles at his disposal. He took a moment to take in the sights, looking at everything with the same enthusiastic gleam in his eyes as a kid would have when he stared down the aisles in a toy store. Slowly, he walked down the first row, looking at all the suits, sweaters, shirts, jeans, and sport slacks. The next aisle was where the undergarments were. They had everything from socks to boxers to T-shirts. The final aisles held the accessories...ties, cufflinks, handkerchiefs, belts and watches.

Thurgood loved watches and his heart skipped a beat when he saw the selection. There were *Chopards*, *Blancpain*, *Vacheron Constantin*, *Audemars Piguet*, *Breguet*, and *Parmigiani Fleurier*. Although the *Chopards Super Ice Cube* was his first choice, and no wonder because the entire watch was covered with 66.16 carats, he

Nationhood

decided to go with the *Breguet*. Better to remain conservative, especially when this was someone else's stuff.

He found a nice pair of dress khakis, a blue Oxford shirt and a pair of *Tanino Crisci Italian Noslers*. He grabbed some cotton boxers, a white T-shirt, a belt and a pair of socks that matched the color of his shoes.

As he exited the closet, he saw the bathroom off to his right. He walked to the bed, placed the clothes neatly across it, then walked into the bathroom and began getting undressed.

After removing the last of his garments, Thurgood saw that a nice warm bath was already run in the Jacuzzi whirlpool bathtub. A nice thick layer of bubbles floated on the surface of the water, enticing him to come in and enjoy. He stepped into the tub, his body sinking beneath the water's surface, the warmth seeping into his muscles and stripping all the dirt and stress from his body.

He reclined against the side of the tub, allowing his head to rest inside the pillow-like headrest affixed to the rim. Bubbles erupted from the jets and pelted his body with massaging streams of air and water. Thurgood could feel his tensions drifting away. The soothing warmth along with the rhythmic jets of water quickly alleviated the tension that gripped his body earlier. The stench of the sewer was chased away by the fragrant aroma of the bath and he began to sink into a state of relaxation, forgetting that an attempt was made on his life earlier. For now, he was in paradise and he was going to enjoy it, even if it was short lived.

"Ah," he said satisfyingly. "Now this is the life. A brother could get used to this."

~~~

Carla was still grieving over the loss of Constable Al-Shahir. Although she'd ceased crying, her heart still ached, the pain increasing instead of seceding. She kept sighing through her mouth, feeling some relief from the building emotions in her chest and the welling of tears in her eyes. As long as she could keep exhaling like this, she might be able to keep it together—at least, that's what she thought.

Al-Shahir's body had been removed from the room, taken to the area where all the other bodies were. They were starting to stack up. Almost three dozen corpses lay in the darkened room at the end of the hall. The place was turning into a veritable morgue.

Although she wanted to look at him one last time, she was told not to go into the room and by the way they said that to her she dared not

181

violate those commands. Aside from being killed if she did, she didn't think she could handle the crushing emotions she would feel when she looked at the Constable's body as well as the rest of the unfortunate souls that had already died from the disease.

She sat on the floor, her legs curled to her chest and her arms wrapped tightly around them. She could hear herself whimpering, but she couldn't stop it. She was scared and grieving at the same time, a combination that felt worse than anything she could imagine.

Although Al-Shahir had given her another inoculation of the serum, Carla knew that it was only a matter of time before she was dead. The only difference was that she would not have anyone around to care for her when she died. She would outlive them all, watching them turn into blood-vomiting victims, dropping like flies one by one until she was the only one left. She wasn't sure if the Constable had done the right thing by giving her the shot. The horror she would certainly see would leave an indelible mark in her mind for the rest of her life.

Abraham opened the door and saw Carla sitting on the floor. He walked into the room and sat down beside her, carrying his camera in his right hand. He placed it on the floor. Carla did not look at him, but instead continued to whimper and stare straight ahead.

Abe reached for her, wrapped his arms around her shoulders, pulled her close to him and began rubbing her shoulders. Carla released a cry, her tears falling like rain, her moans resonating inside the empty room that now seemed more like a tomb than a conference room.

"Shh," Abraham said softly. "It's going to be all right. Everything's going to be all right."

"No," said Carla tearfully. "We're going to die, just like Al-Shahir did."

"No, we're not. We're going to make it. The government is going to find some way of dealing with this and we're both going to walk out of here alive."

Carla pushed away and sprang to her feet. She stared at Abraham with cold, terrified eyes. "Wake up, Abe! Look around you! The government isn't going to deal with this! We're all dead——you just haven't accepted it yet!"

"And I won't accept it, not until the time comes!" Abe fired back. "I have a wife and a child I want to go home to and I'm not about to give in to some damned virus!"

Nationhood

"You're a damned fool! You're living in a fantasy world!"

"Maybe! But I will not give up!"

The last words he said sounded familiar. They were the same words that Al-Shahir used before he died, the very words she repeated when she held him in her arms. She vowed that she would not give up and that she would keep on fighting no matter what. To hear those words again made Carla realize that she was allowing her fears to get the better of her.

She looked away from Abraham, staring blankly into space. A few moments passed and Abraham began feeling a little anxious due to the startled look on her face.

"Carla, you all right?" he asked.

"You're right, Abe," she replied softly.

"About what?" he said, his brow furrowing.

"We can't give up. We have to keep fighting. We owe it to the people who died to keep on fighting until this thing is done. I'd forgotten that, allowed my fears to mess with my head. I'm sorry I snapped at you."

She turned her head and gave him a look of gratefulness.

"Thank you for reminding me," she said.

Abraham smiled. You're welcome."

Just then, a commotion arose outside of the room doors.

"Damn," said Abe. "Must be another one dying."

He stood from the floor, brushed is hands across the back of his pants. He gave Carla a glance, then they walked to the door to see who the unlucky person was that would soon be going to the great beyond.

As they opened the door, Abraham and Carla saw guards racing up the hall. They stepped out of the room a little further and saw a man racing toward one of the exits followed closely by the agents.

"STOP HIM! DON'T LET HIM GET OUTSIDE!" screamed one of the men.

Suddenly, there was the rattle of gunfire. Carla and Abraham covered their ears with their hands, trying to block out the deafening pops of the semi-automatic weapons. The running man's body shook as the bullets ripped through him. Blood spurted from his wounds and he seemed on the verge of falling. But then, he made a huge lunge and crashed through the door. A burst of sunlight shined inside, blinding everyone in the hallway.

"GET HIM BACK IN HERE AND CLOSE THAT DOOR!" screamed one of the agents.

James Gordon

Covering their eyes, the agents raced up the stairs and grabbed the body of the man that lay prone on the ground. They quickly closed the door and dragged him back down the steps. One agent kneeled, checked his vitals, lifted his head and shook it. The lead agent looked perturbed, angrily grasping his communication device and lifting it to his mouth.

"This is zero-one-Charlie. We have the boggy but he did manage to break the seal to the outer perimeter, over."

The scratch of the walkie-talkie echoed down the hall. Then came a reply.

"Base to zero-one-Charlie. Information received. Prepare for code sandman."

The agent lowered his head, shook his fist angrily. The rest of the agents all had spooked looks on their faces. Slowly they turned to face the lead agent, continuing to stare at him with wild looking eyes.

"Did he say what I think he said?" asked one of them.

"Affirmative," replied the lead agent.

Carla continued to stare at the group, trying to figure out what was going on. But then, Abraham pulled her by the arm and yanked her back into the room.

"Abe," she said alarmingly. "What are you doing?"

"Shh," said Abraham, placing his finger in front of his mouth.

"Don't shush me, you almost yanked my arm out of the socket."

"Carla, will you shut up and listen. We've got to get out of here."

"Get out of here? What the hell are you talking about? We are quarantined. There *is* no way out."

"Then we better find one because if we don't we are going to be dead in a matter of moments."

A look of shock, puzzlement and fear coated Carla's face. "Abe, you're scaring me."

"Good, because your fear just might save your life."

"Quit talking in riddles."

Abraham attempted to gather his composure long enough to explain his frantic behavior.

"The conversation in the hallway, when the agent was talking on his communicator, remember that?" he asked.

"Yeah," Carla replied skeptically.

"The guy on the other end said prepare for code sandman, right?"

"Yeah?"

Nationhood

"What do you suppose that means?"

Carla pondered for a moment. "I really have no idea."

Abraham started becoming frantic again. "It means that they are about to exterminate us! The sandman... as in lullaby... as in putting us to sleep, permanently!"

Carla developed a wary look on her face. "C'mon, Abe. You don't think they'd really try to kill us?"

"That crazy idiot who ran outside may have spread the disease. We were quarantined, which meant as long as we were contained in this place we were not a threat. But now that one of us has tried to escape and potentially infected the rest of the population, the government isn't going to take the chance of someone else trying to escape, or jeopardize exposing this situation to the rest of the international community. They are going to kill us all and then probably destroy this building and blame it on terrorists."

Carla didn't say anything, shocked from the theory Abraham just laid upon her. But then she began to think about what he said. Could he be right? Was the government about to kill them all and cover it up by blaming this on terrorists?

A lump tightened in Carla's throat. She didn't want to believe her government would do something like that. But the more she thought about it, coupled with what she was told about the Illuminati by Constable Al-Shahir, the more she began to see that Abraham's suspicions weren't that far fetched. In fact, the idea sounded logical.

Carla thought back to the agents in the hall and the horror that covered their faces when the person on the other end mentioned the code. This helped to fortify Abraham's theory and the fear she felt earlier was suddenly increased exponentially.

She looked at her comrade with fear-filled eyes. "I think you're right!" she said. "What are we going to do?"

"Like I said, we need to get out of here," Abraham replied.

Abraham began scanning the room, looking for an alternate exit. As he walked around the perimeter, his eyes scanned the walls and the ceilings. There were no windows and no vents of which to crawl out of. There were no exits except for the one door where the guards were now standing in front of. The room was literally sealed off with no escape and no place to hide.

Feeling a sense of hopelessness, he stomped on the floor. The sound of a hollow echo returned from beneath his feet. He looked down at the floor intently. He stomped a couple more times, quickly zeroing in on the hollow area.

A beautiful Persian rug covered the spot of the echo. Abraham grabbed the end and pulled it back, revealing a trap door beneath.

"This is probably an electrical manhole or something like it," he said.

"An electrical manhole?" Carla quizzed.

"That's what I call them. It's the place where all the circuitry for this room and the other parts of the building are kept. We should be able to crawl down it and lay low until this thing blows over."

"But won't they find us? I mean, we both can't go down there. It was covered by a rug and if the agents come back in here and see the rug pulled back…"

"Yeah, yeah, you have a point. Listen, why don't you go down there and I'll find another route."

"Abe, I don't know. I mean, what if that isn't an *electrical manhole*? What if I go down there and find something else."

Just then, the rattle of gunfire was heard. It sounded like it was coming from the room where the other news crew teams were. Screams and shrieks, blood curdling cries and even loud booms could be heard through the walls.

Carla and Abraham looked at each other, fear permeating their pupils. Abraham reached down and grabbed the latch leading to the manhole. He pulled it open, revealing a shaft leading downward.

"Listen, we are out of time. I need for you to get down there and keep quiet. I'm going to cover you up and slide a table over this area. You should be safe."

"What about you?" asked Carla, concern woven into her voice.

"I'll find a way out. You just keep this with you," he said, pushing the camera toward her.

"No, you have to come with me."

"Carla, we don't have time for this. There's a good chance this virus is going to take me within the next twenty minutes anyway. You have the best chance of surviving this, seeing as the Constable gave you an additional injection. Now please, get down there and keep quiet."

Indecision was written on Carla's face. She looked down the hole and then back at Abraham. Another round of shots were fired and more

Nationhood

screams and bellows were heard.

"Go!" said Abraham.

With great reluctance, Carla grabbed the camera and descended down the manhole using the metal ladder attached to the side of the wall. Once she was halfway down, she stopped and looked back up at Abraham, who gave her a fearful smile. Then, he replaced the top and sealed Carla in darkness. She could hear the scraping of the rug being pulled back over the cover and then the rumble of furniture being moved around and positioned over her.

Carla resumed her descent down the ladder, feeling her way in the darkness, her feet testing the stability of each rung before she placed her full weight on it. After several more steps she made it to the floor, where she sat the camera down and knelt.

She began to pray, unlike any prayer she'd ever spoken before.

"Dear God, I know you're listening. I don't know what's going on or why this is being allowed to happen. But I'm scared, I'm really, really scared. I need for you to help me and Abe. Somehow we stumbled into something we do not know how to get out of. I don't want to die, I really don't. But if it is your will, please help me to accept it. Help me to embrace it with dignity and without fear. But if it is not our time to go, please help us with this. Please, help us."

She exhaled forcefully and allowed her back to rest against the wall. Suddenly, she heard the rattling of more gunfire, this time it was coming from overhead. She heard a loud scream and it sounded like Abraham, then a muffled thud crashed on the floor overheard.

Carla covered her mouth, fear instantly clutching the breath in her lungs. A slight whimper escaped her lips as her mind raced with the obvious possibility. Had Abraham been shot? Was that really his scream she heard and was that his body that fell on the floor?

Curiosity provoked her to climb back up the manhole and see if her fears were real. But she knew that if they were, she would have given his killers the opportunity to kill her as well. Logic prevailed and Carla remained curled on the floor burying her face in her hands. In the darkness, her fears were enhanced, her mind racing with thoughts of the unknown. Would they find her, and if they did would they kill her? How much longer could she remain in this manhole and how much longer did she have before the virus started to overtake her?

She felt herself losing it, her emotions starting to rip her sanity

James Gordon

from her mind. The darkness had thrown off her sense of direction. She didn't know which way was up. Vertigo began to play with her equilibrium, making her head spin. She felt sick and wanted to vomit. However, her deep breaths and the coldness of the floor helped to control her anxiety. As she regained her composure, she ran her fingers through her thick hair and turned her head in the direction she thought was up. She muttered another prayer.

"Please God, don't let them kill Abe," she said.

~~~

It didn't take Reverend Aziz long to get a line back to the states, especially since he was calling from Senator Pollins' personal phone and was using the emergency access to get through. He called the main line that would have connected him to Ramses, but was told that the leader of Exodus had already left. He now sat waiting on hold as the operator attempted to ring Aziz through to his personal line.

Meanwhile, Pollins sat behind his desk with an anxious look on his face. Already the proposed bill granting President Landau DeVeaux authority to declare war on the US had been rushed to the senate floor and most of the remaining senators were in favor of it. They simply needed to cast their vote. When that happened, the coalition of nations, along with the entire nation of AUNK, would declare war on America and potentially begin the third World War.

Just then, one of Pollins' aides entered the room. He stopped at the door as the Senator and Reverend Aziz turned to look at him.

"Pardon my intrusion, Senator, but there's a man in the hallway who said he needed to speak with you," said the aide.

"Have him make an appointment," Pollins replied.

"He told me that if you said to make an appointment, he said to tell you that, and I quote, November would have one hell of a rain."

Pollins eyes became full with recognition, for he knew who his visitor was. He stood from behind his desk, then turned to Aziz who was still on the phone.

"Will you excuse me, I won't be but a moment. If you happen to get Mister Ramses on the phone, please have him wait for me," he said.

"Certainly," said Aziz.

Pollins walked with the aide out of the room, down the hall and to the waiting area where Clarence Bolo was sitting patiently, his hands braced on the handle of his cane, which he only used for show. When he

Nationhood

saw Pollins, he stood to his feet, extended his hand to the senator. They both shook.

"Elijah, good to see you again," said Clarence.

"My old friend. This is an unexpected pleasure. Won't you step into my study," said Pollins gesturing toward a room just off to the right. He then turned to the aide and said, "That will be all. Keep an eye on the good reverend, would you?"

The aide bowed and walked back toward the office.

Inside the study, Clarence looked around at all the paintings and the African decorations that filled the room. He nodded in approval as he strolled to one piece of artwork in particular, a perfect rendition of the first day Blacks returned to their home continent after their departure from the United States. Tired people of color marched from the Atlantic Ocean and into the welcoming arms of every African tribe on the continent. The piece was called *Home At Last*, and was the official national artistic piece of the nation.

Clarence's eyes seemed to well with tears as he stared at the mammoth picture, his chest swelling with pride. Pollins walked to his side and stared with equal pride at the mural. He, too, seemed moved as the two men stared at it for several moments in silence.

"Never ceases to inspire me," said Clarence finally. "No matter how many times I see this piece it always stirs my soul in a way I can never describe."

He exhaled, biting his bottom lip to contain his emotions.

"Yes, I found myself looking at this same piece no more than a day ago. It helps me to keep things in perspective," Pollins added.

"You know," said Clarence turning away and taking a few steps. "I'd often wondered what would have happened to us as a people had we not returned here and created this new nation. Perhaps we would have drifted abroad like nomads, living off the good graces of other nations for our survival."

Pollins turned and faced his friend. "I believe that was the subject of your thesis when you were studying for your doctorate at New Kemet University, was it not?"

Clarence nodded agreeably. "Ah, yes. Seems as though my mind forgets these things at my tender age."

"Tender would not be the word I would use to describe any part of you, old friend. You've always been one of the toughest dogs in the

189

James Gordon

fight and one of the smartest men I've ever known, which is why I'm most intrigued by you being here. Certainly you've heard about the bill I've proposed to the President?"

"Indeed. Which is why I decided to drive down here instead of calling you. Elijah, I've never been one to meddle in political affairs and in return you and the senate have allowed myself and my nephew to aid the government in anyway they needed. I've always trusted the minds of each of the men and women who were nominated to the senate, for I knew that without trust in one's government, there is sure to come chaos, anarchy and the eventual coup d'état. You must know this first and foremost."

"Your patriotism has never been questioned, Clarence."

"Good. That's good to know. Unfortunately, I must ask whether this current course of action is necessary."

Pollins seemed bothered by the question. "Why would you ask such a thing?" he retorted, walking closer to Clarence.

"Because I do not believe the repercussions of this course have been evaluated. To risk war with the American Empire is to risk everything our people have struggled to attain."

"Would you have us sit idly by and let the Americans poison our people and destroy us with their diseases?"

"No, but you do know there is another way to combat this form of terrorism. We don't even know if the Americans are the ones responsible for all of this."

"Oh, come on, Clarence! Of course the Americans are behind this! They've been trying to infiltrate our government for the last twenty-five years, sending spies and trying to create sanctions against us when we wouldn't accept their form of aid! Had it not been for our plentiful oil supply and the ability to create clean alternate sources of energy for our people which, might I add, has benefited ninety percent of the global populace, we would have fallen like so many other nations have who tried to be independent of both the UK and the US!"

"I understand all of that. You will remember it was my organization that caught most of the spies and potential infiltrators. I know well the oppositions our nation has faced. Which is why I'm coming to you. There's something about this that doesn't make sense."

"Like what?"

Clarence walked to the wet bar and poured himself a drink,

Nationhood

brandy. He lifted the carafe as a gesture to pour Pollins one, but the senator waved it off. Clarence sipped his brandy, then walked back toward his friend.

"Just last night, the Americans tried to kill one of their own people, a spy who was sent here to steal the Romanian jewels," said Clarence.

"I know about the attempted heist. Remember I was the one who told you about it," Pollins replied.

"Yes, but did you know the spy was none other than Katura Ishtar."

Pollins seemed stunned by the info. "Are you serious?"

Clarence finished his drink, winced as the brandy burned the back of his throat.

"I am very serious," he replied.

"But that doesn't make any sense. Why would they kill their top spy?"

"That, my dear friend, is the question. We've been trying to get that bit of info out of her for the last couple of hours."

"You have her?"

"Yes. You could say Mbaku helped her get away from her would be killers."

"Then you must turn her over to the government. She must be placed under arrest."

"Hold on, Elijah. No good would come if I were to do that. Besides, she is feeling a little scorned and wishes to have a little revenge on the people that tried to kill her."

"She's willing to work for us?"

"For the time being. She's one of those individuals who work for herself and her own purposes. In any event, back to my question."

"Yes, why would they try to kill her?"

"I'm guessing it is because she knows something they don't want anyone else to know."

"A plan or some code perhaps?"

"Just what I was thinking. When she heisted the diamonds, Mbaku managed to chisel away one of the smaller diamonds. Vee ran a check on the diamond and found that it wasn't a diamond at all, but instead a very sophisticated crystal."

"A crystal?"

191

"Yes. But this wasn't an ordinary crystal. Located inside was a series of letters which, when unscrambled, turned out to be part of a formula."

Pollins looked puzzled. "What kind of formula?"

"We don't know. But I'm guessing that Ishtar does."

"Then why not ask her?"

"Because she wouldn't tell us if she knew. However, I don't believe she does. I figured the best way to get to the bottom of all of this is to get the rest of the diamonds in order to get the rest of the formula. Mbaku and Ishtar are on their way to the embassy to retrieve them now."

"They're back at the embassy?"

"Yes, odd that they would take the crystals back there. Anyway, Mbaku and Ishtar are on their way to get them."

"You sent her with him? What if this is a trap?"

"That's a chance we'll have to take. Besides, Vee is watching him via sky link. If anything goes wrong, Mbaku and Vee know what to do."

"So, what do you think this formula is?"

"If I'm right, it could be the antidote for this accursed virus. Did you know who Ishtar's adopted father was?"

"Nope. Should I?"

"And you call yourself a senator," said Clarence with his tongue in cheek.

"Can you just tell me?"

"Durst Weinkaufen."

Pollins thought for a second, realizing the name sounded familiar. Then, like a light bulb was turned on, he remembered. "Wasn't he the nuclear bio-physicist, the one who found a cure for cancer?"

"Indeed. Now, how much of a coincidence do you think it would be that the adopted daughter of the man who found the cure for cancer and a virus strangely similar but infinitely more aggressive than cancer would be in the same country at the same time?"

"Remote."

"Now you know why I'm here."

Pollins rubbed the back of his neck. "So, where does this leave us?" he asked.

"All I'm asking is that you buy me some time. Give Mbaku and Ishtar the chance to regain the jewels. Let us see if we can stop this virus without endangering the lives of our citizens and our people still enslaved

Nationhood

in the US."

Pollins exhaled deeply. "I wish I could help you, my friend. But the bill is already on the floor and the votes should be complete any moment."

Clarence placed his hand on Pollins' shoulder. "If you could find funding to open the nuclear research plant when AUNK was nothing more than grass huts and bamboo fields, I know you can stall your colleagues."

Pollins laughed. "I hope you're right about this."

"So do I. Now, I must be going," said Clarence.

Just then, the aide who was with Pollins earlier came to the door. "Excuse me, Senator, but Reverend Aziz has Ramses on the phone."

Clarence stared at the aide and then at Pollins, who simply smiled.

"Ramses, as in the leader of Exodus?" asked Clarence.

"Come, let's go talk to him together."

The two men walked toward the door and followed the aide up the hall and back to Pollins' office. Inside, Aziz had placed the call on the speaker system and he was having a very lively conversation and chuckling. When Pollins and Clarence entered the office, Aziz turned to them, braced his hands on his hips.

"Ah, the Senator has returned," he said.

Pollins walked to his desk and addressed the speaker. "Mister Ramses?" he asked.

"Senator Elijah Pollins. It's an honor to be speaking to you," Ramses' voice replied.

~~~

James Gordon

Chapter Thirteen: Zero Hour

A beautiful citrine sunrise broke across the distant horizon in the east. The place known as the Babylonian Marshes were some of the most scenic spots in all of AUNK. It was five-thirty, ante meridiem, long before the rush of early morning traffic and the hustle of another business day. Although it was located within miles of the major roadways, you would never know you were any where near the city due to the proliferation of natural beauty saturating this location.

Seemingly far removed from the rigors and torrents of the nearest metropolis, this sweet, secluded spot was the perfect getaway for anyone who needed a break from the concrete jungle. Serene was the oasis-like setting, a picturesque cornucopia of greenery and exotic flowers, the likes of which grew only in the moist, tropical climate of the marsh. Everything was still and quiet, except for the distant trumpeting of the elephants and the cry of herons that were lounging near the eastern banks.

This oasis was the result of the revolutionary fertilizer that was created when the nation of AUNK was in its infancy. Countries that had turned their backs on the Black race lent no assistance in providing food for the huddled masses that returned to the continent of Africa. Realizing that they would gain no help, the people used various minerals and the dung of animals to create a fertilizer that turned the harsh, dry sands of the desert into fine, fertile soil that produced some of the best produce anywhere.

The lush swampland was one of the places that benefited from the ingenuity and resourcefulness of a people who had nowhere to turn and nothing to barter with. It was a source of pride for the nation's citizens, which is why the crisis involving the virus was such a sore spot for the ones trying to find the antidote.

Crouching atop the roof of a building near the inlet to the city's main river, Mbaku and Katura peered through binoculars at a very old, but distinguished-looking mansion that sat just off the marshes a little over a mile away. A cool breeze blew the morning air into their faces and a sweet scent of fresh water tantalized their olfactory senses.

James Gordon

Mbaku was anxious, his mind racing. He knew better than anyone what the consequences were for failure. Already his country had suffered and the odds were that before this ordeal was over many more would suffer. He thought about the families of the murdered senators, how they mourned and grieved, totally unaware of the events that were unfurling. He also thought about the people still held at the airport, wondering how much longer they had before the virus took their lives as well. It was difficult for him to stomach the fact that the very people responsible for all of this were in the building he spied upon.

Although he was a man who could normally push aside his pain at a time like this, he had to admit that right now he found it difficult doing that. He grew even angrier over the fact that he was unable to detach himself emotionally. Mainly his irritation was because this was the first time his country had been so openly and viciously attacked.

There was no cover up, no covert activity that kept the country's integrity intact. This attack was performed out in the open, in plain view of the international community. It was an act of sabotage, a ploy used to break the spirit of his nation and bring its people into subjugation. That bothered him more than anything.

It took a long time to raise the pride and spirit of his people, longer than he even realized. Now, as he and Katura Ishtar prepared to launch a counter assault and raid the terrorists' stronghold that just happened to be on his country's soil, Mbaku's objective grew darker in purpose and more vicious in potential execution.

His mind was already made; there would be no survivors. He would go in, retrieve the crystals and slaughter every single person inside the compound. No compromise would be shown and few words would be spoken. Even Katura's counsel would not be tolerated and he was prepared to kill her if he needed to. Despite the fact that she was ambushed and double crossed by the very people inside the mansion, she was, first and foremost, a spy, which meant, like him, she could not be trusted.

For now, he would keep his eye on her, allow her to play her part and see where her loyalties lay. He removed the binoculars from his face, allowed the morning breeze to dry the perspiration from around the areas where the eyepieces rested.

"How many do you count?" he asked.

"Seven," Katura replied. "However, I am getting thermo readings on the inside, perhaps nine more."

Nationhood

Vee had the lines of communication open and Mbaku's communicator was live. She chimed in with her input. "She's correct, Mbaku," she said. "I'm picking up the same thermo readings. I'm a little surprised that they took the diamonds back to the embassy mansion."

Mbaku remained silent. He didn't want to give away the fact that his earpiece was broadcasting their every move and conversation. He looked at Katura, who now removed her binoculars and studied the area without so much as a blink of her eyes. He examined her for a moment, remembering how quickly she'd revived from the injuries she sustained. He had to admit she was a medical marvel, but she also made him uneasy. If there were more like her, it could cause potential problems should the American Empire decide to try their espionage tactics again. He had to know more, find out all he could about her.

"So, how much of you is enhanced?" he asked.

She turned her head, flashed him a glance that displayed her perplexity in him asking such a question now.

"You do realize there may be surveillance detection equipment nearby?" she asked.

"If it is, they're probably already aware we're here. So answer the question."

She turned to look at the mansion once more. "I've had visual and audio augmentations, strength enhancements, sinus and oral sensor upgrades."

"Anything else?"

"Nothing you need worry about."

"Just wanted to know what I'm working with. You could show a little gratitude. In my country it is considered to be quite flattering," said Mbaku with a flat tone.

Katura exhaled deeply, bowed her head slightly. His words made her remember something. He did help save her life and she felt badly for her behavior just now. Katura was not good with showing her emotions, particularly since she never had to do so before. Being cold and distant were the tools she used to keep people at bay. She didn't allow anyone to get too close because doing so made things uncomplicated, simple and painless.

However, she came to see that she could, at least, show some manners to Mbaku. After all, he was the one who helped her get away, whether she wanted to admit it or not. She lifted her head, turned to face

James Gordon

him, a look of uncertainty cloaking her features.

"I want to thank you for saving me. Gratitude isn't something I'm good at showing," said Katura.

Mbaku almost didn't want to accept her gratefulness. But he knew what she meant because he was exactly the same way. He nodded his head and said, "You're welcome. Gratitude isn't something I'm used to getting."

Katura smiled. "Yes, we do have thankless jobs, but you can't beat the adrenalin rush."

"Sometimes I'd like to."

Katura pruned her lips, then turned to look through her binoculars again. "Ever thought of settling down, raising a family?"

"Yeah, I've thought about it," Mbaku replied.

"Wendy's a nice girl, would make a real good wife."

Mbaku turned and looked at her, scanned her from top to bottom. He was a little put off by her comment, bothered by the fact she knew there was something between he and Wendy. She must have seen something when Wendy was giving her a check up. But he couldn't think of what that was. He tried to be careful and not place Wendy in harms way. But somehow he'd slipped, and now this cunning woman knew something about him, something that could come back to haunt him if he should ever find himself at odds with Katura.

He was about to say something when he noticed her symmetry. She had a strong, tight body, her black fatigues hugging every curve and dip. She had the figure of a model and a warrior, someone who knew how to use her shape for more than just fighting. She was a woman, and being such he knew that she would not hesitate to use her feminine charms to get an advantage. Yet he could ill afford to discredit her fighting abilities. He heard about her casualties in the embassy, after she stole the crown jewels. Bodies were found all over the place and it left the consulate very uneasy. She'd also done a number at the docks, bodies she left scattered all over the pier and a scene that was reminiscent of a war zone.

Mbaku quickly summed up her strengths. She could swoon the average man into a love-struck daze, then kill him with a cobra-like strike in the very next instant. He admired her deadly beauty, entranced by the dangerous pleasures he envisioned. But then, he quickly regained his senses and remembered she was off limits. She was like a delicious sundae that made his mouth water, but was tainted with a poison so lethal that

Nationhood

looking at it too long could kill you. He turned away, attempting to reclaim his focus on the mission and becoming angered by his temporary loss of concentration. He decided to comment on her statement about Wendy, hoping to disarm her theory about their relationship.

"She's a friend. But, yes, she would make a fine wife," replied Mbaku.

"You sound so robotized," Katura said playfully.

"What about you? Ever think of starting a family?"

"Nope."

"Never?"

"Nope."

"Not even with that Thurgood guy?"

Katura's shoulders dropped in disgust. In her mind Thurgood was just someone she might consider playing with. She would toy with his emotions, get whatever she needed from him and then drop him like a bad habit. That was the sacrifice she made for being in the line of work she was in. It was a lonely existence, but perhaps when all of the bad guys were killed and the world was a safer, gentler place to live, maybe she would consider the probability of perhaps settling down.

She lowered the binoculars, flashed Mbaku a blushing smile, then lifted them to her face again.

"Maybe," she said.

"Was Jaquimo ever able to get in contact with him?" Mbaku asked.

"No. For some reason the tracer card I placed on him was left at his apartment. Jaquimo did some checking and found out that he might be in some trouble. Reports indicate he is wanted for questioning about a car bomb that exploded in midtown D.C. The car was registered with the state department, had a couple of passengers in the vehicle when it was turned into an impromptu bonfire."

"How are they linking that bombing to him?"

"They were on their way to question him. Their last radio transmission said they were chasing him in another vehicle. Shortly after that, the feds were turned into crispy critters."

"You think he did it?"

"No. I think he was set up but I don't know by whom. I just hope it isn't who I think it is."

"Who do you think might be behind this?"

"Some very bad people."

Just then, Vee chimed in on the communicator. "I'd watch the idle chatter if I were you," she warned.

Mbaku's mouth twisted into a semi smirk, a little embarrassed that his comrade had been listening to the conversation and bothered because he had more questions to ask. But Vee was right. This wasn't the time or the place to be conducting a conversation of this level. He would continue this discussion some other time. Right now he had to get back into focus.

Seconds later, two men exited the mansion and walked onto the patio.

"They're doing something," said Katura quietly. "Two of them just came out of the mansion."

"Gotcha," said Vee in the communicator to Mbaku.

"Let's move," he said.

The two assassins slid from the roof and lowered themselves to the ground using hooks and fishing line cable that extended from their wrist pulley devices. Once they were on the ground, they raced through the marsh like swamp foxes, making no sound at all and barely moving any of the camouflaging vegetation.

They made their way to the outer gates of the compound, ducking behind a huge column of cement that resembled the rook on a chessboard. From their vantage point they saw a partial view of the entire mansion. It was enormous, larger than what either of them remembered, probably because it was now daylight.

The thermo-optic sensors in Katura's eyes switched on and she saw the entire layout in infrared, detecting the small details that would have been missed using normal sight. Three guard dogs rested near the far side of the enormous brick patio, Dobermans, one bred with a wolf and the other two normal. Their heartbeat was slow and they showed no signs that they detected their presence. They could thank the wind for that, for it blew away from the mansion, placing them downwind and thus avoiding the canines' sensitive noses.

Katura scanned around the area, in the trees above and the surrounding grounds, checking for anything unusual or potentially harmful. She saw some smaller heat patterns in the nearby brush, probably creatures of the marshes lounging on the duckweed, lily pads, reeds or cattails, basking in the morning sun before the savage heat drove them into

Nationhood

the water to avoid being burned alive.

She switched back to normal sight, the redness fading into the normal color of the surroundings.

Mbaku watched her the entire time. When her eyes went infrared, they actually had a hue of crimson in the sclera, giving her the look of a vampire or some other hideous demonic creature he'd seen in the movies. Nonetheless, it was an impressive gift, one he would have to discuss with her at a more appropriate time.

"So, what did you see?" he asked.

"Dogs," she replied flatly. "Three, near the back patio. They haven't detected us due to the wind."

"Any more guests that we need to attend to?"

"Not inside, but you already know that."

"By chance did you detect any heat patterns in the surrounding woods?"

"Small blips, probably some wetland creature."

Mbaku nodded, seemingly satisfied with her answer. He then swiftly removed a four-inch hunting knife that was attached to his left shin and flung it into the brush. An agonizing grunt resonated and was followed by a thud and a splash. Katura looked in the direction of where Mbaku threw the knife and then back at him.

"Guess they know we're here," she said. "But how did you..."

"Africa looks out for her sons and daughters. The land spoke to me, told me where they were."

"Spoke to you," Katura replied disbelievingly.

"Let's move," said Mbaku.

He leaped into the air and scaled the outer wall. Katura was impressed by his prowess and followed without hesitation. They hit the ground running, racing toward the house like bandits. The dogs had now caught their scent and were rounding the corner of the house at full speed, barking and showing their fangs. They were followed by the guards toting their guns in firing position and trying to keep up with the Dobermans.

Katura removed some throwing stars called Shurikens from her belt and launched them at the advancing guards. She caught each of them in the throat, slicing their necks open and causing splashes of blood to shoot out. They quickly crumbled to the ground and attempted to stop the copious bleeding, but their efforts would be in vain.

Katura and Mbaku continued on to the mansion, the dogs now

James Gordon

closing in. Realizing they could not outrun the beasts, Mbaku dropped three grenades on the ground, and he and Katura leaped onto the porch. As the dogs drew closer, the grenades released a potent sleeping gas that stopped the dogs in their tracks and forced them into a state of immediate unconsciousness. As Katura made it to the door, she glanced back at the slumbering dogs, a smile faintly appearing on her lips.

"That was humane of you," she said to Mbaku with a passing comment.

He said, "No need to kill the dogs when they are only doing what they've been trained to do. Besides, it's their masters I want."

They broke through the front door and were met with a rain of bullets. They each went in different directions, drawing some of the gunfire toward them. Their actions were quick, their reflexes sharp and perfectly executed. Katura removed her Sais that were lodged inside holders fastened on both sides of her thighs. She ducked and dodged, avoiding every shot of the automatic weapons, moving with the grace of a ballerina and tempered with the determination of an assassin.

Her first strike caught her victim in the throat, a full lunge resulting in her weapon's tip braking through the back of his neck. She retracted her Sai and swiftly delivered a roundhouse kick to his face, knocking the gunman to the ground like a sack of potatoes.

Her next victim was the recipient of multiple strikes, her Sais slicing his throat and puncturing his lungs, stomach, liver, various sections of his intestines and finally finding his heart. His body quivered from the rapid succession of stabs that rivaled the firing of his automatic weapon. He slumped forward, collapsing in her arms. Katura clutched him close, using his body as a shield as she charged toward the other men that were firing at her.

Meanwhile, Mbaku had pulled out his .44 Smith and Wesson Magnum and a pearl handled Wildey Gas Action Auto with an 8-inch barrel. His shots were deadly accurate, nailing his targets with lethal one-shot hits and propelling their bodies through the air like leaves caught in a violent updraft. He managed to kill six men in under ten seconds, stopping for an instant to survey the chaos.

His eyes rested on Katura crouching on the far side of the room. She was pulling one of her Sais from the chest of a dead agent and rising to her feet. She looked at him, rage and bloodlust evident in her eyes and scrolled in the scowl on her face. She was getting even for the pain they'd

Nationhood

caused her and Mbaku realized in that instant why she used hand-to-hand combat as opposed to merely shooting them like he was. She wanted to feel their life being taken with her own hands, witnessing the horror in their eyes when they saw that even with the finest weapons they could buy and equipped with all the best training the government could supply, they still weren't good enough to stop her. Their attempt on her life was simply the metaphorical act of them chiseling their epitaph across their tombstone.

Mbaku holstered his Wildey, but kept his Magnum in hand. "Are you okay?" he asked.

Katura turned her head to face him, nodding with a degree of uncertainty, almost like she was deeply satisfied with her actions but horribly disturbed that she could perform such deadly viciousness with ease. She slung the blood from her Sais, then slid them back into their holsters. She walked over the bodies she's stacked on the floor and proceeded down the hallway.

Mbaku tapped twice on his communicator, his way of signaling Vee. She heard his comment and her equipment alerted her to the change in Katura' heart rate and biorhythms. She said, "Be on your guard. No telling what she could do in her state of mind."

Mbaku didn't answer. Instead, he followed his comrade down the hallway, taking care to be extra alert. By his count they'd killed eleven men, which meant there were five more to go. If he'd calculated the situation correctly, which he did most of the time, the rest were guarding the crystals, probably held up in a room where they were being stored. But there was another danger that needed to be considered; Katura. There was the real chance that she could snap, attack him and leave with the crystals, an option he knew was just as real as her giving them to him. His only hope was that she wouldn't betray his trust, however little that trust may be.

She crept up the hall like a cat on the prowl, taking well-placed, cautious steps and scanning the area for traps. Her eyes shifted sharply to the left. A bust of someone unfamiliar sat on a Greek styled pedestal against the far wall. She moved toward it, still taking careful steps. She arrived at the bust, checking it over like a curator examining a piece of artwork.

Mbaku moved toward her, glancing at her but continuing to scan around him for signs of other agents. He came to stand next to Katura, who was spellbound by the sculpted head.

"What is it?" he asked.

"This piece has heat residue patterns, like someone placed their hands on it. I'm thinking this is some sort of keypad that activates a hidden doorway. But there are booby traps on it. It also has a coating that helps to cool the heat signatures, making it hard for me to see just how to activate it," said Katura.

Mbaku removed an aerosol can from his belt and sprayed it on the face and head of the sculpture. He then removed his lazar scope and shined it on the bust. Instantly Katura could see the pattern and mocked the placement of her hands on the head and face. Seconds later, a huge panel opened on the wall next to them and a massive corridor was revealed.. With surprise, the two assassins looked at each other, then proceeded into the hallway.

Once they entered, the panel closed and now they were cloaked in darkness. For several yards they took it slow and easy, shuffling through the darkness like blind folks, refraining from using any light for fear of giving away their position. Katura used her night vision enhancements while Mbaku placed a like pair of goggles over his eyes. They froze in place when they heard what appeared to be a thundering boom.

"Did you hear that?" Katura asked in a whisper.

"Yes," Mbaku replied.

The sound repeated itself over and over, like a cadence or...

"Footsteps," said Katura.

Frowning, Mbaku asked, "Are you sure?"

"Yes. We need to move, now."

She began trying to find a place to seclude herself, but the corridor had no place to go. The footsteps grew closer and closer, shaking the very foundation they stood upon. Mbaku listened intently, trying to make out if the sound he heard was indeed footsteps. He looked at Katura, who now had a slightly frightful look replacing the near euphoric expression she donned when she killed the agents in the foyer. Her behavior was odd, acting more like a cornered and fearful beast instead of the merciless killer he knew her to be.

Then, he saw something in the distance, it's movement matching the boom of the footsteps. Mbaku could see something, the outline of something huge. Tiny beams of light broke the darkness, shining through fissures in the hallways roof. He stood there watching, his mind trying to

Nationhood

make out what was coming toward him.

Katura steadied her stance, shifting her weight from one foot to the other. She'd removed her Sais and twirled them in her hands like an anxious gladiator waiting for the lions to be released. Seconds passed and her anxiousness grew. She backed up and was even with Mbaku, who now stared at her with bewilderment.

"What is it, Katura?" he asked.

"He's coming," she replied.

"Who? Who's coming?"

She shook her head. "Why. Why did they have to bring him?"

"Katura, what are you talking about?"

Just then, the footsteps stopped, and a blood-curdling roar resonated in the arched hallway. Mbaku covered his ears, as did Katura. The roar was like a cross between a battle cry and a bellow of agony. A thunderous boom shook the ground and parts of the corridor crumbled and fell, opening a hole in the roof. Light from the outside shined into the darkened hallway, finally revealing what had been concealed in the shadows.

A hulking creature possessing human qualities stood before them. He towered several feet in the air and leered at the pair of assassins with utter disdain.

"What the hell is that?" asked Mbaku.

"This is what I'm fighting for," Katura replied. "This is what the US government does to the indentured servants. They use them for experiments, turning them into these creatures and then sending them out to do their bidding. He was a friend of mine, someone I thought had been killed a long time ago. It wasn't until recently I learned what they did to him. His name was Cho."

She slid her Sais back into their holsters, stepped closer and extended her hands out to her sides.

"Cho, it's me, Katura. Do you remember me?" she asked.

The creature, whose face was deformed and twisted, snarled at Katura, causing her to stop her advancing. A low guttural growl was released and his hands opened and then closed into fists. Mbaku cocked the hammer on his Magnum. Katura heard up her hand.

"Don't," she said. "I'll handle him. You just need to get passed him and retrieve the crystals. Let me take care of Cho."

"Are you crazy?" Mbaku retorted. "That thing is three times your size. You could be killed."

"No," she said, shaking her head. "I know what I'm doing. Besides, this is how we IS handle our disputes. Now, when we commence battle, I want you to take off down the hall and retrieve the diamonds, understand?"

Mbaku lifted his gun and pointed it at the beast's head, who turned and gave him a menacing sneer.

"No!" Katura insisted. "He is mine! Let me handle this!"

Mbaku debated for a moment, uncertainty etched in his expression, unsure of what to do. Then, acting against his better judgment, he un-cocked the hammer and lowered his gun. He glanced at Katura, whose eyes stared unflinchingly at her massive opposition. "Are you sure?" he asked.

"Absolutely," she replied.

Cho released a deafening roar, lifted his fist in the air and drove it down towards Katura's location. A fraction of a second before it would have struck her, she dodged to the right, causing the monster's blow to miss her completely and crashing into the floor of the hallway, sending mounds of rubble into the air. As she regrouped, Katura looked over at Mbaku. His eyes were wide and filled with astonishment. For an instant his fear had gotten the best of him, freezing him in stunned disbelief.

"GO!" she exclaimed.

His face snapped and he quickly came to his senses. He shot her a quick glance, then raced passed the creature who was now getting ready to throw another punch at Katura. His mind was reeling with the thought of what he'd just witnessed. Incredible as it may seem, he never thought he'd see a being as massive as Cho. However, he also realized that he could not allow himself to be distracted from his objective. His mission could not be impeded. Katura seemed sure she could handle the over seven-foot tall monster. He, on the other hand, had to get the crystals so the antidote could be created. Only then could the people of AUNK be saved from total annihilation.

Katura was now face to face with her old friend. She didn't want to fight him, but understood that if she couldn't reason with him she would have to.

"Cho, don't you remember me? It's Katura," she said.

The beast growled, possessing a look in his eyes that indicated he was about to attack any moment. Then, as if a light switch had been

Nationhood

flipped, he seemed to have a moment of clarity. Katura's voice triggered it. He looked at her, his eyes showing a hint of remembrance. There was a familiarity in her face, the soft lines of her beautiful features recognizable. Yes, he did remember her. He leaned closer, got a better look at the stunning, honey-colored woman before him.

"Ka-tur-a," he said hoarsely.

"Yes, Cho. It's me."

"Ka...tur...a."

The pain in Katura's heart from seeing her friend like this grew worse. She remembered Cho when he was a happy and enthusiastic young man, so full of life and hope. Like her, he was an IS. However, unlike her he believed that one day he would be free of his enslavement and that his indentured status would become a distant memory, a nightmare that would fade over time. *How wrong he was*, she thought to herself, looking at the monstrous figure he'd been turned into.

She stared into his eyes, seeing the compassionate, gentle being that lay just behind the grotesque exterior.

"What have they done to you?" she asked with pain embedded in her voice.

"Ka...tur...a," Cho replied. "Friend"

A comforting smile bloomed across her lips, happy that he did, indeed, remember her. "Yes, Cho. I am your friend."

"Ka...tur...a?"

"Yes?"

"Cho...hurt. Cho...in pain."

His words instantly brewed a powerful anger in her chest. Whoever did this to him was causing him anguish, hurting him more than they'd already done. In that moment Katura realized what she needed to do. She had to get him out of there. She had to save her friend from whoever was hurting him.

"Let me help you," Katura replied. "I'm going to get you out of here."

Katura was about to reach for Cho's hand when he suddenly grabbed his head, clutching the sides as if someone was sending a bolt of electricity through his brain. He bellowed in pain, squeezing his temple areas and grimacing.

"No hurt!" he yelled. "Cho no hurt!"

With his last scream, he returned to his primal and incoherent

207

state, growling at Katura as she slowly began backing away.

"Cho, fight it! Don't let them take control!" she screamed.

But the beast was far from rational. He slammed his fists onto the floor, snarling and becoming more volatile by the moment. Katura continued to shout her friend's name, but the influence of those who controlled him was now absolute. He grew hostile, his murderous intent written in his scowling face.

Realizing she was left with no alternative, Katura readied herself for the worst. She understood what was happening. The individuals who were hurting Cho had now caused him to revert to a destructive, wrathful monster who could no longer determine right from wrong. It was clear that she would either have to fight her friend or die by his hands. With reluctance, she removed one of her Sais from the holster and prepared to defend herself. With saddened eyes, she made one request.

"Forgive me, old friend," she said.

Meanwhile, Mbaku continued his race up the hallway. As he rounded the corner, he quickly slid to a stop. Standing before him were the five remaining agents, all armed with automatic weapons and each of them pointed at him. A sudden burst of gunfire exploded and Mbaku quickly ducked back into the connecting hallway. As he removed his guns from their holsters, he realized that not all of the bullets missed him. One had nicked him on the leg, nothing severe but it was burning like hell. He checked the cylinder of his .44 and the magazine of the pistol. Three bullets were left in his Magnum and five were left in his Wildey.

Just then he heard Katura moan and then the sound of a thunderous boom. *The beast must have gotten her*, he thought. He wanted to go back, but knew that wasn't wise. He had to take care of this first, had to get the crystals before he did anything else. He could hear her release another moan and another thunderous rumble shook the floor. His attention was then interrupted by one of the five agents that waited around the corner.

"You can come out now," he said. "There's no where for you to go. I assure you your death will be quick."

Just then, Vee chimed into Mbaku's communicator. "The creature is beating Katura. My sensors indicate she's badly hurt. You have to help her," she said.

"Vee," Mbaku replied. "I'm pinned down. There are five agents standing between me and the crystals. You know that's my mission. I have

Nationhood

no time to play savior."

"Come out!" screamed the agent. "I will count to three and then we are coming after you! One!"

Mbaku tightened his grip around the handles of his guns. "Time to go down in the history books," he said.

"Two!"

"Mbaku, what are you doing?" asked Vee.

"You'll see." He stood up, bracing his back against the wall.

"Three!"

"All right!" Mbaku screamed. "Hold your fire! I'm coming out!"

He rounded the corner, initially acting like he was going to give up. Then he raised his guns and fired five shots in a nice tight pattern. Seconds later, five dead agents fell on the ground. He ran toward the doorway at the far end of the hall, the one they were obviously trying to protect. As he turned the knob, he heard a click which made his stomach instantly nauseous.

"God, I hope that wasn't what I thought it was," he said.

"Mbaku," said Vee. "Get out of there now! My system is telling me you just activated a bomb! It was a set up! Get out of there!"

At the other end of the hall, Katura was fighting with everything she had. But Cho was just too strong. In his enraged state, he only wanted to kill, which Katura was trying not to do to him. If there was a chance to bring him back to normal, she wanted to take that risk. But she had to survive the beating she was now taking. She'd sliced his body, stabbed the non-lethal places on his torso in hopes of incapacitating him for a while. Nothing seemed to work. His adrenaline was blocking out all the pain, making him nearly unstoppable.

He swung at her again, this time she dodged the blow. The same thing happened with his subsequent attacks. She leaped out of harms way, allowing Cho to hurt himself as his punches and lunges caused him to collided into the walls and floors of the corridor. He swung again, this time his hand embedding into the side of the hallway. When he jerked it loose a piece of rubble smashed into Katura and nearly knocked her unconscious. Cho turned and slowly moved toward her. He released a loud growl, lifted his hand in the air and prepared to deliver the deathblow.

As Cho was about to secure his victory, Mbaku hustled toward the hulking monster. He began firing the last of his rounds at the creature, backing it up as he raced toward a nearly unconscious and battered Katura.

James Gordon

The beast stumbled away, allowing Mbaku to kneel beside Katura, scoop her in his arms and race toward the entrance they came. Cho immediately followed, his thundering steps shaking the ground and causing Mbaku to stumble slightly as he ran. Somehow he kept his footing and soon arrived at the sliding panel. He tried to find a button to push that would open it, but there was nothing.

The mammoth Cho was now in a full charge, his head low and his feet pounding the ground like a drum. Mbaku turned and face him as Katura's limp body began showing signs of life once more. He would normally be amazed at her swift recovery if he didn't have a nearly five hundred pound human rhino bearing down upon them.

With nowhere to go, Mbaku waited for the final impact. But just as the creature closed within mere feet, Katura reached up and touched the wall with her hand. As if she was the woman with the magic touch, the panel slid open and Mbaku wasted no time racing through the doorway as it closed immediately behind them. Seconds later, the loud crash of Cho colliding with the other side could be heard. The panel split and was almost broken in half by his impact.

Mbaku raced for the exit, trying to get out of there before the entire place exploded. As he reached the foyer and leaped over the dead bodies, Cho broke through the panel and was now in the main hallway. He quickly located the fleeing assassins and raced after them, grunting and salivating as he ran. Katura, who'd now regained some of her faculties, raised her head and saw the behemoth closing in. Seeing that severely hurting him was the only way they were going to get away, she removed her last Sai from the holster, clutching it tightly in her hands.

"Keep running," she whispered to Mbaku.

Now mere inches away, Cho reached out and was about to grab Mbaku by the head when Katura reared back and lunged the point of her weapon into the right eye of her one-time friend. Cho abandoned his chase, grasping his eye and bellowing in pain. Mbaku reached the front door and crossed the threshold just as the entire mansion exploded into an eruption of fire, smoke, hurled bricks and wood.

The two of them fell to the ground as their bodies were pelted by debris. A shower of wreckage fell and the mansion, which was so stately and beautiful, was gone. Clouds of smoke rolled into the sky and the shockwave from the blast leveled the outer effects of the yards. The roar of the blast faded into the winds and soon only the crackle of the fire was

210

Nationhood

heard.

Katura lifted her head and looked around, amazed that they'd made it out of the mansion in time. She saw the devastation and wondered how they hadn't been killed. However, there was no time to think about this. They needed to get out of there before the authorities arrived.

Her eyes looked around and found Mbaku. He was lying still, faced down on the ground. She crawled toward him and shook him. He did not respond. She checked for a pulse in his neck. It was weak, but, at least, there *was* one. Using her augmented strength, she lifted him up and threw him over her shoulders, lugging him away in a fireman's carry position.

As she reached the perimeter of the yard, she stopped to look once more at the remains of the mansion, remembering her friend and perhaps hoping that Cho had somehow survived. She was heartbroken to see what had become of him, how the government had turned him into a monster to serve their vile purposes. But then, she realized just how selfish her hope for his survival was.

Although she knew that the thought she now had was cruel, she found herself hoping that he was dead. At least he would no longer be in pain and the people who'd experimented on him couldn't hurt him anymore. One day, she would find the people responsible and make them pay for what they did. As for now, she had to get Mbaku and herself out of there.

She kicked down the remnants of the fence and stepped over the rubble. Moments later, they disappeared into the marshes as the sound of elephants trumpeting resonated in the distance.

~~~

211

James Gordon

Chapter Fourteen: The Seeds of War

With his luxurious bath complete, Thurgood was now in the process of getting dressed. He slid on the khakis and the oxford shirt as well as the Italian shoes that fit his feet like a glove. He made the necessary adjustments, slid on the *Breguet* watch and walked to the door.

The panel whirred and slid open. He entered the hallway feeling refreshed, but no more at ease. There was a lot going on, more then he realized. Right now he was in, what he could only imagine, the bowels of one of Exodus' compounds. He was surprised by what he saw. The place looked like something off one of those Sci-Fi movies where the people all lived underground in sterile-aired environments eating foods grown in some form of hyperbolic chamber.

His steps echoed in the barren corridor, giving him an eerie feeling. His eyes scanned around him, looking for the cameras he knew had to be around somewhere, spying on him and watching to see if he was going to do something stupid. Oddly, he could find no such devices, which he thought to be quite peculiar. Surely a place like this had to have security. Perhaps the technology was so advanced that he could not detect it. They had to have the kind of cameras with lenses the size of pin needles, he thought. Couldn't image Exodus having anything less than the best.

He made his way to the end of the hall and the open bay where all the experiments were taking place. He stood there, trying to absorb all he could. *This was amazing*, he thought. All of this and right under the government's nose. What made this even more appealing to him was the fact that most of the people in here were Black. The scientists, the guards, even little Black children were here. It was unlike anything he'd ever witnessed before, seeing all this progress and all of it being done by his people.

If only his mother could have seen this, he thought. She was a strong woman and had often spoken about how Blacks used to work together and how they were able to do so much back in the day when her great-grandmother was alive. There was pride in the community and there was a sense of family regardless if you were kin or not. People looked out for each other and made sure to watch each other's backs.

But over the years, greed took over. Black people became more interested in making money, having cars and doing whatever they could to get ahead. They'd forgotten the teachings of the motherland, to maintain the village and make sure it was safe for the entire tribe.

Drugs infected the community and the civil leaders kept looking to the government to police the streets and make their neighborhoods safe. But the law and the government were the ones polluting the community, selling guns to the dangerous people as well as the drugs and telling the weak-minded that it was okay as long as they were keeping to their own kind.

The children of the sun were a lost tribe for many years, decades even. Some even cursed their own people by making fashion statements of derogatory slang that further oppressed the spirit of a once proud and regal people. Many leaders were slain, while others simply gave up and joined the ranks of those who simply looked out for themselves.

For years, Thurgood believe that the native residents and descendants of Africa were a doomed people, destined to wander the earth without a home or a purpose. But now, standing in the hallway and looking at the progress that was made despite the hand of oppression, he felt more proud than ever and more ashamed that he never knew that the struggle hadn't been abandoned, just modified.

Just then, Huey approached. Thurgood snapped out of his euphoric daze and smiled.

"This is magnificent," he said "So many of our people are right here working together for a single cause. It's the most uplifting thing I've ever seen."

Huey smiled. "I'm glad you approve."

"I never knew all of this was going on. I simply thought most of us were still indentured or were scrounging around trying to stay alive. I never expected to see this."

"We each have done our part. You fought for the freedom of the people on the surface, trying to end the oppression that has haunted our native brothers and sisters since the day our continent was invaded by outsiders. They called us primitive and spoke about us as if we were uncivilized and uneducated. They do not realize that ages ago we were building temples and erecting monuments that still stand to this day and are mocked by the very government that raped and defamed our people. The Washington Monument was a direct rip off of the obelisks in Egypt. The pyramid graces the back of the one dollar bill. Even our speech and our style have set trends over the history of this country. And yet, our rights and freedoms are taken away simply because someone went to court and won a lawsuit. Amazing how things happen."

"Yes, quite amazing."

"But I guess our God works in mysterious ways. Had it not been for that simple act of discrimination, we would not have formed Exodus and none of this would exist. We would still be a lost people, foraging through the trash and leftovers of a race that still refuses to acknowledge our existence and our contributions. There is no place we can go without ridicule. Russia, Germany, Spain, France, even England. We are not welcomed anywhere. Our people have constantly been oppressed, beaten, murdered and mistreated. The moral majority will claim that we should stand up on our own two feet and rise. They have a point. But now that we have risen to our feet, they want to tear us down. However, we have become too strong and the mistakes of the past will not happen again."

"You're quite the orator, Huey. You know there was another brother who went by that name who was just as opinionated as you are."

"Yes. He was one of many who tried to warn our people of the horrors to come. Thankfully, some of us listened."

"Perhaps I could have a tour?"

"Certainly. But I would have thought you would've preferred something to eat first."

"You're right. I am a little hungry. Is Lela around?"

"Right here," her voice resounded from behind.

Thurgood and Huey turned to address her.

"Hey there," said Thurgood as he walked toward her and gave her a hug.

"You okay?" she asked.

"Good. I'm good."

They released each other.

"I heard you were shot at?" Lela continued.

"Yeah, but thanks to Huey, I'm fine."

Lela inhaled deeply, shaking her head ever so slightly. She looked as if she was going to cry any moment.

"This is too much, Thurgood. I can't take this. All this cloak and dagger bullshit, people hijacking our car or having meetings with you on the plane. I was in the middle of a bath when these Exodus people burst into my apartment and pulled me out of there, saying I was in some kind of danger. I can't do this anymore."

She was becoming emotional, her eyes watering with tears. Thurgood pulled her close, wrapping his arms around her like a protective brother.

"It's okay. We're safe now," he said with an assuring tone.

Lela pulled away. "How can you say that? We don't know these people! They could kill us for all you know!"

Thurgood looked at Huey, who seemed bothered by her comment.

"I can assure you, Miss Washington, no one here will harm you," he replied.

Lela shot him a bitter glance. "And I'm supposed to believe you?" she fired back.

"If not them, who?" Thurgood interjected.

Lela's eyes eased back to Thurgood, giving him a wary look. "You aren't actually thinking about joining these people?" she asked.

Thurgood faced the bay filled with people. "Look around you, Lela. What do you see?"

Her eyes drifted across the room quickly. "A lab."

Thurgood laughed. "You know what I see? I see our people doing something that hasn't been done in over fifty years. We're actually working together, in unison. Striving to make our lives better and the lives of those still in bondage free. These people are risking everything to ensure there is a future for Black people. They're the ones busting their asses while we do our part to help overturn the laws that have placed our people back into bondage. I see a community embracing the very core values that all descendants of Africa hold dear, and that is looking out for the tribe. I see promise and I see progress. I see achievements that have blown my mind and opportunities that have yet to be capitalized upon. Yes, I see all these things. But to answer your question, yes, I can see me joining the struggle, joining the movement, joining the community."

Lela stood in shocked revelation. With his words, Thurgood showed her that there was more happening here than mere work. There was a purpose being fulfilled and a dream being reborn. She stared out at the people, her people, and for the first time she saw them in ways she

Nationhood

hadn't envisioned since she was a little girl.

All her life she'd been raised in the environment of Jack Crow, where Blacks were treated as inferior beings and only worthy of respect when they were released from IS status. But now, she saw free men and women, free brothers and sisters, fighting to regain their independence and putting in place the safeguards to protect that freedom once it was regained.

The sight reminded her of the time when she used to dream of being a doctor. She used to tell her mother that one day she would become the best neurosurgeon the world had ever known. But reality struck when her mother died and the bills from her funeral caused her to spend a brief and uncomfortable period of time as the indentured servant of a woman who made her clean her home. The embarrassment of being placed in such a belittling position and made to feel she was nothing emptied her dream into the wastebasket she emptied every night. For three years she was this woman's handmaiden, her slave, a thing she used whenever she felt like it, all because of the color of her skin.

That was two years ago. A tear welled in her eye. She folded her arms across her chest. Looking out on the people that hustled in a more respectful manner made her see a glimmer of the dream she once had, a glimmer she hadn't seen in a while and thought she'd never see again. Perhaps, she began to think, that dream could be resurrected.

Huey removed a handkerchief from his pocket and handed it to her.

"Perhaps we should move to the dining room and have some dinner," he said.

"Yes, I think that would be best," Thurgood replied as he placed his arm around Lela.

They began walking down the hallway and toward the place where they would eat as the clattering, clanging and chattering of the dedicated brothers and sisters of Exodus continued behind them.

~~~

Carla was scared, curled on the floor of the electrical manhole fearing the worst for her friend and co-worker, Abraham. Earlier, she heard shots fired when he secured her in this compartment and covered it to ensure she would not be found. Since then, she heard additional pops, which she could only assume came from gunfire. Her mind was abuzz with terrible thoughts, but sitting in a place that now seemed more like a prison

217

cell than a hiding place she knew there was nothing she could do.

It was quiet most of the time. Occasional she'd hear a scrapping sound, the kind that reminded her of something being dragged across the floor, slow and scratchy. It sickened her when she heard it, made her wonder who'd died. She even began to wonder whether it was her mind playing tricks on her, that perhaps what she heard wasn't that at all and that maybe it was something else, like rats scurrying inside the walls or a wire shorting out. Oddly, those explanations were more acceptable than her initial thought. Even though she didn't like rats or the thought of some sort of electrical explosion happening while she was in this confined place, it was less disturbing than thinking that someone had been killed.

But at this point she couldn't be sure what to think. In fact, she couldn't be sure about anything. She's been in this dark and musky hiding place for some time now and that alone could create unbelievable distress. It could also create a degree of madness, which Carla felt was slowly consuming her. Her mind would settle on different thoughts, dreadful thoughts, the kind of thoughts that allowed terror to grip her chest like a vice and nearly suffocated her.

She would realize that her fears were getting to her and the only way to counter them was to stay focused and be prepared for anything. She asked herself questions, thinking that her mental exercise was just a form of preparation, trying to think of things before they happened. What if they found her down here? Would they kill her? Would they do something else to her? What could she do to be ready for them if they did find her? When would they find her?

Soon, Carla found out that her attempts to prepare were doing more damage than her fears. Her anxieties were getting the better of her and she decided to try and relax by closing her eyes and sitting motionlessly in complete silence. It was something her yoga teacher used to make her do as a result of the panic attacks she had when she was a teen.

But instead of calming silence, there were humming and whirring sounds all around her. Ironically, the noise seemed more of a comfort than a distraction, easing some of the tension after a while, like a note or a song that was continuously being played. Her shoulders relaxed and her mind drifted. She felt her anxiousness fading and the tension lifting from her mind and body.

She allowed her thoughts to drift to a calm and peaceful place,

Nationhood

like Liberty Park, which was a massive recreational area located in the middle of the city of Independence. Larger than Central Park in New York City, Liberty Park stretched for over three miles in each direction and was filled with trees and plants of all varieties.

Carla recalled the times she went there as a child. Her parents would take her there on Sundays. She and her other family members consisting of cousins, aunts and uncles would meet and have an impromptu family reunion. It was a fun time in her life and she loved the memories she had there.

In the center of the park was an observatory where visitors would be able to see clear images beamed down from the Hubble telescope. The dome-shaped room would be transformed into a planetarium as laser-sharp images of space were displayed on the walls, ceiling and floors. She loved going there because when the show commenced she felt as if she was floating in space, like an angel looking at the grand universe that God had created.

The area also had a theme park with rides, games and the best food around. Her favorite was the mammoth carousel called Safari, which had life-sized animal replicas that you had to climb up a ladder to get on. Tigers, lions, zebras, elephants, giraffes, gazelles and hippopotami were among her favorite. They even moved like the creatures as she whirled around the disc-shaped platform.

Just as she was starting to settle, Carla heard a thump or a knock on the floor above. Her body jerked, her chest tightened and a knot of anxiousness constricted her throat. She waited like a panther preparing to pounce. After a few moments had passed she slowly loosened her tightened body and attempted to calm down.

As she attempted to relax once more, she tried to revisit the peaceful memories of her childhood. But the knock she heard had caused a degree of anxiousness that now kept her on alert. She couldn't get herself back to that serene frame of mind. The noise had brought back the more recent and troublesome memories of why she was down there. The status on Abraham was also on her mind. She wondered if he was still alive, and if he was how was he doing? Had he finally succumbed to the virus that was killing everyone or was he suffering alone?

Her thoughts were scrambled, unable to focus on anything in particular due to either the rebuilding stress or fear. She couldn't be sure what the dominant emotion was because clarity was beyond her grasp.

James Gordon

Uneasiness was her constant companion as she clutched the camera that Abe had given her like it was her life's blood. She began to wonder what would become of her. Would she die in this restricted compartment? Was it her fate to end up a soiled and rotting corpse found years later by some electrician who came down here to change a circuit, only to find her decomposed remnants clutching the very camera in her arms?

She shuddered to think of such a thing. Yet, the possibility of that happening was very real.

The circuit boards were humming with tons of current, causing an increase in temperature inside the small, confined space of the manhole. With the latch above sealed and covered, the humid air had nowhere to go.

Carla loosened her blouse and allowed it to drape open. Growing tired of holding the camera, she laid it on the floor, allowing her arms some reprieve from the developing cramps. The warm air was beginning to lull her to sleep. She rested her head against the wall, right between two control switches. She could hear the slight hum of the electricity, felt the gentle wave-like tremors in the wall. It was just like a tender massage, vibrating ever so slightly. She closed her eyes, allowed her mind to drift. It was quiet, very quiet and still.

Upstairs, nothing was moving and nothing was making any noise. Only the drone from the circuits surrounding her was all she heard. Soothing, calming, casting a dreamy spell over her, pulling her into the comforting arms of slumber.

In her state of relaxation she thought about Al-Shahir and what he did for her. With his remaining strength, he injected her with the remaining dose of the vaccine. It all happened so quickly that she didn't know what he was doing until it had already been done. He could have kept the vaccine, used it on himself to increase his chances of making it out of here alive. Instead, he gave it to her, hoping that she would survive long enough to reveal the truth about the people who were truly responsible for all of this.

It was all right there on tape, on the very camera that lay next to her.

She couldn't help wondering what it would have been like had she and Al-Shahir met under more favorable circumstances. Would he have been as charming, as alluring, as gentlemanly as he was today? Why did he really give her the vaccine? Did he know he was going to die and that using it on himself would have done little good?

Nationhood

Then again, perhaps it was because he truly like her, cared for her and wanted her to be okay.

The thought puzzled her, messed with her head. It was beginning to make her crazy, forcing her to remember other things she tried to dismiss from her mind, like the sight of him dying in her arms. She never felt so helpless and angry in all her life. Why him? Why did he have to die? What did he do to deserve such a fate, to have to face death on a cold hard floor bleeding profusely and suffering immensely? It wasn't fair, not fair at all. He was a good man and he deserved better than what he got.

She opened her eyes, allowed her senses to come back from the depths of her subconscious and into the realm of reality. Slowly, she looked at the camera and thought about the information it held on its videotape. Ironically, the information it recorded caused the deaths of everyone that died here today. This seemingly insignificant piece of electronic equipment was the source to all the problems she currently face. The idea angered her, made her want to pick up that camera and smash it into a billion pieces.

She stood to her feet suddenly and snatched up the camera, lifting it over her head and readying herself to drop it and watch it break. But then, like phantoms screaming from the shadows, she heard voices, voices that sounded just like Abraham and Al-Shahir.

"Carla," said the voice of Abraham. "What are you doing?"

"Abe?" she replied.

"Think about what you are doing, my love," said the voice of Al-Shahir.

Carla became panicky. She heard them, she actually heard them, just as clearly as if they were standing next to her. It made her wonder if she was going even more crazy. Their faces floated through her mind and she recalled how they both gave so much to protect her and the information on the camera.

"I don't know what to do," she said sobbingly. "So many people have died...so much needless death. I can't handle this. It's too big for me."

"We believe in you," said Al-Shahir. "You must stay strong. You must hold on for a little longer."

"But it's so hard."

"Yes, it is," said Abraham. "But we are with you. You must not allow our killers to escape judgment. Hold on, Carla. Hold on for just a

221

James Gordon

little longer."

Their voices faded, and a moment of clarity dawned on Carla. Thanks to Abraham's last words, she now knew what she needed to do. It was very simple, actually. Releasing this information would bring the people responsible for this nightmare to justice, or would, at the very least, reveal to the world their identity. It would also be a just and fitting homage paid to the memory of the two men who saved her life by forfeiting their own. They paid dearly for the exposure of this information, made sacrifices to ensure this was aired. To smash it would be to spit on everything they died for.

They were real men, heroes, not cowards. They faced death even though they knew there was a chance the information they sought to expose would never see the light of day. However, their convictions made Carla see something else. They believed in her and that belief gave her the strength to go on. Gradually, her resolve was being restored and she now knew she could not allow her faith in herself to waiver again. Too many lives were riding on her slender shoulders and she had to remain strong for the sake of her people and her nation.

But there was a bittersweet message in the conversation she just had. Hearing Abe's voice gave her the realization he was no longer alive. The hope he'd survived was dashed and he'd become another casualty, an innocent victim who fell prey to the actions of the terrorists who orchestrated this attack.

Tears rolled down her cheeks and her breath shuddered. In a matter of one day she'd lost two very influential people in her life. Abe and Al-Shahir gave their lives for this information and for Carla, believing that she would do what was best and that somehow she would find a way to get this information to the right people. She was known for doing that; Al-Shahir so much as said so when they spoke. Abe even confided his belief in her when all of this started. He said she was being strong and that he admired her for that.

But now, as she lowered the camera from over her head and trembled with the urge to drop it to the floor and watch it explode into shards of debris, another thought entered her head. She wondered whether to crawl from inside this manhole and take her chances or stay inside and wait for something to come looking for her. These were her choices and neither one of them sounded appealing.

Her lip trembled. She knelt to the ground and placed the camera back on the floor. She wiped the tears from her eyes, still feeling confused and emotional. She wanted to break something and somehow release the anger and resentment that had built inside her heart and soul. She needed a release, this much she knew, something to help her refocus and get her head straight. Regardless, it had to be something physical. Once she did that, she might be able to figure out her next step.

With one quick move she lifted her hands and slammed them against the floor. An echoing rumble resonated. Her palms stung, but the pain was cathartic. It cleansed her, made her senses tingle and forced out some of her anguish.

"I will not stay here like a coward. It's time to leave this place," she said.

She was about to pick up the camera when she thought of a better idea—leave it here, protected inside the confines of this secluded spot. This was her proof that bad people had done bad things and she understood that she had to guard this information at all costs. This was her way of thanking Abe and Al-Shahir for the sacrifices they made and the contribution they'd given to the people of AUNK. For certain, this videotape was a prize that would be sought long after her death and she could not let it be destroyed, no matter what.

After removing the tape, she slid it between two insulated pads that lined the floor panel. Then, she placed the video camera along the wall. She grabbed the rung of the utility ladder and slowly began climbing to the top of the manhole. All the while she kept asking herself, was she being smart leaving this place or was she succumbing to the fear that made wise and resourceful people irrational? Common sense would suggest she stay in the manhole and wait for someone to come. But who knew when that would be. She could be there for days or weeks before anyone knew she was down there. Her best chances were outside in plain view. That way if something were to happen to her, at least she would be found.

Carla made it to the top. The door was secure, but there was an inside latch which she grabbed and cranked to the right. Whatever Abraham had placed over the door was weighing it down. She strained as she pushed upward, taking care not to allow her feet to slip or it would be a nasty tumble to the floor below. She managed to ease the door open slightly, feeling the weight of whatever was on top of it starting to shift. The light shining inside was dim, which indicated that the lights had been turned off. With a grunt she gave one hard push. The door flung open as the sound of tumbling furniture resounded.

Panting heavily, Carla emerged from the manhole, then dropped on all fours as she attempted to regain her strength. Her head hung low, feeling like a pendulum that had lost its momentum. With a sigh, she looked up and did a preliminary scan of the room. The lights were off, but at the far side for the room she could see the light from the hallway.

She stood to her feet, feeling a slight degree of joy from being freed from her pit-like cell. She closed the trap door, then proceeded to the entrance on the far side of the room. She took a couple of steps, then tripped over something lying in the darkness on the floor. Carla fell hard across whatever it was that caused her to trip. The air was knocked out of her, but she soon scrambled to gather her senses and get back to her feet. Her hand rested on the item that caused her to fall. She frowned. It felt lumpy, almost like…

She stood again in a rush, her heart racing and her mind consumed with fear. Slowly, she continued to make her way toward the doorway. Whimpers escaped her mouth as she shuffled her feet across the ground, feeling more and more of the lumpy obstacles in her path. She couldn't make out what they were, but she feared the worst. Using her feet to feel her way, she finally made it to the door, circumventing the objects until she was standing in the entrance to the hall.

Next to the door she saw the light switch. *Did she dare*, she asked herself.

Carla turned her back toward the path she'd traveled. With trembling hands, she placed her fingers on the switch and flipped it up. The lights came on in waves, totally illuminating the room. She almost didn't want to look, but her curiosity had gotten the better of her. Cautiously, she turned to see that what she'd feared was indeed the case. Bodies, dead bodies, lying on the floor, bloodied and still.

She almost vomited on the spot, bending over and retching violently. After a few moments, her breathing returned to near normal. She stood upright and looked at all the corpses that filled the room. There had to be at least sixty to seventy of them. This explained the dragging noises she heard when she was in the hole. The room had been turned into a morgue, housing the bodies of all who'd fallen victim to the virus.

Their remains were still fresh, hadn't begun decomposing yet.

She immediately fled the room, racing into the hallway and covering her mouth with her hands to avoid throwing up. She made it

Nationhood

halfway up the hall before collapsing to the ground on her knees. The image of all those bodies was embedded in her mind, disabling her ability to think. There were dozens of them. She didn't even remember that many people being in this place. Her whimpers turned into sobs, which echoed in the barren hallway. She was close to hysterics, unable to control the feeling of horror that was overtaking her entire being.

As Carla fought to hold on to her rapidly diminishing sanity, the clop of footsteps could be heard. They went virtually unnoticed by her until the image of a man could be seen walking up the hallway. His stride was labored, almost as if he were in pain. Carla finally saw him, he was about twenty feet away. Her fear grew even more, wondering if this person had come to kill her. She struggled to get to her feet, bracing her hand against the wall in order to stabilize herself.

"You're not going to take my life!" she yelled in a low roar.

The approaching man stopped. "Carla?" he asked.

The voice sounded familiar, too familiar. She thought for a moment. No, it couldn't be. "Abe?" she replied.

The man took two more steps and stood under one of the overhead lights of the hallways. Carla's eyes widened as her friend, Abraham stood staring at her.

"Abe, is that really you?" she asked.

"Yes, Carla, it's me," Abe replied.

She ran to him, hugging him tightly around his neck and laughing in a near hysterical, but greatly relieved, manner. Abe returned the favor, holding Carla close to his body; their embrace lasting for minutes. Carla released a river of tears, thankful that her friend was still alive.

"I thought you were dead. I thought they'd killed you," she said in a muffled tone.

"No, I'm okay," he replied.

She pulled away and looked at him with wild eyes and spoke in a frantic tone.

"Abe, the bodies in that room. There's dozens of them. Those people are all dead..."

"Yes, they are," he interrupted with a solemn tone. "They're all dead."

"Yes. I know. None of those people are alive..."

"No, you don't get it, Carla. Everyone is dead. The agents, the other news teams, everyone is dead. You and I are all that remains."

James Gordon

Her eyes displayed the shock her mind could not handle. She was overwhelmed by the news that she and Abe were the only people left alive in the entire facility. Her body stiffened and an icy chill raced down her spine. Abe saw her difficulty handling the news. He placed his arm around her and began guiding her down the hallway.

"C'mon, let's get you something to eat," he said.

~~~

Chapter Fifteen: Napalm Sunrise

The food was delicious. They had everything; lobster, steak, crab and shrimp. There was filleted fish of all kinds; cod, whiting, catfish, salmon and trout, just to name a few. Chicken was grilled, baked, fried and stewed. Vegetables were steamed to seal in the flavor. Snow peas, corn on the cob, succotash, collard greens and several stews with thick liquors of broth or tomato sauce were kept in warmers as the steam swirled slowly from inside. Cakes, pies, pastries and an assortment of ice cream were set on a different table. It was a feast fit for a king, a banquet that could feed more than the two people who it was intended for.

While eating, Thurgood couldn't help but think to himself how scrumptious everything was. He and Lela had multiple plates in front of them and each plate had a sampling of everything. But while they consumed their meals without so much as a word, a conference call was made, one that connected Thurgood with a very secret, yet powerful conversation, a conversation involving Pollins, Clarence, Aziz and Ramses.

They'd finished their meals and now Lela and Thurgood sat before holographic images of all the distinguished members. Their faces possessed deadly serious expressions, their eyes showed glimmers of anger. Each one of them was a man of strength and purpose, and there was no more meaningful discussion than the one they were about to have.

Ramses had just been given the news about the virus. His response was nothing short of rage. His feelings were mirrored by Pollins.

Moments before, the president of AUNK signed the order to declare war against the United States. Troops were being recalled and planes were being prepped. Jets were having their pre-flight checks performed and bombers were having their payloads coordinated. Battle ships were being stocked and readied. Long-range missiles were activated and satellites were beaming down pictures of the air force and navy bases located on American soil.

It was 4:00 PM. Three days had passed since the IS Victor Johnson released the virus at the airport. Intelligence was being delivered

James Gordon

from all regions of the world. Every single nation who'd been at odds in one form or fashion with the American Empire was now making a donation of some sort to the movement. Countries in South America, the Far East, the Middle East and in Europe were on standby, waiting for the nation of AUNK to give the signal and commence the attack.

Pollins was pleased by the response, but there was still one more piece to be placed. He turned and looked at Ramses' image on the viewer.

"Brother Ramses. I'd like to make a request of you," he said.

Ramses leaned forward, smirking, his interest piqued by the powerful senator's statement.

"What is this request?" he asked.

"I request that Exodus begin its assault on the major cities of America."

Upon concluding their meal, Thurgood and Lela had been watching the ramp up in the coalition forces as well as the various communications between the heads of state in all the aiding nations. The entire nightmare unfolded like a well-written novel, both of them too shocked to utter a single word. Lela sobbed quietly, covering her mouth with her hands and trying to contain her remorse. She was upset because she knew the pain and suffering this war would bring. Although the entire situation seemed too unbelievable for words, the last sentence spoken by Pollins almost made Thurgood choke. He stood up abruptly and addressed the three-dimensional images.

"You can't be serious!" he exclaimed.

They each turned to look at him like he was standing in the room with them.

"Is there something you'd like to add, Mister Thurgood?" asked Pollins.

"Yes, there's something I'd like to add!" Thurgood shot back. "This is a mistake! You can't just send your troops into war against the United States simply because a virus was released on the populace of your country! You don't have any proof that the Americans are responsible!"

"We have all the proof we need," said Pollins. "They sent over the IS Victor Johnson and contaminated our people with a virus so lethal it could kill us all if it were ever to reach the outside world. Right now we have it contained in the conference building at the airport. There it will remain until we either force the Americans to give us the antidote or we find a cure ourselves."

Nationhood

"Just because the IS was a carrier of the disease doesn't make the United States responsible! Did it ever occur to you that there might be other entities involved, like shadow players who are attempting to orchestrate this entire ordeal?"

"His conspiracy theory does have merit," said Clarence. "Perhaps we should explore the possibilities a little further."

"Clarence, don't tell me you are going to let this American lapdog sway you to side with him," said Pollins.

"I resent that comment!" said Thurgood.

"Dully noted," said Pollins.

"He echoes what I tried to tell you when I arrived, Elijah," said Clarence. "Mbaku is currently trying to retrieve the crystals, which potentially holds the antidote inside its shells. If we can only give him time…"

"Time?" interrupted Ramses. "Time is all we've given these bandits of humanity, Mister Bolo. For eons, America and those of their ilk have stripped our people of our riches and our dignity. We were never a people who provoked war. We were creative and industrious, powerful and majestic. Now look at us, reduced to groveling servants who struggle everyday to survive."

"I lost three friends," said Pollins. "Three good men who only loved their country and tried to bring a degree of acceptance for our nation in the global climate. Now, they rot in a morgue while those who put them there roam free and unpunished. The Americans drew first blood in this war, my friend, not us. But this time, the oppressed and the mistreated will not turn the other cheek for them to slap that also. This time, we take back what was rightfully ours and we will show a level of strength that will be unrivaled on this planet."

"Gentlemen, please," Thurgood intervened. "We sound like a group of thugs planning to rob a convenience store. They did this and they did that. Aren't we supposed to take the higher road and call a summit to discuss the matter?"

"And what good would that do?" Ramses asked. "We've tried that route before, remember? We marched on Washington and New York, and Montgomery and Little Rock. We protested and rallied, shook our fists in the air and laid our lives on the line. All it did was cause the truly powerful to scrape some scraps on the floor for us to nibble on and distract us from the real atrocities they were performing."

James Gordon

Thurgood was about to fire back. "Listen, Ramses..."

"No," Ramses retaliated. "You listen, Mister Thurgood. We deserve more than scraps. We deserve respect. But no one is ever going to respect us unless we stand up for ourselves and do what we must in order to gain that respect. No being or entity of power could ever respect someone or something that comes to them asking for permission to do anything. Only those who challenge the norm, who challenge the establishment, only those individuals will gain respect and be treated as an equal and as a human."

"We as a people should never have to have legislature that grants us voting rights for a period of time," said Pollins. "Do they have such legislation for Whites? No, they don't. Do they have Whites as indentured servants? No, they don't. Yet, with all the contributions we as a people have made to this world, our American brethren are still treated like children asking the evil task master for permission to do something that should be their God-given right to do."

"But still," Clarence interjected. "We should appeal to our higher selves as a nation to approach this issue with diplomacy and intellect. To rush into war could be more damaging than any of us think."

Just then, the aide who was with Pollins earlier came back in. He made a beeline to the senator and passed him a folded note. As he turned and left the room, Pollins opened the folded paper and began reading it. His brow furrowed.

"Is anything the matter, Elijah?" asked Clarence.

He paused for a moment, batting his eyes to fight back his grief. He looked up at Clarence, then allowed his eyes to scan at the other holographic members in attendance.

"The virus," he said, his voice breaking. "It's loose."

"Loose?" asked Aziz, who'd been rather quiet throughout most of the conversation. "What do you mean by *loose*?"

Pollins swallowed hard. "One of the quarantined people broke through the barrier and made it to the outside. The virus is now airborne," he said.

Each of the men and Lela instantly had shocked expressions on their faces.

Ramses shook his head. "Well, that settles it," he said.

"Settles what?" Thurgood asked.

"What we need to do."

Nationhood

"And just what might that be?" asked Clarence.

"C'mon, brothers. The virus has been set free. It's only a matter of time before our people begin to see the signs and feel the pains this virus will cause. Soon, the entire country will be littered with dead bodies and then the oppressors will come through and take over, just as they've always done."

"Ramses is right," said Pollins. "The time to act is now. We must send out our troops before they contract the disease. We must deploy everyone right away."

"Then we will do our part," said Ramses. "We will attack the major cities and keep everyone off balance. That should give you time to deploy your people and attack the bases. With the country being hit by both of our groups, they won't know what is going on."

"Gentlemen, please. We're being a bit too rash," said Clarence.

"There's a fine line between rash and reason," said Pollins.

"Is there? I'm not so sure anymore," Clarence retorted.

"So, is this your final decision?" asked Thurgood.

Pollins looked at his image. "Yes, Mister Thurgood, this is our final decision. Our president has signed the order and our plans have been set."

"I see. Then I am of no further need here."

"Ah, but you are," said Ramses. "Your words and behaviors have led me to believe that you would undermine our mission, perhaps betray us to the US government."

"If you're saying that I would do my best to stop this from happening, then you'd be right, even if that meant involving the government," Thurgood fired back.

"Then, you will understand why I cannot allow you to leave."

Both Lela and Thurgood gave questioning leers at Ramses.

"What do you mean you can't allow us to leave?" Lela finally spoke.

"Just what I said. This war has been a long time coming and now that we are on the threshold of the final battle, I cannot not allow either of you to go off and reveal our plans before we can execute them. I'm fully aware of your in-flight meeting with Senator Green, Mister Thurgood. As I said, we would be watching."

"Spying on me, Ramses? My, that's a little beneath you, isn't it?" said Thurgood.

231

James Gordon

"It wasn't beneath me when I saved your ass in Los Angeles. Fortunately for us, Senator Green will not be getting a call from you telling him anything. However, the information he gave you to investigate, did you find out anything?"

Thurgood's brow furrowed. He realized just how in depth their investigation of him went. Ramses was obviously referring to the information about the Illuminati, the secret organization Senator Green alluded to. But Ramses, seeing the eyes of Thurgood and knowing that the wheels were turning and the pieces of the puzzle he'd collected were being shuffled into place, did not give Thurgood time to answer.

"He was correct in pointing you in the direction of Elbert, Georgia. There is something of interest there, but the secret is far more stunning that you'd ever believe."

"How so?" asked Thurgood.

Pollins turned and gave a smirk toward Aziz and Ramses. Clarence, however, was just as lost as Thurgood. He looked at his longtime friend with a puzzled expression.

"Elijah, is there something you aren't telling me?" asked Clarence.

The three men chuckled. "My old friend," said Pollins. "As educated as you are and with as many connections as you've made in your life, how is it that you do not know who the real power in this world is?"

The cryptic comment was still lost on Clarence. He turned and looked at the image of Thurgood, who now seemed to finally piece the whole thing together.

"Are you telling me that the Illuminati is not a clandestine organization of Whites, but is, in fact, an organization of Black people?"

"By George Washington Carver, I think he's got it," said Ramses.

Thurgood looked at Clarence, whose eyes were as large as saucers. The elder Bolo leered at his longtime friend, Elijah, his mouth agape and his body frozen in place.

"Come now, Clarence. Don't look so surprised," said Pollins. "Haven't you ever wondered why so many Egyptian symbols are located in so many different areas or on so many different objects around the world? The Pyramid on the back of the one-dollar bill, the obelisk as the Washington Monument, even the Vatican's involvement in combating the secret organizations like the Masons is all because of the our involvement."

Nationhood

"But the Illuminati?" asked Clarence.

"Well, not exactly. The Illuminati is the term given to a branch of this global organization of order. Our branch is called the Inner Circle, the main body and the single most powerful organization on the planet."

"We are connected to more agencies, more banks, more power than anyone," said Ramses. "Even the ruling by the Supreme Court over twenty five years ago was our doing."

"We've been planning this war for some time now, building our resources and our connections until the time was right. Now, with the president signing the bill I introduced to him, we can completely annihilate all nations that have had a hand in the oppression of our people," said Pollins.

Suddenly it all became clear to Thurgood. "My God," he said. "It was a set up. *You* released the virus."

Pollins puckered his lips and looked down his nose. Slowly, he began to nod his head.

"But, the other senators, they were your friends, Elijah," said Clarence.

"When going to war, some sacrifices must be made," Pollins replied.

"And do those sacrifices include the loss of the lives of your fellow countrymen? Are you willing to kill our people just to win some damned war?" said Clarence as his voice escalated.

"I'll do whatever I have to, Clarence! Don't lecture me on the ills of war! I know better than you do the price that must be paid! Our time has come to reclaim that which is ours! For far too long we've sat back and watched White Europeans, Americans and South Africans reap the benefits of raping this planet and taking whatever they wanted! Now, the time has come for us to get our share, if not the whole damned pot!"

"This is genocide!" said Lela. "You're sending our entire race to their graves!"

"No, Miss Washington," said Reverend Aziz. "We're only doing what is our destiny. This plan has taken decades to orchestrate. Now, the crescendo and the climax are almost here."

Clarence was still looking at Pollins. "So, am I a prisoner, too?" he asked.

"I'm afraid so, my friend. Even now, your nephew and his companion, Miss Ishtar, are probably in the great beyond. We know about

233

the mansion and we had a little surprise waiting for them."

Clarence's face was blanketed with alarm. "No, you didn't!" he exclaimed.

"Yes, we did," said Ramses. "Mbaku and Katura should be fish food right about now. With them out of the way, there's no one that can stop us. Wake up, world! The revolution is about to be televised!"

~~~

Unbeknownst to Pollins, Ramses or Aziz, Clarence had some idea about what was going on before he met with Pollins. As a precaution, he instructed Vee to monitor his communication device's frequency. Luckily, she was right on queue and heard every single comment that was made. She informed Clarence that Mbaku and Katura made it back to headquarters alive. She also informed him that Mbaku was unconscious, but Wendy was attending to him.

Upon listening to the conversation, Vee realized that things had gone from bad to worse. They were no closer to finding the cure for the virus and with the country getting ready to go to war it was doubtful there would be anyone left after this was over. With the virus being airborne and no antidote, it would only be a matter of time before the entire country fell victim to the horrors that were once contained inside the conference area.

Meanwhile, Wendy was in one of the spare rooms checking the vital signs of Mbaku, who lay in a bed and was connected to a heart monitor. He was still unconscious, but his readings showed that everything was okay. Using her stethoscope, she listened to his chest, checking his breathing and the rhythm of his heartbeat. She stood upright, removed the earpieces from her ears, jotted a few notes in his file and then placed it on the hook connected to the bed's footboard. She stared at her unconscious patient who was also her lover. He was still and he looked so peaceful, almost as if he was sleeping. She folded her arms across her chest, a worried look covering her face. Tears welled in her eyes and for a moment the magnitude of him not awakening descended upon her.

Like a drizzle of rain, her worry and pain sprinkled upon her thoughts. Mbaku was the only man who'd ever seen passed her light complexion and saw her for the woman she was. She was a doctor, attractive and sleek, smart and sexy. But she was also a person, a living breathing person, not someone whose sole purpose was to make someone else look good in the eyes of his colleagues. Men in her past considered her more of a trophy or an arm ornament instead of a person, but that

Nationhood

seemed to be the accepted place for women in this country.

However, Mbaku was different. He talked to her, listened to her, shared things with her, solicited ideas from her, treated her like a person, like a woman. He respected her, made her feel special and not just someone to help him release his tensions. Seeing him like this and knowing that he, the man she loved, now teetered between being on life support or emerging from his unconscious state stronger than he'd ever been tormented her unlike any other thought she'd ever come across.

As Wendy stood there, silently allowing her grief to flow in the form of tears, Katura quietly stood in the doorway. She'd been watching Wendy and her caring and meticulous handling of Mbaku. She, like Wendy, was concerned about him, not because she cared for him as deeply as Wendy did, but because she had developed a degree of respect for Mbaku. He'd helped her on more than one occasion and never once did she feel threatened by him. He'd proven his loyalty as a friend and comrade and she owed him much. In fact, had it not been for Mbaku, she might not be alive right now. Instead, she would have been black bagged with a toe tag attached to her foot.

She leaned against the doorframe and recalled the time at the Romanian Embassy when they first met. He was handsome and charming, and the way he assisted her in getting the fake diamonds out of the building was nothing short of genius.

She remembered when he came to rescue her after the agents who were supposed to be her backup double-crossed her at the pier. Once again Mbaku came through like a valiant mocha-colored knight, saving her when it seemed she was on the brink of death.

Even this last caper, when the entire mansion was falling down around them and her former friend, Cho, was thrashing her about like a rag doll, Mbaku was there, carrying her in his arms as he leaped over the dead bodies they'd laid on the floors and dodging the falling chucks of the rapidly crumbling manor.

She owed him a lot and she appreciated everything he'd done for her. She wished he would wake up so she could tell him just how grateful she was. Somehow, she felt she was to blame for all of this and she was certain Wendy felt that way. Truth be told, ever since she'd come into his life there has been nothing but drama and danger. Perhaps it was time to leave and spare him and those who cared about him any more grief.

Just then, Wendy turned her head and made eye contact with

James Gordon

Katura. The lady assassin stood from her leaning position and returned a stare of her own. Wendy walked toward her as anxiousness began to build inside of Katura. She wasn't sure what Wendy would do. Wendy came to a stop in front of her as her tear-filled hazel eyes stared deeply into Katura's green pupils.

"Is there something you want?" Wendy asked.

Katura seemed at a loss for words. She didn't quite know how to answer. Her mouth moved, but nothing would come out. She paused for a moment and bowed her head. A deep sigh hissed from her nostrils and then she looked Wendy in the eyes as the anguish she'd been feeling over Mbaku's condition began to show.

"I just wanted to see how he was doing," said Katura somberly.

Wendy breathed in heavily and released it hard. Her exasperation could be felt in her released breath and was beginning to show on her face.

"I don't know what's going to happen," she said. "His vitals are stable and he seems to be okay right now. However, he is still unconscious and everything is touch and go for the moment."

Katura looked at him, seeing how still he was. She nibbled her bottom lip, trying to think of something to say to ease Wendy's obvious tension.

"Tell me what happened," said Wendy abruptly.

Katura looked at her once more. "I already did," she replied.

"You say an explosion destroyed the mansion and that Mbaku was carrying you when it happened. Why was he carrying you?"

Wendy's tone was becoming more assertive, like she wanted to accuse Katura of something.

"I had gotten injured and Mbaku picked me up and carried me out of the mansion," Katura explained.

"And you're America's dangerous weapon, huh? How is it that you're constantly in trouble and Mbaku has to be the one who consistently bails you out?"

"I can't explain why this is going on and I never asked for his help."

Wendy laughed due to her disbelief in Katura's lack of appreciation. "Your gratitude is astonishing," she said.

"Listen, I never meant for Mbaku to wind up like this. In fact, I didn't anticipate any of this happening. I didn't ask to be double-crossed by the very government that turned me into a lab experiment. I didn't want

Nationhood

to be a part of any of this. All I ever wanted was to live in peace and have a happy life. But then I became indentured and since then I've experienced nothing but sheer hell. Mbaku is a good man and I respect him and appreciate everything he's done for me. Don't think for one second I wouldn't trade places with him."

Wendy leaned in closer. "Don't think for one second I wouldn't want you to."

As the two women stared menacingly at one another, a groan came from the bed where Mbaku laid. Their eyes widened simultaneously and they slowly began looking toward the bed. To their amazement, Mbaku had regained consciousness and was looking at the two women.

"How's a man supposed to get any sleep around here when the two of you are making so much noise," he said.

Wendy quickly walked to his bedside and looked at him. Her expression was a mixture of pain and relief. She sat gingerly next to him and cupped his hand in hers.

"How are you feeling? Are you okay?" she asked.

"My head hurts but other than that I think I'm all right," said Mbaku.

"You have a mild concussion. Your headache is to be expected."

Mbaku nodded. Wendy pressed her lips together tightly, trying to fight back the tears in her eyes. "You had me so scared," she said.

She began crying as her head rested against Mbaku's shoulders. He held her in his arms, stroking her head and doing his best to console her. Across the room, he saw Katura standing next to the door. The two of them made eye contact. She smiled faintly and nodded once, as if to say she was glad to see that he was all right. Mbaku nodded once also, returning his thanks and appreciation for helping him.

Katura turned and left the room, allowing the two of them some time together. She quickly found Jaquimo standing next to a desk in the hallway talking on the phone. She walked to him as he turned and displayed an expression that he was glad to see her.

"Yes, she just arrived. Hold for just one moment," he said. He removed the phone from his ear and covered the mouthpiece. "Madam, I managed to contact your mother."

Katura frowned. "Marina?" she asked.

"Yes. But I'm afraid she is speaking in code. It appears that there are some uninvited guests in her midst. However, she is most anxious to speak to you."

"I see. Let me talk to her."

Jaquimo passed the phone to Katura. She lifted it to her ear and took a deep breath. "Hey, Marina."

"Katura, I'm so glad to hear your voice. Is everything okay?" said the voice of Marina on the other end.

"Yes. I heard about Dad. I'm sorry I wasn't able to be there for you."

"It's okay. I understand you have things to attend to. Just hearing your voice makes me feel so much better."

"I miss you so much. I wish I could be there."

"Well, when you get back I'll fix you some gumbo with pork, just the way you like it."

Marina's last comment was one of the codes Jaquimo was talking about. Katura liked gumbo, but not with pork. In fact, Marina didn't put pork in her gumbo. Pork was slang for cops. Her comment meant that there were agents there and they were listening to her phone call.

"I can't wait. You make the best gumbo," Katura replied.

"You know, your father loved you so much. We used to talk all the time about you, hoping you were all right and that one day you would be able to come home and be free of all this stuff," said Marina.

"I know. I wish I could have done that before he died."

Emotions began to tug at Katura's heart. She felt that somehow she'd let Durst and Marina down by not being able to free herself prior to his death.

"The fact is you're going to do it. You were always stubborn like that, always doing what couldn't normally be done. That's why he called you his little Blue Jay, because your presence did the same thing as a Blue Jay's, you always brought about change," said Marina.

As those words came out of Marina's mouth, Katura's eyes widened. Inside the technologically enhanced portion of her brain, which was nothing short of a super microcomputer, information began being processed. Marina had said the code words that began unlocking a secret and hidden file stored in Katura's techno-brain. It had been downloaded there by Durst prior to his death as a precaution in case the worse case scenario had taken place.

For decades he'd been a part of the government's project to develop a virus so terrible that it would make the world bow in fear before

Nationhood

them. Knowing that the release of such a virus would be catastrophic if it managed to fall into the wrong hands, he created the antidote, converted the formula into a file and stored it inside Katura's enhanced brain. The sentence that Marina said contained code words that, once heard by Katura, would unlock the file and download the antidote's formula into her head. Now, Katura knew how to stop the virus.

"Marina, thank you," said Katura. "I'll be home soon. Try to hang in there until I return."

"I will," Marina replied.

Katura hung up the phone and looked at Jaquimo.

"You look pale, My Lady," he said. "Would you like a sherry to calm her nerves?"

"No," said Katura flatly. "But I would like to speak to Vee. Do you happen to know where she is?"

"I would assume she is in that monstrous place she calls her lab."

"Take me to her. Marina just gave me exactly what I needed to stop this virus."

~~~

James Gordon

Chapter Sixteen: All Or Nothing

It wasn't the tastiest meal she'd ever had, but it definitely stopped her stomach from growling. Carla had eaten three packages of beef jerky, a bag of potato chips and some Skittles, swallowing it down with a grape soda, all of which was courtesy of the trashed vending machines in one of the waiting rooms in the lower chamber. Commandeering the food was simply a matter of survival and since it appeared no one was coming to save them, she and Abraham had to look out for themselves.

She felt her intestines clogging from all the sugar, fructose, syrups and other preservatives and additives that gave these poor excuses for junk food shelf life. But, it was better than starving to death. Given the choices, though, she would gladly choose starvation over the agony she'd seen so many others suffer as a result of the final stages caused by the virus.

Abraham sat quietly against the wall, his mind seemingly miles away. Carla rubbed her stomach, feeling a stomachache coming on. She glanced at her friend, the one she was sure had been killed when she sat in the cramped quarters of the electrical manhole. Now, with her hunger somewhat satisfied, somewhat, and her mind a little less troubled, she had some questions that needed to be answered and Abraham was the only one remaining who could give her any information.

"Abe," she said. "How're you doing?"

Abraham nodded. "Okay," he said with a sigh of exasperation.

Carla knew he was worried, worried about how much longer he had before he became one of the corpses in the other room. She looked at the clock on the wall, taking note of how much time was left before they met their fate.

"You wanna talk?" she asked.

"Nope, not particularly."

Carla stared ahead into the distance. "Well, I do. You mind if I tell you something?" she asked.

"Go right ahead," Abraham said.

"First of all, I'm glad to see that you're still alive. I heard some strange things while I was in that manhole. I heard gunshots and noises of things being scraped across the floor. Being in the dark and roasting amidst electrical currents nearly drove me close to insanity."

"I can imagine."

"But you know what kept me going?"

"What?"

"You. When I heard those shots and all those noises I thought they had gotten you. I remembered what you said about them killing everyone, that this was going to be some form of extermination. I thought they shot you and killed you, then dragged you off somewhere. I said to myself that you gave your life for me and that you and Constable Al-Shahir would not die in vain. I was going to make sure that tape aired and that the true people responsible would pay for what they did. I was going to fight with everything I had to stay alive because of you, Abe, you and Al-Shahir."

Abe was looking at Carla, stared at her the entire time she spoke. A part of him was happy to see her still alive and he was very appreciative of her words. He was also flattered how she used his actions as a form of strength. He only hoped she would maintain her courage and continue her fight.

But truth be told, he was in tremendous pain. Even now he struggled to keep his focus. His lack of conversing wasn't because he was traumatized or was having difficulty handling the situation. Those mental agonies had long since passed. What he dealt with now was physical pain and fear. He simply didn't want to become like the quivering beings he'd witnessed in the hours passed.

Every one of those bodies that lay in the room down the hall he helped carry there, right down to the last person who'd collapsed in his arms just as they finished helping him drag in the last body.

The vaccine he'd been given by Al-Shahir was starting to diminish in effect. Up until now he'd had no symptoms, felt no pain. He'd been strong and in his mind he believed he had a chance of getting out of here alive. However, the last person who'd not been inoculated with the vaccine he and Carla had been given died hours ago and now he was starting to experience the symptoms that signaled the beginning of the end.

"I'm glad to see that my actions helped you," said Abraham, attempting to switch his mind onto something more upbeat.

He felt a pain in his right side. He grimaced, an act that did not go unnoticed by Carla. Instantly she knew he was beginning to suffer from the ravages of the virus. She stood to her feet and walked toward him. She sat on the floor next to him, wrapping her arm around his shoulders and pulling him close.

"I'm here for you. I'll be here till the very end," she said.

Abraham allowed a tear to roll across the bridge of his nose.

"You know," he began. "The only thing I ever wanted out of life was to see my daughter grow up. I didn't have to be rich and I didn't have to live until she had grandchildren. I simply wanted to see her make it to adulthood. Now…"

His emotions choked him, prevented the rest of his words from being said. Carla wrapped her other arm around him and rested her head against his.

"You may still see her grow up, Abe. Don't give up hope yet," she said.

"They all had stomach cramps before their health took a downward spiral within minutes."

"Do you have stomach cramps?"

"I don't know what you go through during your periods, but if it is anything like what I'm feeling right now I've gained a whole new respect for women."

Carla couldn't help but chuckle. "That doesn't mean you're done. Remember, you had the blocker vaccine. It may slow down the effects," she said.

"Yeah, that's what I keep telling myself. So, what if it does slow it down? That doesn't mean we are going to be rescued, it just means I have a longer time to suffer. They've got armed soldiers surrounding this place and no one has come in here yet. Hell, they killed one of us when he made it to the outside."

"All that means is that we are going to keep fighting for our lives until there is nothing left."

"If I had the strength, I'd run right out there and let them shoot me."

"Thank goodness you don't have the strength. Now, stop all this foolish talk and get some rest."

Abraham pulled away from Carla and stood to his feet.

"No, thanks. I have the feeling I'll be doing all the resting in peace I'll ever want to do real soon," said Abraham solemnly. "Besides,

I have a phone call I need to make. Might be the last opportunity I have to do this."

"Do you want me to go with you?" Carla asked.

"Nah, I'll be all right. And don't worry about me doing what I said about running out and getting shot. I'm not that desperate or that ready to die."

He sucked in a deep breath and then headed out of the room. Carla sat there on the floor staring at the door he left out of. She wanted to go with him, but she was certain that the phone call he was going to make was to his wife and daughter. The conversation was going to be hard enough without her gawking at him like some mother hen. She decided to wait right where she was and hoped that wasn't the last time she saw him alive. She pulled her knees to her chest, hugged them with her arms and began praying.

~~~

The exchange of information was done quickly. Vee had told Katura what she overheard from the meeting Clarence Bolo had attended. Conversely, Katura rattled off the formula that had been stored in her head. With both of them realizing the urgency of the situation, Vee began to work the components of the formula, but was puzzled by some of the properties and their compatibility.

"I'm a little uncertain about mixing some of the elements you named. Are you certain about the information you gave to me?" asked Vee, turning toward Katura as if she could actually see her.

"Yes, I'm quite sure. Is there a problem?" Katura replied.

"Well, it's just that some of these compounds, when mixed, can be rather lethal."

"These people are going to die anyway if we don't do something. Perhaps the lethality of the mixture will counteract the virus."

"Perhaps. But it's very risky. I simply don't want to worsen the situation."

"Tell you what, you mix the concoction and I'll deliver it. That way if it doesn't work your government can blame one more thing on the Americans."

"It's not that simple, Katura. We're talking about my people, my countrymen. I don't want them being used as some sort of guinea pigs," said Vee with a little hostility in her voice.

"I don't see where we have much of a choice," Katura fired back.

Nationhood

"She's right, Vee," said a husky voice from the doorway.

Katura turned and saw Mbaku standing near the entrance to the lab, being assisted by Jaquimo and accompanied by Wendy.

"How are you feeling, Mbaku?" asked Vee.

"I've been better and I've been worse," he said, as he made his way further into the lab.

"It's good to see you up and walking," said Katura.

"It's good to be seen. By the way, thank you for getting me back here."

"Well, thank you for saving my life and getting us both out of the mansion."

Katura's eyes gravitated toward Wendy, who stood silently at Mbaku's side returning a slightly seething stare. Katura cleared her throat and turned her attention back to Vee.

"So, Vee, is there another way to test this formula?" Katura asked.

"Perhaps," said Vee. "Maybe if we could find someone initially infected by the disease, like one of the people at the airport. But after studying the molecular structure of the virus from the forensic reports of the murdered senators I managed to attain from the coroners office, everyone there should be dead by now."

"Still, what if we are able to spray the area and take a sample of the air content. If it shows counter effects on the airborne pathogens, then perhaps it will do the same in some of the victims."

"That's a fool's theory," said Wendy. "You can't equate the effects on a free flying pathogen to that attached to the host."

"It's the only choice we have," said Mbaku. "No one in the free populace has begun to experience the effects of the virus yet, and if we wait until they do it will be too late. It's a long shot and very risky, but we have to chance it. Otherwise, we'll have a full scale epidemic on our hands."

Wendy still wasn't excited about the idea, especially since Katura had thought of it. But in her professional opinion and given the current state the country was in, she saw no other way. Reluctantly, she nodded. "Need any help with the components, Vee?" she asked.

"I could always use an extra set of hands and eyes, Doc," Vee replied jokingly.

Mbaku grunted as he turned to exit the lab.

James Gordon

"And just where are you going?" asked Wendy.

"To get dressed. Someone has to deliver the antidote," he said.

"You aren't going anywhere," said Katura. "This was my idea and I'm going to be the one to administer it."

"You? How are you going to administer the antidote? You don't know anything about the airport," Mbaku questioned.

"You forget that I'm connected," said Katura, tapping the side of her head and reminding him about her cerebral implants.

"She's right, Mbaku," said Wendy. "You are in no condition to be out there right now. Besides, she's supposed to be this great American spy. Let her take the risk since it was her government that started all of this."

A tense moment filled the room as Katura and Wendy stared at one another. But to Vee, it was time to reveal the truth.

"Actually, Wendy, it wasn't the Americans who dropped the virus," she interjected.

Mbaku turned toward her. "What do you mean?" he asked.

"Before your uncle left for the Senate to talk to Senator Pollins, he asked me to monitor his communication frequency. I eavesdropped on the conversation and found out something very interesting."

"What did you find?"

"It was a set up, Mbaku, just like the set up you and Katura ran into at the mansion. Pollins and some guys named Ramses and Reverend Aziz are behind all of this."

Katura's ears perked up along with Jaquimo's.

"Did you say Ramses?" Katura asked.

"Yes. Know him?"

"He's the head of an organization called Exodus. They are a believed terrorist group, at least that's what the US government called them."

"Actually, they're a part of a much bigger group. Ever heard of the Illuminati?"

Mbaku's brow furrowed. "You can't be serious," he said.

"Afraid so. It seems that Aziz, Ramses and our own beloved Senator Pollins are a part of a major splinter group called the Inner Circle. They released the virus, although I'm not sure how. Their intention is to start a war that will bring about the rise of the Nubian race. They've gotten the president's approval on a declaration of war Pollins initiated on the

Nationhood

Americans."

"Dear God," said Jaquimo.

"Yes, my thoughts exactly," said Vee. "The troops are being recalled and all the ships and jets we have are being prepared. In a matter of hours we and a coalition of nations are going to be launching the biggest attack in the history of the world."

"All because of this virus," said Mbaku.

"Then, it's settled. Vee, please put together the antidote so I can kill this virus and we can stop this war before it starts," said Katura.

"Maybe we should wait until my uncle gets back," said Mbaku. "He would know the best way to handle situations like this."

"That could be a problem," said Vee.

"What's that suppose to mean?"

"Your uncle is being held prisoner by Aziz and Pollins. Someone named Thurgood is being held in one of Ramses' strongholds."

"Pollins has my uncle?" asked Mbaku with surprise.

"Yes. He's okay, but I don't know what's going to happen when this whole thing pops off," said Vee.

Katura looked at Vee, a disturbed expression covered her face. "Did you say Thurgood, as in Thomas Thurgood?" she asked.

"I don't know his full name," said Vee. "They only said Thurgood."

Mbaku was seething over the news that Pollins had betrayed his country and was now holding his uncle hostage. But he held his temper, trying to keep a clear head about things. He turned to look at Katura, remembering she'd mentioned a person by that name earlier.

"Thurgood. Isn't that the name of the person you had some connection with in the US Senate, the one you tried to get in contact with?" he asked.

"Yes, it is," said Katura. "Guess I was right about him being in trouble."

"I can't believe they have Clarence and are holding him hostage," said Wendy.

"I believe my mother is also being contained," said Katura. "When I spoke to her earlier she informed me that she wasn't alone."

"How'd she do that?"

"We have a code," said Katura, refusing to elaborate any further.

"Then we've got a lot at stake. It seems that our opposition has

James Gordon

been one step ahead of us and this conflict has more going on than we know. They managed to start a war and have potentially neutralized us by holding hostage the very people that we care about, not to mention releasing a virus that could potentially kill every living soul on the planet," said Mbaku.

"Well, here's the good news," said Vee.

"There's good news?" asked Wendy.

"Yes. Pollins and his group believe you're dead. That whole mansion situation was a set up to kill you."

"And that's supposed to be good news?" quizzed Mbaku.

"It could be," said Katura. "If they think we're dead that means we have the element of surprise."

"Indeed," said Mbaku with a tone of revelation. "Perhaps we can use this to our advantage. But we've got our work cut out for us. Vee, get started on that antidote. Wendy, please help her. Katura, you get prepared to go to the airport."

"And what are you going to do, Mbaku? I'll repeat that you are in no condition to go anywhere. But I know you. Trying to talk you out of whatever you plan on doing is completely out of the question," said Wendy.

"Yes, you know me well, love. I *am* going to do something. I'm going to the Senate building, rescue my uncle and bring Senator Pollins and his compatriots to justice," said Mbaku.

~~~

For someone who was being held hostage, Clarence was unusually calm. Although he tried to *look* distressed when his captors turned their eyes toward him, it was all a façade, his attempt to not let on that he knew something that Pollins and Aziz did not. He sat in a silk-tufted, high back chair that had a nice Victorian design to it. A cup of tea had been brought to him along with a slice of chocolate-layered cake. He nibbled on the cake and sipped some of the tea. However, his eyes remained glued on Pollins and Aziz, his chest aching with disappointment and his mind ravaged by thoughts of his friend's betrayal.

When he decided to come to the Senate Building, to the place he suspected he would find most of his answers, he knew he would uncover information that would be terribly disturbing, but not to this level. His previous observation of the events that had unfolded led him to the conclusion that there was something about this entire situation that didn't

Nationhood

seem right, like an equation that didn't add up properly. There were variables that led him to believe that the state of affairs were being coerced, like a theatrical drama that was playing out right before his eyes.

It was all too clean, too perfectly executed. The way everything was so conveniently placed—strategic, timely and exact. The senators falling victim to a virus, the incident with the diamonds being stolen, the arrival of Katura Ishtar and her connection with the man who worked for the government and helped to create the very virus that was running rampant in his country. He dared not think that such things could happen due to sheer coincidence. He, unlike so many others he'd known, did not fall victim to the theories of chance. Not even luck could be this fortuitous.

This was a plot, an elaborate ploy that was pulling this country toward a conflict that was otherwise avoidable. He began to wonder who stood to gain the most from a war erupting between the American Empire and AUNK. Scholars of warfare knew that most of the time the individuals who were pushing for war often were the ones who would profit the most. Pollins was one of the most vocal and was the individual who authored the bill that the president signed to declare war on the US. However, Clarence, although suspicious, wasn't exactly sure of his friend's involvement prior to his arrival here but decided to take the extra precaution of having Vee monitor his communication device, just in case his fears were correct. Sadly, he now knew that his longtime friend was a terrorist and a traitor, two words he never thought he'd ever say about him.

Pollins seemed happy and there was a reason why. As he gazed at the television, the medias' elite were in a frenzy. All the top networks had their most popular personalities pumping up the need to go to battle against the US. Men and women, young and old, conservative and liberal were all a part of the circus surrounding the conflict that was growing more out of control by the moment.

With his gaze firmly on the television while armed guards kept an eye on Clarence, Pollins watched as the pieces of his plan slowly began to settle into place. Rallies were being held to gather support for the troops, riotous crowds converged and burned American flags in protest of the believed attempt to subjugate the nation of AUNK. This was all music to Pollins' ears, a sweet melody of chaos with the climax being the total destruction of the very nation that was instrumental in the oppression of the enslaved descendants of Africa.

Reverend Aziz also watched with enthusiasm, but not quite as much as Pollins. He seemed delighted that such an event was taking place. However, as Clarence observed his mannerisms, his body language painted a slightly different picture. His posture suggested he was more like an observer whose curiosity had been piqued as opposed to someone who was an active participant in the planning of this ruse. He often looked at Pollins with a somewhat disdainful glare, almost as if he was a little jealous of the wily senator. With those observations, identifying that series of involuntary reactions, Clarence knew exactly what was going on. He realized that Aziz had been planning something like this and wanted to be the person who orchestrated this coupe de tat of America. But somehow, Pollins had beaten him to the punch.

Meanwhile, Aziz had a smile on his face, but there was a simmering anger in his chest. Unknown to him, Clarence had surmised the situation accurately. This was to be his plan, his way of putting his name in the history books. Now, he had to play second fiddle to the man that sat next to him gawking at the television with glee.

Aziz knew that the person who could perform this feat would be heralded as a conqueror, a person that would eclipse the likes of Alexander the Great, Julius Caesar, Cyrus the Great or Genghis Khan. Then again, he could be linked to such names as Napoleon Bonaparte, Attila the Hun or Adolf Hitler. Either way, the fame would be historic on an unparalleled level.

His plan was to attack the country from within, weaken its defensive capabilities and then hold the country hostage until their demands had been met. This dream of conquest was born a long time ago as a result of what took place on an early September morning in a city called New York.

When the event happened, and for a long time after, the conscience of America and its allies couldn't come to grips with what had occurred. Four planes changed the world forever. For decades it was believed that Arab terrorists were behind the attack that brought America and the world to a screeching halt.

For years, the world lived in denial, buying into the belief that a rogue group of Muslims were responsible. Then, a small group of hackers tapped into a database and revealed to the world that a splinter cell of revolutionists, both in America and abroad, had staged the entire event and blamed the chaos and terror on individuals who had no part in the horrific catastrophe called September 11. That's when all hell literally broke loose.

Nationhood

It became public knowledge that many of the top military and governmental leaders had a hand in what happened, planned the event and kept buried the information until well after their deaths. It was the single greatest cover up in American history, one that, once revealed, sent the country into a downward spiral of chaos and anger.

The government vehemently denied the information, but the people of the world were no longer listening. Despite the attempts by the government to discredit the information and the people who exposed it by unleashing a campaign of patriotic propaganda and counter reports that supported the uncovered lies, suspicion and doubt had already latched onto the minds of the American people, as well as the people of the international community.

America was never the same after that. No longer was it the shining beacon of hope or the land of opportunity. It became known worldwide as the land of deception and lies. A vast coalition of countries from Russia to Korea refused to do business with the US as a result of the uncovered truth. Caricatures of Lady Liberty's burning torch becoming a water hose that sprayed its unrelenting and powerful jets upon all who dared to speak against the policies and principles of the US were scattered throughout the world. The Bald Eagle was referred to as, *The Swooping Avian of Death*, a jab at the US military's might that descended from the skies and pounced upon all who did not embrace American ideals. America as a whole was called, *The Modern-day Sodom and Gomorrah*, becoming the most despised country in the history of the planet.

These were the opinions of those who lived outside of the country. However, for those within the US borders, life became even more intolerable. Taxes increased, living conditions got worse, food prices rose exponentially, and if you weren't in debt you were considered to be a terrorist conspiring to overthrow the government. Properties were seized, assets were frozen and the liberties that were admired by people of other countries once considered to be third-world civilizations were gone.

Underground resistance groups were formed and skirmishes between citizens and police or military units were an everyday event in some of the more impoverished areas of the country. Poor Whites huddled amongst themselves, becoming servants to the wealthy elite just to stay alive. The Latinos returned to Mexico where they could work in factories that were established due to American outsourcing.

The Scottish, Irish, Russians, Asians and every other non-Black

ethnicity returned to their homelands where they also found opportunities
to put their American-learned skills to work and improve their nation.

However, the descendants of enslaved Africans in North America
had nowhere to go. This was the only country they'd ever known, the only
place they considered home. Collectively, they became a race of nomads,
a traveling band of impoverished citizens who had no resources to draw
from and no land that would claim them. Instinctually, they all migrated
to the cities that had the largest Black populations. Atlanta, New York,
Washington, D.C., Los Angeles and Chicago became massive tribes where
Blacks could stand some chance of survival.

The individuals who still had jobs became targets of
discrimination. Everything that was considered racial discrimination under
the Civil Rights Act was performed against them. Promotions were denied,
layoffs were performed and trumped up investigations that built cases
against Black employees were conducted. Finally, when the employment
situation had grown to the point where Whites could no longer find jobs,
the Affirmative Action policy was challenged and subsequently
overturned. When this happened, an all out war was declared upon African
Americans. The need to unify had never been greater, however, there were
no resources of which to pull from and their basic human rights were
consistently violated. Now, Blacks were no longer considered citizens of
the country, and without citizenship many were deported.

When it was finally discovered a year later and pointed out by a
host of financial institutions that most of the individuals that were being
deported still owed significant debt to their companies, a halt was placed
on allowing the Blacks to leave. When subpoenaed to repay the debt,
many Blacks did not have the ability to do so. That's when everything
went from bad to worse.

Covert groups called Erasers were created to find and place into
custody those individuals who could not pay their debts. The government
referred to them as Indentured Servants, or I.S., for short. Either they
worked for wealthy White people or groups to slowly repay their debt or
they were volunteered to be subjects in various government experiments.
Either way, they were never heard from again and the road to freedom for
them was excruciatingly slow and unbearably agonizing.

Aziz had seen many atrocities during that time. At age 20, he'd
witnessed his own twin sister gunned down by police simply because she
fought to get away and not become another victim of the Black Bag Ops,

Nationhood

the term given to the disappearance of people that were being hunted by the Erasers. Friends and relatives, tribal members and associates disappeared and were later discovered as being captured or *black bagged*. The grief was just as strong as if they'd been killed and drove many people to the brink of insanity. He'd often thought that there had to be some way for them to fight back, someway for him to bring relief to his people and keep their hopes alive. That's why he became a preacher. He brought the word of God to those whose faith was waning and strengthen those who fought to free the enslaved.

Then one day, he met the young man who orchestrated the information hacking about September 11. His name was Ramses. When he met him it was like meeting the Messiah himself. The light he brought to the world from the release of that information was so extreme that many referred to him as the second coming of Christ. Ramses asked him to be a part of his organization and introduced him to what was known as Exodus. Fifteen years have passed since then and he never looked back.

Although the dream of Ramses was to bring down the tyranny of the American Empire and free the people who were enslaved by the unjust practices of US diplomacy, it was not the overall dream of Reverend Mohammed Aziz. His dream was revenge. He wanted to get back at the country that murdered his sister and treated him like a piece of meat. Many friends and family were lost because of what the corrupt and racist government had done and now it was time for them to pay. Aziz was going to use Exodus as his personal army to destroy America from within and bring the cleansing spirits of vindication and reparation to his people.

But there was a fly in the ointment. Someone else was executing his plan. In fact, the plan Aziz had was smaller in scale compared to the one Pollins managed to construct. Not only did the crafty senator utilize Exodus in his plans, but he also managed to include AUNK and many of the world's countries that formed the coalition of nations against America. In some respects he admired Pollins for what he was able to accomplish. But there was an equally bitter jealousy for the senator because he had outdone Aziz, something that gnawed at the reverend's pride and his hunger for revenge.

His eyes once more eased toward Pollins, narrowing slightly, his brow faintly furrowing.

Across the room, still seated in his Victorian style chair, Clarence spied Aziz's subtle, but noteworthy, expression. The right side of his

James Gordon

mouth turned up a little. He'd found the chink in the armor. He hooked his finger inside the loop of his teacup, lifted it to his mouth and took another sip. Instantly, his mind began drawing up a plan, a plan that he hoped would stop this war before a single missile could be fired. But he had to do it swiftly, because if he didn't the lives of his countrymen and so many others throughout the world would be at stake.

~~~

Chapter Seventeen: If I Don't See You Again...

Thirty minutes had passed since Wendy and Vee began working on the antidote. But for these supremely gifted women, thirty minutes was twenty-nine point nine minutes longer than what they needed. They'd synthesized and processed the formula, prepped it for delivery and had given it a preliminary analysis through the computerized simulator. Everything turned out as expected, the results extremely promising. Now, with a completed batch of the antidote ready to go and another massive lot being processed, Wendy decided that she needed a break.

"Vee, I'm going to take a few minutes to close my eyes," she said.

"Okay, Doc," Vee replied.

She walked over to a stool and sat, allowing her body to slouch slightly from exhaustion. She'd been on the go for the last several hours. She attended to Mbaku earlier. Checking his vital signs and nursing him back to health was a chore in and of itself. Now she was helping Vee with the antidote to the virus. The entire run left her feeling very fatigued. In fact, she was so tired that if she were near the bed Mbaku had been lying in she would have collapsed across it and gone right to sleep.

As she pondered that thought further and attempted to summon the energy to perform one last ditch effort to make it to the very bed she envisioned, Mbaku walked into the room dressed in a sharp jet black suit with a cream-colored collarless shirt. He stood in front of a full-length mirror and was placing the finishing touches on his outfit. Wendy, stunned by the heavenly vision of the man she loved standing before her, suddenly found the energy to stand and walked toward him, eyeing him from top to bottom like a tigress hungry for antelope.

"My, don't we look handsome," she said, stopping next to him and running her hand down his arm.

The feel of the fine silk of the suit combined with the tightness of his muscles sent a shiver down her spine. She wished he could make love to her once before he left. But time was of the essence. He turned to stare at her, his eyes showing the same desire she wanted so much to share with him.

"Thank you, love. I'm glad you approve," Mbaku replied.

"Love? That's an unusual word to hear you say," said Wendy

"Sometimes it takes a few traumas to wake you up and show you what you have."

Wendy smiled, then brushed her hands across the front of his suit "This fits you nicely. Hard to believe it's a full-on assault outfit," she said.

"No kidding. This thing has everything from a refrigerator to a missile launcher."

She scoffed. "Just make sure you don't blow off something you're going to need later."

They gave each other warm smiles. Then Wendy's face went from happiness to a cold, pained expression. Mbaku knew she was worried. She always got this way when he went on a mission. But he had to admit that this one was a little different and even made him feel uneasy and concerned. This wasn't a mission that was secretive like the other covert operations he'd performed in the past. This mission was out in the open and was so important that he couldn't afford to make any mistakes.

Hooking his index finger under her chin and lifting her face upward, he stared into her eyes like a man searching for that last bit of inspiration, that one thing he needed to help carry him through. He saw the pain and the worry in her moist eyes, felt the anxiousness in her warm breath. He had to set her mind at ease, had to let her know that everything was okay and that he had everything under control.

"Don't worry, I'll be back," he said reassuringly.

Wendy tilted her head away and gave him a somewhat skeptical look.

"Don't worry, he says," she replied. "My man is about to go into the lion's den to retrieve his uncle knowing he will face men with guns who would much rather kill him than to talk to him and he tells me not to worry."

"I've faced worse odds before."

"And *that* is supposed to make me feel better?"

Mbaku flashed a look of exasperation and blew out a hissing exhale through his nose. "What do you want for me to say?" he asked.

Wendy stared silently into his eyes as her mind searched for the right phrase that would give her some relief, some solace, some

256

Nationhood

reassurance that everything was going to be okay and that this wasn't the last time she would see this beautiful man of hers alive. But she knew there was nothing he could say, there was nothing that anyone could say that would relieve her of the fear that, even now, was binging her to the verge of tears.

She reached up, stroked the side of his face with her left hand. Mbaku turned his face into her hand and kissed her palm. They locked eyes once more, the emotions building in both of them, but showing more on Wendy's face as a tear streamed down her cheek.

"I had to watch you lying in a bed unconscious for an hour, wondering whether you were going to wake up or not. That was the scariest sixty minutes of my life. My mind went through all sorts of scary thoughts that kept coming like a flood. I literally felt myself losing it because I couldn't bare the thought of not having you in my life, not being able to touch your face and hold your hand or kiss your mouth again. It literally tore me up inside. I don't want to go through that again. I can't take that again," she said emotionally.

Mbaku brushed away her tears and held her face in his hands.

"I give you my word, you'll never have to go through that again," he said.

"I just need to know, are you sure about this? Are you absolutely sure that you know what you're up against and that you'll come out of this without a scratch?" she asked in a near frantic tone.

"Yep!" he replied.

"Liar," she said with a chuckle.

They both smiled. Their lips met and the sweetness of their love was shared in that one instant. Wendy knew he only said what he said to not make her worry. But if this was to be the last time she ever saw him, ever felt his warm body close to her, ever felt his sweet kiss and his loving touch, then she wanted to savor it for as long as she could.

She nestled her face against his chest, his tight body felt good to her. He enclosed her in his arms, holding her close and tight.

"Remember when we met, how you looked at me and turned your nose up at me?" she asked.

Mbaku frowned. "I don't remember turning my nose up at you," he replied.

"Yes you did. I recall how you looked at me at the Governor's Ball and how you later mentioned when we bumped into each other on the

257

patio how you thought I was White just because my skin was so light."

Mbaku hummed as he recalled the conversation.

"It was always like that. When I was back in the states, women used to hate me because of my color. They used to call me a high yellow bitch and that I thought I was so high and mighty. They never knew the pain I went through behind some of the comments they made."

"I see."

"White men used to try and pick up on me because I was dark enough for them to have sex with without being called a nigger lover and Black men used to come after me because I was close enough to White but not quite. It made me feel so unloved, like I was some sort of damned trophy, a piece of property whom the owner would have bragging rights and status."

Mbaku sighed hard.

"I felt so lost, Mbaku, like I didn't know where I belonged. I wasn't White and I wasn't Black. I was in between, like a child in limbo, a throw-away kid without any place to call my own."

She lifted her face and looked into his deep dark eyes.

"Then I earned my freedom and I came here. For the first time I felt I was somewhere I belonged. But I never felt completely whole until I met you. After we talked on the patio, you apologized for your initial observation. When you discovered I was studying to become a doctor and I found out you worked for the government, we grew closer and got to know each other better. We shared our thoughts, our dreams and we fell in love. You made me feel special, needed. It was like seeing the person who would finally accept me for who I was without labels and without some sort of racially ulterior motive. It was just me, and you saw me for who I was, not for what you could get out of me. You made me feel like a person, someone who had a purpose. I never forgot that and I never want to. That's why you have to come back, because I need you. I need you in my life. I need you to help me live."

A compassionate smile came to Mbaku's lips. Just like he made her feel wanted and needed, she did the same for him. Before she came into his life, he'd gotten lost in the rigors of his job. He felt like nothing more than a tool, something his government used to accomplish their mission. There never seemed to be a show of appreciation or gratitude for the sacrifices he made or the risks he took. They simply compensated him for his time and work, then he disappeared into the shadows until they

Nationhood

needed him again.

Wendy was the first person to see him as someone who made the world a better place, not just for the citizens of AUNK or the international community, but for her. She was always there for him, even if he was half way around the world. If he needed her, she would hop on the first thing smoking and be there for him. It truly seemed as if he was her purpose for living. She definitely was his. He couldn't imagine life without her and he hoped he never would.

As he stared back into her eyes, he understood her message. But, he also realized the torture she was putting herself through thinking he would not return. His eyes were warm and sympathetic. He understood her pain and shared her feelings. She was the first woman he truly loved and to not have her in his life would take away his reason to live. He cupped her face in his hands, planted a gentle kiss on her lips once more, then pulled back just enough to let her see the seriousness of his expression.

"I promise you, I will be back," he said.

On the other side of the room, Katura returned dressed in black combat gear that looked more like an outfit a hip-hop video dancer would wear. Her midriff was showing and the tube-style top accentuated her round and full breasts. Her hair was pulled into a long braid and her pants had that hip hugger look to them, sitting low, just above the hips.

She walked over to Vee, who was busily finishing up with preparing the rest of the antidote. Jaquimo walked in after Katura and stopped just behind her as Katura looked expectantly at Vee.

"Are we ready?" she asked.

Vee turned her head into her direction. "Just about. We're finishing the last of the second batch now," she said.

"What's the deal with this second batch? I thought we were going to test this and see what it does."

"If it works, we won't have time for you to come back and get a second application. You'll need to spread this into the air as soon as possible. If we wait too long it could have a disastrous outcome. Every moment this virus is left unchecked places our people in deeper danger. You'll need to get the antidote airborne as soon as possible after we determine that it can do what we want it to."

Katura had a disbelieving look, but understood the logic that Vee was explaining to her.

"Very well," she said. "I'll spread the cure."

James Gordon

Using her walking stick, Vee made her way to another table where a gun the size of an M-16 lay. It had a moderate-sized canister attached beneath the barrel. Katura surmised that this was the gun she would use to administer the antidote, at least the smaller application.

Vee said, "This will be the gun you will use to target the area in the airport. According to my calculations you should need to spray..."

"Only fifteen seconds worth, considering the size of the area and the length of time the virus has had to incubate," Katura interrupted.

"Yes," said Vee, slightly annoyed by her interruption but amazed at her ability to calculate the dosage. "Until you know the results, I would limit the amount of time you're exposed to the virus. Although we've run our tests through various simulations in the computer, there's no guarantee that things will go as planned. There's always that X-factor to be considered."

"Are you saying that it is possible for the virus to be even more aggressive?" asked Jaquimo.

"There is that possibility. The calculations were based on a mild form of the virus. But with the time it has taken for us to get the antidote and prepare it, the virus could have undergone a variety of transformations. There were a number of hosts in that conference area and there is a good chance the virus could have mutated into something far worse than its original composition," said Vee.

"In other words, spray for fifteen seconds and get the hell out of there," said Katura.

"In a manner of speaking," said Vee.

"So, if this stuff works and we kill all the little airborne critters, how do you want me to proceed."

"Glad you asked. Jaquimo, would you be so kind as to open that case to your left."

Jaquimo looked around and saw a black case measuring about three feet in length, three feet in height and two feet in width. Latches secured the case and a nifty handle made it easy to carry. It looked more like a massive attaché case. He picked up the case and sat it on the table. He and Katura flashed each other a look. Then, his hands began popping the latches open until he was able to slowly lift the lid and reveal its content.

"Holy Moses," said Jaquimo.

Inside the case was a device that appeared to be a bomb.

Nationhood

Attached to it was the same style canister, which had to be filled with a concentrated version of the antidote. Jaquimo's eyes slowly raised and his head turned to face Katura, who was still looking at the bomb.

"You couldn't house the antidote inside some sort of aerosol can or perhaps a nice automatic dispenser?" asked Jaquimo.

"No, they couldn't," Katura replied. "In order to get most of this stuff dispersed in the air in the shortest amount of time they needed to put it into a device that could spread this stuff quickly. A bomb was the most likely solution."

"We could load it in a plane and do crop dusting or something like that. But a bomb, Katura?"

"It's not our call, Jaquimo," said Katura turning to look at him. "This country's people are in danger and this is the best solution. We just need to make sure that we clear as many people from ground zero as we can."

"Don't think we haven't questioned our own decision on this, Jaquimo. We've wondered whether we were doing the right thing by handling things this way. But as Katura said, this was the only logical solution to disburse the antidote quickly. Any other way would be allowing the epidemic to manifest," said Vee.

"Very well," he said. "But just so you know I'm against the whole idea."

"Dully noted."

Vee walked over and showed them how to set the timer. "It will give you one minute before it explodes. I suggest you clear away the by-standers before you set it."

Katura studied the bomb, stored its schematics into her central processor. She now knew everything she needed to know about the device. She turned and looked at Jaquimo, whose eyes were large and fearful. His expression almost made her laugh, but this was not the time for jokes.

"I really don't think you should go with me," she said. "This mission is proving to be more dangerous than I imagined."

Jaquimo turned and faced Katura. "My Lady, I would disgrace myself if I were to allow you to go into such peril and you not have me there to escort you. Besides, I'm tired of sitting around. It's high time I got out and did some good in the world. Can't have you constantly grabbing all the glory."

"Jaquimo, I'm serious. This is a very dangerous thing we're about

James Gordon

to do."

"I'll try not to embarrass you, My Lady."

Katura snickered. She closed the case, then turned to Vee.

"Can you have this stuff ready in fifteen minutes?" Katura asked.

"It will be ready in two," Vee replied.

Just then, Mbaku and Wendy walked over to Katura and Jaquimo.

"Everybody ready?" Mbaku asked.

"A little overdressed, don't you think?" asked Katura.

"There's never an occasion not fit for a suit," Mbaku replied. "Vee, is everything set?"

"Yes, Mbaku. Katura and Jaquimo are going to the airport and run the test. If all goes well they will set the timer on the bomb and release the antidote into the air," Vee explained.

"Good. Katura, is there anything else you need from us?" asked Mbaku.

"I don't think so. But thanks for asking," Katura replied.

"You be careful."

"You, too. Good luck in getting back your uncle."

"Thank you." There was a moment of uncomfortable silence as everyone looked at each other, perhaps waiting for someone to make the first move and commence their part of the plan. Then, Mbaku spoke once more.

"I don't know what's going to happen, but I just wanted to say that it's been good working with the both of you. Jaquimo, you are a real gentleman and I'm glad I met you. Katura, you are a great partner and if there was anyone I'd want to be with me in battle, it would be you."

Katura seemed touched by the comment, as was Jaquimo.

"Thank you, Mbaku. It was a pleasure working with you. But let's stop talking as if we're not coming back. When this mission is over we'll all sit down and celebrate. Just send me an invitation when you and Wendy decide to get married."

Wendy's eyes widened, like she was surprised that Katura would say something like that. The two women exchanged glances, then Katura gave Wendy a wink, turned and walked to the table to grab the gun with the antidote attached to it.

"Let's go, Jaquimo!" she called as she walked toward the door.

Jaquimo looked at Mbaku, clicked his heels together and bowed

Nationhood

slightly. He turned, closed the case and secured it with the latches, then picked it up by the handle and followed Katura out of the room. Vee moved closer to Mbaku. Wendy snickered as she watched them walk out of the door.

"You know, I don't like her. But I have to say I have a lot of respect for her," said Wendy.

"The two of you are a lot alike. Perhaps you'll have the opportunity to work together again," said Vee.

"Not if I've got anything to say about it," said Wendy.

"Well, one things for certain. If we are successful in stopping this madness, me and this entire country will owe her a debt of gratitude," said Mbaku.

~~~

Abraham was about to conclude his call to his wife and daughter. It had been a very emotional conversation and lasted for over thirty minutes. His face was wet with tears and the sobbing voice of his wife on the other end didn't help matters. He braced his arm against the wall, trying to find the right way to end the call.

"Listen, sweetheart, I have to go," he said.

"No, you can't leave! Please stay and talk to me! Please," his wife, Loren, begged.

"Tell LaShelle I love her and that daddy misses her so much. Tell her that, Loren. Please do that for me."

"I will! But Abraham, don't go, please!"

"I have to. I love you, sweetheart."

"Abraham!"

He quickly hung up the phone as his tears poured from his eyes. He braced his back against the wall and slid down it until he was sitting on the floor. He cried openly, bellowing his pain into the echoing hallway. In his mind that was the last time he would ever talk to them again and that was a pain far worse than the one that ate at his body.

Physically, he could feel the virus destroying his organs and the pain was growing by the second. He couldn't let Loren hear the agony he was going through, didn't want her to visualize him being in pain as the last images she would have of him. He wanted her to remember him as the strong man he'd always tried to be. She deserved that, as did LaShelle. If he could give them nothing else, he would ensure they had that.

Carla, realizing that Abraham had been gone a while, made her

James Gordon

way up the hall. She could hear him crying and knew he was suffering from a pain that was worse than the physical one he was enduring. This pain was emotional, spiritual and mental. It hurt more than the physical pain and there was nothing she could do to soothe it.

She rounded the corner and saw him sitting on the ground crying out in Arabic. He was asking Allah why he was allowing this and what had he done to earn such a fate.

Carla walked to him and knelt beside him as he continued his mantra to God. He stopped and buried his face in his hands. She wrapped her arms around him and comforted him. It was all she could do, wishing silently that she had some way of making this all better.

Secretly, she feared that this is how she would end up, huddled on the floor while the virus ravaged her system. The only exception was she wouldn't have anyone to comfort her. She would be alone, going through her personal hell without any support or assistance. The only thing that comforted her was that no one would be around to see her become the blood-gagging pile of flesh she would eventually turn into.

Suddenly, Abraham began coughing violently, so violently that he couldn't catch his breath. Retching fiercely, he could feel his stomach and his other organs being tightened to the point of agony. He clutched his stomach and chest, trying to fight the involuntary constricting of his muscles as they attempted to counter the effects of the virus. After several seconds, his breathing returned and he gasped for the life-giving breath that had been so viciously stripped from his lungs.

Carla rubbed his back, hoping it did some good to help alleviate the pain and the distress. Deep down inside, she realized that Abraham didn't have much time left. The best she could do was make him as comfortable as she could, for as long as she could. If for nothing else, he would keep her company until it was her time to endure her pains.

~~~

He looked around the room, his eyes scanning the faces of the guards. They each had blank stares, looking like they'd been brainwashed and were nothing more than zombies dressed in military gear. Their guns rested on their shoulders or were being toted in the carrying position. They wore no insignias, not even the official AUNK defense badges all the nation's military members were required to wear. Just black fatigues, armored breastplates and caps, like SWAT members.

Clarence was a little uneasy. Why wouldn't he be? A man he

Nationhood

once considered to be his friend was holding him hostage. But his uneasiness wasn't because he felt his life was in any danger. He was uneasy about the events that were taking place. In a matter of moments, New Kemet's armed forces would be pulling out to join other nations' military forces in the largest attack against the United States of America the world had ever witnessed.

Up until now, the US was considered to be the juggernaut, the invincible nation who did what they wanted, when they wanted. AUNK was able to match America's might in economics, but it lacked the military means to go to battle with them, as was the case with most of the other civilized countries of the world.

Outside of the former Soviet Union, no one had ever been able to match the US when it came to the power of its defense forces. However, at no other time had there been a cause to create a coalition of forces against them, until now.

The release of the virus was considered an open act of terrorism, a threat that, left unchecked, would violate numerous articles of the UN governing terrorism and germ warfare. But it wasn't just this incident that provoked the international community to rise up against the 'Land of the Free' and the 'Home of the Brave'. Albeit the last straw, there had been simmering resentment against America since the attack they made on Baghdad, Iraq, when they dropped a shower of bombs that later became known as the *Shock and Awe* campaign.

Since then, nations were a little wary when dealing with the west. They considered America as the deceptive country who would do business with them so long as it served their purposes. Smaller countries were especially concerned because if they had something the Americans wanted they would suddenly have the tables turned on them. They feared being deemed terrorist nations and having campaigns commenced against them that would leave their people trembling in fear.

Fear, a word that had become all too common in this day and age, Clarence thought. All the efforts the American-aligned countries took to eliminate fear and to bring order and structure to their nations only perpetuated the fear, turning the governments into socialist entities that thought for the people and censored everything that didn't comply with the status quo.

The liberties and freedoms once flowing in abundance like rivers of information and expression had been reduced to mainstream tributaries

James Gordon

that flooded the minds of the populace with patriotic drivel and brainwashed those too simple to decipher truth from fiction. They clung to empty platitudes like *United We Stand*, all the while raping the truly patriotic of their dignity and their God-given rights.

Yes, America had done a lot of that and, on some parallel scale, deserved the potentially impending attack that was moving toward it. But if that was all there was behind this movement, Clarence would gladly watch from the sidelines with a bag of popcorn in one hand and an AUNK flag in the other gleefully cheering on the coalition. He was in no way a fan of American diplomacy, especially when it was America that still enslaved his brothers and sisters, treating them like lab rats instead of human beings. But, he knew this was a set up, a façade, an elaborate display of smoke and mirrors. America had not committed this crime against the people of this nation. The man he now stared at, Senator Elijah Pollins, did.

Just then, Clarence heard a buzzing in his ear. It was his communicator.

"Elder Bolo," said Vee's voice in his ear.

Clarence was given the title of Elder, which is similar to a lord or a knight in European cultures. He cleared his throat, his way of informing Vee that he heard her.

"Mbaku is on his way. He should be there shortly," she said.

He sighed, his way of letting her know he understood. He picked up his cup and finished off his tea.

"He's using your communicator to hone in on your location. How many captors are there?"

Clarence lowered the cup and looked at his friend.

"Elijah," he said.

Pollins turned around and looked at his friend, trying to stifle the glee on his face. "Yes, Clarence?" he replied.

"Do you mind terribly if I had some more tea? Perhaps one of your goons would be so gracious?" said Clarence, lifting the cup and jingling it.

"But of course, my friend." Pollins pointed to one of the soldiers. "You, go get my friend some more tea."

The soldier looked perturbed that he was being made to do servants work. However, he walked over to Clarence and snatch the cup away from him, then turned and marched out of the room and down the

Nationhood

hall. Clarence seemed somewhat offended by the soldier's actions, giving Pollins a look of bewilderment.

"After this is over I'll give him to you to properly train him. Consider it a gift," said Pollins.

"How generous," Clarence replied.

Unbeknownst to Pollins, the conversation he had gave Vee all the information she needed. It was actually relayed with his first word, the utterance of Pollins' first name. When Clarence said Elijah, he'd given Vee the exact number of people in the room with him. The mentioning of the name was the key and each letter in the name represented a captor. Six letters in the name Elijah meant there were six people in the room with him.

"I got the information," said Vee. "I'll relay it to Mbaku."

With that, Vee pressed a few sensor buttons on her brail circuit board and connected with Mbaku.

"Yes, Vee?" he answered.

"You should already have your uncle's coordinates. There are six people in the room with him. One should be Pollins and one should be Reverend Aziz. The rest should be nothing but lion food," she said.

"Gotcha."

Mbaku pulled to the front of the Ambassador Regency Towers, the luxurious 50-story grand hotel with art deco architecture. It was located in the heart of downtown Mecca City, which just so happened to place it one block away from the capital building where Senator Elijah Pollins held his uncle captive. He gave his keys to the valet to park his car, tipping him handsomely with a one hundred dollar bill.

"Make sure to have it back in this exact spot in fifteen minutes," said Mbaku.

"Yes sir!" the valet replied enthusiastically.

Accented with sparkling diamond-crusted cufflinks, a Super Ice Cube Chopard watch and custom made leather shoes from Kenya, Mbaku looked like a model on the cover of handsome-Black-man-whose-rich-and-proud-of-it magazine. But aside from his cool demeanor, his polished and flawless appearance, and his neatly suave and debonair grooming, he had only one thing on his mind. Get his uncle and kill anything else that moves.

His eyes looked up at the skies above. Evening was starting to settle and the warm African climate would normally have someone in a black suit regretting they wore something that dark in this heat. But this wasn't any suit. It was a Vee original, the kind of suit that had its own climate control, keeping his body at a perfect seventy-six degrees. This was just one of its many amenities and before the night was over Mbaku knew he would probably use every single one of them.

He slipped on a pair of stylish Versace glasses and touched the temple with his fingertip, activating the Infrared scope built into the lenses, another one of Vee's inventions.

"We are live," he said.

"I got you in my sights," said Vee.

"Cute."

"How are they working?"

"Excellently. You did a great job in designing these glasses. I might want to use these when Wendy takes another shower."

Vee chuckled. "I'll tell her you said that."

The lenses penetrated the outer wall of the building. He could see images moving, not many, but more than what should be in there right now. Vee informed him of how many people were in the room with his uncle, but that didn't mean those were all there were. For what was going down, Pollins had to have considerable backup.

He followed the bulky images, the ones that looked as if they had on body armor and were sweating profusely. The Infrared readings showed up well with them. They also showed him where the heat patterns of firearms were being concentrated. If he found that, his uncle was sure to be near. In a matter of moments he'd located what he was looking for. They were in the northwest corner of the building. He pressed the temples once more to turn off the scanner, then pressed on his communicator in his ear.

"Vee?" he called.

"Yes, Mbaku," she replied.

"Did you reach you-know-who yet?"

"No, I'm still trying."

"I'm going in. Keep trying and let me know the moment you get him."

"I will."

"All right. I'm going silent."

This was the signal that meant he would have no further communications with her until his mission was over. Slowly, he began

Nationhood

walking toward the building, the very building where so many of his country's laws had been deliberated, lobbied, discussed and passed. It seemed ironic or even poetic that he should be going in and potentially breaking the law in order to stop someone from sentencing his country and all its people to a horror it didn't deserve. Chances were he might not come out of there alive and perhaps all of this would be in vain. But Mbaku was a man who loved challenges. He enjoyed beating the odds. He remembered what Katura said about the adrenaline rush that was felt when they performed their duties. She was right, you just couldn't beat it.

The sides of his mouth turned up and a vicious looking grin appeared. It was time to hunt, time to bring justice to those who'd betrayed him and his uncle and the people of his nation. It was time to end this war before it started, before anyone was senselessly murdered for a war that didn't need to take place. He'd made it to the front steps, raced up them and walked to the side entrance. *No perimeter guards*, he thought to himself. *Surely it can't be this easy.*

Using his senses and his training, he scanned the entire area. No one was around. Either Pollins was really stupid or he was holding something that ensured he would not be challenged, which meant to Mbaku that the stakes were higher than he thought. He ran his fingers across his lips, tasted the flavor of a supreme test on his tongue.

"Now, the fun begins," he said.

~~~

James Gordon

Chapter Eighteen: The Final Overture

They were unseen, staying close to the ground and scurrying across the landscape like rats. Katura and Jaquimo had arrived at the airport and were now a few yards away from the guarded entrance of the quarantined area.

"This is the spot," said Katura.

"Quite perceptive of you, My Lady," Jaquimo replied sarcastically.

"We need to get in there. To shoot the antidote from this distance would be useless."

"Maybe a subtle approach would work, say delivering a pizza, perhaps?"

"No, smartass. But maybe we should try a more direct approach. You watch the stuff. I'm going in for a closer look."

Katura lowered the gun, then waved her hand suggesting that Jaquimo remain where he was. Slowly, she eased around the debris that formed a perimeter barricade, making her way toward the far wall of the building. She eased her head out to take a peek. No one was around. Switching her visual mode to infrared she tried to get heat readings of where everyone was located. She did a scan and saw twelve guards roaming the outside, their guns ready to fire at the slightest reason. They had on gas masks, no doubt attempting to shield themselves from being affected by the virus.

Katura was about to move on one of the individuals when her enhanced hearing picked up a voice that didn't sound masculine or military. They sounded as if they were sobbing, or close to it, and frantic.

Katura did another visual adjustment, switching from infrared to x-ray. She penetrated the walls of the building and peered inside, quickly locating two bodies in one of the inner chamber. She switched to sonar sight, an enhancement that allowed her to get a more detailed image of the individuals by using sound waves. It was a man and a woman and the man seemed to be in distress. They were both sitting on the floor while the woman appeared to be providing some consolation to the man.

Katura listened to the conversation and heard the woman saying

James Gordon

'hold on'. She quickly realized that they were victims affected by the virus, perhaps the last two remaining. She did a sweep of the entire building and saw what appeared to be bodies lying in a room down the hall. She choked back the lump that developed in her throat, a little disturbed by the image of all the corpses.

"Hey you!" screamed a husky voice.

She switched her eyes back to regular mode and saw one of the perimeter guards pointing his gun at her.

"Don't move," he said in a sinister tone.

He lifted the mouthpiece attached to his collar and pressed the transmission button.

"Unit three to zone. We have an unauthorized individual near sector 11," he said.

Katura was a little angry that she allowed her attention to slip to the point where someone had gotten the drop on her. She leered at him, her body tensing like a coiling cobra, her eyes focused as she prepared to strike. Slowly she began to crouch in preparation of her pounce.

But then another thought entered her head. Why kill just one person when she could get a group of them? No doubt his comrades would be rounding the corner soon and they would certainly want to take her into custody, an act she had no interest in allowing. She could eliminate the entire lot without having to scout around and find them before she could administer the antidote. She decided to play it coy, perhaps even innocent, lure them in and then take them out. Her outfit was not the kind that would give these soldiers the impression that she was some sort of assassin. At most, she would be viewed as some wayward traveler who'd wandered into the wrong place by accident. She walked toward the soldier as his instructions were relayed.

"Apprehend target and contain until backup arrives," said the person on the other end.

"Roger that."

The scratch of the communication device echoed off the building. Katura continued to approach the soldier, nice and slow. She was only a few feet away.

"Hold it right there, Miss," said the soldier, pointing his M-16 rifle.

Katura decided to use a ploy, something that might allow her the time she needed until the others arrived. She didn't want him to fire his

Nationhood

gun because it meant she would have to kill him were he stood. She would get no satisfaction from that because there was no challenge to killing just one person. She wanted to go on a spree, taking out several at one time. She loved to be tested, lived for the thrill of overcoming insurmountable odds and proving that she was unequaled in any aspect. Right now her adrenaline was beginning to kick in and the rush of excitement increased due to the idea of combat.

"I'm unarmed," she said, raising her hands. "I'm a dancer. I was thinking about doing a dance routine near this wall for an upcoming video."

"I don't care," the soldier replied. "Stop where you are."

Katura halted, but continued to sport a sly smile on her lips. Just then, a few more men arrived, each pointing their guns at her. Katura's eyes widened, the surge of exhilaration taking a jump exponentially. This was more like it, the type of odds she loved facing____six men total. She studied their posture, the way they held their guns, their eyes behind their masked faces and the stance they took. She felt a degree of disappointment. From what she saw they weren't going to be much of a challenge. She extended her arms outward, like she was expecting a hug, her fingers tightening into fists and then opening again.

"My, so many guns and so little time," she said.

"Get down on your knees and put your hands on top of your head!" one of the soldiers shouted.

Katura propped her hip to one side, lowering her arms in the process. "That's a little suggestive, don't you think?" speaking in a ditsy tone.

"NOW!"

Slowly, she raised her arms and proceeded to place her hands behind her head, which she layered them one atop the other. Suddenly, she removed two razor-sharp arrowheads that were concealed in her long braid. She slowly bent at the knees, but she wasn't going to kneel on the ground before these men. She was crouching, preparing to strike. She wasn't going to give them the satisfaction of seeing her in a groveling position. In fact, in a few seconds they wouldn't be seeing much of anything.

Two of the soldiers approached her and one prepared to frisk her, draping his gun across his shoulder while the others kept her in their crosshairs. As she crouched to the depth she wanted, the soldier had now come within striking range. Her hands suddenly flew from behind her head holding the arrowheads. Then, she launched into action and struck like a lightning bolt.

The first soldier began squirting blood from his neck before he even knew he was cut. Katura had used the arrow's point to slice his jugular, then repeated the process to his accompanying comrade. She then threw the arrowheads at two of the other soldiers, lodging the weapons into their foreheads. She grabbed one of the men struggling to stop their bleeding throat and pulled him in front of her as a rain of gunfire exploded. The soldier's body convulsed as the bullets pummeled his body armor and eventually ripped into his flesh. Katura pushed him toward his firing teammates, crashing him into one and knocking him to the ground. The trapped soldier screamed as his now dead and still bleeding buddy flopped lifelessly on top of him.

Only two more left, and one of them was trapped beneath the weight of his dead comrade trying to get from under the body before she was able to kill him.

Katura quickly knelt to avoid the shot made by the final standing officer. But while she was crouched on the ground, she removed one of the arrowheads from the forehead of one of the other agents and hurled it at the soldier with an underhand toss. The diamond-shaped weapon entered through the front of his throat and exploded through the rear, completely destroying his medulla oblongata. A stream of blood erupted from the back of his neck. He stood motionless for a few moments, his eyes wide and wild looking behind the mask, trickling crimson flowing out of the entry wound where his Adam's apple used to be. He teeter for an instant, then collapsed to the ground.

Just as his body fell, Katura pulled out her eight-inch blade hunting knife and placed at the throat of the soldier who'd managed to free himself from under his dead teammate. His eyes bugged, his breath shuddering and he shook with fear, scared to even exhale. He lay on his back, staring up at the woman who would either be his merciful angel or his executioner.

"Now, get on *your* knees," she said.

The soldier turned on his stomach, then slowly pushed himself up and sat on his knees. He raised his hands in the air, while his eyes showed fear for the woman that stood before him. Scowling, Katura used the tip of her knife to apply pressure under his chin, making him stand, all the

Nationhood

while staring him in the eyes. She motioned with her other hand for him to drop his weapon, which he quickly flung to the ground.

"Do you want to live?" she asked.

"Yes," he said in a scared, quivering whisper.

Katura's scowl tightened slightly.

"Is there any more like you?"

He nodded his head. "Six more. But they are in the command bunker."

"Good. Tell them to leave this place unless they wish to end up like your friends. This will be the only time I will warn you. You think you can remember that when you wake up?"

With befuddled eyes, the soldier asked, "Wake up?"

She removed the knife from his throat, then delivered a powerful knockout elbow shot to the side of his face. The soldier fell to the ground unconscious. Katura did a quick twirl of her knife and slid it back into its holster. She surveyed her handy work, proud that she could still take out a group of soldiers without breathing hard. But her time for gloating was not to be had for very long.

She remembered there were people still alive inside, live hosts who'd been affected by the virus. If she was able to get to them and administer the antidote, perhaps she would be able to save them. She turned and walked back to Jaquimo with a determined stride, grabbing her gun with the antidote and then turning to walk back toward the building. Jaquimo picked up the larger briefcase containing the bomb and trotted off behind her.

"I say, My Lady. Don't you think this could be most unwise, walking into the building like this?" he asked running along side of her.

"What do you mean?" she asked.

"Aren't you afraid of there being more guards?"

"No. In fact, I know there's not going to be any soldiers inside because most of the people in there are already dead."

"How do you know this?"

"The guard I knocked out told me."

"And you'd believe a man who was just shooting at you?"

"If I was holding a knife to your throat while all of your buddies lay dead on the ground around you, do you think you'd lie?" she asked giving in a snide look.

"Good point, My Lady."

275

James Gordon

"Besides, almost everyone inside is dead."

"And how do you know this? Don't tell me, let me guess. You held a knife to one of the other men's neck, right?"

"You really are silly sometime," said Katura, stopping a few feet in front one of the entrances to the building. "I saw them."

She slipped her arm through the holster strap attached to the antidote gun and allowed it to drape over her left shoulder. She removed a small vile from one of her fatigue pants pockets and tossed it at the door. It was a chemical grenade, one that was more sophisticated that those given to the military. It changed the elemental components of whatever it touched into a combustible combination, literally turning the entire door into a miniature bomb.

The doors imploded and a vacuum of air forced it's way into the building. Jaquimo passed Katura her nine-millimeter as the two of them slowly walked inside and made their way into the main hallway. After a quick perimeter sweep, Katura began walking with a little more urgency, remembering the pathways she saw when she x-rayed the building earlier. Those two people were just around this next corner. She quickly made it to the location where she'd seen them last, only to find they were no long there. Katura looked around, baffled and wondering where they went. Jaquimo saw her slight confusion and voiced his concern.

"My Lady, are you all right?" he asked.

"There were people right here earlier," she said. "I saw them. It was a man and a woman. The man looked hurt, like he was in a lot of pain."

"I thought you said the only people in here were dead."

"I said *almost* everyone. There were two people still alive."

Just then someone bellowed a cry. Seconds later, the blade of a knife appeared across the throat of Jaquimo, causing him to huff in terror. Katura jumped and pointed her gun in his direction. Jaquimo had a scared look on his face while Katura's eyes eased down to stare at the knife blade being held at his neck. She tilted her head slightly to the right and saw a petit woman standing behind him. Katura couldn't quite see her entire face, but she *could* see her eyes. They had a scared glaze in them, like someone who'd been through a lot of trauma and was at the border of crossing into insanity.

It was Carla. She'd removed one of the combat knives from one of the dead soldiers in the next room. She did so just in case someone

Nationhood

came in here and tried to end her life before it was time. It was her weapon now and she gripped it with deadly intent. She'd heard the gunfire and the explosion, believing that it was someone coming to kill her and Abraham. She held the knife firmly across the windpipe of Jaquimo, flexing when Katura raised her gun and pointed it at Carla's forehead.

"Let…him…go," said Katura with a determined tone.

"WHO ARE YOU?" screamed Carla, keeping herself secluded by trying to hide behind Jaquimo.

"Someone you don't want to trifle with."

"You're here to kill us aren't you?"

"If I wanted to do that you'd be dead by now."

"I don't believe you! I'm not going to let you kill us! I'll kill him before I let you touch us!"

"Us? There's more of you?"

"I'll never say! But you have about five seconds to explain yourself or I'll slice his throat!"

They continued their standoff for a few seconds more——Katura with her gun pointed directly at Carla's head and Carla snugly holding the knife across Jaquimo's throat. As she shifted positions, Katura was able to see enough of her face to recognize her. This was the woman aiding the man that she saw lying on the ground. With that realization, the reason behind her frightened behavior became obvious. All the deaths and the resulting rotting corpses whose smell now reeked within the halls of this building had traumatized her, driven her to irrationality and made her into a primal beast hell bent on self-preservation. Of course, the gunfire and the explosion didn't help matters. She had become a terrified animal who was fighting to stay alive, using Jaquimo as a bargaining chip.

Katura knew she had to defuse the situation and help this frantic and near-crazed woman to understand that she wasn't here to harm her.

"Listen," she said. "I know you don't want to do this. You've been through enough and I'm betting that all you want to do is go home. That's why I'm here, to help you go home. In order to do that, to save you so you and your friend can go home to your families, I need to get rid of this virus."

"What guarantee can you give me that you aren't lying to me, that you're not just saying this in order for me to drop my guard?" asked Carla.

"My word."

"Sorry. Not good enough."

James Gordon

Katura realized that she needed to do more in order to show her good intentions, but doing that would risk not only Jaquimo's life, but hers as well. However, it was a risk she had to take. Time was running out and she needed to administer the antidote soon.

She loosened her grip on her nine-millimeter, allowed it to dangle on the edge of her trigger finger. She held it in front of her like an offering to Carla. It was her way of showing her that she wasn't here to harm her.

Carla continued to look like a frightened and panic-stricken animal who'd resorted to hostage taking in order to stay alive. But seeing that Katura had relinquished her threatening posture, as well as her grip on the gun, made her feel less threatened and she began to loosen her grip on the knife a little.

"Place it on the floor," said Carla.

Katura nodded, then slowly knelt to the floor and placed the gun down. She stood to her feet and held out her arms.

"I'm not here to harm you," she said.

"What about the gun on your shoulder?" Carla asked.

"This gun sprays the antidote to the virus that is ravaging you and your friend's bodies. If you let me spray this, I'll be able to help you. I know you don't have a reason to trust me, but as you can see I have no mask, which means I have just as much to lose if this stuff doesn't work."

"Why would you do that? Why would you risk your life for us?"

"I have too many enemies to kill, like the people who are actually responsible for this, and I don't want some stupid virus to stop me from doing that. The longer this stuff is airborne, the more people it will kill. Eventually, it will slaughter everyone on the planet and that is something that doesn't set well with me. So please, let my friend go. I'll release the antidote and we can all live happily ever after."

Carla was torn with indecision. She wanted to believe Katura, wanted to be able to walk out of here with her life and start all over again. Abraham could go home to his wife and daughter and the both of them would be able to tell their story and reveal the individuals responsible for the holocaust that had taken place in this country.

But what if this was all a lie? What if this woman was actually here to kill her and Abe? Perhaps this woman was someone that knew about her and Al-Shahir's conversation, the things he revealed and shared. Maybe she was here to make sure that none of that information ever reached the media? How could Carla be sure? If she trusted her and she

Nationhood

was right it could save both her and Abe's lives, not to mention the lives of billions of people. But if she was wrong, it could cost both of her and Abe's lives and the truth about this incident would be forever buried. With Abraham at death's door, what was Carla going to do? Could she take that chance? Would she dare take that chance?

~~~

It had been a hot day, and as was customary on days such as this the birth of a thunder storm was eminent. The distant rumble could be heard and the building trembled mildly as a result. In that moment, Clarence turned his head and listened to the residual growl of the impending storm as if he was listening to the gods conversing. Then, he turned forward and stared at the television as the media continued their coverage of the military forces preparing to leave.

Vee had already given him the news about Mbaku's arrival at the Senate building. But despite his calm and collected demeanor, he was still concerned, not so much for the state of affairs his country was in anymore, but for his nephew. Mbaku was walking into dangerous territory. Although Pollins suspected he was dead, certainly the crafty politician would not leave anything to chance. He knew his longtime friend well and to think he didn't have a contingency plan was complete lunacy. The only problem was finding out what that plan was.

Clarence needed to do something to generate a conversation. He needed to occupy the interest of the others, hoping to give Mbaku some advantage and perhaps glean some information that would allow his nephew to get the drop on Pollins and Aziz. With his two-way communication link still open, Vee could let Mbaku know everything that was said. He simply needed to stall for time, and as he looked at Aziz he figured out just how to do that.

Earlier, Clarence realized that Aziz was harboring some resentment toward Pollins. Now he would use that information against him, make him bring those feelings to boil. He looked at Pollins and cleared his throat.

"I have to hand it to you, Elijah. I would have never thought anyone could pull off something like this. I'm beginning to see the amount of work you put into this plan of yours," said Clarence.

Pollins turned his attention from the screen and looked at his friend. "Thank you, Clarence," he replied appreciatively.

"I mean I'm really impressed. To get all the countries involved in this took some doing. I take my hat off to you. You are an absolute genius."

"You really think so?"

"I do. At first I couldn't see the intricacies, the details in your plans. At first look I thought you'd gone mad and placed the country in jeopardy. But now, as I look at everything coming together, I'd have to say that this was nothing short of brilliance."

A smile came to Pollins' lips. "Those are mighty generous words, my friend. But I've never known you to be so munificent with compliments. What are you up to?"

"Nothing. I'm merely saying that although I might not be totally supportive of your actions, I can't help but admire the complexity and depth of your plan. This took quite a bit of work and years of preparation. Only great men are able to pull off something like this."

"Right," said Pollins disbelievingly.

"If you don't believe me, ask Reverent Aziz," said Clarence nodding toward him. "Reverend, wouldn't you agree with my assessment of Senator Pollins' genius?"

Aziz's eyes were filled with venom. His lips were pressed together tightly and he stared at Clarence with a hateful leer. Clarence's words fueled the anger and envy that already existed in Aziz's chest, feeling that he should have been the one responsible for the eminent attack on the US. However, he managed to repress his anger and supported his comments.

"Yes, the good senator has done a remarkable job with pooling the forces," said Aziz.

"Pooling the forces?" replied Clarence wryly. "The man literally assembled the greatest coalition of armed services since the Gulf War. Surely you have to see that."

"I see that he has been instrumental in bringing everything together, but he didn't do this alone. It took a combined effort of other factions to make all of this possible."

"Sounds to me you believe you should be taking some of the credit for *his* plan."

"I'm only saying that he is the figurehead."

"Oh, and I'm sure you would have been able to do something like this?" said Clarence with a tone of sarcasm.

"Yes, I could have," said Aziz sharply.

Nationhood

"You must be out of your mind," said Clarence with a chuckle. "How can you, a mere foot soldier, even think you have the mental acumen to pull off something like this? You're a follower, Aziz, not a general. This man has mastered a level of brilliance you could not imagine. Then again, I would expect such disrespect from a mere American."

Aziz was about to move toward Clarence when Pollins intervened, pressing his palm against Aziz's chest to hold him back.

"Easy. He's just trying to get inside your head, Aziz," said Pollins.

"I'd like to place my fist inside of his," Aziz replied.

"Don't mind him. He's just trying to come between us, cause us to turn on one another."

"Am I?" asked Clarence.

Pollins turned and looked at his friend. "Yes, you are. All this talk about me being cleaver and brilliant is all a bunch of bull. You know you aren't impressed by my plan. In fact, I wouldn't be at all surprised to know that you have your own plan to try and stop me."

"And why would I do that, knowing that you are about to take our country to a level surpassing that of the Americans."

"Call it a hunch," said Pollins with a smile.

"You have me all wrong, Elijah. I was simply congratulating you on a well-planned onslaught. But I'd be careful if I were you. That little outburst by Aziz gives one pause to believe that he might not be as supportive as you think."

"You pitiful, stupid dog!" exclaimed Aziz. "How dare you question my loyalty!"

"I question everything about you, Aziz. You come over here without an invitation and suddenly you are a part of something so big that it reeks of brilliance, pure Black brilliance, and not the second-hand slave thinking of a man who imitates Blackness."

"You gutless slug! What makes you think you're more of a Black man than I?"

Clarence knew it was time for the hard stuff. He couldn't pull any punches and he had to make his argument so convincing that it would even startle Pollins. With a smile, he settled against the back of the Victorian chair and stared at Aziz menacingly.

"First of all, color. You are mixed with milky whiteness. The mere sight of you nauseates me and offends me that you could even be considered a member of my people. In fact, I wouldn't be at all surprised to know that you're working against our interests."

"What the hell is that supposed to mean?" asked Pollins, his brow furrowing.

Clarence turned to look at his friend. "Think about it, Elijah. You didn't invite him. Remember, I have the ability to obtain all sorts of information and he was a last minute reservation that happened to show up and provide you with a way to escalate your plans."

"There's where you are wrong, my friend. He wasn't some last minute addition. He's been a part of the plan from the start. Him being here was all arranged."

"What?" asked Aziz, looking at Pollins with wonder.

"Just what I said," replied Pollins, turning to look at the reverend. "I've had people in your organization since its inception. They've been working for me, guiding you to the point to where everything you've done was according to my plans. Your every move, speech, demonstration, right down to the very hand gestures your junior ministers suggested was under my orchestration."

"No, this can't be," said Aziz backing away.

"Oh, but it is. I've been planning this little tea party for over twenty years, ever since we began to build this city from little more than a pile of dirt. I vowed to make the American Empire pay for their disrespect of our people and now that everything is in place I intend to see this promise through till the end."

"But Exodus, I helped to create that. You had nothing to do with that!"

"If Ramses were still here I'd let him tell you himself just how much you actually contributed to the creation of that organization. But since he isn't I'll tell you myself. Zilch, zip, zero, nada. You called me the figurehead, the one who helped organize everything. You foolish diluted man. You were the figurehead, the front man, the puppet I used to distract the Americans while Ramses and I constructed one of the mightiest organizations on the planet."

Aziz began shaking his head in disbelief. Even Clarence's eyes were widened by Pollins' boastful and brash comments.

"You were right, Clarence. Perhaps he is someone who can't be trusted," said Pollins.

Nationhood

The Senator reached into his coat pocket and removed a small hand gun, pointing it at Aziz. The reverend stood with widened eyes, a fearful expression and trembling like a leaf.

"Elijah, Senator Pollins, don't do this. I've been faithful to the cause," said a begging Aziz.

"And you will be remembered for your selfless acts and dedications. Even now a memorial is being constructed in your honor. Although when everything is said and done, I doubt it will hold much significance, seeing that I'll have an even bigger statue when I become the grand potentate of this world."

Three shots were fired, and with those shots everything seemed to be reduced to slow motion. All Clarence could do was watch as the bullets ripped through Aziz's shirt and replaced their entry holes with spurts of blood. His body jerked with each shot, the impact knocking him backwards. He stumbled into a bureau, knocking over a lamp and nearly turning a table over. A stunned expression was painted over his face, no doubt caused by the unbelievable pain that burned his lungs and chest. He clutched his wounded area, his index finger sinking into one of the bullet holes that now had swirls of smoke coming out of it.

Aziz slumped against the wall. He panted heavily, his eyes looking as if he were trying to keep his focus and remain alive for as long as he could. He removed his hand from his chest and stared at his blood-covered palm. Slowly, he lifted his head to look at Pollins, who stared at Aziz stoically. With a gasp, the reverend dropped his hand on his lap, his head falling forward. He wasn't moving.

Pollins inhaled sharply and released a huge exhale, seemingly relieved that whole episode was over. He turned to the two guards in the room.

"Dispose of him," he said.

The two guards grabbed Aziz's lifeless body and carried him out of the room. Pollins turned with a start and pointed his gun at Clarence as the two guards disappeared into the hallway. Clarence didn't appear surprised. If he could kill Aziz, someone who was from his own organization, there was little doubt what he would do to him.

"So, this is the true you, Elijah?" he asked.

"No hard feelings, old friend," said Pollins. "But I can't have any loose ends messing things up. Like I said, I've been planning this for over twenty years. This is the culmination of all my works. For too long I've witnessed mankind's inhumanity toward its brethren. It's time for the oppressed to have their day in court."

"What are you talking about?"

"You know. Each day that goes by our people grow closer to enslavement. In the states, brothers and sisters are treated like lab animals or property, their basic liberties stripped from them. How long do you think it would be before their tyrannical hands reach across the ocean and strangle the life out of this country?"

"So this is about our people in America?"

"It's always been about them. But now, it has become so much more. Ask the Black men and women who fought for the American Empire how it feels to be spat on by White folks who came from another country and now call America their home. Ask them, when they were fighting Russia or Germany or all the other countries, what it feels like to see them being treated more like US citizens then they are, all because of the color of their skin. It is a shame for that country to turn a blind eye to all that is going on, pretending like nothing is wrong."

"Then talk to them, Elijah. Tell them how you feel. Try to handle this diplomatically."

"No. The time for talking is over. They should have never overturned that policy, Elijah. They should have left well enough alone. Now they are going to see how their greed and insolence is repaid. But first, I need to make sure no one is able to stop me. You're the only person standing between me and total victory. I can't risk you compromising everything I've worked for."

Pollins lifted his gun, pointed it at his lifelong friend.

"Elijah, listen. You don't need to do this," said Clarence.

"I'm sorry, old friend. I just can't risk it," Pollins replied.

His finger tightened on the trigger, squeezing. A whirring sound echoed. A thud resounded. The gun flew from Pollins hand, twirled through the air and fell to the wooden floor, sliding to a stop a few feet away.

Pollins grabbed the hand that had clutched the gun. A Japanese throwing star was lodged into the back of it. Blood poured out of the entry wound, a vicious, burning sting ripping through every fiber from his hand to his elbow. He screamed in agony, clutching his wrist as his face contorted from the pain.

As he attended to his injury, his eyes turned toward the door. A

Nationhood

figure stood inside the doorway. Was it one of his men? No. Through the tears caused by the shooting pain inflicted by the star, he began to make out the culprit. It was Mbaku.

Rage surged in Pollins chest as he backed away from Clarence, attempting to distance himself in his seemingly handicapped condition.

"No, I thought you were dead," he said between pants.

"Wishful thinking, I'm afraid," Mbaku replied.

"GUARDS!" Pollins exclaimed.

"My apologies," said the younger Bolo as he entered further into the room. "I dispatched your sorry excuses for security a long time ago. For the last minute or two I stood in the doorway listening to everything you said, even witnessed you killing Reverend Aziz. Although I'm no fan of the man, but he didn't deserve the death you gave him."

Mbaku stood next to his uncle.

"You okay?" he asked.

"Never better. Next time don't cut it so close," Clarence replied.

~~~

James Gordon

Chapter Nineteen: Ace Up My Sleeve

Ramses rode in a black Hummer equipped with armor plated panels in the doors, dark-tinted, bullet-proof windows, steel floor plates and reinforced tires. The vehicle was also loaded with an assortment of rocket launchers and assault rifles, making it virtually a tank with eloquent style. The vehicle was escorted by a couple of Cadillac Escalades, one in front and the other behind, both black and both equally loaded with all the trimmings. It didn't take long before Ramses arrived at the compound and immediately went to the room where he visitors were being kept.

Thurgood didn't say much once Ramses arrived. He pondered the potential impact the war was going to have on the country as well as the rest of the world. Armed guards surrounded him and Lela, only allowing them to go to the restroom and then back to their seats.

When Ramses arrived, he entered the room like the commander-in-chief, a posture Thurgood found intriguing and disturbing. He and Lela stared at him like a man with the plague. He was a plague, as far as they were concerned and somehow Thurgood had to find a way to stop this madness before it could start.

The conference room was a designer's dream, surrounding them with luxury and status. An extensive mahogany table that was smoothed, polished to perfection and glossed with an enamel finish sat in the middle of the room. Plush high-back leather chairs encircled the table. The walls were a deep sea-blue trimmed with pure ivory crown molding. The floor was made of blue marble polished to a stunning shine.

Surrounding them were five of Ramses' most menacing-looking guards, each of them toting AK-47s. Thurgood's eyes gazed at all of them, seeing if their facial expression or body language showed signs that one of them was an undercover agent who was there to save them. None of them gave any hint of such intent. Realizing there would be no cavalry coming to save them, he decided he had to make his move now. But for the life of him he didn't have the slightest clue what to do. He decided that he would start a conversation and hope that something would come to mind.

James Gordon

"So, you plan to attack the US military installations?" probed Thurgood.

"That would be the plan right now," Ramses replied, sipping on some cognac.

"Then why do you need us?" Lela chimed in. "Why not let us go? Obviously there's no way for us to stop you."

Thurgood was surprised by her interruption. But, he was glad that he would not have to go it alone in this situation.

"I'm keeping you here because I want you to witness something that will be truly incredible," said Ramses. "In about two minutes my forces around Washington DC and every other state capital from Florida to Alaska will put in motion the first successful coupe in the history of this country. We are going to make the Civil War look like a footnote in US history."

"How? You intend on bombing the states' capitols and the nation's capitol?" asked Thurgood.

"No, something better than that. Just keep watching the television. You'll see what happens."

~~~

"I don't know if I should trust you!" said Carla, still holding the knife to Jaquimo's throat.

"Listen," said Katura. "I placed my gun on the ground. I've told you what I need to do in order to save our lives. You have a knife at my friend's throat. I'm not sure what else can be done to let you know that any attempt by me to trick you would be of little good. I don't want to die and I know my friend doesn't want to die. I'm sure you want to live but in order for that to happen I need to release this antidote."

Carla felt her heart beating faster. God, how she wanted to believe this woman was being honest. "I don't know," she said shaking her head.

"If you don't believe me then go outside. I'll spray the stuff in here, take an air sample and then leave."

"No! You see I know there are people out there who will kill us if we set one foot out that door! Now I know you're trying to kill us!"

"No, there's no one outside. I killed most of them just to get in here, to help save you. Please, there isn't much time. Your fellow countrymen will begin to show the signs of this disease. If we don't get this stuff in the air soon, a lot of people are going to suffer."

Nationhood

Just then, Carla could hear Abraham coughing violently. Her eyes flashed toward the room she'd placed him in, discomfort and concern written in her expression. He was getting worse and soon he would be puking blood and it would be too late to do anything for him. However, she still didn't know whether to trust Katura.

One thing was for certain. If she was going to do something, she had to do it now. She pondered for a moment longer, realizing that either way, whether she was right or wrong, she would be freed from this predicament she was in. If she were dead she would not have to deal with the discomforts she would encounter if the virus began to eat away her insides. Abraham's death would be quick and neither of them will suffer any further indignities.

But, if Katura was being truthful and she did have the antidote, there was a chance that both of them would get out of this alive and could continue the fight they were committed to. With one more look into Katura's eyes, Carla slowly removed the knife from Jaquimo's neck, then pushed him forward, almost causing him to collide with Katura.

"You okay?" she asked.

"Yes," Jaquimo replied.

With arms outstretched, Carla leered wearily at Katura. "So, I guess this is where you shoot me, huh?" she asked.

Katura pulled the rifle from over her shoulder and pointed it at Carla. "Yes, it is."

Carla gulped, the knife dropping from her hand and clanging on the floor. She closed her eyes tightly and waited for the shot. An explosive hiss resounded in the hallway. Carla felt her lungs fill with something that felt like cement. She couldn't breathe, thinking that she'd been shot in the chest and this was how it felt to have your insides turned to mush. It didn't hurt quite as badly as she thought it would—no pain, just a tingling sensation that burned slightly.

With her arms still outstretched, Carla anticipated that she would fall any minute and feel the hard slap of the floor against the back of her head. Still, no pain ever came. Her brow furrowed, opening her eyelids slightly and peeking through the tiny slits. She saw light, perhaps the one everybody sees when they died, she thought. She saw something moving, two images, a guy and a woman, the ones that she saw before she was shot, Katura and Jaquimo.

She opened her eyes fully, her brow still furrowed. Katura

lowered her gun as Jaquimo pulled out a small black instrument and held it in the air. Faint beeping sounds cold be heard. Anxious eyes stared at its readout.

"Looks good," said Jaquimo. "Already the readings are lower, down by four clicks per second."

"Good, then we're ready for phase two," Katura replied.

Carla looked perplexed, befuddled. Still frowning, she looked at Katura, who met her gaze as she prepared to leave.

"Wait for about five minutes before you try to leave. That way if some of the disease is still on your clothes or on your person, the mist should kill it, makes it less likely of a re-infection," the sleek spy explained as she walked passed Carla.

"Wait a minute," said Carla, causing Katura to stop in her tracks and turn to face her. "That was it? No shots or no strip searching? You mean you sprayed that stuff in the air and that was it?"

"Yes. I told you that's all I needed to do," Katura replied. "Of course, if you want to be strip searched, Jaquimo, here, would be most anxious to oblige."

Carla's eyes looked at Jaquimo, who had one of those *trust me* smiles on his face. She shook her head. "Never mind."

Katura snickered briefly. Jaquimo looked offended. Katura turned to her assistant. "Jaquimo, why don't you check on her friend and see how he's doing," she said.

Jaquimo nodded, then with a gesture of his hand asking Carla to lead the way, they walked down the hall toward the area that she'd taken Abraham. Katura stood there with one hand propped on her hip and shaking her head. A pleased look covered her face, but then it turned serious. This was a ploy, a way to get Jaquimo away from her so she could do what she needed to do. The real job was now at hand—she needed to set off the bomb.

Having Jaquimo around would only complicate things. She wanted him to be safe, nowhere near the place where she would detonate the device. If she didn't get rid of him he would only insist that he come with her, something she could not allow. She reached to the floor, picked up the case containing the bomb and proceeded to the door. She kicked it open and walked outside, trotting until she got a few hundred feet from the building.

She sat the case down and opened it, slowly pulling the top back.

Nationhood

She reverently gazed at the bomb, sucking in a deep breath through her nose. She was excited and scared, ready to do what had to be done and disregarding the chance that she wouldn't make it out of there alive.

As her hand rested on the keyboard, her mind drifted to thoughts of Durst Weinkaufen, her father. He was tall and strong and very opinionated. If he didn't believe in something, he didn't do it, no matter how you threatened him. He was a gifted man, played the violin and the piano. His voice was amazing when he sang, a strong baritone bass that gave his singing just a touch of pain when he performed opera. He'd always been a peaceful man and it troubled her that someone would take his life-long work and trash it by turning it into a virus.

"I'm sorry, father. I'm sorry they did this to your work," she said.

Suddenly, as if a voice had spoken to her and revealed the truth, another thought struck Katura. Could it be that the virus wasn't a manifestation of his work? That, in truth, the very serum that sat in the container before her was what he'd perfected to cure the disease that was now being used as a biological weapon. Yes, that had to be it. The virus didn't come after the cure, but the other way around. All this time Katura was led to believe that her father's work had been corrupted and turned into a living nightmare as it relates to germ warfare. But the truth was her father found the cure knowing what the military was up to. That's why he was killed, because he would not give up the secret of his invention. That had to be it and now that she understood why and how he stored the antidote in her head. He wanted her to be able to expose the truth and show the world the horrors that happen behind closed doors.

Looking at the container, Katura realized more than ever that her being there wasn't a coincidence. A plethora of possibilities flooded her mind. Somehow Durst was responsible for her being placed in the government IS program so that she could stop them from destroying the world with this virus. Yes, that would certainly make sense. How else could she explain being given all the abilities she has in order to carry out this mission. Her father turned her over to the government and, in turn, was given everything she needed to stop this virus from being spread—her physical abilities, the mental enhancements, even the formula. It was providence, her fate, her destiny to be the one to release the antidote. It was all so clear to her now, like pieces of an intricate puzzle being slid into place and seeing the entire picture in all its intricate magnificence. However, it was not the time to gloat over this revealing data. It was time to bring this terrifying ordeal to an end, to fulfill her purpose.

As her hand began to press the start codes on the timer, a bullet struck the control panel. Sparks flew from the shattered and utterly destroyed keypad, sending slivers of glass flying into the air. Katura drew back her hand, but she moved too late. Her flesh was instantly burned by the exploding sparks and blood flowed from the lacerations caused by the flying shards.

Acting on pure instinct, she quickly hopped behind the case cover, using the metal lining as a shield. A rain of bullets screamed through the air and pounded against the protective lining of the lid. She quickly realized what was happening. The guard she'd allowed to live didn't do as she instructed. Instead, he and his comrades now sought revenge for the assassination of their buddies. They continued to approach her location, firing rounds of bullets that battered the case containing the bomb, a sticky situation that could wind up detonating the bomb any moment.

Katura was pinned down and there was nowhere for her to escape. With very few options remaining, she realized she would have to kill the rest of them. That was the only way she was going to get out of there alive. She reached to her side to retrieve her firearm. It was then she remembered she left her gun in the building on the floor, not thinking that she would have to fight the remaining guards that didn't take her advice and leave.

There is no time for this, she thought. She had to release the antidote now or risk an epidemic that might not be reversible. But there was a bigger problem. If the advancing soldiers didn't stop shooting they might set off the bomb by accident. At this range, Katura knew she would be vaporized if it went off. However, if she left from behind the protection of the case top she would most certainly be killed. With time running out, Katura had a decision to make, and none of the choices seemed acceptable.

~~~

"I should be angry with you," said Mbaku as he began stalking Pollins around the room. "Kidnapping my uncle, your longtime friend. How despicable you are."

Pollins removed the star from the back of his hand with a yank and a bellow of pain. Panting, he pointed the bloody tip at Mbaku.

"Do not pretend to be my judge and jury, young one," said

Nationhood

Pollins. "The things I've seen would make you cry out in your sleep—nightmares beyond your wildest fantasizes."

"Be that as it may, it still doesn't give you the right to play God with people's lives. You killed Aziz and those other senators at the airport, not to mention anyone else who contracted that disease. You threatened my uncle. You even tried to have me killed. I have every right to skin you alive right now."

Continuing to back away, Pollins found that he'd run out of room, backing himself into a wall. Mbaku approached, looking menacingly at him, rage painted in both pupils. A ninja sword slid down his coat sleeve and rested in his palm, one of the weapons that came with the suit. He swung it and stopped the cutting edge right at Pollins' neck.

"WHY SHOULD I ALLOW YOU TO LIVE?" he shouted angrily.

Although he was breathing heavily with flaring nostrils and a fearful expression, Mbaku saw something that slightly unnerved him—Pollins' eyes. They were devoid of fear—clear, like he wasn't afraid. Although he seemed terrified on the outside, something told Mbaku that Pollins was calm and cool on the inside, like whether he died or not didn't matter to him.

The young assassin had seen that look before in the eyes of suicide bombers, people who would blow themselves up for the causes they stood for. That was a dangerous sign because that meant he would not think twice about killing anyone when given the opportunity, even if he had to take his own life. He was a Black Mamba, a killer without care. Mbaku now saw that he could not let him live, for he was a threat to every living being on the planet. He brought back his sword and prepared to deliver the killing stroke.

"MBAKU, NO!" shouted Clarence.

The bellowing of his uncle caused an immediate reaction in the younger Bolo. He stopped his blade just inches from slicing into Pollins' throat, the razor sharp blade hovering just in front of his Adam's Apple. Mbaku looked into Pollins' eyes. The senator never once blinked. The two men stood there, frozen in time, their eyes locking, challenging each other in silent combat. They understood each other, realizing that if one of them didn't get killed, the other would be sorry for it.

The hunger to kill him was overwhelming to Mbaku. He knew that Pollins was a threat and to let him live would invite another chance for him to do something like this. He rested his blade against his flesh, watching it slice his skin upon touch, a trickle of blood oozing from the cut.

"I said that's enough," said Clarence.

"Don't be easy on him, uncle. He doesn't deserve your generosity," said Mbaku, continuing to hold the sword at Pollins' neck.

"He's right, Clarence. I don't deserve your kindness," said the near motionless senator.

"SHUT UP! My uncle should not be lowering himself to talk to you. I say we should kill you right here and now," said Mbaku.

"And what good would that serve?" asked Clarence. "You would allow him to leave this world without punishment. He should pay for his crimes so that those whose families suffered from his malevolence can have closure to their losses. You cannot allow your anger to cloud your thinking. You must do the right thing and turn him over to the authorities."

"We both know that he would be out in a matter of days, planning his next coupe in even less time. No, uncle, I cannot...let...him...pass."

Mbaku pressed the sword a little deeper. More blood rolled down the senator's neck. Pollins' voice squeaked.

"Mbaku!" Clarence exclaimed. "If you kill him you will become what he is. You will be a man who no longer fights for the honor of his country, but is nothing more than a vigilante, a thug, a murderer who waits to take his frustrations out on his next victim. Don't let yourself sink to his level. You must rise above it. Please, think about it, son."

His teeth gnashed and grinded, his jaw tightened, his hand anxiously waited to finish pressing the sword through the soft tissue of Pollins' neck. But, as much as he wanted to dismiss his uncle's words, Mbaku held back his desire to kill, his inner strength coming through in the end. Against his better judgment, he eased the sword from Pollins' neck. The senator released a deep sigh as a group of agents raced through the chamber door.

"Yes, now you'll pay for what you've done. Guards, arrest these men," said Pollins.

"I'm afraid you're under arrest, Senator," said the lead guard.

A baffled look came to Pollins face as the guards maneuvered his hands behind him and read him his rights.

"But, how? What is the meaning of this?" asked Pollins.

"See, that's the problem with you bad guy types. You talk way

Nationhood

too much, and when you do that you give up all the info anyone needs to bring you down," said Mbaku.

A look of revelation came on Pollins' face. "You were bugged. Very ingenious. You are shaping up to be quite a little surprise, young Bolo," Pollins said.

As they secured the cuffs and marched him toward the door, he stopped just inside the entryway and turned back to address Mbaku.

"Perhaps we shall duel wits again," he said.

"Not in this lifetime," Mbaku replied.

Pollins scoffed. "You never know, lifetimes can be so short sometimes."

Mbaku frowned. The officers manhandled Pollins away, taking him toward the front door where a SWAT vehicle was waiting for him.

Not giving the senator's comment a second thought, Mbaku turned to look at his uncle, allowing his sword to retract back into his sleeve.

"I'm not so sure we did the right thing," said Mbaku.

"Sometimes doing what's right isn't doing what's easiest," Clarence replied.

"You sound like a Buddhist or a Tibetan Monk," said Mbaku, smiling at his uncle.

"But no less sound advice."

Mbaku huffed. "So, you feeling okay? I mean, he was one of your oldest friends."

"He will always be my friend. Indeed, he has made some poor choices, but he has a purpose, Mbaku, even if it is to raise the ire of our people. Sometimes anger can lead to action."

"Perhaps you are right, Uncle. I just wonder about him. Something in his eyes didn't seem like he was all there."

"He was all there, I'm afraid, more there than most people give him credit for. He's a brilliant man, Mbaku, never...under...underestimate him."

Clarence started having trouble breathing, clutching his chest and kneeling to the floor. Mbaku quickly grabbed on to him and tried to keep him from falling. He assisted him to the floor, lying him on his side and trying to comfort him as best he could.

"Uncle, what's the matter?" Mbaku asked frantically.

Clarence had trouble speaking. He was gasping for air and a

gurgling sound emanated from his throat.

"HELP!" Mbaku screamed toward the door. "SOMEBODY GET AN AMBULANCE!"

He looked back at his uncle, who was gazing around the room wildly and still attempting to catch his breath. He managed to focus his stare on his nephew, his breathing becoming more stable.

"M-Mbaku," said Clarence wheezing. "You...are...on your...own now, son. Please...remember what...I taught you. The safety...of our country...depends on...you."

His eyes became fixed, his breathing slowed to non-existence. The weight of his head became heavier.

Mbaku, still supporting his uncle's head, shook it lightly. "Uncle, speak to me," he said. There was no reply. Over and over Mbaku called to his uncle, each call louder than the last, shaking him more aggressively with each shout. Still, nothing.

Paramedics scrambled into the room, locating Mbaku and his uncle. They raced to them, but the young spy knew it was too late. His uncle was gone.

The emergency team still did their routine, taking vitals and hooking him up to a defibulator monitor. They scooped the elder Bolo on the gurney and whisked him out of the room. Mbaku continued to sit there, slumped on the floor in disbelief, not sure whether to scream or cry or kill something. He watched the attendants leave, shock covering his face, disbelief trying to convince him that this wasn't happening. But he'd seen death far too many times and he knew it when he saw it.

How did this happen, he thought. He could see no injuries on his uncle's body, heard no distress in his voice until the last instant. Regardless of his assessment or his bewilderment, he prayed for a miracle. He prayed that somehow his uncle would pull through this and everything would turn out all right. But, if something managed to kill his uncle, Mbaku was going to find out what.

He stood from the floor, sucked in a deep breath and raced out of the door after the paramedics.

~~~

Lela was beginning to grow impatient. Thurgood was antsy and Ramses grew more pleased as each moment progressed. They stared at the television screen, the national news, for what neither Thurgood nor Lela had any idea. But their captor knew and he wasn't telling—at least, not

Nationhood

yet.

For several minutes Lela had been watching the screen as unimportant and uninteresting segments about the economy and restlessness in the urban areas was reported. After another minute went by, Lela had had enough and decided to speak.

"What are we watching for?" she asked with great annoyance in her voice.

"Only a few seconds more," said Ramses holding up his index finger. In that same instant, Thurgood held up his middle finger and pointed it at Ramses, who merely chuckled.

"I know this has been unpleasant, but I assure you we will all be much better from what I'm about to do," he said.

Thurgood swung his head in Ramses' direction. "I don't care what it is you're trying to do here, Ramses!" he said. "You think holding us hostage is winning you any approval points in my book? Hell, no! You've kept us in the dark playing this cat and mouse game! You disgust me!"

Meanwhile, Lela turned her attention back to the television. Suddenly, her eyes widened as a newsbreak came across the screen.

"Uh, Thomas?" she said, tugging on his sleeve.

"I thought you were someone who was really trying to make a difference!" Thurgood continued to shout at Ramses. "But now I see what you really are!"

Ramses didn't look at him, but kept his eyes on the television screen, a smile now blooming across his lips.

"You think that's funny?" screamed Thurgood louder.

"Thomas!" said Lela a little louder.

"That's all this is to you, isn't it!" Thurgood continued. "Just a big-ass game, huh? Well some of us aren't amused and now the world will know that none of Exodus can be trusted!"

Finally, Ramses replied. "For however long that lasts," he said.

"What?" asked Thurgood. "What the hell is that supposed to mean?"

"THOMAS!" screamed Lela.

"What?" he asked, turning to look at her.

She pointed to the screen, eyes wide with fear, mouth slightly agape.

Still fuming, Thurgood turned and looked at the screen. The

James Gordon

blood drained quickly from his face as he read the headlines. 'TRAGEDY IN WASHINGTON D.C.' He listened as the reporter relayed the information.

"The nation's capitol is locked down tonight as a result of a string of mysterious illnesses that struck Washington D.C. with a vengeance. On Capitol Hill, seventy-five senators and over four hundred congressmen and women have suddenly fallen ill to a vicious disease that has already taken the lives of Congresswoman Linda Grace and Senator Tom Greene. It is unsure at this time how many more members have been infected, but the entire body of the legislative branch has been quarantined and the virus has doctors at Walter Reed stumped."

"A shame what happened to Senator Greene," said Ramses.

Thurgood fell against the back of his chair, stunned beyond all words. His breath trembled, his eyes watering.

"No," he said in a whisper.

"Now, that's the kind of publicity you just can't buy," said Ramses. "But wait, there's more."

The reporter went on to say that only moments ago a massive explosion ripped through New York's financial district, destroying everything including the New York Stock Exchange, all of Wall Street and the World Financial Center. In a heartbeat, everything was gone.

In a separate segment there was a report of wildfires destroying farmlands in the Midwest. Entire crops were lost and the incident had weather people and meteorologists shaking their heads. They were expecting rain on the forecast, but somehow their predictions were wrong. A searing heat wave hit the heartlands, reducing the crops to cinder in a matter of hours.

Ramses continued to stare smugly at the television. However, tears were streaming down Lela's face, her hands covering her mouth. She was breathing heavily, trying hard to believe that what she'd seen and heard weren't actually happening. She turned and looked at Ramses, who finally removed his eyes from the television screen and looked at her and Thurgood.

"Dear God," she said softly. "What have you done?"

Ramses stood from his seat and began to walk the floor.

"I am the cleansing hand of our God, the redeemer who has come to set his people free," Ramses boasted. "Exodus is but a small part of this grand scheme. In fact, much bigger players have invested in this little exhibition."

"You are insane," said Lela.

Ramses stopped and looked at her. "I believe history will see things otherwise." He resumed pacing. "You call me insane. Was it insanity when Hitler killed all of those Jews? Yes, it was. But he was also considered a genius with a penchant for the extreme. Some have even created Neo-Nazi parties right here in America with one intent in mind, to kill our people and erase us off the planet. For years Blacks have suffered while the unjust get away with everything. They grow richer, more powerful, more destructive and more oppressive as the days go on. They've even allowed immigrants from Russia and Germany and France to come to this country and be treated better than us. What you just saw was only the tip of the iceberg. There is more suffering to come."

Thurgood stood to his feet and leered at Ramses. "You are a monster," he growled.

"Why? Because I have the fortitude to do what must be done. Think about it, Thurgood. All this time those in power had the opportunity to make things right. But they didn't do a damn thing while we, the poor pitiful Black folk, have another rally, another protest, another boycott, another Million-Man March. When will enough be enough? When are we going to stand up and face our enemy and say, no more. I'll tell you when, today. We make our stand right here and right now. That little virus that spread throughout the airport in AUNK was only a teaser compared to what just ravaged the nation's capitol. Notice anything peculiar about the senators who are ill?"

Thurgood thought about it, but couldn't find the connection. However, Lela did.

"They're all White," she replied.

Thurgood flashed her a look of surprise.

"All of the senators who have no shred of Blackness in them are sick. The ones that have some pigmentation to their skin aren't suffering from it quite as badly," she further explained.

"Very perceptive, Miss Washington," said Ramses.

Thurgood wheeled his head back around. "You made a virus that can specifically kill all White people?" he asked.

"Not all. Just enough to let the world know that we aren't going to stand for this second-classed citizen shit any longer. The wildfires in the Midwest, all a part of the satellite weapon system the US has had trained

James Gordon

on us for the last several years. We simply used it's mirror dish, made some minor programming adjustments and, voile, instant roasted corn for all those corn huskers. You see, Mister Thurgood, the time is now and we are going to get what is rightfully ours, even if I have to kill every pale-skinned person on the planet. But, there is only one way to make this right, and you are going to be a large part of this."

"I will not be a part of this," Thurgood replied with clenched teeth.

"Oh yes, you will. In a few short hours you are going to carry a note to Senator Decker, that lousy racist Senator from Alabama. On that note will be the set of demands that must be met before I release the antidote and stop my war against this country. If they aren't met, then by tomorrow night every last person who doesn't have at least one Black parent will be dead."

This is insane!" screamed Lela, jumping to her feet. "Not everyone is like that! There are still some good people in this world and you're killing them! You're no better than those bigots you spoke of!"

"Oh, but I am so much more," said Ramses. "I am the apocalypse, the rapture, the one who shall be rising in the east. I've brought them war by blowing up their financial district. I brought them famine by burning their crops. I've brought them pestilence by giving them the very virus they intended to use on us. Now, all I need to do is wait and death will surely come."

"All four horsemen rolled into one, huh?" asked Thurgood.

"Enough of this idle prattle. I have a world to conquer," said Ramses. He nodded to the guards who lifted their guns and pointed them at Thurgood and Lela.

"I thought you wanted me to deliver a message?" asked Thurgood.

"I'm not going to kill you, Mister Thurgood. Your roll in all of this is much bigger than you know. When you wake up, your instructions will be clear."

Ramses walked out of the room, nodding at one of the guards as he left. Thurgood and Lela huddled as the guard aimed and fired a single shot. Their bodies flinched and their eyes squeezed shut. Oddly, neither of them felt the burn of a gunshot.

Seconds later, however, Thurgood felt a stinging sensation in his right arm. He looked down and saw a dart sticking out from his shoulder.

300

Nationhood

He lifted his hand to remove it, but before he could pull the dart out his body went completely numb. His hand dropped to his side, his knees began to buckle. The room spun at an incredible rate and everything was fuzzy. As Lela attempted to reach for him, Thurgood fell to the ground on his back and lost consciousness.

~~~

Any moment now this thing is going to blow, Katura thought. She knew she needed to get out of there. But with no guns, advancing soldiers and a rain of gunfire she was virtually out of options. She had only one choice. She would make a run for it, hoping to draw their gunfire away from the bomb. She knew the chances of her getting shot were great, but at least it would be better than being blown to bits. She turned on her stomach and got ready to make her dash.

As she waited for the right moment, Katura had to admit she was disappointed in herself, feeling that she lost her focus and allowed herself to get into this predicament. How could she be so stupid as to forget her gun and leave it on the floor. Now she was defenseless and seconds away from being blown to smithereens. So much for the great plans of her father, Durst. If he could see her now he would be most disappointed. If it weren't for the fact she was scared out of her mind she would actually cry. But there was no use crying over spilled milk. It was do or die. She crouched to all fours and prepared for her sprint for life.

Just as she was about to run, the gunfire stopped. Faint yelps of pain were heard followed by a deafening silence. Katura wondered why they stopped firing. Did they run out of ammunition or were they waiting to see if she would make a run for it? Perhaps they realized they were shooting at a bomb and decided to back away before they blew themselves and her into the outer atmosphere.

Although she knew it was wishful thinking on her part, Katura hoped that a miracle had shined upon her. It was then she heard a voice calling to her.

"Lady Katura, where are you?" the voice of Jaquimo shouted.

With a furrowing brow she slowly peeked from behind the case top. To her wonderment she saw Jaquimo and Carla, both toting guns standing next to the dead bodies of the guards that had been firing at her. Disbelief was all she could think of. Here she was trying to keep him out of harms way and Jaquimo ends up saving her. What irony.

She slowly rose to her feet, the sand falling from her clothing.

James Gordon

"Are you all right?" asked Jaquimo yelling.

"Yes!" Katura yelled back. "Did you happen to bring my gun?"

"Indeed! I have it right here!"

Katura began walking toward Jaquimo and Carla, brushing the sand off as she drew closer. She stopped in front of them and gave each one a stern look as Jaquimo passed her the nine-millimeter.

"That was rather dangerous what you two did out there," said Katura.

"Consider it my way of thanking you for saving my life," said Carla. "Abe has got a lot of healing to do. But I think he'll be okay. I'm sure I speak for him when I say, thank you."

Carla stuck out her hand. Katura looked at it, then lifted her eyes to stare once more into Carla's brown pupils. She lifted her hand and shook it.

"This isn't how women normally express their gratitude. But after what we both went through, I wouldn't consider us to be just women anymore," said Carla.

"You're wrong," Katura retorted. "We *are* women. We're just not froufrou."

The two women smiled at each other.

"Now, I suggest you two find a place to hide," said Katura. "The keypad controls are gone and since that was the easy way to detonate the bomb it looks like I'm going to have to do things the hard way."

Carla nodded, then turned and walked back into the building. Jaquimo stayed behind for an instant.

"Are you sure you know what you're doing?" he asked.

"Nope." Katura replied. "Now, get going."

Jaquimo seemed reluctant to comply, but also knew he couldn't argue with her. She was a marksmen and one of the best spies in the world. If anyone could pull this off, Katura could. As he walked into the building, Katura checked her surroundings. She was pretty much out in the open and shooting a bomb from this distances was sure to be suicidal. But, it had to be done.

She checked behind her, the door to the building was slightly ajar. A smile came to her lips and a look of determination appeared on her face. She lifted her gun and took aim at the triggering device. She only had one shot at this and her timing had to be flawless. One miscalculation and she would be dead. She took aim, adjusted for the wind, placed the target

302

Nationhood

in her sights. She sucked in a slow, deep breath, then she slowly squeezed the trigger.

~~~

James Gordon

Chapter Twenty: We'll Meet Again, Someday

The plume of smoke rose into the air and spread across the upper stratosphere, the proverbial mushroom cloud. The wind that was created from the blast was strong, but caused minimal damage. Most of the area near the detonation site was consumed in sand, a few vehicles were overturned and a fair amount of the airport had to be shut down due to clean up efforts and for the removal of the bodies stored in the conference area. In spite of that, the air was clean once more and all traces of the virus had been eradicated.

The sun was shining brighter that ever. Blue skies and fluffy white cumulonimbi created a beautiful overhead tapestry, giving hope that better days were on the horizon. A new beginning had dawned, a beginning that brought both promise and global awareness of what lied in store for this proud nation. Now it was time to rebuild.

There were no signs of sorrow, no teary eyes or wails of despair. Instead, life was moving on, just as it always has. The high optimism of the nation was an amazing feat, considering the fact that the citizens of AUNK had just been through one of the worst situations in recorded history. They were taken to the brink of war, a scant hair's breath away from conflict, and only by the intervention of a few brave people were they able to avert it.

Rebuilding the small damaged portion of the city was nothing compared to the near catastrophic destruction that would have been brought by the war that almost happened. That was the thought that lived in the minds of those who were helping to restore things to normal. Brick by brick the eastern portion of the airport would be rebuilt, bigger and better than before. Brick by brick the surrounding buildings would be reconstructed, perhaps there was even the possibility of a completely new look. The restoration was going to be costly and time consuming, but it would be infinitely easier compared to the repairs that would take place in many of the citizen's lives.

Although the majority of the populace tried to look at the positive side of things, the crisis caused losses, created fears and chaos. Yet, it

James Gordon

opened a new chapter in the evolution of the Nation of AUNK, a chapter that would be remembered for many centuries to come.

Those whose lives were lost in this holocaust would be immortalized. Their heroism and self-sacrifice would become legend in the pages of AUNK's history books. They would be remembered as patriots, warriors, soldiers, heroines and martyrs. Monuments would be erected in their honor and ballads would sing of their greatness and of their devotion to their country. Schools would be named after them and great halls of research would be dedicated to them. And then, there would be gardens, lush and colorful and brimming with life.

Snapdragons, sunflowers and lilies. Traditional arrangements of gladiolas, white carnations and white daisies abounded. Spectacular displays of red roses trimmed in Ti leaves and dagger ferns. White mums with lemon leaves and tulip vine wreaths. These arrangements filled the area along with pink, yellow or white roses accented with a full stock of baby's breath. It was a bouquet of color, creating a fragrant and festive air. To many, this beautifully convivial collection of flowers would bring inspiration and peace to those who gazed at the plethora of flora. But to Mbaku Bolo, all of this meant one thing—his prayer wasn't answered.

He stared at his uncle as he lay in his casket. He looked like he was sleeping. He didn't know what to say, couldn't find the words to explain what happened and why he didn't see this coming. In some respects he felt that this was his fault, that he'd somehow caused all of this and was responsible for his uncle's death.

As he inhaled deeply, he felt himself losing his composure. His guilt was getting the best of him, ripping at his heart and tearing him apart inside. He searched his thoughts, looking for a way to regain control of himself and find a justification why his uncle was lying in a coffin mere inches in front of him. But there were no easy solutions. This was all too unbelievable, too surreal, too painful to accept. His uncle couldn't be dead. This had to be a dream that he would be waking up from soon.

His remorse made him feel as if everyone else blamed him for this. His head turned and he looked around the room. There were a lot of people there, friends of Clarence who'd come to pay their last respects. Although they each had solemn faces, Mbaku's insecurities made him feel that their whispered conversations were about him, ridiculing him for not protecting his uncle and cursing him for allowing him to die.

He wanted to find a way out, some side door that would allow

Nationhood

him the ability to escape. But there was no way he could leave. In fact, he really didn't want to be alone, just away from the gawking eyes and the air of blame. He wanted to talk to someone and tell them that he'd done everything he could to ensure his uncle's safety. He wanted to commiserate with someone and share stories about a man he had the utmost respect for. Then again, he wished he could go to some remote place where he could think. He needed some space, a place where he could hide from his shame and run from his pain. In short, he wanted to go home.

The toxicology report showed that Clarence died from the same thing the people at the airport died from, the cancerous disease that ate its hosts from the inside out. But when the results were given, there was one question that could not be answered—how did he catch the virus? He hadn't been anywhere near the airport, was never in contact with any of the individuals who'd been infected with the virus. That could only mean one thing, he'd been infected while he was at the Senate building.

No one at the hospital had a clue as to how this could happen. But Mbaku had an idea. With the help of Vee it didn't take long to find out how the virus was administered. Through deductive reasoning and some sharp investigative work, they surmised that if the virus were airborne it would have infected everyone in the Senate, including the guards and Pollins. Since that wasn't the case, that left the obvious conclusion—the virus was introduced into Clarence Bolo using an exclusive medium—the tea.

Somehow Pollins, or someone he was affiliated with, managed to convert the virus into a form that remained active in liquid. Once ingested, it immediately entered the bloodstream, killing off the white blood cells and preventing the body from being able to create antibodies to fight the disease. Within a few moments necrosis would take place in the organs and it would be a matter of time before death came.

The liquid version was much more potent and very difficult to detect in comparison to the airborne version. But with careful research and patience, they found it and concluded that that was how it was done, how Pollins murdered Clarence Bolo.

Mbaku continued to stare at his uncle's face. He looked so peaceful, eyes closed and his hands resting one atop the other across his chest. However serene the setting, Mbaku was anything but peaceful. He was angry and hurt, but knew this was neither the time nor the place to let those emotions show. He would deal with them soon enough, as well as the person responsible for what happened to his uncle. He knew exactly who to go to, the one person he knew without a shadow of a doubt did this—Elijah Pollins.

Vee walked up next to Mbaku, tapping her walking cane lightly. Her hand cupped his elbow. He turned his head toward her.

"You okay?" she asked.

"Are you kidding?" he replied.

"I know this is tough. We all loved Clarence like he was our own father. He was a good man, taught me everything I knew." There was a pause as they both stood there lost in the moment, Mbaku staring at Clarence. Then Vee spoke again. "We'll get him, Mbaku. He will not get away with this."

Mbaku kept staring at his uncle.

"He was smarter than we were, Vee. Pollins set this whole thing up. The virus, the coalition, everything. If we hadn't gotten in contact with the president and allowed him to listen to him bragging about what he'd done via our communicator we would be at war right now."

"Thank goodness the president called off the attack when he found out."

Mbaku thought a little more. "He wasn't going to shoot him."

"Who?" Vee asked.

"Pollins. He had no intention of firing his gun. He knew my uncle was already at death's door. The question is why all the theatrics?"

Vee turned her head toward him.

"He wanted your attention, Mbaku. For whatever reason this was not directed at Clarence. This was directed toward you. He wanted you to know that he took away your uncle and there was nothing you could do about it."

"When I looked into his eyes, I saw it, Vee. I saw that he wasn't all there. It was like staring into an empty vase, there was nothing left inside, just a huge empty shell."

"We're dealing with a devilish individual, Mbaku, and from now on we need to be very careful."

"You're right, this was intended to hurt me. But why? Why would he come after me?"

"Who knows? Perhaps you pose some sort of challenge. All I can say is you have a very dangerous and crafty adversary, and with Clarence

Nationhood

gone you are going to have to be extra careful. Even though he is locked up and it will be a long time before he ever gets out again, he has people working for him and I wouldn't be too shocked to see some of them coming after you in the near future. We know he can be depraved and his brilliance is off the charts. If he were to ever get out he would be a very deadly foe, to say the least."

"Then let him and the rest of his minions come, because when they do I will have their graves waiting for them," Mbaku replied menacingly.

Just then, Wendy walked up with the commissioner, Gregory Oboro. She hugged Mbaku tightly, but his arms barely encircled her shoulders. She stepped back and took a deep breath.

"I've prescribed your mother some medication should she need to use it later. But she's holding up pretty good right now," said Wendy.

"That's good. Thank you," Mbaku replied.

The commissioner stepped forward. "My condolences, Mister Bolo. I knew Clarence for a long time. He taught me everything I know about law enforcement. I'm going to miss him," he said.

"Yeah. Me, too."

The commissioner suddenly displayed a disturbed look. He glanced around the general area, as if he wanted to make sure none of the other family members were around. Then, he leaned toward Mbaku and spoke softly.

"I know this would not normally be a good time to bring up matters such as the one I need to discuss, but I was wondering if I could speak to you in private for a minute," said Oboro.

"Sure," Mbaku replied.

The ladies excused themselves as the two men walked off to a semi-secluded spot. The commissioner seemed worried and uncomfortable, fidgeting with his hat as if he was debating whether to relay his information.

"What is it, Commissioner?" asked Mbaku.

"I don't really know how to say this," Oboro replied.

"Just spill it."

"It's about Pollins."

Mbaku frowned, his posture becoming more erect. "What about him?"

"Well, he's, um, missing."

309

James Gordon

Mbaku's eyes widened. "Missing? What the hell do you mean he's missing?" his voice rising a bit.

"He was in the maximum security section in Independence Penitentiary. The guards did their customary night checks when they noticed he was already in bed. They didn't think anything of it until they went to check him the next morning. That's when..." his voice trailed off.

"How long ago did this happen?"

"Just this morning. We think it was an inside job, perhaps one or more of the guards could have been working for him or his organization. We're interrogating the ones on patrol last night and every other available agent is out searching for him as we speak."

Anger boiled inside of Mbaku. He didn't know whether to punch the Commissioner or tell him to call off his search for fear of losing more men. By now, Pollins could be anywhere and combined with the fact that he was connected to such a clandestine organization as the Illuminati, finding him would be like looking for a needle in a haystack.

It now appeared to Mbaku that his worse nightmare had come true. A madman was loose and there was no telling what he had planned next or when and where he would strike. Indeed, his last words spoken to him had come true. Lifetimes *can* be so short sometimes.

Mbaku's mindset was unstable. The man who helped raise him after his father died was now laying in a casket a few feet away. The man that put him there was free once more, the same man that betrayed his country and it's citizens, placed innocent people like his mother, Vee and Wendy in jeopardy because they were a part of the population he was infecting. Such actions were grounds for execution on the spot.

However, Mbaku allowed his uncle's words to convince him that he should turn Pollins over to the authorities instead of killing him where he stood. Now, hearing that he was out there somewhere planning or preparing his next act of terrorism, Mbaku got a sick feeling in the pit of his stomach. He could only imagine what Pollins would do next.

If there was one thing he knew for certain it was this. When Pollins resurfaced he would be deadlier and more calculating than he was before. Many people would die and the fate of the world would rest on how prepared he, Vee, Wendy and the rest of his organization was. In that instant, everything became clear. It was time to prepare and this time he would not allow anyone to convince him that killing Pollins wasn't the right thing to do. When they met again, Pollins would die.

310

Nationhood

He lifted his head and gave an angry scowl toward Oboro.

"I'm going back in and I'm going to finish paying my respects to my uncle. When I'm done here we will sit down and discuss this. This past incident was a clear indication of what Pollins and his people are capable of, and we are going to have our work cut out for us. We need to prepare now," Mbaku said.

"I'm sorry about this, Mister Bolo. We will do everything we can," said Oboro.

"Don't be sorry, Commissioner—be prepared. Something tells me we are going to be in for a long hard battle."

Mbaku turned and walked back toward Vee, Wendy and his mother. Commissioner Oboro slid his hat inside his armpit and watched as the procession of people began paying their respects to Clarence Bolo. But as the march of mourners continued, Oboro began to feel tension in the pit of his stomach. Mbaku's words held much truth. Should Pollins return, there would be hell to pay. There would be much bloodshed and destruction, and his wrath would be unholy. But Oboro had someone on his side, someone that beat him once and could surely do it again. Whatever Mbaku needed, he would have. Oboro only prayed that it would be enough.

~~~

Katura couldn't believe her eyes. Prime, the leader of the organization she worked for, the same organization that attempted to assassinate her, had just given her a proclamation of release. She was no longer an indentured servant. Her ties to the military and any part of the government were severed. The moment almost made her want to cry.

She looked at Jaquimo and showed him the notice. "I'm free," she said, choking back her emotions.

"Yes, My Lady," said Jaquimo. "Should we make plans for a celebration?"

"Absolutely."

"You did an excellent job on this last mission," said Prime. "You managed to release the antidote and save the people of AUNK. You helped to avert an attack on the United States and aided in defusing a potentially global conflict. The American government owes you a debt of gratitude, Miss Ishtar. If there's anything you should ever need, please let us know."

"What's my severance pay again?" she asked.

James Gordon

"Seven point five billion," said Prime.

"Nice." A big cheesy smile appeared.

"I will leave you to begin preparing for your new life," said Prime.

"Thank you."

Primes turned and walked toward the door when Katura called to him.

"Before you go, there's just one more thing," she said.

Prime stopped and turned toward her, a curious expression cloaking his face. Katura slowly approached him, her walk sexy and sultry, her eyes filled with lustful hunger. Her body language screamed out sexual innuendos like a woman who'd been deprived for so long that this day she was not going to be denied her just desserts. She came to within inches of him, her hot breath drifting across his face. Her sweet fragrance tantalized his nose and her body heat was making him excited. That's when he found out the real reason behind her sensual antics.

She struck so quickly he didn't know he was hurt until she was backing away from him. Anger was embedded deeply in her scowling face and her fists were clenched tighter than any knot every tied. While she was chest to chest with him, her knee went north, caught him in his privates, the pain radiating from down under all the way to the top of his head. He doubled over, clutching his manhood in his hands and wondering if all she did was knee him.

As he grunted in agony, struggling to keep himself from crashing to the floor, his face turned upward and he stared at the seething beauty who would just as well kill him as to speak to him.

"Why did you do that?" he asked grunting.

"Be thankful that is all I do to you," she said. "But hear this, Prime, and suffer no delusions about this. If you ever send anyone after me again—in any way, shape, form or fashion—I will find you, and when I'm done there won't be enough of you left to fit into a matchbox, is that clear?"

Prime nodded, still clutching himself.

"Now, get out," said Katura, her head motioning toward the door.

Prime straightened himself as best he could, then turned and walked out of the room, leaving Katura and Jaquimo standing in her palatial bedroom.

As the doors closed, Katura looked down at her proclamation, the

Nationhood

bittersweet feeling of anger and joy simultaneously assaulting her senses. Jaquimo came to her side, nudged her with his elbow to awaken her from her daydreaming state.

"So, you're officially free," he said, nodding toward the paper.

"Yeah," said Katura mildly.

"You don't seem happy."

"I am," she replied listlessly. "It's just that all this time I've had people watching my every move, telling me what to do, feeding me information and controlling my life. I felt like a lab rat. It just feels odd that I'm my own person now."

"It's not like you haven't already experienced this," Jaquimo replied. "The entire time you were in AUNK you were acting under your own volition. This will be no different."

"Perhaps. I just never thought I would see this day."

"Well, you have. So enjoy it."

Katura nodded as Jaquimo smiled at her. "Are the bags packed?" she asked.

"Yes. I've even taken the liberty of contacting Marina and letting her know you are on your way there. She sounded very excited."

"Good. I owe her for helping me stop that virus. Had it not been for her using the key words to unlock the file Durst hid in my brain we might not be alive right now." She paused for a moment, stared off into the distance. "God, how I wish he could have been here to see this."

"I'm sure he's looking down and smiling right now. He's very proud of you, as we all are."

Katura looked back at her friend with emotional eyes. "Thank you, Jaquimo," she replied.

"Of course, as you mentioned, Marina does deserve some of the credit. I'm certain she wouldn't want you beating yourself up for not being there to handle Durst's affairs. After all, she knew exactly what to do when you called her and I'm even surer that she understands more than you think. But now that everything is done, let's not go there with a doom or gloom attitude. This is a time for celebration. There will be plenty of time for worrying later."

Katura released a heavy sigh, then gave Jaquimo a hard stare. Just then, the phone rang. Jaquimo walked to the desk and answered. It was Vee. After exchanging a few pleasantries, a troubled look came to his face. He said he would relay her message and said goodbye. He turned to look

313

James Gordon

at Katura, his face laden with fear and uncertainty.

"What is it?" she asked.

"Well, as you know that was Vee. She just gave me some disturbing news," he said.

Katura didn't need to quiz him. By the look on his face she already knew what the message was. She knew it didn't have anything to do with Mbaku or Wendy. She already knew about Clarence and had given her condolences to Mbaku for his loss. That meant it could only mean one thing.

"He's free again, isn't he?" she asked.

Jaquimo nodded.

"I know what you're thinking, and yes, things are going to get worse," he said.

"Indeed," Katura replied. "According to Vee's information, Exodus and the Illuminati are in cahoots with each other, and now that Pollins is on the loose there's no telling what will happen next."

"I don't like this, My Lady. Pollins nearly took over the world and Exodus is still active. Both Pollins and Ramses have proven themselves to be ruthless and determined men with aspirations that surpass megalomania. Now that they have been exposed, there's no telling what they'll do next."

"Or what they've already done."

Frowning, Jaquimo replied, "I beg your pardon?"

"Think about it, Jaquimo. What if Pollins' real intentions had nothing to do with starting this war, about avenging the stripping of our people's rights and paying back America for its abandonment and abuse?"

"What do you mean?"

"What if his intent was something else, something we overlooked because we were too hell bent on stopping him."

"I think I see what you're saying," said Jaquimo with a tone of enlightenment. "He tried to start a war by spreading a virus amongst his own people, then blamed another country for doing this. That is a rather diabolical diversion. What else do you think he had planned?"

"I'm not sure. However, if there's one thing I've learned during this last mission is that nothing is as it seems. I wouldn't be at all surprised to know that he had a secondary plan in the works, something global, and I'd be even less surprised to know he accomplished whatever it was he set out to do in this phase of his plan. The only problem is we just haven't

314

figured out what he's done yet."

"He is a sharp man. I guess time will tell."

"Indeed," said Katura taking a few paces away.

She stared through her open bedroom patio doors. Her chateau in Senegal faced the beach and a gentle breeze was wafting inside, dancing with her white sheer gossamer panels. A tropical sunset was fading into the horizon, a rust-colored core with bands of burnt-yellow radiating around it. Her eyes stared at it, directly into the sun, her optical sensors compensating for the intense light. She marveled at how many colors were actually in a beam of sunlight. An entire spectrum existed and displayed colors more spectacular than anything seen on earth. But normal eyes couldn't handle this much light and are, therefore, unable to witness the beautiful prismatic lightshow that was put on every night before dusk.

"That's the part that scares me, Jaquimo," said Katura refocusing her thoughts. "By the time we find out, things may be well out of our control."

"What do you suggest we do?"

Katura released a deep sigh, then turned and face Jaquimo.

"I think the time has come for us to move things to a higher level," she replied. "We need to be mindful of everything; every accident, every skirmish, even the smallest, most insignificant feature in the newspaper. From what I've learned about him, he loves to operate under the radar."

"The devil is in the details," Jaquimo replied.

"No kidding. When we get back from visiting Marina, we need to contact Mbaku. I have the strangest feeling that the real hunt is about to begin."

Jaquimo detected a slight gleam in Katura's eyes when the name Mbaku exited her mouth.

"You liked him, didn't you?" he asked.

Katura frowned. "What are you talking about?" she asked.

"Mbaku. You kind of like him."

For the first time since he'd known her, Jaquimo could swear Katura Ishtar, one of the deadliest assassins on the planet, a woman who'd stared death in the face many times over and spat in it, was blushing.

"Why would you ask me that?" she replied embarrassingly, her arms stiff by her sides.

"Everyone could see it. You two were smitten with each other.

315

James Gordon

That's why Wendy kept close watch over you the entire time you two worked together," Jaquimo explained.

"He's a great spy and a hell of a fighter. I admire him for that, that's all."

"Oh, sure." Jaquimo nodded in sarcasm.

Once again, she blushed, but this time a cute smile bloomed across her lips. With a shrug of her shoulders she looked at Jaquimo with a soft expression.

"Would you please put the bags in the car?" she asked.

"Yes, My Lady," said Jaquimo.

~~~

Kashmir, India. Escorted by several guards, Pollins strolled into a beautifully palatial and ornate chamber room. A light, enchanting Hindu song played as an assortment of beautiful women in exotic sheer gossamer garments of every color lounged on huge plush pillows smoking opium and writhing like harlots in heat.

He was ushered to the bed where he reclined between a bevy of beauties who playfully caressed his head and face, tracing their hands across his body and showering him with loving attention. For several minutes he basked in the glow of indulgence as the women prepared to strip him of his garments. Just then, the guards returned. The women quickly climbed off the bed and scurried through an open door a few feet away.

Perplexed, Pollins slowly slid to the edge of the bed and, to his surprise, saw amongst the guards a slender man standing before him. A white turban was wrapped around his head and a fiercely black beard adorned his face. His eyes were like black pearls staring at Pollins like a panther ready to pounce.

"Outstretch your arms," he said.

Pollins gave him an uncertain look, then did what he was asked. The turban wearing man nodded to one of the guards to frisk him. The guard did a pat down of Pollins' body, then gave a nod indicating that he was clean.

"What is the name of the bird that never dies?" the turbaned man asked with a snobbish tone.

Pollins tilted his head to the right, shooting him a skeptical look "The same as the name of the bird that never lived," he replied.

The turbaned man stared at Pollins for a few moments more.

Nationhood

Then, a broad smile came to his lips. "I see you fulfilled your mission," he said.

"Did you ever doubt I would, Singh?" Pollins replied.

"Not really, Doctor. That is why I serve you."

"Yes. And soon shall the rest of the world." Pollins paused in thought for a moment, a satisfying smile covering his lips. "Doctor. How long it has been since I've heard someone call me that."

"A title befitting an individual as brilliant as you," said Singh. "You will soon bring order to this world, restore power to the rightful people. Only a man of infinite intelligence could think of such a plan and then manipulate so many people into doing the things you wanted them to, just to exercise a fraction of your mental attributes."

"How I hated being called Senator. The very sound of that name saturates my mouth with a foul taste."

"Never shall you hear that title again, I shall see to it. How is your hand?"

Pollins looked down at his bandaged appendage, the result of Mbaku's throwing star that dislodged his gun when he pointed it at Clarence.

"Better. Thank you, Singh," Pollins replied.

"Do you think the plan was uncovered?" asked Singh as both he and Pollins walked toward the chamber door.

"The Nation of AUNK is clueless and the Americans are even more in the dark. As you know, the war was just a farce to cover up my real plan. Far too long have I watched countries fight over territories that aren't theirs. I've witnessed how money corrupted the righteous, innocence being offered up for a price. Greed is rotting this world and ignorance is perpetuating its progress. Only when there is a common enemy does humanity rise to a more nobler level. And since the only way to make them work together is to create an enemy so powerful that it makes them lose sleep, I decided to create this monster. By this time next year, the entire world will be one. I will save humanity and usher in a new era, a new order, a new world order. I can't wait to spring phase two."

"You are a genius, sire. It is a pleasure to watch you operate."

Pollins stopped in his tracks, causing Singh and the rest of the guards to halt.

"What is it, my liege?" asked Singh.

"I'm simply taking a few moments to bask in my glory. America,

317

one of the most manipulative and powerful countries in the world has just been given a taste of its own medicine. I infiltrated their government, corrupted their laws and ruptured their financial infrastructure without having to do anything more than release a virus."

"It was poetic justice, if you ask me. Countless times the world has watched the American pigs do things to lesser countries, use all of their resources and push these countries around like a bully on a playground. It is high time that they get what they deserve."

"Not just them, but Europe, Russia, Germany and every other industrialized nation that has instituted injustices against the people. The art of winning a war, Mister Singh, is to defeat your opponent before they even know they're in a battle."

"Do you think they know they're in a battle now?"

With a smile Pollins replied, "I'm absolutely sure of it."

Singh nodded. "So, Clarence Bolo is dead, I see," he said.

A bittersweet expression covered Pollins' face. "You should have seen him, his nephew; the way he looked at me when they took me away. He was so righteous and cocky, like he actually felt he did something marvelous when they caught me. Little did he know he was a part of my plan, as well, just like Clarence was a part of my plan. Every enemy needs a hero, someone to help maintain the faith."

"But the nephew, he is not in your league, Doctor. He is but a child. I would have thought the senior Bolo would have been more your level."

"The virus in his tea was the test. Had he gotten around that, he may have been my formidable foe. But now, his rambunctious nephew must shoulder the burden. However, you are correct, he isn't my equal—mentally, that is. But his eyes, Mister Singh, you should have seen his eyes. They were filled with fire and passion, almost seething with pure contempt for me. He had me once, wanted to kill me so badly that I could almost see my life flashing before my eyes when he held his sword to my throat. Had it not been for Clarence's words to calm him, I might not be standing here before you now."

"I doubt he would have done anything to you. Besides, the loss of Clarence Bolo's life had to be done. AUNK must keep up with the rest of the world as it relates to preparedness. This incident will ensure they make the necessary adjustments to their operations to compete with and protect itself from the other countries. Mister Bolo's death ensured them

Nationhood

at least one champion who would keep fighting until the bitter end."

"He has unbridled passion, the kind that can allow a man to walk through the fires of Hell to accomplish his mission. He will make a great opponent."

"And do you really see this young upstart as someone who will give you a challenge?"

"Never underestimate this guy, Mister Singh. What he lacks in intelligence he more than makes up for in skill. There are more than enough countries out there with people who think they're brilliant and have the aptitude to figure out what I'm up to—professors, doctors, investigators, inspectors; a whole smorgasbord of froufrou men. So, I'll have all the mental challengers I'll ever need, not that they'll be successful against me, mind you. It'll hardly be a challenge proving myself supremely superior intellectually when I thrash these pretentious and pompous learned men. But to challenge someone with prowess and cunning, that should be quite interesting."

"The proverbial brawn-versus-brain contest. This should be rather interesting. He will come after you, now that you've murdered his uncle."

"Yes, I know," said Pollins with a hint of despair. "I wish I hadn't killed Clarence. He was such a good friend, the only man that truly understood my brilliance, my vision. However, sacrifices have to be made, which is why we need to prepare. The Bolo lad has already had a taste of what is in store for the world. If he's as enraged as I think he is, he will try to kill me the next time we meet. And I have the feeling that encounter will come very soon."

"I saw your picture on the television. You are officially a fugitive now, a dangerous terrorist," said Singh wryly.

"I'm surprised they thought they could hold me in a maximum security prison. That place is for dangerous criminals who lack the mental acumen to use soap when they bathe. Escaping from that place was like putting an adult cat in a child's playpen. The irony that they could put someone like me, a man who could pull off what I did, inside a mere prison is totally ludicrous. In fact, I should be insulted by the idea."

"They know not with whom they are dealing."

"Ah, but they will, Mister Singh. They will. Come, we have much work to do."

Followed closely by the guards, Pollins and Singh exited the room and continued down the hall. Now free to continue with his plans, what new events will Pollins have in store for the world. Only time will tell.

~~~

She sat impatiently in the examination room as the doctor finished his review of her lab results. All Carla wanted to do was get out of there and go home. She was tired of the examinations, the blood work, the taking of her vital signs, the constant prodding and poking they were doing to make sure that all traces of the virus were gone from her system. It was becoming irritating and she'd been through enough irritation to last her a lifetime.

She thought about the first thing she would do once she was released. She would go to her mosque and do some serious praying. She was going to thank God for blessing her with another chance at life, for her and Abraham. She still didn't understand how they were able to dodge the bullet of being killed by the virus. When Katura finally showed up with the cure, just before both of them would have taken a turn for the worse, it was like a scene out of a movie, the cavalry showing up just in time. There was no way to assign this to luck; she didn't believe in that anyway. In the end, she was left with resigning herself to the thought that it was all a part of the master's plan. There was no other way for her to logically explain such a miraculous feat.

It had been ten minutes since the doctor concluded his final analysis. Now he was waiting for the lab results to return and then she would be released. A few more minutes passed, then finally the doctor returned carrying her files in his hands, followed closely by his nurse. Carla looked at them both, her eyes wide with anticipation.

"Am I free to go?" she asked with eagerness.

"Yes, the tests came back negative. There doesn't seem to be any traces of the virus left in your system. But we are going to want to set up regular visits with you," said the doctor.

"Sure, I would expect that. To make sure that the virus doesn't return," Carla speculated.

"That, too," the doctor replied with a degree of hesitance.

Carla heard how he said that. Her observation skills were still at work.

"That, too?" she asked.

"Miss Snipes, you're pregnant," said the doctor.

Nationhood

His words had the stunning and unnerving effects of a thunder clap. Carla sat there, her mouth agape, her amber eyes wild looking. She could have been knocked over with a feather had one been available. She shook her head, disorientation taking a serious increase. She wanted to be sure she heard the doctor correctly.

"Could you repeat that?" she asked in an uncertain tone.

"You're pregnant," the doctor repeated.

At that moment, a warm sensation shot throughout her body. The shock she felt from the doctor's words had frozen her in place and sent her mind spinning. She couldn't believe she was going to be a mother!

A surge of emotions erupted inside of her. Her body shook with nervousness. Her breath trembled and she could actually feel her heart beating at an accelerated rate. With moistening eyes, she looked at the doctor, a fearful expression blanketing her lovely features.

"Are you sure about this?" she probed.

In a jesting tone, the doctor replied, "I'm a doctor, Miss Snipes. I'm paid to know these things."

"And there's no way you could be mistaken, like the virus fooling the lab work and giving you the impression I'm pregnant."

"That's why we kept you here for the last three days. We needed to make sure we were absolutely certain about this before we told you."

"Is this good news?" asked the nurse, trying to read passed Carla's confused expression.

She didn't answer right away, but stared into the distance as she allowed the news to settle in her brain. She thought back to the time in the airport, when she and Constable Al-Shahir had shared a moment of surrender in one of the back rooms. She remembered how they loved and how she enjoyed being with him. She even confessed how she wished she could have started a family and if she were given a second chance how that would become her priority.

She also remembered the valiant efforts of the Constable, giving her the last of the serum to slow the effects of the virus. He told her how he'd been an admirer of hers and how he wished he'd come to her sooner, that perhaps they could have had a relationship and shared their lives and love. She also remembered his last few moments on this earth, how he fought to stay strong, even as the virus tore his insides apart. She admired him and even in that briefest of time, loved him dearly.

Now, as she sat on the examination table, she realized that her

James Gordon

prayers had been answered. Her right hand autonomously came to rest on her stomach, the first conscious connection between mother and child. Her mind was a maelstrom of thoughts, ranging from pure joy to terrifying fear. She had escaped the clutches of death, was given a chance at a new life and was now presented with something far more valuable than what she could ever ask for. She was pregnant, and she was carrying Al-Shahir's baby.

Slowly, her head nodded, a faint smile appearing on her lips. She looked down at her stomach and cradled it lovingly in her hands. She now had an even better reason to go to the mosque and thank God for his mercy. She looked up at the nurse, who'd asked her whether her pregnancy was a good thing.

"Yes," said Carla. "This is very good news."

At that moment, she understood the choice in songs Al-Shahir used as his life faded away. Just before he died, when she was holding him in her arms, he hummed the song entitled, *Born Again*. Carla realized he couldn't have picked a more appropriate ballad.

~~~

He did what he was told. He delivered the letter to Senator Decker. Now Thomas Thurgood sat at the desk in his house staring at a slip of paper, his reading lamp shining its light down upon it. Beads of sweat covered his forehead and his eyes were filled with disbelief. With his brow wrinkled and his posture slumped forward, he examined the paper, his body language giving the impression that something was terribly amiss.

His eyes were firmly fixed on the slip he held. But this was no ordinary note. It was a direct result of his actions, his part in the grand scheme of which he had no clue. Before he delivered the message to Senator Decker, he read the communication he was to deliver. On it, Ramses had promised to release the antidote if certain conditions were met. Those conditions were written in great detail and would set in motion the very events that would change this world forever.

Among the list of demands was the unconditional surrender of all governmental and financial controls of the United States of America to a small group of African Americans, namely Exodus. This included all its territories and international interests. Although on the surface the running of the country would appear to be left in the hands of the elected officials, the true power now belonged to the people connected to Exodus.

Nationhood

At first, the officials didn't want to acquiesce to the demands. But when the virus began to wipe out almost all of the non-Black populace, which included eighty percent of the elected government officials, they quickly changed their minds.

Exodus now controlled one of the most powerful countries in the world. Blacks now held the reigns of control and influence, determining the political and economic future of the world. No longer would they be treated like second-class citizens, but as the chosen people, the blessed people and the meek that now inherited the earth.

As a result, Thurgood was seated at his table staring at a piece of paper that seemed more unbelievable than real. It represented his part in the grand coupe that was performed, his compensation for all the trials and tribulations he went through.

Although the preceding events marked a huge victory for civil rights and balancing the scales of equity, he felt ashamed about the loss of life. Many people died as a result of Exodus' actions and he couldn't help wondering if things could have been handled differently.

Then again, would any of this be possible had there been no loss of life? Should there be any shame when a populace did what they had to do in order to regain the rights and freedoms that were so pompously taken and vehemently denied? The liberties that had been stripped away over twenty-five years ago had been restored, irrevocably restored. From now on, Blacks in America, and the world for that matter, were equal citizens, free to roam wherever they pleased without fear of retaliation or racial discrimination.

Thurgood thought about Ramses and what he'd done, what he'd managed to accomplish. All this time he thought the Exodus leader as being nothing more than a common terrorist, a thug, a person who attempted to take violent measures for a cause he was truly powerless to support. But now, still looking at his piece of paper, he had to ask——was he right? Did it have to come to this in order to make the oppressors see that their treatment of his people was inhumane and unjust?

There was no sure way to answer that question. However, Thurgood knew that Ramses was celebrating this moment. What made his victory evident was the slip of paper he held in his hands. It was the very thing owed to Black people since the birth of this nation. It was a reparations check in the amount of two hundred and seventy five million dollars. Thurgood un-furrowed his forehead and smiled.

James Gordon

"Ramses, have you really set our people free?" he asked.

~~~

Made in the USA